Away

A Keaton Series Novel

B.A. WOLFE

To my husband, family, and friends.

All of your support and encouragement has brought me to where I am today. Without it, I would have never had the courage to chase my dreams. I love you all to the moon and back.

Away

A Keaton Series Novel

Chapter one

THE TERM 'AWAY' COMES IN many forms and phrases. Get away, stay away, far away, go away, went away, and move away, but the term that best fits my situation... Run away.

Girls like me don't run away. We've had our lives handed to us on a silver platter. So why was I running away? All because of one night — one stupid night that ruined every little thing that I had worked so hard for. I needed someone to tell me that life wasn't ending and that things would be okay. I wanted a Band-Aid to cover my injuries, but no bandage was large enough for the wounds I'd inflicted upon myself. What I truly needed was my best friend.

So I headed to Alamosa to see Melanie. She was the only person I trusted to know what I should do. Life wasn't turning out the way I had planned. I was going to school and had a 4.0 GPA. I was little 'Miss Perfect', just how my parents raised and wanted me to be. Now, everything was in jeopardy, and my mistake threatened to haunt my future. If it weren't for my blunder, I wouldn't have realized how messed up my so-called perfect life actually was. That's why I needed to see Melanie. Unlike my parents, she wouldn't judge me or tell me how she expected more from me.

The only problem? I had never actually been to Adams State College to visit her. With GPS in tow, I felt positive that I'd be okay. Considering I was always decent at taking directions and orders from everyone else, following the GPS commands should be no different. The only enjoyable part was that it wasn't making me call it Mother or Father.

"Hey, Mel," I said into the phone.

"Hey girl. I hope you're on the road." Mel's tone was somewhat somber. She knew that desperation was what prompted this visit.

"Yeah, I'm on I-25 right now. I just wanted to let you know I'm on my way. I need you right now, Mel," I confessed in a shaky voice.

"I know. Just get here and we'll figure it out."

She was my rock, the only person who ever loved me for being me. I didn't want to go to school to get a Bachelor's in finance, let alone a Master's degree too. I had other dreams for my life, but they weren't acceptable, or allowed in my family. My parents had expectations for me, and if I delivered, I was their perfect daughter. If I deviated from their plan, there would be hell to pay. That's what I was told the day that I applied for colleges. I didn't have a problem getting into school. I was smart and enjoyed learning. But, the chosen path of finance had no interest to me whatsoever. I felt trapped, and now my mistake was forcing me to drop everything and run to Melanie, my lifeboat. She was the only thing that was keeping me from drowning a long torturous death. This time, Melanie was pulling me to shore.

"Thanks, Mel. I don't know what I'd ever do without you."

"You'd be lost and scared. Same as me, Cass. Drive carefully. Call me when you get close to Alamosa, okay?"

"You got it. I'll call you soon. Love you," I replied and ended the call. I tossed my phone in the cup holder in case it rang again. It wouldn't be my parents, of course. They never called until after my grades had been posted for the semester. I had grown accustomed to that though. The 'less is more' theory applied to every situation when it came to things between my parents and me.

The drive down was uneventful and somewhat torturous. It was turning into the very definition of what a Sunday afternoon drive would feel like. I never ventured anywhere outside of the

Denver area. The further south I drove, the more differences I noticed. There were farms, more trucks on the road, and the heat was just a little more unbearable. My exit was coming up, so I veered left and continued down the ramp, finally leaving I-25. I had never driven a longer stretch of highway in my life. The little digital box displayed that I needed to head east for at least another 100 miles. Leaving before sunrise was the only thing going for me. The towns I zipped through were small and brought to mind a time before there were city skyscrapers, fancy cars, or technology.

An hour or so later, my monotonous drive changed to terrifying. A loud pop stung my eardrums as my wheel shook erratically in my trembling hands. My stomach dropped. I gripped the steering wheel tighter, trying to fight the force that was veering me left, but it wasn't working. My body stiffened as I saw what was in front of me. I tried to slam my foot on the brake as an impossibly large tree stood firm in my path. It was no use, too little, too late. We collided, and my body flew forward. My head bounced into the steering wheel, and then my seatbelt locked which jerked me back into the headrest. Steam poured from the hood of my car like an awakening volcano. The throbbing in my head immediately settled in. My breathing became uncontrollable, and I felt trapped beneath my seatbelt. I wanted to escape from its tight hold, and as simple as unlocking it should have been, panic was leaching in. I pulled at the belt and fought as it kept me contained like a prisoner. The harder I tugged, the more I realized that my head wasn't the only part of my body in massive amounts of pain. My neck muscles had tightened and barely wanted to turn my head. I forgot about my seatbelt and put my hand to my chest as the pounding increased. If others were around, they would have been able to hear the beating. It didn't take long for a second wave of terror to set in. My body was shaking uncontrollably as I realized I was alone and helpless.

Hearing a small tap on my window, I looked over to see a guy about my age with eyes as wide as I imagined mine were.

"Hold still. I'm calling for help right now. You were just in an accident. Your airbag didn't deploy, and you hit your head pretty hard. I need you to stay put." The young guy pulled his phone out of his pocket.

I lifted my hand to my throbbing forehead, and when I pulled it away, sure enough, blood covered it. I couldn't help but let the welling tears uncontrollably trickle down my face.

"I know you're scared, Sweetheart, but help is on the way," he said calmly.

Scared didn't even begin to cover it. I looked down at the seatbelt and sighed when I realized that all I had to do was unlock it. Clicking the buckle, and finally releasing myself from the strong grip it had on my body, I felt an ounce of freedom as I pushed it to my side. The door wouldn't budge when I tried to open it, and so, the torment continued. I pounded my hands on the window with all my remaining energy, drawing the guy's attention back to me.

"I need you to calm down. You're going to be okay. The cops are going to help get you out."

"NO! I need out of here. I need out now!" I yelled through the glass.

He pulled on the door handle with no luck. When he walked over to the other side and tried to open the passenger door, he motioned for me to unlock the door. I reached over, opened it for him, and got my first close look at him. A belt with a large, western-style buckle looped through his body-hugging jeans. Pearl snaps decorated the center of his shirt and all he was missing was the cowboy hat. Without question, a country boy had come to my rescue.

He looked around and then bent down, leaning halfway into the car. "Hi there," he said, with a smile on his slightly scruffy face. His short, wavy, light brown hair was blowing in the breeze.

"Hi," I replied quietly, focused on the gorgeous green eyes that stared into mine. They were dark and so exquisite, reminding me of emerald stones you would see showcased at a jewelry store.

"I saw the whole thing happen from across the street. Your tire blew, and you hit the tree. You seriously need to stay calm, okay."

"I just want out of the car. Can you please help me?" I knew I was begging, but the enclosed space was beginning to suffocate me.

4

"Alright." He nodded his head. "Let's get you out then. I need you to climb over your console and come out this way. Can you do that for me?"

"Yeah... I... I can do that," I said, my voice hitching. Reaching for his hands, I grabbed on tightly as I slowly swung each leg over the console. I let out a sigh of relief as he effortlessly picked me up. With one quick swoop, I was out of the car and held close in this helpful stranger's arms, and for a split second, I felt safe and calm.

"See, you're out, and you're okay. What's your name, Sweetheart?" He continued to hold me tightly against his chest.

I let out a deep breath. "It's Cassandra. My name is Cassandra. At least I can still remember my name." I tried to reassure myself.

"Cassandra, that's a great thing." He cocked his head to the side, allowing me to see his face more clearly. His eyes were even brighter in the sun. "Mine's Jason. I'm the town's knight in shining armor," he said, his lips curling to the side as he kept a strong hold on me.

"Thanks for the rescue, Jason." I smiled back at him. "I have a splitting headache right now though," I said, closing my eyes and hoping the tension in my forehead would ease.

"No, no, no. Don't close your eyes. You need to stay awake. You hit your head hard. In fact, here." He pulled a handkerchief from his pocket and put it on my lap. "Press that firmly against your forehead. It'll help stop the bleeding."

I studied the handkerchief for a moment. He barely knew me, yet he treated me as if I were his best friend who'd just been in an accident.

"It's clean, Cassandra. I promise," he said.

"No, it's not that. I've just never met someone so helpful to a complete stranger before."

"I don't know where you're from, but that's how we do things around here. But, it's not every day that I get to help out a pretty girl like you."

"Does the town pay you to say that?"

"I wouldn't need to be paid to tell you that," he whispered against my ear.

5

"Thanks." My cheeks warmed instantly. I kept my eyes forward, and knew that if I continued looking at him that I would melt through his arms. He was gorgeous, helpful, and sweet. Talk about a trifecta. I wish I had come here two months ago before I found myself in this predicament.

He gently set me down on the sidewalk and sat close to me until the ambulance and police arrived. A guy had never treated me as if I were something fragile that needed protection, and had certainly never taken care of me unless taking me out to a fancy dinner counted. I thought of myself as a strong girl, but this fragile, helpless Cassandra was emerging more frequently, and it was all too foreign to me. Navigating the new roads, both literally and physically, left me feeling uncertain because running away was an entirely new concept to me.

"Please, I don't need to go to the hospital. I'm just a little sore," I tried to convince the EMT.

"Ma'am, we need to check you out. At least get in the back so we can bandage up your head wound, and look you over." The older EMT reached for my hand before I could tuck it behind me.

"No, really, I'm fine."

"Cassandra, they need to check you out," Jason said.

Before I could beg, I cupped my mouth with my hand, ran over to the side of the street, and released all the contents of my breakfast, right in front of everyone. I dropped to my knees, both half-embarrassed, and half-relieved to be feeling slightly better. A hanky appeared at my left side, and I knew it was Jason being helpful again. I grabbed the now-used hanky and wiped my mouth before taking in a deep breath and lifting my head. He knelt beside me and placed his hand lightly on my back.

"I don't think you want this back," I said, contemplating whether *I* even wanted to be touching it.

"Well, you're right about that. You can keep it," he said, a soft laugh escaping him. "But you're going to the hospital now.

You could have a concussion, Cassandra. They need to check you out."

Feeling even more defeated, I gave in and stood. "I can walk to the ambulance." I gazed at the grass I had ruined, and clenched my fists, angry that they were taking me where I didn't want to go to yet.

"I know you can. I just want to be here to catch you in case you fall," he said quietly.

I couldn't help but feel the knots growing in my stomach. He was my 'knight in shining armor', and I was dismissing him out of anger over my need to go to the hospital. Some grateful girl I was.

He walked the short distance to the back of the ambulance with me, keeping his hands close as if he were putting a protective shield around me.

"Thanks for your help, Jason," I said. He raised his hand to wave goodbye, keeping his eyes on me as they closed the ambulance doors. I wasn't in the mood to go with them, and wished he were going with me. The warmth of his touch was comforting compared to the cold feeling of the ambulance.

Chapter

two

THE ER, IF THAT IS WHAT they wanted to call it, was the size of my doctor's office back home. When I arrived, the only other person there was a spouse dropping off lunch for one of the nurses. I waited in a small room, and when the curtain opened, a lady in brown-colored scrubs walked in. Her curly hair was in a ponytail, and a pendant that read 'Mom' swayed from a delicate chain around her neck. She looked to be close to my parents' age.

"Cassandra Pierce? I'm your nurse, Trish. I'm just going to check a few things before the doctor sees you." Her voice was gentle and warm, and helped to take away an ounce of the fear that was settling inside me.

"Trish?" I asked after she finished checking my vitals.

"Yes?" Her soft, honey-brown eyes looked down at me.

"I'm pregnant. Well, I was before the accident. I need to know if the baby is okay." She looked as if I'd just set off a fire alarm. I had to say something though. I was curious and almost too hopeful that, with some small miracle, I was no longer pregnant.

"I'll get our OB in here so we can check." Compassion flowed through her soft words. "Everything will be fine, Sweetie. Don't worry," she said before walking out of the room.

My heart sank as her words settled in because I didn't want everything to be fine. I wanted this over with and my freedom back. I wasn't ready to be a mother. I needed to know if my accident happened for a reason and took care of my problem for me. An immense pang of guilt twisted in my stomach. My thoughts ate at me, haunted me. Everything about them and my situation was awful in the worst possible way.

Trish came back with a machine and the doctor. I gulped as I felt my nerves coursing through my body, anxious and anticipating the coming news.

"Hello, Cassandra. I'm Dr. Rich." He was an older doctor with a comforting smile, thick salt-and-pepper hair, and glasses that emphasized thoughtful eyes. Though he appeared to be the kind of doctor you'd want in a nerve-wracking situation, nothing was going to ease my traumatized nerves.

"Hello, Dr. Rich," I muttered, ready to get this finished. I was familiar with standard checkups on my lady parts, but something told me this exam would be far different.

"Trish tells me you were in a car accident, and you're pregnant?"

I nodded, finding the words were too hard to repeat. Saying it out loud once was bad enough.

"Do you know how far along you are, or when your last period was?"

"I haven't been to the doctor to confirm anything yet. I took a few pregnancy tests at home." My period had been like clockwork since I had started the pill. "I missed my period last month. It was supposed to start the 25th, but it didn't."

"Very well. I'm going to do a quick exam to make sure everything is okay with the baby, and then we'll get another doctor in here to check you over." He moved the machine closer and pulled the stirrups out of the end of the bed.

"Trish?" I asked.

"Yes, Cassandra?"

"Can you stay in here with me please?" I was scared to go through this type of exam alone. While she wasn't my mother, she was someone's mom, and that was enough for me.

With a small smile and a nod of her head, she stood right by my side. She grabbed hold of my shaking hand as Dr. Rich continued to set up the machine.

The anxiety in my body increased when he placed my feet in the stirrups. "Deep breaths, Sweetie," Trish whispered, squeezing my hand tighter.

I was trying. God was I trying.

"Okay, we're all set." He wheeled his chair closer to the end of the bed. "Because it's so early in your pregnancy, we'll have to do a vaginal ultrasound," he said as he put a condom and gel on the wand that was about to deliver my fate. "Just relax." He pulled the screen closer to his face while moving the uncomfortable wand around inside.

He squinted at the screen before giving a nod to Trish. I glanced at her, and then Dr. Rich turned the screen around for me to look. I didn't want to see anything. I just wanted to know if the accident had solved my problem.

"Your baby is fine," he said, and Trish squeezed my hand even harder. "Your baby is measuring at about 6 1/2 weeks. While it's a little too early to hear the heartbeat, it's showing strong at 112 beats per minute." He pointed to the little dot on the screen.

"See, Sweetie, I told you everything would be okay," Trish whispered.

My heart sank as I struggled to hold back the stinging tears. This clearly wasn't the reason I'd gotten into an accident. I closed my eyes as Dr. Rich continued spouting more information that neither my head nor my heart desired to hear. I was back to square one, and even worse than before, I was without a car.

Before I knew it, the wand was out, the screen was gone, and Trish let go of my hand. "Dr. Rich is coming back with some goodies for you, a bottle of prenatal vitamins, and some reading materials about your baby." She acted as though a baby was the most exciting thing in life.

"Great," I muttered.

"You don't seem relieved Cassandra. This is good news," she said.

"This was unplanned, Trish, very much unplanned," I confessed.

She took my hand again. "You'll get through this, Sweetie."

The problem was that I didn't want to get through it. I didn't want this baby. I may have ruined my life right now, but it was also going to ruin my future. As horrible as I was for thinking that, it was the unfortunate truth. I felt nothing but guilty and awful for my honesty.

The second doctor was in and out quickly. He looked over my chart, checked me over from head to toe, and gave me the concussion rundown before speaking to me about filling out paperwork. Once he left, Trish returned.

"Looks like Dr. Montgomery would like you to stay until your blood work comes back. That way, we can keep an eye on you for a bit. I'll be back to check on you soon." Putting my chart under her arm, she turned and looked at me with kindness. "No need to be scared. We may be a small hospital, but we have excellent doctors," she said before leaving.

Twenty minutes later, the curtain swung open, and I opened my eyes, hoping it was Trish. I liked her. She seemed to be the kind of mother who would be happy to receive a necklace that said 'Mom' on it. My mother wouldn't dare wear such a display around her dignified neck. But it wasn't Trish. It was someone that I didn't think I would ever see again.

"Jason?" I questioned as I saw him closing the curtain behind him. "I didn't think I'd see you again." I was surprised, yet relieved to see him.

"I wanted to check on you and see how you were doing," he said with a smile tugging at his lips. He turned toward me as he stood in front of the curtain, his eyes gazing me over from head to toe.

"Only a couple more hours."

Both of his eyebrows rose, and his voice went up an octave. "Until you die?"

I let out a soft chuckle. I liked how he was trying to ease the tension that was clearly taking over my stressed body and mind. "No, no, no. Just until I'm able to leave."

He walked over to the end of my hospital bed, his cowboy boots clacking against the floor with each step he took. He sat down beside my feet as if he were at ease.

"I'm just teasing you. You look far too healthy to die in a few hours," he said.

"Yeah, well, I don't feel so healthy, but thanks." I looked down at the blanket.

"Really, this hospital gown is a good look on you." He winked.

I tried my best to take my gaze off him. I didn't need him getting the wrong idea. I was a mess right now.

"So," he said as he scratched the side of his face that looked as though it hadn't been shaved in a few days. "Your car." He cringed.

"Do I want to know how bad it is?" I asked, closing my eyes, not ready to hear the answer.

"It's fixable, so that's good," he said, before rubbing the back of his neck. "But the bad news is that you like foreign cars," he said, giving me a soft glare. I didn't like them; my father did. "The parts aren't in stock at our mechanical shop, so you'll be waiting a while."

Ugh. "This is bad. This is so bad," I said, shaking my head. I tried my best to hold back the tears that were sitting impatiently behind my eyes wanting to release themselves yet again.

"I assure you that they're working hard to get it fixed. The mechanic is a close family friend. I'll make sure it gets repaired quickly, Cassandra," he said.

"Thanks, but right now, can I just have a little time alone? I just need to let all this process, okay?" I asked him, struggling to keep the tears from pouring out and my voice from shaking. This poor guy didn't need to see another breakdown.

"I understand. I'll be back later to check on you before you leave," he said before he left through the curtains.

I. Was. Screwed. There was no other way to put it. Life kept throwing obstacle after obstacle in my path to test me, and I was failing each one. My spirits were low. My positivity had turned to negativity, and my thoughts had become jaded. I didn't fail. Cassandra Elizabeth Pierce never, EVER failed anything. It wasn't an option, but at this moment, I felt as though I didn't have options. It was failure, nothing else.

My pity party continued for quite some time, two hours, a box of tissues, and a couple of nurse visits later to be exact. It felt weird just to sit and cry, and let it all out. I don't think that, in all my years, I'd ever done that before, and it felt right.

"How's it going in here, Sweetheart? You doing okay?" Jason asked as he poked his head through the curtain. I shot him a quick grin as he made his way to the foot of my bed.

"For the moment I guess. I just needed to have a breakdown by myself this time. You didn't need to witness another freak show again," I explained to him.

"Ah, I quite enjoyed the entertainment." He chuckled. "I'm kidding, Cassandra. I don't mind being here. I don't want you to be alone."

I was so thankful for him. He didn't know me, and I wouldn't have known him from Adam, but something about him was strangely comforting.

"I appreciate your being here, but really, you don't have to stay." I couldn't lie though. His presence was a pleasant distraction from my thoughts.

"Cassandra," he said with a hard look on his face, yet his eyes were soft and connected with mine. "I'm staying. End of subject." I gave him another smile. This time though, it went from ear to ear.

"So what are you doing here in town anyway?" He leaned against the edge of the bed.

"I'm headed to Alamosa. I wasn't supposed to be in town, just passing through."

His eyes got wide as he craned his neck, looking at me even closer. "Alamosa? Really?"

"Why is that so hard to believe?" I asked, giving him a questioning glance. What, a girl can't go to Alamosa?

"Cassandra," he said, trying to contain his laughter. "Alamosa is in the complete opposite direction. You're not even close; it's at least three hours away. You're in Keaton right now."

No. No. No. That wasn't possible. I closed my eyes and tried to remember seeing Keaton on the GPS before I wrecked my car.

"What do you mean I'm not even close?" I needed him to explain before I started screaming in frustration.

"Well Sweetheart, Alamosa is west. We're east. Clearly someone gave you the wrong directions," he said with an apologetic look.

"Are you kidding me?" I yelled out. "Are you freaking kidding me? Goddamn GPS, stupid thing, I hate it. Dumb, horrible, lousy, good for nothing, piece of junk!" I screamed out before dropping my head to my hands in defeat.

I felt a hand gently resting on my lower leg. "Hey, don't be upset. It's okay. You'll get your car fixed, and then I'll give you directions. You'll still get there," he said softly.

I raised my head, trying to give him a fraction of a smile since he was trying so hard to be polite during my mini-tantrum. The least I could do was calm down for him, but my emotions were getting the best of me.

"I've never heard of Keaton. It wasn't even on my GPS," I told him, not surprised that the dumb piece of junk didn't display this city on its map.

"We like to keep our city a secret. Saves more trees that way." I couldn't believe he just went there. It hadn't even been 12 hours since I hit a tree and my head. "Too soon?" he asked.

I continued to gaze at him. His warm eyes, charming smile, and that laugh had me feeling as if I wanted to laugh with him. Something about him, about his presence left me awestruck.

I opened my mouth to answer him. "Yes, but–" I froze. What was I supposed to tell him? *But, you have a real appealing smile, and I can't help but feel the need to smile around you, so what you said doesn't bother me that much.* Hell, no. I was not about to say that.

"But what?" He raised a brow waiting for me to finish my sentence, the grin on his face still present.

I had nothing, and luckily, I didn't have to answer. Trish came to my rescue by walking in with my discharge papers, which prompted Jason to stand.

"Okay, Cassandra, you're good to go. If you have any more issues, then come right back, or call an ambulance to bring you in."

I nodded my head. With that, Jason and Trish both left my room. I slowly put my clothes back on and sat myself on the edge of the bed trying to figure out what I needed to do next. I began to look around to find my purse, but it was missing from my room. It must still be in my car... My wrecked car.

"Damn it!" I yelled to myself. At that moment, I could hear Jason's voice on the other side of the curtain.

"Everything okay in there, Cassandra?"

"No. I can't find my purse. I think it's still in my car. I need my phone to call my friend," I explained.

"Are you dressed yet?" Jason asked calmly.

I looked down at myself, gazing from my shoes to my shirt. It was as good as it was going to get. I've never been this not put together in my life. My hair was a disaster. My clothes had blood on them from the cut on my head, and mud covered my shoes. Not my finest hour, but at least I was dressed.

"Yes," I mumbled. Before I could finish answering, he was pushing a wheelchair into my room. My eyes widened when I saw my purse on his shoulder. "Thank you, thank you, thank you, Jason!" I all but screamed. "You're a life saver, seriously." I reached for the purse he was handing over to me.

"Of course, what are friends for?"

"Friends already, huh?" I teased back.

"Well, we can't be best friends yet. I've only known you for approximately 8 hours," he said, looking down at his wristwatch.

I couldn't help but feel as if he were a friend. I sat back down on my bed, digging through my purse for my phone, pushing too many other items aside that I didn't need. I was angry to find it wasn't in my bag.

"Where is the damn thing?" I said to myself.

"What's wrong?"

I dug through my purse one last time, checking every square inch without my phone turning up. Damn it. I set my purse to the side in frustration. "I can't find my phone, and I need to call my friend to let her know what's going on."

"We'll find your phone. In the meantime, here." He reached into his front pocket and handed me his phone. "You can use mine."

As thoughtful as the gesture was, I didn't feel right using his phone. I would have to find a payphone or a phone in a hotel room since I clearly wouldn't be traveling today or tomorrow. I shook my head at him. "No, that's okay. I'll figure it out. Right now, my head really hurts; I'm exhausted, and ready to leave the hospital. Do you think you could take me to a motel?" I watched as his face went flat with no emotion. Oh, God. "You do have a motel, don't you?" I asked nervously, praying that they did.

"We do. I just wanted to scare you a bit," he confessed.

"Oh, thank God," I said in relief as he walked toward me.

"But I'd rather you didn't stay there. I want you to come and stay with me," he said.

Say what? Oh, I don't think so. Talk about being taken aback. I wasn't prepared to hear that answer, let alone to be okay with it. I barely knew the guy, and he wanted to take me home. Talk about a scene right out of an investigation show.

"I don't think so, Jason," I told him, gripping my hands in my lap.

"I do. My mom insisted. You'll be much more comfortable at our house than at a motel. We have a spare bedroom. You can stay with us until your car is done, and it'll save you money. You don't even want to know what kind of bugs are creeping around in that motel," he said, giving me a reassuring nod.

Bugs. Money. Spare bedroom. I kept running through the words that he just spewed. Yep, I was going to a motel, bugs, or no bugs.

"Jason, I appreciate it, but I don't know that much about you. Honestly, you could be a genuinely nice guy just wanting to help a girl out, but then again," I shrugged, "you could be one of those guys that preys on young girls, does unspeakable things to them, and then kills them, disposing their bodies in trash bags," I said, watching his face go from shocked to amused.

"Really? You think I'm a killer, huh? You watch way too much TV, Cassandra. I'm just trying to be polite here," he said. "I'm offering you a much better room than the one you are about to pay for."

"Yeah, but I might be saving my own life right now by having watched too much TV," I said to him. "Do you guys have a cab service that I can call to take me to this bug-infested motel?"

He walked over to the bed, standing in front of me. "No, we don't, but I'll take you there." He continued to stand there with his thumb tucked in the front pocket of his jeans, his other hand reaching out for me to take. "I'm not happy about it, but if that's where you want to go, I'll gladly take you."

I looked at the hand that was waiting for me. He didn't look like a killer. Quite the opposite, in fact, but I needed to be smart with all of this.

"You can trust me," he said softly.

I didn't know what it was inside me that was allowing myself to trust this stranger, but something was telling me it was okay to place my hand in his, and let him take me to the motel. And that is exactly what I did.

He guided me into the wheelchair, and I looked at him with confusion.

"The wheelchair is a little overboard. I can walk you know." He grabbed my purse and placed it gently in my lap as he began pushing us through the ER to the exit.

He continued pushing me. "I know, but it's policy. You have to be escorted out in a wheelchair. No ifs, ands, or buts about it."

I guess today was my day to be carried from my car, and pushed in a wheelchair by this stranger, but after a short time, he didn't seem to be such a stranger anymore. Right now, I was glad to have such a compassionate person come to my rescue. If I couldn't have my best friend by my side, then I was more than okay with Jason.

Chapter
three

"ARE YOU SURE ABOUT THIS?" He put his truck in park as we sat in front of the ancient motel. No, I wasn't sure about it at all. It looked just as horrid as my mind had envisioned, the outdoor room entrance, the old paint, the vacancy sign illuminated by the front desk 'check-in'. I took a big gulp and turned to face him. "Yeah, I'm... I'm sure," I said before reaching for the door handle. As I gripped the handle, I felt a hand on my arm. I whipped around to see Jason with worried eyes fixed on me and his jaw clenched together.

"I really don't feel comfortable with you staying here by yourself," he said.

I took a deep breath and tried to give him a smile even though I was scared shitless of what I was about to get myself into. "I'll be fine," I assured him as I stepped out of his truck. It was old, rusty, and surprisingly, a comfortable ride.

I watched Jason as he got out and walked to the back. He pulled something over the side of his truck bed, and I immediately recognized the black luggage. I let out a relieved sigh, and shook my head in disbelief as I approached him.

"They pulled it out before they towed your car. I didn't want you to be without your stuff," he said, keeping a grip on the handle.

"Jason, thank you, really," I said, all too eager to have my belongings, and yet ready to cry just seeing something of mine back with me.

"You're welcome," he replied. "All right, if you're ready for this, then let's go," he said, motioning with his head toward the front desk office.

I wasn't sure, but I also wasn't an idiot. Staying with him wasn't in the cards for me.

"Hey Jeff," Jason said to the guy at the counter.

Jeff stood to shake Jason's hand, and gave him a strange look. "Hey man, what are you doing here?"

"I need a room for the night for this one right here," he said, pointing in my direction. "I need you to do me a favor though. Can you keep an eye on her, please?" He gave Jeff a steady look. I wasn't sure how to take his protectiveness if that's what that was.

"Yeah, of course man," Jeff grabbed one of the silver-plated keys from behind him and laid it on the desk. "That's one night."

I walked up to the counter. "It could be more than one night. I'm waiting for my car."

"It's only on a one-night basis, so just come back tomorrow, and we can book it for you again," he said.

After paying for my one night and taking my key for room number eight, Jason grabbed my luggage, and we headed for what could possibly be the most frightening room I've ever stayed in.

"Is this one of those small towns where everyone knows everyone?" I asked as we walked side-by-side.

"You could say that. I grew up with Jeff. We graduated high school together. His parents own this motel and make him work it for the most part. He's a good guy." He unlocked the door with my tagged key. "Here we go," he said as he opened the door for me.

When I flipped the light switch so I could see, moths flew around over our heads and then out the open door. "Gross." I shivered as I walked in further. The old motel smell made me want to pass out, but I figured I could keep the window open to let fresh air circulate. The bed to my left appeared okay, at least on the outside anyway. A beat-up dresser with a small television on top that had rabbit ears poking out of it sat beside the door. I continued to the bathroom crammed in the back corner, peeked in it, and all but ran back to where Jason stood. "Holy crap," I said cringing.

"You are braver than I gave you credit for, Cassandra." Jason walked in the room, setting my luggage on the floor. "I feel terrible for leaving you here."

"I'll be okay," I said, peering around the room, but not believing a word of what I'd just said. This was my only option, aside from staying with a complete stranger. The latter was certainly not happening, even though he was amiable and I felt safe with him. I knew what happened when I let my guard down. I didn't need to backtrack.

"Alright." He raised his brow as he walked over to the nightstand, writing something on the notepad. "Here's my cell number, call me if you need anything. I only live about ten minutes away. Seriously, if you need anything, just use the motel phone."

I took the ripped piece of paper he handed me. "Thanks." I knew I needed it so I could talk to him about my car, but that's as far as it would go.

"I mean it, anything," he said as he walked to the door, resting his hand against the frame. "Can I get you something before I leave? Dinner?"

"No, I'm not hungry at all, but thanks for offering. I think I'm ready to get some sleep," I admitted.

"I'll keep you posted about your car," he said.

"Thanks," I said, thankful that I would get to see him again, but feeling like a mixed up basket case for not trusting him. I was a freaking mess.

"Goodnight Cassandra," he said quietly before closing the door and walking away.

Yeah, right. Goodnight in this place was going to be hard to come by. I locked the door after he left and walked over to the bed. I drew the covers back and found exactly what I'd pictured... Stains. Gross. I pulled the covers back over the bed and decided to sleep with a towel over me instead. I walked into the filthy bathroom, quickly grabbed a towel, and ran back to the room like a scared child. I put on a pair of yoga pants and a t-shirt and was ready to get some rest. It had been an unusually long day between the long drive, the accident, and the hospital. Too exhausted for continued thinking, I let my brain off the hook and laid down on the hard mattress. As I pulled the towel over my body, I noticed my feet were going to be hanging out all night. *Great.*

I gently laid my sore head back onto the pillow and blinked my eyes a few times. I was right. Sweet dreams were extremely hard to come by in this place, but I tried. I closed my eyes and fell asleep.

Based on the way I felt the next morning, I'd gotten only a few hours of sleep at the most. Between the noises, the creaks, and the foul smell, I didn't know which was worse. *That was, by far, the worst night's sleep I've ever had.* The morning sun shone brightly through the yellowed curtains, and I decided to give up on trying to get any more sleep.

I ripped the towel off of me and was about to put my feet on the floor and there it was. Staring back at me as if I were invading his turf was an oversized, nasty, grey rat. "OH MY GOD!" I screamed as I jumped up and stood on the bed, unsure of what to do if he were to start climbing up. I let out another loud scream as it raised itself up with its beady little eyes staring, making it scurry off under the bed. This was even worse; now I couldn't see the damn thing.

I jumped off the bed and collected my belongings faster than I even realized I could. I threw on a jacket before making a mad dash for the door, slamming it behind me.

"Holy shit, that was gross," I said breathlessly. I took a moment to compose myself, and to think about what to do next. I was not going back into that room. That was for certain.

"Are you looking for a place to stay yet?" I heard his familiar voice from afar. I peeked over the railing, and there he was standing with his arms crossed, wearing a sexy grin, faded jeans, and a tight white tee.

"I don't know whether to think you're a creeper for being here or thank you for being my savior and hug you majorly," I shouted over the railing.

"I'll take being a savior and a hug," he said, giving me an approving smile. "I was driving by, heading back from checking on your car and I thought I'd see if you were finally ready to give in and stay with me," he yelled back. I could hug this man.

"Yes and yes. I'm so ready to get out of here. I have my luggage already behind me," I said, ready to make a dash down to him.

He unfolded his arms and headed my way. "Stay there. I'll come grab it for you," he shouted.

"No need, I walk fast. Let's just get the hell out of here, please," I said, practically running to him.

He grabbed a hold of my luggage and grazed his hand on top of mine before I let go. "I tried to tell you," he said.

"Yeah. Next time I'll listen. I'd rather take my chances on being killed than ever have to experience that again," I said, relieved to be out of that hellhole.

Chapter four

THE RIDE TO HIS HOUSE was short. When I commented that I was used to seeing stoplights on every corner, he told me that there was only one in town, and we wouldn't go through it. We pulled up to a cream-colored ranch style house. The lovely wraparound porch had a swing to the left of the door and two rockers to the right. Jason drove his truck onto the gravel driveway that was in front of a two-car detached garage.

"We're here. Already looking better, huh?"

"You have no idea," I said, relieved to see this beautiful house and not a neon vacant sign.

Jason parked the truck and quickly stepped out. I didn't even have an opportunity to let myself out. He opened my door and put his hand out for me to hold as I slid off the seat.

"A little higher than my car, sorry," I apologized.

A small smile played on his lips as he continued helping me out of the truck. "Don't apologize. It's cute," he said quietly.

Yeah, real cute, I'm sure.

Once I was out, he closed the door behind me, guiding me to the front of the house.

Just as I'd expected, the inside was quaint and country. The living room was to my right and a small dining room decorated with red apples was to the left.

"Your house is really nice," I said in awe of its homey feel.

"Yeah, it's a good house. Small, but it works for us. We've lived here since I was a baby."

I had never been in a house that long; my family moved all the time. They were extremely 'keep up with Jones' type people. This house was cozy, and I liked it.

"This way Sweetheart," he said, grabbing my luggage and leading us down a small hallway.

There were four doors, all closed. He let go of my hand and opened the first door on the right, showing me a bathroom.

"Obviously, it's a bathroom," he stated with a soft laugh. I couldn't help but let out a chuckle. This was quite the tour I was being given.

He walked away, leaving the door open, and led me to the second door on the right. We walked into a small bedroom with a queen size bed, a short dresser and a nightstand to complete it.

"This will be your bedroom," he said, placing my suitcase next to the dresser. He walked over to the closet doors on the left of the bed and pointed at them. "You can put your clothes in the closet or the dresser, whichever you prefer."

The closet? How long was I going to be here? I took another glance over the room. It was small, but it had a warm feeling. I particularly liked the peach colored quilt that covered the bed.

"Will this work for you?"

I turned my eyes to him. "Yes. It's perfect," I assured him.

A satisfied look took over his face as he walked to the door. "Good, then I'll let you settle in, and then meet you in the kitchen. It's just through the hall and to your right," he said. He dropped his head a little and arched his brows. "Make sure to use my directions and not a GPS though."

"Get out," I said, pointing to the door, trying to hold back my smirk.

He laughed and shut the door behind him. I looked around the room, but not a single mirror was in here. That could be a good thing. I didn't even want to see the mess staring back at me.

I opened my suitcase and pulled out a pair of shorts and a t-shirt. I slipped my clean clothes on and immediately felt ten times better. I dug a hair tie out of my make-up bag and pulled my hair into a messy bun. I wasn't one for messy anything, but with the state that my hair was in, messy was my only option. I just hoped my hair was still blonde and not dyed red from any blood that was on my forehead.

I zipped up my suitcase, contemplating if I should actually hang up my clothes. With no idea exactly how long it would take to get my car back, feelings of anxiety swept through me. I had no clue what was going to happen, when I would be leaving, or how long I would be staying here. I took a few deep breaths to ease my nerves and decided to leave my clothes in their luggage for now.

Closing the door behind me, I walked out of the room and made my way to the kitchen, following the exact directions Jason gave me. I wouldn't have needed them because the house was small and I would have found the kitchen sooner or later. But seriously, who needs to get lost two days in a row? Not me.

"And she made it without any injuries," he said, looking up at me from the kitchen table, his hands clasped around a tall blue cup.

"Eh, someone gave me some good directions." I teased back.

"Good? They were spot-on Sweetheart." All I could do was shake my head at him.

He stood up from the table and walked over to pull my chair out for me. He missed nothing. I sat down, and he pushed me up to the table. I was relieved to be sitting again; my body was exhausted.

"Something to drink?" he asked.

"Water would be great, thanks," I replied and within seconds, I had a tall glass of ice water sitting in front of me. Jason sat back down in his chair and took a few sips out of his blue glass.

"So, yesterday at the hospital, you mentioned my being here was okay with your mom. I take it she doesn't mind a complete stranger staying in her house?" I knew damn well my own mother would never do something like this. His mother was a saint. His eyes found mine, and he looked as though I was missing something.

"You already met my mom, Cassandra," he reminded me. Unfortunately, I had no clue who he was talking about because I couldn't recall meeting any mother of Jason's. I gave him a questioning glance.

"Yes, your nurse, Trish," he said. "That's my mom."

"She is?" I was stunned. No one mentioned anything about those two being related while I was at the hospital. How was I to know this?

"She is. And she's pretty wonderful, I might add." You could tell, just from the look on his face, he loved his mother deeply. I wonder if it was him or a sibling who gave her that 'mom' necklace that she wore around her neck.

I thought back to how much she helped me and soothed my frazzled nerves at the hospital. "I had no clue she was your mom," I admitted, now slightly apprehensive to be staying in their house. Trish knew my secret. I didn't know whether she would approve of a girl like me staying in their house. I dropped my gaze to my hands that held my glass of water.

"Are you sure," I started to ask him until he interrupted me.

"She insisted," he answered me without letting me even finish my thought.

"She did?"

"Yes, at the hospital when I was waiting for you. She came out to talk to me, telling me that she didn't want you to be alone, to see if you would stay with us in our spare room," he answered.

I sighed in relief and took a sip of the cold water. It felt good running down my throat. It was hot here today. We both sat in awkward silence until I finished my sip of water.

"And your dad? What's his name? What does he do?" I asked, then immediately regretted it. I just assumed he had a father, and I would feel like the world's biggest jerk if he didn't.

"His name is Bart, and he works on the farm," he said with a distant look in his eyes.

"Oh you guys own a farm?"

"No. We used to own it, but we sold it awhile back and now my dad just helps run it," he answered.

"Why did you sell your farm?" I asked, intrigued about his life here, I wanted to know more. The small town country life was nothing I was used to. I watched him as he looked at the wall behind me, keeping his eyes steady as he sat there for a moment before answering.

"We just couldn't keep up with all the work. It had been in our family for a few generations. It was hard, but sometimes there are just things in life that you have to do," he said quietly. He focused his eyes back on mine, and they looked distressed, like he was bearing something but didn't want to share.

Trying to divert his attention elsewhere, I changed the subject. "Any siblings?" I asked in a more chipper voice.

"Do you always play 20 questions when you meet someone?" he asked.

"Yes, as a matter of fact I do. I like to know everything about a person, about a family, especially one that I'm staying with," I stated.

"Cassandra, that's just called being nosy."

I shot him a crusted look and crossed my arms over my chest. "I just wanted to know more about you."

He held up a hand in front of me. "You're real inquisitive. I get it."

I sat there in silence; his tone was getting a little snippy, and felt as though I was crossing a line that I shouldn't be. The need to know everything gets me in more trouble than it's worth. He got up from his chair and started leaving the table. Maybe staying here was a bad idea and an even worse decision on my part to accept.

"Have you eaten anything since yesterday?"

I shook my head. I hadn't eaten anything since before I left for Alamosa, and I could tell it was starting to wear on me.

"You need to eat then. What can I fix you?"

I raised my head up to see him standing in the kitchen. I was more than stunned to hear him ask that. I thought for sure he was ready to help me pack and take me back to the bug-infested motel again.

Unfortunately, the idea of food was starting to make my stomach turn. So much, in fact, that I thought I was going to heave on this very table. I looked over at Jason who had his eyes already on me. They had a look of panic in them, and I contemplated what to do next, shifting my head from him to the hallway. He was getting ready to speak when I decided now was a good time to run again. I dashed from the table and went straight to the bathroom, kneeling before the toilet, and purging up nothing but bile. Nothing was left in my stomach to come up. It was yellow and acidic and burned my throat to the point of tears. I laid my arm across the seat and rested my forehead against it. I reached over for some toilet paper to wipe the streaming tears from my eyes when I saw his silhouette standing in the doorway. He bent down, handed me a towel, and rested his hand on my back.

"I'm taking you back in," he said quietly. I wiped my eyes first, then took the towel down to my mouth, wiping away any last remnants of bile I could.

"No, Jason, I'm fine," I tried to convince him.

"Clearly," he said quietly, in a sarcastic tone. I knew this looked bad to him. I did. There was nothing I was going to be able to say to him though.

He grabbed the towel from my hand and ran it under the faucet. I lowered my eyes back to the toilet I was hugging. Nasty. I immediately flushed the contents down, seeing it was just making me more nauseated. He knelt down in front of me and delicately put his hand underneath my chin, raising my head up as he wiped my face. I closed my eyes, and enjoyed the feel of a cool towel over my face and having someone take care of me. I opened my eyes only to meet his directly in front of mine. I could tell I was going to have to fight this battle of going to the hospital again. I moved his hand down from my chin and began to ease myself up from their toilet that I was certain I'd need to clean up. His hand grabbed a hold of my arm, helping me up.

"Your mom will be home tonight, right?" I asked him.

He peered down at me cautiously as we stood still in the bathroom. "Yes, why?"

"She's a nurse so she can look me over. I don't need to go to the hospital again," I said. He took in a deep breath, narrowing his eyes as though he was thinking it over. He released his breath and started walking us out of the bathroom.

"Okay then, I can agree with that," he answered. Yes, I won a small battle. "Don't get too excited though. If she says you need to go back, then you're going back."

We continued back to the room I was staying in. I sat down on the bed and could feel the tension as he stood close to me watching every move I made.

"I'm not going to break Jason. I really am okay," I tried to tell him, gazing down at my hands that were fidgeting nervously in my lap.

He cleared his throat and walked over to the bed, kneeling down in front of me. I couldn't help but look down at him. "You must think I'm crazy," he said, rubbing his hand over his scruffy face. "I just don't like to mess around with this kind of stuff." He said it so quietly that it was practically a whisper; almost as if he was uncomfortable telling me how much he cared.

"I'm not used to having someone take care of me or worry about me. I've never been in this sort of situation before, so I'm not taking this very well," I confessed.

He closed his eyes for a split second and let out a long exhale. "I'm sorry no one has been there to take care of you," he replied, finally moving to sit down next to me on the bed.

It made me sad that he felt the need to worry about me. Not having even known this guy for two full days, he was only the second person I'd ever met that I knew genuinely cared about me.

"Hey." I turned my head toward him. "I don't even know your full name."

He looked at me while running his hand through his soft wavy hair. "Jason Dean Bradley," he told me.

"I like it," I said.

"What's your full name Sweetheart?"

"Cassandra Elizabeth Pierce," I revealed to him.

"I like *your* name," he said in a low voice as he nudged my shoulder with his.

I could feel my lips curling up into a cheesy schoolgirl grin, and there was no stopping it. There was just something extraordinary about this guy, and I couldn't put my finger on it, but I knew I not only enjoyed it, hell, I admired it. I could bet money he was one of those guys who had a lot of friends and a lot of girls chasing him down. He was the guy everyone knew and loved to be around. He literally could light up an entire room, and erase any tension floating around.

"So do people call you J.D.?" I asked, curious about any nicknames he might have.

"No, definitely have never been called JD," he told me with a slightly disgusted look on his face. Well then, I guess I would definitely not be calling him JD. "Do people call you Cassie?" he asked with a teasing voice.

"No, they don't," I said. I couldn't deny I kind of liked it though.

"Well, that's a bummer."

"Why is that?" I asked.

He brought his face closer to mine, positioning his mouth by my ear. "Because it fits you, and your pretty face," he whispered.

Cue the flutters that were going crazy in my stomach and the goose bumps that now covered my body. I didn't know whether I should confess I was a mess, and he should stay as far from me as possible, or if I should shut up and embrace the compliment. It's been a long time since I've received one that felt real, and that one did. Too real. I couldn't make up my mind, so I flashed him a grateful smile and began to rebut his nickname choice for me. Before I knew it, I realized we had hung out the whole afternoon when both our heads turned to the sound of the front door unlocking and opening. I knew in an instant that it was his mother returning home from work. Our conversation ceased, and it was apparent that the ease from this afternoon was gone the moment we heard the door open. Jason quickly motioned with his finger that he would be just a moment and got up from the bed. He would be returning, with his mother to come look me over more, even though we both knew the real problem that was haunting me.

Chapter five

WHILE JASON STAYED OUT of the room at Trish's request, she sat on the side of my bed next to me. Her eyes were steady on me. I tried hard to stay calm, but my eyes looked at everything but her.

"Trish, p-please don't say anything," I pleaded with her, not wanting anyone else to know how much I messed things up.

She put her arm around my shoulders, "Sweetie, it's patient confidentiality. I'm not allowed to. Not only that, I would never say anything. That's your news to share."

"Thank you," I said with a deep sigh.

"I'll tell Jason you're fine and that you just had a rough couple of days, which you did," she said. I was thankful she was on board with my request.

"In the meantime, ginger ale and crackers will help with the upset stomach. Help yourself; they are in the kitchen, and anything else you would like too. And don't forget your vitamins," she said, giving my shoulders a quick squeeze before getting up from the bed.

"I appreciate it Trish, I really do," I told her.

"I'm glad you decided to stay here. I know Jason was worried about you, he said you were pretty scared when he found you."

"I'm glad he was there to help," I said, thinking about my 'town rescuer'.

"Me too," she said before walking out and leaving the door open behind her.

"See, I'm fine," I announced to Jason as I saw him peeking around the corner once Trish finished telling him my 'cover' story.

He stood by the door, his arms crossed over his chest. "I guess," he said, as if he didn't believe his mother or me.

I couldn't blame him, but it wasn't something I was ready to tell the world. I yawned and put my hand over my mouth, covering the obnoxious face I made. Nothing is even remotely attractive about a yawn. I noticed Jason covering his mouth while he yawned.

"I didn't sleep well in the motel as I'm sure you already knew," I said, waiting for an 'I told you so', but it never came.

"I'm pretty tired too. If you need anything, I'll be downstairs, and my mom is just on the other side of the hall," he informed me.

"Downstairs?" I questioned him, not knowing there was a basement. I never got that part of the tour. Some tour guide he was.

"Yeah, sorry I never got to show you. It's probably best if I give you directions though," he joked.

"I think I'll be okay, but thanks."

He was extremely persistent in making sure I knew how awful of a direction taker I was. I was never going to live this down, probably not even from Mel. MEL. Holy shit. I sat up in panic mode causing Jason to take a step back from the bed.

"Cassandra?" he asked, sounding apprehensive. I got up, pushed past him, and started for my luggage, hopeful it would be in there.

"My phone. I need to call my friend to let her know what's going on Jason. Oh my God, she is probably freaking out. I was supposed to be there last night!" I told him, feeling my stomach multiply in knots as I thought about how worried Mel would be. I couldn't believe that I didn't think of this last night. For all I knew, she could have called the police, or worse, my family, to start a search for me. Oh no. This was too much to think about. My head began immediately throbbing as the room started slowly spinning like a merry-go-round. I watched as everything passed by me. My chest grew tighter; my breathing got shorter and soon far surpassed becoming rapid. It all hurt; the shortness of breath was too much for me.

"Whoa," I mumbled as the walls around me were starting to slowly cave in. I felt hands on my shoulders and a voice speaking to me, but the thoughts of Melanie continued to take over my body and mind. Her name ran rampant through my mind. Melanie. Melanie. Melanie. It was all I could focus on. I was dropping lower and lower, until I felt myself being laid on the bed.

"Cassie…" I heard his voice more clearly as he continued to say my name while stroking the side of my face. "Cassie…"

The vision of his face was faintly coming into sight. I tried to focus on it and relax myself as best I could. A few moments later, his face was in full view, and I could finally catch a decent breath.

"That's it, stay with me," he said calmly, but the look on his face said he was ready to pack me up and either take me to the hospital or the looney house. I clearly scared him.

"I'm here, I'm here," I said. "I think I just had a panic attack." Unfortunately, I'd been having them more frequently these days.

"I'm going," he started to say as I shoved my hand against his mouth, his lips touching the palm of my hand. His eyes got wide, and his head moved back while I kept my hand held against his lips.

"No, I am not going to the hospital!" I yelled to him. He calmly took my hand in his and lowered it to the bed, keeping a loose hold on it.

"I'm going to get you some water," he said, slowly arching his eyebrows.

"Oh, sorry." I was thoroughly embarrassed.

His hand finally let go of mine, and he left the room. *Get it together, Cassandra.* This was ridiculous and childish. I mean, what would my parents think of me if they saw me like this? They would for sure have me committed. Jason came back into my room after a few minutes carrying a large glass of water in one hand and something wrapped in a paper towel in the other. He set the water on the nightstand next to the bed and pulled his flip phone out of his pocket, setting it next to the water.

"Drink this and use that," he said, peering down at me. I nodded my head in acceptance. "And eat this, no questions asked." He handed me what was in his other hand. I opened it to find a sandwich.

"I will," I told him.

"I'll be downstairs. It's the door in the back of the kitchen."

"Thanks Jason, again."

"You're welcome."

Once he left the room and closed the door behind him, I nearly drowned myself in the water. It never tasted so good. I put the finished glass down on the nightstand and ate my sandwich. Something so simple was entirely too satisfying. I put the empty paper towel aside and picked up his flip phone. I was just not going to get over his phone. I flipped it open to a small screen with the time and date in the corner and a picture in the middle. I brought the phone to my face to look more closely at the picture, being that the screen was smaller than the phones I was used to. The picture was of a tree, a large one. Squinting more I could tell that it looked damaged. Oh My God, you have got to be kidding me. I shook my head in utter shock that he would take this picture, and then of course let me see it on his phone, knowing darn well I would notice it. He was undeniably atypical in all the right ways.

When I was done being amused with the tree on his screen I navigated my way through his phone. I reached the contacts, and I was starting to feel a little too invasive. I wanted to know more about this stranger who was hardly a stranger any longer. He was too intriguing. He looked about my age if not a couple years older, he lived at home, and he had a life that I was not used to seeing. I wanted to understand it. I wanted to know if he had siblings, a girlfriend, a best friend, and then I wanted to investigate his photo albums. But, I knew deep down that I had to stop. The line would be crossed in bright red if I didn't back off now. This Cassandra would have never let a stranger's phone that fell into her inquisitive hands go unturned, but this felt wrong. A family I didn't know, a guy I barely knew, welcomed me with open arms into their home, cared for me, and let me hang on to his phone without hesitation. I wanted to be like them and not question every little thing. I didn't want to be intrusive. Letting out another breath, I decided that I did well on closing out of the contacts icon and instead started to dial Mel's number.

On the second ring, Mel answered the phone sounding terrified. "Hello?"

"Mel, it's me." I started choking up just hearing her voice. I wanted so much to be with her right now. I was supposed to be with her in her warm embrace right now.

"Oh my God, Cassandra, where in the hell are you? I've called every hospital from Alamosa to Boulder. Please tell me you aren't in some ditch on the side of the road. I was just getting ready to report you missing. What's going on? Are you okay? Where is your phone? Whose phone is this?" She spouted off question after question until she ran out of breath.

"I don't even know where the hell I am. My GPS got me lost apparently. They said I'm like 4 hours from Alamosa, my tire blew out, I hit a tree with my car, I ended up at the hospital, they thought I had a concussion, I went to a rat infested motel last night, I was exhausted beyond words and forgot to call you, then I came home with this family, I'm staying in their spare bedroom, I can't find my phone, this is Jason's phone I'm using, and my car is in the process of getting fixed," I spewed out to her until I ran out of breath and had to stop to catch it.

"What?" she asked confused.

"Exactly," I said just as confused as she was. We sat on the phone for what felt like forever in silence, but I'm sure it was only a minute or so. Trying to get a grip on what happened.

"I'm coming to get you, can you please find out where you are?" She finally asked, breaking the silence between us.

"What about my car, Mel?" I reminded her.

"We'll come back to get it. Cassandra, right now, I just want you safe with me," she said hastily.

I held the sobs back that were ready to escape. Just hearing that she was ready to jump in a car tonight to come and get me was enough for me to remember exactly why this girl was my best friend and my sister. Even if not blood related, she was family enough for me.

"Who's this Jason guy and what family are you staying with?" she asked eagerly.

I wasn't surprised she asked, in fact, it would be the first thing I would ask her if she were in this predicament. I began to think about Jason and this family I was staying with, and I could tell a smile was spreading across my face. They were nothing like my own and I was pretty sure I was more than okay with that.

"Well, are you locked up in some basement, Cass? Do I need to call the cops?" she asked quickly and frantically. I must have stayed deep in thought too long.

"No, Mel, not at the moment anyway," I tried to reassure her. "Jason's the one who saw me crash and called the cops and ambulance to come to the scene of the accident. Then I was taken to the hospital." I paused after hearing her gasp. "I'm six weeks."

"That's okay. We'll figure out that stuff when you get here," she said calmly.

She clearly couldn't see me, but it felt good to hear the reassurance from her. "My nurse just so happened to be Jason's mom. They offered me their spare bedroom to stay in while my car…" I stopped to shake my head in anger. I still had a hard time accepting what happened yesterday.

"It's okay, Cass," she said in a soft voice.

I swallowed my anger back and continued. "While my car gets fixed, but I don't even know how long that will be. They said the parts aren't in stock, and I'm positive it needs major body work," I said in frustration. I could hear Mel doing the same on her end of the phone while we just sat there in silence again.

"Where are you at? I'm coming to get you," she stated.

I looked around the room I was in. It was a luxury hotel compared to the motel I stayed in last night. The Cassandra I used to be would have NEVER in a million years stayed in a stranger's house, but there was something about this family I couldn't help but feel at ease around. Now was my chance to speak up and have Mel either come get me out of this town or hold my peace and accept that I was staying here with complete and utter strangers until my car was fixed. I took a deep breath in and pulled the phone down from my ear, looking at the picture of the damaged tree on the screen once more. It was weird and truly out of character, but I was going to stay. I put the phone back up to my ear and told Mel my decision.

"Like hell you are, I'm coming to get you right now. Give me the address," she demanded.

"I'm fine here. This family, oddly enough, is genuinely kind, and I'll be okay, honestly. I promise to call you every day, as soon as I find my phone that is," I said, peering around my room wishing the damn thing would appear out of thin air.

"Are you serious, Cass?" she asked, sounding upset. "Can you rent a car maybe?"

I never thought about that, but with the town being as small as it is, I doubt they had one. "I have to use all the extra money I have to pay for the repairs on my car. I couldn't afford one even if they did have a place."

"So you're staying with this family then? I don't feel right about this."

"I'm sure. I'll be okay. You have Jason's number. I called you on his phone remember?"

"Oh yes, and I intend to call it every day until you are back on the road," she sassed. "What's their last name? I need this information in case–in case of an emergency."

"It's Bradley. I'll call you tomorrow then?"

"I guess, Cass. You aren't giving me any other choice," she said, sounding defeated. "You okay otherwise?"

I knew where she was going with this question, and I was glad she asked in a roundabout way; I wasn't ready to accept anything yet. "Eh, okay, I suppose. Not great, that's for sure," I told her the truth.

"Okay, call me tomorrow love." I told her I loved her and flipped the phone closed, placing it on the nightstand next to the bed.

A deep sigh escaped me, deflating my body as I weighed the decision I had just made. It was deeper than just waiting it out for my car and not wanting Mel to come pick me up. Not only did Mel have a life of her own to attend to without wasting a day to come and rescue my ass, but also something inside me made me want to stay here for other reasons. It could have been the kindness of Trish and Jason or the fact that I could be this lost girl around them and not have to worry about it. It didn't hurt that Trish would be here to talk to if I wanted the chance to discuss my pregnancy with someone. She already knew what was going on and could be a lending shoulder, ear, or voice.

Perhaps it was something about their warm hearts and open arms that screamed to me because I missed having that in my life. I knew deep down in my core I was craving that sort of affection, and here it was, magically landing in my lap. I'd be a fool not to at least accept the attention and wait for my car, all the while, enjoying their company. I guess we would find out just how big of a fool I really was when all was said and done.

Chapter
six

I FINALLY LAID MY HEAD down on the pillow and thought about what a journey this was turning into. Here I was, thinking that things couldn't get any worse, and then life laughed at me and threw a damn tree in my way. I was grateful that I wasn't sleeping in a motel like last night. I needed to get some rest. My body was mentally and physically exhausted. I let my eyelids shut and fell fast asleep only to wake up parched a couple hours later. I tore the covers off of me thinking that maybe I was just overheated. I lay there for a few minutes contemplating the thought of needing versus wanting water. It was needed. I stood up out of the bed, slipped on a pair of cotton shorts and tiptoed out into the hallway. I couldn't help but feel a little strange about walking around their home while they were asleep.

"Hello there." A shadow from the kitchen table with a deep husky voice said.

"AHHH!" I screamed and all but jumped out of my skin when the voice rumbled through my body.

"Easy does it little lady, I didn't mean to scare you," he said calmly, still sitting at the table.

There was enough light from the rising sun peeking through the windows that I could slightly make out his features. He was older with a full head of hair, and I couldn't help but guess that it was Jason's dad, Bart. I breathed out deeply, and quickly wiped around my frontal area, making sure I didn't piss myself when he scared me from out of nowhere. I was good. I slowly made my way to the kitchen table where he was sitting.

"You must be Bart," I said, still breathing heavy from being so frightened of the shadowed figure at the table.

"You must be Cassandra, the girl from the hospital," he said in a husky voice that could give some actors a run for their money. It reminded me of one you'd hear in an old western movie, slow and easy.

"Yes, that'd be me," I answered back. I wasn't sure what to expect of his dad, and I thought we would have met in an entirely different way. Definitely not in the wee hours of the morning like this.

"Here, have a seat," he said, pointing to the chair he just rose from.

"Okay," I quietly said, walking over to the chair awaiting my arrival.

He slid my chair in as I sat down then walked over to the chair directly across from my seat. His eyes were squinted while he looked me over. I swallowed a deep gulp and let out the breath I had been holding when he shifted in his chair, putting one arm behind him on the back of it.

"Well, the good news is you definitely look a lot better than the tree, Darlin'," he said.

He was just like his son or vice versa. They just couldn't help but tease me. I felt relieved to know this man wasn't as scary as his deep voice led me to believe. I let out a slight chuckle. I guess I had to get over the fact that I was forever going to be known as the girl who hit the tree.

"Thanks Bart."

"How are you feeling, Darlin'?" he asked.

I was scared, lonely, lost, desperate, needy, and pathetic. So many emotions. I had never felt this way before, and I wasn't enjoying feeling any of it. I needed to get back to being me, but that was half the problem. The Cassandra I was before may have been stronger and much less scared, but that girl lived for everyone else and was just as pathetic in a much different sense. I gazed up at Bart.

"I'm okay, just a little…." I sat, thinking of the right word to tell him.

"Lost?" he asked with a raised brow.

Bingo. I felt like he didn't know exactly how lost I really was. Instead, he just knew I ended up lost in this town I've never even heard of.

"Something like that," I replied.

"We'll get you back on track. You're in good hands. Jason is as good as they come, and well, Trish, she is the rock of this family. I'd be lost without those two," he said as he stood up from his chair.

"They've been really helpful," I told him, glad to hear how much he cherished his family. "Thanks again for letting me stay here, Bart."

"Don't mention it, anything we can do to help. Water? I presume that is what you were coming out here for." He was good. I nodded my head eagerly.

"Yes, please," I said kindly while he poured some water into a tall glass.

"I couldn't help but notice that you're up pretty early," I mentioned to him, curious as to why he was up.

"You don't miss a beat do you?" he asked, bringing my water to the table and taking a seat back in his chair.

I shook my head. "No, sorry." Once again, I was being too nosy as Jason would say. This family didn't seem like the type for questions, and here I was full of too many. He let out a soft chuckle; it was just like Jason's, very contagious.

"It's quite alright. I was actually just letting myself wake up before I head out for work," he said, peering out the kitchen window at the moonlit sky. Work? That was extremely early. I was an early riser, but holy crap.

"Farm life. Up before the sun," he said.

I hadn't ever been around a farm before. I've seen them in movies, the hot guys with their tractors, boots, and cowboy hats, but that was as far as it went.

He got up from his chair and put his hands on the back of it.

"Get some rest, okay? I heard you had a pretty rough accident." He peered at me, and, with the light from the window hitting his face, I noticed that his eyes were green. Even though they didn't appear to be emerald stones like Jason's, they were still comforting to look at.

"Thank you Bart, I will," I assured him. "Don't work too hard."

"I always do, Cassandra." He patted the back of the chair before making his way out of the kitchen.

I wasn't sure what to expect from his dad. Jason didn't give me much information on him other than that he worked on the farm, but he seemed nice. He was a little intense at first, but definitely a dad who just seemed to have a lot on his plate and his mind.

I sat in silence for the next few minutes sipping my glass of water, before going back to bed, when I heard the door in the back of the kitchen creak open. I held my breath and quickly turned in my chair. It was faint, but I could see Jason stalking out of the doorway through the kitchen. I put my hand to my chest, trying to catch my breath.

"You scared me," I panted.

"That's not hard to do," he said, sounding amused. "I heard you scream when I was headed upstairs and I heard my dad talking to you." He walked over to the cabinet and grabbed a glass, filling it with water.

"I was wondering if my scream woke anyone up," I said.

He turned from the sink, and he made his way over to the table, sitting down in the chair his father had sat in.

"I would have saved you, but you needed to meet him and I figured he'd like you enough not to scare you away," he said.

"He seems nice. A little intimidating at first, sitting at the table in the dark," I said. "He does have a strong voice though. It was very…" I sat trying to think of the right word as Jason leaned toward me.

"Intense," he whispered.

"Yes, exactly." I agreed.

He leaned back into his chair. "He definitely does have a profound voice, but deep down he's a sensitive guy. He is a hard worker, and he likes things to be in order, but that's just because of the way he was raised. The only time I've ever heard his voice go soft was when he cried," he said, gazing out the window, getting lost in his own words. Just like his dad was doing.

"So deep down, he's a teddy bear?" I asked teasingly, trying to ease Jason.

He quickly returned his gaze to meet mine. "I've never heard anyone call him that before. I wouldn't go that far, but you get the idea."

"I understand the term teddy bear, but I've actually never seen a dad act like one. Especially..." I stopped myself. I didn't know how much I should discuss my family. It wasn't as though I was going to see this family ever again once I got my car back and hit the road in the *correct* direction, but it also wasn't something that was worth discussing, not like he could do anything to help.

"Especially what?" he asked, breaking the silence as I sat thinking about how I understood now why it was hard for Jason to discuss his family with me. We barely knew each other. It wasn't normal to just word vomit your life story to strangers, but I started now, it would be impossible not to finish.

"Especially my father." I shrugged. "No teddy bear there. He and my mother are very firm and strict. They want things done their way, or it literally would be the highway for my ass, no questions asked," I finally told him. I let out a heavy exhale. "I don't normally share information like that. I don't know why I just did." The look on his face made me regret telling him.

"For starters, don't be sorry, Cassandra. It's good to share things like that. Sometimes, it can help take away the pain and frustration bottled up inside," he said, pausing long enough to take a sip of water. "Secondly, sharing details about family is hard for *all* of us." I knew exactly how he must have felt now. I leaned back in my seat; embarrassed by all the uncomfortable questions that I put him through yesterday. "And lastly, are they why you're running?"

The words slipped out of his mouth like water coming out of a faucet, fast and in full force. I didn't know how he knew I was running. All I told him when we met was I was headed to Alamosa to see a friend. I didn't want to share anything else about my situation with him.

"I'm not running Jason." I said, trying to convince him and myself of the lie I was telling. "I'm just going to visit my friend in Alamosa, that's all."

He sat across from me, still and expressionless. There was nothing on his face I could read. It was like looking at a mime that suddenly stopped their act.

"Honest," I said, trying to show him I had nothing to hide. Except I did. I had everything to hide and run away from. How could someone who barely knew you, know you so well? He continued to stare at me, moving his head from one side to the other, as though he was investigating *my* expressions.

"I don't know, Cassie," he muttered. "I just don't believe you. You seem like you're running from something or someone. I know lost eyes when I see them."

Jason was easy to be around, but this secret, being pregnant and running away, wasn't easy to share. He would just have to let it go. "I guess you can think what you want Jason."

"Come here for a sec." He stood up and nudged his head in the direction of the hallway.

I wasn't sure what he was up to, but I followed him anyway. He walked into the bathroom, and I stood next to him quietly as he turned on the light. He took his hand and cupped my chin, searching my forehead. I couldn't help but watch him as he did. He looked my head over diligently, not missing one inch of my face.

"Your cut needs some attention." He removed his hand from my chin and grabbed a tube out of the medicine cabinet. "I'm going to put some ointment on it for you okay?" He arched a brow at me.

This was all new to me, a guy caring for me in this way. I was in a state of shock as he put the ointment on my forehead. He dabbed it on gently and smoothed it over my cut so softly, I would have never known he was doing it if it weren't for him standing in front of me.

"That's better." He finished and put the cap back on the tube.

"Thank you," I said. "And I really am okay otherwise, Jason."

It was a last attempt to convince him, but I could tell he still didn't believe me. Hell, I didn't believe me. There was one thing

I was good at, and that was people-pleasing, because I did it all my life, but lying, I didn't do well. This surprised me because, throughout my life, I did what everyone else wanted, even though I wasn't happy with it, thinking I had no other choice. So why was lying so much different? Maybe it wasn't the lying but maybe lying to Jason. He seemed, in only a matter of a day, to know me better than anyone else had, aside from Melanie. He could see through the façade that I put on all my life.

"It's okay Sweetheart, when you're ready," he said. He definitely didn't believe me, but at least he wasn't pushing either. All I had to do was get my car, go on my way, and he would never have to know.

Chapter seven

THE SUNLIGHT GLARING THROUGH the window hit my eyes as I peeled them open one at a time. I felt more exhausted and bent out of shape than the day before. The meet and greet with Bart, and then talking with Jason made it hard to get much sleep. I sat up and stretched my arms above my head before I rushed to the bathroom. I was ready to relieve myself from the buckets of water I had last night when I heard a light knock on the door.

"Come in," I said, wondering whom it could be. It opened slowly as Jason, dressed in yet another pair of fitted jeans, V-neck tee, and cowboy boots, came walking in. I couldn't help but gaze all the way from his boots to the slight waves that topped his head. Everything just worked. I'm pretty sure it was the jeans that cupped his ass perfectly or the tee that hugged his chest just enough to show his muscles underneath, but either way he was looking good. The look was complete with the same wide smile that seemed to always be plastered on his face. I wished I knew his secret to smiling all the time.

"Good Morning or I guess almost afternoon," he said. I looked around, there wasn't a clock in this room, and I had no clue what time it actually was. "It's almost noon, you must have been tired." He put both arms on the end of the bed, hovering down over my legs, his muscles flexing as he held himself up. It was hard not to take notice.

"Wow, I never sleep that late," I said, still trying to wake up and take my focus off of him hovering over me. I was always an early riser for classes, so this was completely out of sorts for me, but I guess without any classes to attend I was out of sorts.

I grabbed his phone from the nightstand next to me and slid it down the bed to him. "Thanks again, I was able to call my friend last night. All is good, she might be calling you though, and, as in might, I mean will be," I warned him.

He let out a soft chuckle before grabbing the phone and stuffing it in his front pocket. "To make sure I haven't chopped you up and killed you yet?"

"Exactly," I assured him, nodding.

"I'll make sure to let her know I'm keeping you safe."

"Nice picture, by the way," I eyed him with a glare, trying to change the subject so I could stop blushing.

"I thought you'd get a kick out of that. That old tree has been around since I can remember and then you came along and showed it who was boss." He laughed.

"I think it showed me who was boss," I said, still feeling the pain it caused me days later. I sat there for a moment rubbing my neck when a strange but familiar feeling snuck up on me.

"You okay?" he asked, gazing at me with those alarmed eyes I was getting all too used to seeing.

I could feel it again, the need to run, and quick. I cupped my hand over my mouth, shoved the blankets to the side as I ran past Jason, and went straight for the bathroom. Kneeling before the toilet, I purged up nothing but bile again. The acid was burning my raw throat even more today than yesterday. I let it come up twice more before I noticed Jason standing in the doorway holding a washcloth. I leaned myself against the wall across from the toilet, letting myself take a moment to recover. He walked in and bent down right next to me as he began to wipe my mouth off. I grabbed the washcloth from his hands, unsure how to feel about him cleaning my face and finished the job. I wiped my forehead with the other side of it and put it beside me when I was done.

"You really don't need to be this helpful," I told him as I leaned my head back against the wall. I extended my legs out, putting one on either side of the toilet bowl in front of me. This pregnancy was starting to get worse. I didn't know if I had the strength to keep up with it until I got to Mel's. Let alone try and continue to hide the sickness from Jason. I wasn't sure how I was going to explain this one to him without avoiding another unnecessary trip to the hospital.

"I know I don't need to," he said, closing the door behind him and leaning his back against the wall, our legs almost side by side. I kept my gaze forward; if I looked at him and saw those damn eyes staring at me, I didn't know if I would be able to withhold the truth, and I truly needed to.

He cleared his throat and turned to look at me. "I want to, Cassie," he said quietly.

"Why?" I asked curiously.

"You look afraid, and I just don't want you to have to be scared alone okay?"

I lifted my gaze and turned so that I was face-to-face with him. "Okay," I answered him. "I hope you know how much I appreciate it."

"I do." He gently tucked a piece of my loose hair behind my ear. My heart stood still. It was a small thing to do, but he had no clue about the powerful impression it just had on me. "So." He arched his brow, peering at me with eyes that wanted answers.

I should have known that was coming. I needed to come up with a lie and quick. I took in a deep breath and pulled an answer together. "I think I felt sick because I need to eat something," I told him. It wasn't necessarily a lie either. I was so hungry it really was making me feel sick.

He let his brow down. "Good answer. I was about to take you back in, you know? I don't like seeing you sick."

"I know Jase, I know." I was beginning to see even more, how caring he was when it came to my health. I just couldn't understand why.

He cocked his head to the side and peered at me. "What did you just call me?" he asked.

I didn't realize I had, but I guess I just gave him a nickname. I slumped down against the wall, feeling awkward and wondering if he wasn't happy that I just shortened his name for him. "I called you Jase. Is that okay?" I asked coyly.

A smile swept across his face, all his pearly whites beaming just like his eyes. He stood up and lowered his hand in front of me, helping me up.

"It's definitely okay," he said approvingly.

"Good," I replied.

"Breakfast or lunch?" he asked. *Food, yes food.*

"Honestly, you pick, I just need something," I said.

"Okay then, breakfast just so happens to be my favorite meal of the day and one of the things I *can* cook. You better prepare yourself for the best breakfast you've ever had Sweetheart."

"Can't wait," I said, hardly believing I was about to have a guy cook breakfast for me. The only meals cooked for me were either from a chef at a restaurant or the microwave. He started to walk us out of the bathroom, but I wasn't quite finished in there.

I tugged my arm behind him to turn him toward me. "I need to use the little girls' room still." I was now really embarrassed. He let a chuckle escape his throat before letting my hand and body go back into the bathroom.

Chapter
eight

AFTER I RELIEVED MYSELF, I decided a shower was in order. I grabbed a towel under the sink and turned the water on. I got the water to just the right temperature before submerging my body underneath the much needed escape. I started thinking about every single moment up until now.

A few of the moments made me angry for letting myself even be in this mess, then I thought of all the things I still had yet to do. I didn't want to be weak and let all the things I had yet to do consume me and take me down. I had to be strong. I was only twenty-one and felt like I was some young teenager screwing up her life.

The thoughts of getting back on track made me think of the ride down, making me think of Jason. I wasn't sure why my thoughts led me to him. I let the water continue to pour on top of me, running down my face so I couldn't see. But that didn't stop the vision of Jason's gorgeous, green, drown-worthy eyes staring back at me, wanting to consume me. It wasn't bad enough that his eyes got a hold of me first; he also had the biggest heart in the world. I didn't know how many times he had helped a complete stranger before, but something told me it was a lot more than just helping me out. He was a good guy, and as crazy as I was for staying here, I was completely okay with it all and happy I had someone with me. I was changing in more ways than one. And as

I was changing so was the water, it had turned from steaming, to warm, to icy.

I quickly used whatever shampoo, conditioner, and soap they had and once the water was arctic cold, giving me the quick wake-up I needed, I turned the shower off. I dried myself, wrapped the towel around my body, and wiped away the fog on the mirror.

Although I still had a small cut and a bruise on my forehead, I looked ten times better than I felt and I'm sure I looked yesterday. I stared at the spot that had Jason's fingers on it last night, trying to make the cut better. I didn't understand his insistent need to help me, but I also couldn't deny that I hated it either. I let out a sigh and turned my focus to my hair.

I didn't have a brush with me to untangle it, so I ran my fingers through it the best I could. I opened the door, and luckily, no one was in the hallway, so I scurried to my room and closed the door behind me.

I knelt down to my suitcase and unzipped it. I decided on a pair of shorts and a silky tank top that I bought at a boutique in Boulder last month. It was flowy and breathable, exactly what I needed today since the house was already stifling hot. Unfortunately, I didn't pack a blow dryer or curling iron with me, and I was more than regretting that decision. I was in a hurry to leave and against my better judgment, didn't think I would need it. Mel was a hair fanatic and always had too many tools; I thought I'd be fine. It would just have to air dry.

I walked out of my room and the smell of bacon hit me immediately. It smelled delicious and made my mouth water a little more with each inhale. The last time I had breakfast was at a brunch with my parents a couple months ago to discuss the course of action I would take for my senior year of college, and of course, how they were disappointed that I didn't graduate a year early. I remember rushing to my advisor the next day seeing if there was anything I could do to take summer courses to try and graduate even a semester early, but there was no use. I still had thirty credit hours left because of my double major and that was too much to cram into one semester. So once again I disappointed them, and once again they didn't congratulate me on the 4.0 GPA I received last semester. I let out a sigh in frustration as I recalled the meal I had with them and suddenly was ready to start crying.

"Whoa there, Sweetheart, you okay?" he asked as I stepped into the kitchen.

I wiped the corners of my eyes and took a deep breath; I was not going to let them do this to me, not here. I looked up at him, a pair of tongs in his left hand as he stared at me. I pushed away the negative thoughts and let a smile appear on my face, for me and for the kind-hearted man standing in front of me cooking me breakfast.

"Great," I told him.

"Good, I hope you're hungry."

"It smells amazing Jase. I'm starving," I assured him, my stomach starting to growl even louder as the smell continued to linger through the kitchen. He turned back to the stove, using the tongs to turn the bacon as it sizzled in the skillet.

"Go take a seat. I poured you some juice, coffee, and water. I wasn't sure what you wanted," he said, looking over his shoulder at me.

I shook my head. "I'm not that picky, Jase." I watched him in the kitchen for a moment. He looked at ease and completely into what he was doing. There was just one thing missing. "What? No apron?" I teased him.

He turned his head, looking at me over his shoulder once more. "Funny," he replied, playfully rolling his eyes before continuing to cook.

I made my way to the table and sat down. I decided to take a sip of all of the drinks he spread out for me. I needed some coffee though; I was an all-day coffee kind of girl. With the amount of schoolwork I was doing, I had to pull too many all-nighters to keep up. But then a thought triggered in my already overcrowded brain. Was coffee okay for the baby? I let out a huff. I didn't have a clue what was good and what was considered negligent toward this ever-growing fetus taking up residency in my stomach. Again, it was showing me how much I didn't know about being a mother and reminding me that I wasn't ready to be one.

"Cream?" I heard him shout.

"Not anymore," I shouted back. "I used to be a cream, sugar, and more sugar coffee girl. But not these days." I watched as he brought a plate full of bacon over to the table, then returned to the kitchen bringing out more plates of food, enough for the neighbors and the rest of the block.

"Jason, I think you cooked just a little too much."

"You said you were hungry," he reminded me.

"Yup, I sure did, but I didn't expect you to cook a three course meal."

"Maybe I was just trying to impress you with my culinary skills." He winked.

He didn't have to try; he already had impressed me more than he could realize. This was impressive though. He had an array displayed in front of us including pancakes, French toast, scrambled eggs, toast, bacon, and sausage links. I was feeling greasy just looking at it all. I didn't eat at home a lot. Looking at what was in front of me, I started to realize what I was missing out on. It all looked like it was cooked in a gourmet restaurant and presented as though it was something my parents would order at brunch.

"Dig in, or are you one of them fruit and yogurt girls?" he asked with a disapproving look. He was too smart for his own good. "Please don't tell me I'm right?"

"It's just that I rarely cook and when I go out I normally order a salad, but only because I do enjoy them and they're healthy and quick. This, however, looks amazing," I added, placing a little bit of everything on my plate, a little heavy on the bacon; it smelled too good and my body was craving it now. I slipped a piece of it in my mouth, savoring the salty goodness as it crunched between my teeth.

"Oh my God," I mumbled through the bites.

"That's what they all say," he said smiling.

"Oh really?" I asked.

"No. Actually you're the only one I've cooked for before."

I wasn't expecting him to say that, but it more than made me happy. "Is that so? Well you did good. I love it."

"I'm glad. And yes, the only one," he smirked and stared at my eyes for a moment before shifting his back down to his plate.

I didn't know how after the flips my stomach was doing from his comment, but I finished off another piece of bacon as we sat in silence. Normally the silence would be awkward and bother me, but right now, I was too consumed by the delicious food in front of me to care. I started on my French toast when Jason finally broke the silence between us.

"So why don't you have time to cook, too busy warding off guys?" he asked. Was this his roundabout way of asking if I had a boyfriend? He was way off base.

"Not even close. I was busy with school. I guess you could say I was a little obsessed." I'm sure that made me sound like someone who had no life, and it was true, I didn't.

"That busy, huh?" he asked with a surprised look on his face.

"That busy."

"Why?"

I dropped my head and looked up at him. He looked about my age; unless he was sheltered, he should understand.

"Did you not go to college?" I asked curiously.

He shook his head and took his gaze to his plate. "I took a few classes at a community college but decided not to go back, so I never really got into the whole college thing," he said quietly.

I was curious why, but I was learning that things down here were a little different from where I was from. Even though we were in the same state, it felt like completely different countries.

"I was double majoring, and I had a minor. Not only was I too busy to cook, but I was lucky if I remembered what day it was."

He looked back up, his eyes tainted with sadness. I didn't like seeing him upset and I wondered if this was how he felt when he looked at me yesterday. "What's wrong over there?" I asked him.

He shook his head and stabbed another pancake with his fork. "Nothing, I'm just enjoying listening to you talk," he said before eating the pancake.

"What are your majors?" he asked. "You're making me feel a little intimidated over here, by the way."

"Don't. My life is far from intimidating," I told him honestly. "My majors are Finance and Business Management," I tried to answer him with more information, but it was all I could do to spit those words out. They tasted horrible in my mouth, especially considering it was not an 'is' but a 'was'. "Can we change the subject?" I pleaded.

His lips curled up. I could tell he knew that discussing school was making me uncomfortable. It was beginning to feel like a conversation I would have with kids at school, both out of politeness and because there was nothing else to talk about with them.

"So where did you learn to cook like a five star restaurant?" I asked, changing the subject since he wouldn't. He continued to smile, and if I wasn't mistaken, I could have sworn his cheeks were turning a shade of red. It didn't take much to make this guy blush.

"My mom taught me," he answered.

"Well, kudos to your mom, she must be a great teacher," I said, jealous that my mom never taught me to cook. I stopped the hateful thoughts against her before I let the bitterness run through me again.

"My mom used to make me breakfast a lot when I was younger, it's sort of my comfort food," he said after taking a sip of his orange juice. "Then she taught me how to cook it. To be honest, I think she just got sick of me begging her to do it all the time."

"Well maybe you could come to Boulder and teach me how to cook sometime," I said, shocking us both. I could immediately feel my cheeks getting hotter as I sat and thought about what I just invited him to do. The widening look in his eyes made me even more embarrassed; I guess it didn't take much to make me blush either.

"I'm sorry Jase." I laughed nervously. "I didn't mean to say that, or maybe I did, but I guess… I guess what I'm trying to say is that I didn't mean to make you uncomfortable. I honestly don't know why I even just said that." I stopped myself and put my hands over my face. The words were just not coming out right. I was making it worse. I heard a husky chuckle come out of him as I slowly peeled my hands from my face.

"I'd actually really like that," he said, smiling. I wasn't sure if it was a pity response or if he was really being honest, but either way, I was glad he didn't make an embarrassing situation even worse. I gave him a grateful look and finished my breakfast, both of us remaining silent until we were done.

I got up from the table when I finished and Jason immediately started getting up.

"No, you sit. I'm doing dishes," I announced.

He started shaking his head quickly, still trying to get up. I walked over and put my hand on his shoulder.

"No means no. Now, sit and finish your coffee. You cooked breakfast; it's the least I can do," I said, grabbing his plate from in front of him when his hand grabbed onto it too.

"Cassandra, put it down," he demanded. I hadn't seen him so demanding before, and a slight thrill ran through me. I couldn't let him do that to me though. I could be just as demanding.

"NO!" I said frustrated.

We both maintained our grip on his plate and were now competing in a stare down.

"If you don't let go of the plate, then I will when you aren't expecting it, and it will go flying. Then you'll have to explain to your mom how you broke her dish." He glared his eyes at me and slowly released the plate. "Good Jase," I said, patting him on the head before I walked to the sink with his plate.

"You are very persistent, you know that?" he asked, rubbing the back of his neck as I came back to get the rest of the plates on the table.

"And you use a lot of dishes when you cook," I sassed back.

I noticed the lack of a dishwasher and realized this was going to be a hands-on job. I started filling the sink with hot water and soap, and sensed when Jase walked up behind me. It startled me, causing goose bumps to break out on my body. I was so focused on the water that I didn't even see him get up from the table. He reached over my head to the cabinet above us, pulled out a dishtowel, and moved over to my left side. I turned my head toward him, staring at the towel in his hands. I shut the water off while I kept my gaze on the damn towel. He was not going to help me with this.

"What is that?" I asked, tapping my foot.

"Well Sweetheart, it's a towel," he replied. "I'm not sure of the specific definition, but people use it to primarily dry things, such as dishes, which I intend to do."

I shook my head, baffled by his persistence. "And you think *I'm* the persistent one."

"Go sit back down," I told him, reaching my hand out for the towel. "If you don't, I'm not cleaning the dishes, so you'll have nothing to dry." I put a hand on each hip and stood with my back in front of the sink.

"I think you may have met your match, Sweetheart. I can play this game better than you can," he declared, leaning his back against the counter with the towel in his hands, swishing it around.

"So what school do you go to?" he asked, breaking the silence between us. He knew what he was doing; he was going to ask me uncomfortable questions until I broke and caved in.

I wasn't one for failing, well used to be anyway. "University of Colorado," I said with a pleased grin.

"That's a good school," he stated. "Why aren't you there right now?" He was now treading in deep waters.

I turned back to the sink and started putting the dishes in one by one.

"I dry dishes really well," he whispered in my ear, giving me a second round of goose bumps for the afternoon. I leaned my head in his direction as I scrubbed the dishes off.

"Let's hope so," I said firmly. He may have won the battle, but he wasn't going to win this war. There were too many skeletons in my closet to share with him... nice guy or not. And that was just it; he was too nice to have to worry about my problems.

"You know," he said, taking the wet dish from my hands. "You gave up too easily."

"Yeah, but you play dirty," I confessed.

"I clean up nice though," he said in such a quiet voice that I almost didn't hear it as he continued drying dishes.

I couldn't help but envision him cleaned up considering he looked damn good "not" cleaned up. I handed him the last one and walked over to the pile he made of clean dishes. With his help, we got all of them put away rather quickly.

"Thanks again for breakfast, and for helping with the dishes, even though you weren't supposed to."

"You're the guest," he said softly. It made me feel as though I was a longtime friend that came for frequent visits. But I wasn't a guest, I didn't know what I was, but a guest wasn't it.

"So what's the story with my car?" I asked the question I had been dreading. He stopped walking, keeping his back toward me. He stood there still as a statue, a statue that was happy not talking.

"Jase," I urged him on.

He took a long pause before finally clearing his throat to speak, and I was now wishing I hadn't asked. "The parts should be in soon, but I'm not going to lie to you, Cassie. It's going to take a little while. If you want, I could take you to Alamosa and then bring your car to you when it's done," he offered.

I'm not sure what I expected to hear out of his mouth, but offering to take me four hours to Alamosa and then dropping my car off when it was done was definitely not it. Why was he so nice, and why did it feel like I knew him forever and that this was something normal between us?

"I really appreciate the offer, but I can't ask you to do that for me. If push comes to shove, Mel said she would pick me up. But at this point, I don't mind waiting it out for my car," I replied.

His worried expression that haunted his face just a moment ago was now wiped away with a pleased look. I could feel it in my bones, in my mind, and in my heart that he was feeling the same unexplainable connection I was. Our two bodies seemed linked, I just couldn't figure out how. As much as I had learned about him in the past few days, I was hopeful I would learn just as much today and the next. He was growing on me too quickly.

"Okay, if you don't mind sticking it out, Cassie. They are working on it, I promise. In the meantime, I'm glad you're here," he said, smiling at me.

"Well now that I know you aren't going to feed me to the wolves, I'm glad I'm here too," I said, sending him into those contagious chuckles of his.

"You might taste a little too high maintenance for them," he told me.

"I'm far from high maintenance. I'm what we like to call a people pleaser," I confessed, using my hands to make quotation marks when I said people pleaser.

He raised his brows at me and tapped his finger on his chin. "Really? Since you're such a people pleaser, how about you go unpack for me? It would please me to see you not digging out of your suitcase anymore," he said. "I have to go run an errand, and then I'll be back later this afternoon," he said, turning his grin into pressed lips as he stared past me.

"Okay, I suppose I can do that. Are you sure it's still okay that I stay here?" I asked cautiously, already feeling guilty for staying one night. He motioned with his finger to move toward him, so I did. He put his hand on my arm, creating warmth on my skin where he kept his hand.

"Stop asking. You are more than welcome to stay as long as you need. My parents are not the type to kick a girl out on the streets," he told me with his hand still on my arm. "And neither am I."

"Okay, I'll stop asking. Do you work; am I holding you from your job? If you need to go in, I fully understand. I can find something to occupy my time with."

"I do have a job, it's on the weekends though, so that means I'm all yours this week," he said trying to tease, but something was wrong with the way he said it, like he was trying to cover up some sort of unhappiness that was buried inside him.

"Yes, I'm very lucky," I said in a sarcastic tone. "Where do you work?"

"The hardware shop. My dad works there during the week after he gets off from working the morning shift at the farm, and then I take the weekends," he answered.

"God, your dad is busy," I said, feeling exhausted just thinking of all the work he had to do.

"Yeah, he's a hard worker," he replied.

"What's this errand you're running?"

"Just an errand," he said quickly.

Well that answer was vague. "Can I help or go with?"

"No, not this time," he said politely. He was trying to be nice about it but something inside said he definitely didn't want me to go.

"So what's the plan when you get back from your errand that I can't help with and I'm done pleasing you by unpacking?" I asked, mocking him. I hated that he wouldn't tell me what it was, but he wasn't budging.

"We'll just have to figure it out, won't we?" He motioned with his head to follow him as he led us to the front door while he put on his cowboy boots. He put them on with ease under his tight fitting jeans. When he was done, he put his hands in his back pocket pulling out the key to his truck.

"In case you didn't notice, I'm not much a of a 'figure it out' kind of girl. I like to have things mapped out, planned, organized."

"Then this will be good for you, won't it," he said before he walked out of the door, not giving me a chance to argue with him. This wasn't going to be good for me. The last time I didn't plan something or keep to my already mapped out life, I ended up in this predicament.

Chapter
nine

I DIDN'T REALIZE HOW MANY clothes I had actually packed. Maybe I was more high maintenance than I originally thought. I sat up in the bed stretching my arms after I took a quick nap. I tried looking around for the time when I remembered there were no clocks in this room and I was without my phone. I was glued to that thing and felt naked without it, not to mention it was my one security item that I had. I was now disconnected to the world and a way to keep in touch with Mel. It was far more troubling than I previously thought, and I definitely didn't appreciate the fact that I always had my phone when I needed it before.

The more I thought about it, the feeling of not being able to touch base with Mel was the only thing I was mostly upset about. Other than that, I felt a sense of liberation. No one could call me, no one knew where I was, and vice versa. I started nodding my head in approval to myself when I then remembered what happened the last time I felt liberated. I suddenly sunk down back in the bed and curled into a ball. I really had to find a balance between liberation and control. I had to find my medium, my level head, and the stability I desired without weighing the scale too much to either side. I didn't want to be one extreme or the other, and I couldn't figure out why I was. I heard my stomach growl and I knew I needed to eat again quickly before I got the overwhelming sensation to have yet another relationship with their toilet bowl. We were already too close. Ginger ale and crackers were a must right now.

I pulled myself out of the fetal position I put myself in, opened the door, and made my way down the hall. I was almost to the kitchen when I heard Jason's voice and another one crying, almost hysterical, it sounded like Trish.

"Stop crying. It'll be all right, Mom. We'll get the next one, okay?" I heard him say as I inched my way closer to the kitchen. I could see the two of them sitting around the table, his mom had her head in her hands sobbing heavily as Jason sat close, consoling her with his arms around her, holding her tightly.

My heart started to rip right down the middle as I continued to hear her sobbing. As much as I wanted to know what was so emotional for him and his mother, I had to leave before I busted into tears too. As I took a backward step, the floor creaked making Jason's head shoot right in my direction. His eyes were glossed over with tears that matched his mother's.

Shit. "Oh my gosh, I'm so sorry for interrupting," I apologized as I quickly pivoted my feet and started heading back to my room.

I could hear them both getting up from their chairs as I all but ran like a chicken back to my room closing the door behind me. It only took a few moments for him to enter the room I was cowering in.

"Jase, I am so sorry. I was just headed to the kitchen to get something to eat. I promise I wasn't spying."

He looked at me with red eyes, now free of any leftover tears he must have wiped clean. He walked slowly to the bed and sat down right next to me, our legs almost touching as he folded his hands in his lap.

"I believe you," he said with his eyes on the floor.

"What's going on? Is everything okay with your mom?" I asked cautiously. If he didn't want to discuss it, I could accept that, but I needed to make sure he knew I was here for him if he wanted me to be. This wonderful family that took me in was growing on me and it was hard to see them in pain.

He kept his head low, his gaze trained on the floor by our feet. I wanted to wrap my arms around him and hold him tightly, but I couldn't. My body was frozen with fear that I even wanted to hug him, and all I could do was move my hand. I placed it gently on his leg, causing him to break his focused stare on the floor. He raised his eyes to meet mine, they were still red, and I wanted so badly to know what was making them sad.

"If you don't want to talk about it, I understand. I just want you to know you can tell me anything. I'm here for you if you need me," I told him, keeping my hand on his leg. He locked his eyes with mine; blinking his long dark lashes a few times, trying to hold back the tears.

His shoulders came back down as he let out a deep sigh. "Everything is fine with my mom, there are some things going on right now that are not okay; but they will be."

He put his hand over the one I kept on his leg and offered up a resemblance of a smile. "Thanks for asking. I really don't want to talk about it anymore though. Okay?"

"I understand, but if you ever want to, I'm here for you," I reminded him.

"I appreciate it, but I don't need to burden you with our family problems," he said as he removed his hand off of mine. "So now that that's over with." He rubbed the palms of his hands over his eyes. "Let's get out of here," he said quickly, helping me up from the bed. "Why don't you put some shoes on? You did unpack, right?" he asked peering at me, waiting for me to probably tell him no.

"Sure did," I said, sliding open the closet doors.

"You are a very good people pleaser," he stated. I rolled my eyes and grabbed a pair of shoes, quickly putting them on before heading to the truck.

He opened the passenger door, holding my hand as I pushed myself into the seat. I heard a chuckle escape his lips as he shut my door and walked over to the driver side door.

"I heard you laugh," I informed him as he started the truck.

"I've just never seen a girl have such problems getting into a truck before," he whispered to me.

"Well, I'm not like other girls around here," I whispered back to him, latching my seatbelt together.

"No you're not," his lips curled into a sexy grin as he reached over and latched his seatbelt. He pulled us out of the driveway and down the street, not saying a word. It then occurred to me I had no clue where we were headed.

"Where are we going?" I asked him, watching the houses pass by through the window.

"To dinner," he stated, keeping his eyes on the road in front of us. I was absolutely not dressed to be seen in a public place like a restaurant. I didn't care how small the town was; wearing clothes that I was unpacking and napping in was not considered dining material.

"To dinner? Dressed like this?" I gaped at him.

He turned his neck and faced me with a stunned look that took over his eyes and mouth. "Well yeah. What do you want to go in, your pajamas?"

"I feel like that's what I'm already in. Jase we need to go back, I need to change and get dressed in something more..." I looked down at my pants and felt my hair that was frizzy from absence of hair care. "Appropriate. I can't go out looking like this," I said in a panic.

He shifted his eyes to the road and then back to me with a confused expression plastered on his face. "Why would you dress up to go eat dinner?"

"You're kidding me right?" I gawked at him. He shook his head and then turned his focus back on the road. "Jase!" I yelled at him with my body practically turned completely in his direction.

"I don't know why you think you need to change, but we're almost there. I'm not turning back just so you can go put on different clothes." His voice sounded as frustrated as I felt. I wasn't going to win this battle with him.

"Fine, but if people start staring at me, just refer to me as your crazy cousin you just picked up from the hospital." I gave in, folding my arms across my chest. I could see out of the corner of my eye his head was turned toward me with what looked like the biggest grin I'd ever seen on his face. He leaned across the middle seat that divided us as I kept my defeated gaze ahead of me.

"Well, you kind of are, aren't you?" He quietly chuckled close to my ear. I whipped my head to face him dead in the eyes and all the evil that was ready to come pouring out of my mouth suddenly shied away. I couldn't help getting lost in his laugh and the sweet look taking over his face. I shrugged it off as we both turned our bodies forward, Jason still wearing the huge smile across his face.

We pulled up to what I would normally drive by and classify as a "hole-in-the-wall" and parked a few spots down from the door. The sign above the restaurant only said "Diner" and nothing more. The window seats were all full; as I could only assume this was one of the few main places to eat in this little town.

"Come on Crazy Cousin Cassie," Jason said, reaching for my hand as I sauntered toward the door.

"At least give me a fake name," I said in complete honesty, in hopes that he would.

Chapter
ten

"JASON," AN OLDER LADY SAID as we stepped through the front doors.

"Miss Sue," he said, giving her a half hug.

"Just two tonight?" she asked.

Jason leaned in close to her telling her something so quietly I couldn't hear.

She gave me a slightly odd look before taking us over to a booth near the back of the small diner. She set the menus down on the table before giving Jason another hug and leaving us to our booth.

"Thank gosh we're in the back," I said, relieved that no one would be able to see what I was wearing aside from Jason. He got comfortable on the other side of the booth and set a menu in front of me.

"I told her my crazy cousin was afraid of people and needed to be seated far away from everyone."

I smacked the menu back down to the table and gave him a piercing look. He was now officially taking this too far. He was pressing his lips together, but it was useless, he couldn't hold it back.

"I'm kidding. I asked her for some privacy," he confessed with a slight chuckle. "You don't even look like someone who's crazy. You look good, you always do," he said before putting the menu back up in front of his face.

I could feel my cheeks starting to flame as the compliment sank in. I whispered thank you, before hiding my face behind the menu as well.

"So what are you getting?"

I glanced back over the menu once more before placing it flat on the table with his. "The Caesar salad with chicken."

He rested his arm on the booth's edge making himself comfortable. "I should have guessed."

I shook my head at him, appalled that he was judging my food decisions. "Salads are good if you just give them a chance," I hissed back.

The waitress was another older lady who patted Jason on the shoulder when she arrived to take our orders. Yes, I was certain everyone knew who Jason was or the town was just that small.

Before I could say a word, Jason grabbed my menu and handed them to the waitress along with our order. "The usual Peggy, for both of us," he told her, pointing his finger at me when he said 'us'.

I focused my gaze on him and didn't know whether to be disgusted or amused that he just ordered God knows what for me.

"You'll like it I promise." He sat there, looking amused with himself.

"You better hope so, or it'll end up in your lap," I told him. Knowing I would never throw my food at him, part of me was slightly entertained that he ordered for me. I also cringed at the thought of *what* he just ordered. For all I knew, it could be liver and onions.

We were next to a window. The sun was going down and was providing just enough light through the blinds to hit Jason's eyes just perfectly again. The light hit a piece of his hair as well, making the strand appear a light shade of blonde. It made me laugh to think of him with blond hair since his hair was dark. It definitely wouldn't suit him.

"What are you thinking about over there? Or do you just like staring at me?" he asked, tilting his head as he found my eyes.

Busted. I hated to admit it, but he was easy to stare at. He wasn't one of those guys who was busting out of his baby tee shirt with arms that could barely fit through the sleeves. He was better than that. He had the perfect amount of muscle; he was lean and it looked good on him. His wavy hair was in absolutely no way styled, but it worked. His eyes were the main focus, and anyone with a heartbeat would be stupid not to take a moment to stare into them for even just half a second. The jeans he wore snuggled his body in all the right places. The boys that I dated would never be caught in them, and I would have agreed with them, until I saw Jason wearing them. Of course, they had to be paired with a pair of cowboy boots and a tee. It was never the type I gave a second glance to and I'm ashamed, because now it's the only thing I could focus on.

"I'm thinking about too many things," I told him, fidgeting with a piece of my hair, trying to conceal the fact that all my thoughts were about him. "What are *you* thinking about over there?"

"That I want to play a game with you." A sexy grin spread across his face, which not only complimented the thoughts I was having, but also scared me.

"What kind of game?" I was nervous to inquire.

"It's called Diner trivia," he said, bringing his arm that was resting over the booth down to the table.

"What kind of game is that?"

"I'll start, I get to ask you five questions, and you have to answer all of them."

"Clearly I'm getting the raw end of this game," I muttered.

"I'm not finished yet, Sweetheart," he said, leaning over the table with his hands practically on my side. God, I loved that he calls me that. No one has ever called me Sweetheart. "If you answer all five, then you get to ask me five, and so forth. But if you don't answer all five, you forfeit your turn."

I leaned in closer to him, pushing myself into the table. "What's the catch, *Sweetheart?*" I asked, because knowing Jason, there was a catch to this game; he wasn't about to start giving me information that easily.

"We only have until our food comes out," he whispered in a deep voice.

"Well then I guess we better hurry," I whispered back, making his lips curl up.

"Guess we better," he said, leaning back in the booth seat resting his arm again on the edge.

Chapter
eleven

I WASN'T SURE WHAT I was getting myself into, but getting the chance to ask Jase five questions of my choice was all too tempting to not at least give his Diner Trivia a chance. I just had to get through his five questions first. *Lord help me.*

"Do you have a boyfriend and is he the reason you're going to Alamosa?"

That wasn't too bad to start with. Maybe these questions wouldn't be too deep. I mean we were in a diner, not a private home. "That's two questions, by the way," I smirked. "No, no boyfriend, so I guess that implies I'm not going to Alamosa to see him either."

His face was slightly amused as he relaxed his body even more into the booth.

"How long since your last boyfriend?"

I wasn't sure what I was expecting him to ask, but definitely not these. "Two years ago," I responded, very confused why this was important to him.

"What happened?" he asked.

I looked down at my hands; this question was going to be uncomfortable to answer and although I was expecting difficult questions, it still was not something I was eager to discuss.

"You're going to take it the wrong way."

"I'm not judging at all, Cassie, but if you don't want your turn, then you don't have to answer." He shrugged.

Ugh, fine. "He wasn't physical enough, okay?" And if I wasn't blushing earlier, I was full-on firecracker red right now.

He took his arm off the booth and immediately leaned in closer, his body almost covering the table. "You are going to have to elaborate on that or as much as I don't want to, I'll probably take it wrong."

"I knew you would. It's not what you're thinking, Jase," I said, staring out the window as I answered. "It was the little things. The affection, he just never showed it, and I wanted it." I stopped, returning my gaze to Jase, waiting for a response from him. But he sat there with his eyes fixed on mine, listening as if I was telling him some amazing story. So I continued with the truth of what I wanted.

"He never held my hand in his; he never kissed me just because. It was like he was afraid to touch me, like I was going to break or something," I told him, picturing my ex in my head as I spoke of the memories.

"He was a good guy, but I wanted someone who couldn't keep his hands off me. Not in the perverted sense, but in the 'I want to show everyone in the world that you're my girl, that I want to hold your hand in mine because it fits so perfectly, and I want to steal all the kisses I can from you because my lips can't get enough of yours'. That kind of way." I finished and I couldn't help but feel my heart tug at the thought of how bad I desired that from a guy.

I felt his warm hand on top of mine as I looked up to meet his eyes. "You did the right thing because a girl like you deserves all of that and more," he said, keeping our hands touching.

How was it that a guy I met only a couple of days ago doesn't have a single problem showing me contact but a boyfriend of one year couldn't even muster up the desire to show me once?

He took his hand off of mine rather hastily, leaving the feeling of loneliness in its place.

"What's the story with Mel?" he asked, shifting in his seat.

This question was the easiest to answer yet; unfortunately, I could talk about Mel all day if he let me. "She also goes by Melanie, she's my best friend," I answered, trying not to tear up at the thought of how much I missed her. Being away from her was getting harder the older we got.

"You said she's in Alamosa, I'm assuming at college, so why didn't you two go to the same one?"

"You know, assuming is never good," I told him with a teasing look. My parents had said 'assuming' never got anyone anywhere; you would almost always assume the wrong thing. I learned early on to leave it out of my vocabulary.

He laughed quietly. "Just answer the question," he said. "Or are you going to forfeit?" he asked with a mischievous grin.

"Never," I sassed back. "My parents. The answer is my parents," I told him, short and sweet.

"Your parents what?"

"They didn't give me that college as an option. I was given a handful of in state colleges and the one Mel wanted to attend, wasn't on my list," I said with a sigh, remembering the day that Mel and I had to go our separate ways, vowing to never give up on our friendship.

"You always have a choice, Cassie," he said, his eyes steady on mine.

"Yeah well, it's a void subject these days anyway, and would you look at that, our food's here!" I was saved by the waitress.

She set our plates down, serving me first. I glanced down at the plate with a huge hamburger on it instead of a chicken Caesar Salad, and then brought my eyes up to the waitress ready to let her know she got my order wrong when she scurried off. I glanced over to Jase who had a burger on his plate as well.

"I presume this is the 'usual' you ordered?" I asked, forgetting that he had ordered for me. Not that a burger was the worst thing he could have ordered, but I was more than looking forward to *my* usual.

"Now who's assuming?" he asked, giving me a sarcastic glance. "In case school didn't teach you, assume and presume are the same. So don't try and fancy it up okay?"

I hadn't even noticed I said presume. I let out a soft chuckle.

"I'm glad I humor you," he said. "Now humor me and just try your burger, best in town."

"The only in town, and I'm not assuming on this one. I'm pretty confident with my conclusion," I told him as our hands met the mustard bottle at the same time.

He snatched the bottle of mustard up before I even had the chance to grab it first, putting the bottle upside down ready to pour, right over my burger.

"No, no, no." I panicked.

His eyes got wide and he retracted the bottle immediately. I felt ridiculous as I realized how panicked I was over a condiment. "I don't like anything on my burger, the mustard is for my fries," I revealed.

He returned the bottle to my plate, squeezing the yellow goodness right next to my fries. "Ah...so I finally get to meet another fan of mustard and fries," he said quietly. "I can't stand ketchup."

"Seriously ketchup is awful, I can't stand the stuff either," I said, amused to meet another mustard fanatic. When Mel and I were kids and I dunked my fry in mustard, she would cringe telling me how weird I was. Looks like I was no longer the only one I knew who was weird too.

"Tomatoes?" he asked with a lifted brow.

"Love them," I confessed. "I know what you're thinking..."

"Nope, you probably have no clue," he said. "Because I love them too."

"Not many of us around, we have to stick together," I said, getting another chuckle out of him. We were definitely a strange pair, but one that felt awkwardly normal.

He put the bottle down between us and lifted his burger up to his mouth before taking a huge bite. As much as I wanted my salad, the burger dripping with juice and cheese sitting on my plate was now brushing its grilled smell against my nose and I was ready to dig in like Jase. I put it up to my mouth and as the hunger was now taking over, I took an oversized bite. I enjoyed every second of it, not caring at all how un-lady like my appetite was.

"Well?" he asked after finishing off another bite.

"Surprisingly delicious," I admitted, enjoying my burger too much.

"There's just something wonderful about greasy diner food," he said.

"Well, when it's the only place there is to eat at, then yes," I replied. "But it is wonderful. It's greasy and comforting, two words I never thought I'd say in the same sentence together."

I got a loud laugh out of him as he dunked his fries into his mustard.

"Are you feeling generous tonight?" I asked him with a smirk. I knew our game was over, but I wasn't ready for it to be done.

He put his fry back on his plate as he glared at me with one eye. "Whoa, Cassandra. I didn't peg you for that kind of girl!" he exclaimed.

I should have expected that answer. "Generous as in, maybe letting me ask you a few questions, since my turn was cut short? And don't think I didn't notice you asked me more than five questions." I peered at him.

He sat there not saying a word as he twirled a fry in the mustard piled on his plate. "Well, I did make up the game so I can change the rules when necessary," he said playfully.

"Figures." I shook my head at him. "So how about that turn? Please?"

"Only because you're begging and it's pathetically cute," he said.

"Thanks," I replied. "So how old are you?"

"I'm 22," he said.

"Do you have any siblings?"

"Just me, myself, and I in the house," he answered.

Which brought me to my next question. "Why are you still living at home?" I asked, hoping the brunt nature of my question didn't turn him away.

"Do you still live at home?" he answered with a question.

"You are so breaking the rules," I said, giving him a teasing evil eye.

"Yes, but I get to learn just a little bit more about you this way too."

"No, I moved out when I left for college. I live in an apartment in Boulder," I answered, giving him a look that told him I expected an answer in return.

"I haven't found a reason to leave yet. That's my home and it's the only place I've ever known," he finally answered as he quietly took in a few more fries.

"Thanks for answering. I kind of like this game," I told him.

He looked up and smiled at me, not answering, but he didn't have to. I could tell, even though the game was probably made up, he wanted to know about me too.

I started to finish what I could of my meal as I sat and absorbed his answers. I could feel deep down there was more to him than he was letting me see. Normally I would veer far away from guys that were hiding something, but what he was hiding seemed to go very deep, if he was in fact hiding something from me. I could have been totally off base for all I knew, but something inside me was screaming that he was.

I put my napkin on the table when I finished and immediately regretted eating as much as I did, but also felt extremely satisfied.

"Shall we?" he asked, standing up from the booth.

"Yes, I'm now full *and* tired," I replied, unsure if it was because of the pregnancy or eating way too much.

"That makes two of us, again," he said before slipping the waitress some cash and leading us back to his truck.

Chapter twelve

I PUT A HAND OVER MY STOMACH, feeling slightly ill from the grease pit I ingested last night. And the thought of it all was not settling well with my stomach. I needed to find some sort of a clear soda or some water to help ease my upset stomach. I put on a pair of cotton shorts and left my room.

The house was eerily quiet and empty. I walked over to the front window to check and see if Jase's truck was still there. He hadn't mentioned last night when we got home that he had something going on this morning. I pulled back the drapes and could still see his red pickup in the gravel drive. I let out a sigh and walked toward the kitchen. Jason wasn't in the kitchen, if he was in fact here, he was in his room. This was unusual for Jason, even in the couple of days that I've known him he seemed like a very early riser. I decided to go to his room to check on him and make sure everything was okay.

I tiptoed to the back door where he said his room was and opened the door to the basement. The door creaked a little as I tried to quietly make my way down to his room.

It was dark, making it hard to venture down all of the stairs without either falling or making too much noise, but I managed. I looked around to my left, which was full of boxes, and then to my right where there was a door a few steps away. I was hoping I found Jason's room. I was now thinking how I wished I would have taken directions from him; I was worse than I thought.

Thinking that to myself made me chuckle, and perhaps a little too loud. Jason's voice radiated through the white wooden door I was standing in front of.

"Cassie, is that you?" he asked, sounding amused.

So much for being quiet. "Yeah," I answered. "Can I come in?"

"Of course. It's unlocked," he shouted.

I slowly turned the round knob and gently pushed the door open to what was an equally dark room.

"You can turn the light on; the switch is just on your right side," he said quietly, his voice coming from somewhere in front of me.

I blindly stretched my hand to the side of me, reaching around for the feel of a switch to hit my hand. Bingo.

The room became illuminated, hurting both of our eyes as we screamed at the same time. I slowly lifted my lids, adjusting my eyes to the lights and saw Jason across from me in his large bed, doing the same.

"You could have pre-warned me," I muttered to him, finally opening my eyes fully.

"You could have pre-warned *me*," he said back.

I gave him a sarcastic glare before touring my eyes around his room. It was surprisingly large down here, and not at all what I had expected. His bed was in the center and a dresser was to the left. A small two-seat sofa was to the right with a television on a stand facing it. There was nothing resembling the house upstairs in his room. It was all his own. Two racks to the right of his bed held six cowboy hats, each a different color. I turned my gaze back to Jase who was lying on his bed wearing a sexy grin as he kept his focus on me. His arms tucked behind his head full of perfectly messy hair left his toned chest fully exposed to my appreciative eyes. I definitely wanted to walk into his room in the mornings more often.

"Not what I expected Jason," I said. Steering my eyes away from him, I continued my tour of his room. The walls were a light brown that went perfect with his red comforter that was covering up half of his body.

"Yeah I like it down here. It's like my own little retreat from the world," he said.

I walked over to the left side of his room, focusing on a framed picture that was standing on his dresser. The picture was of three young boys; one looked older than the rest, and all appeared very similar in their little cowboy hats and cowboy boots sitting on a haystack with straw hanging out of their mouths as they smiled. It was adorable. "Is this you?" I asked him.

I shifted my gaze over to him as he moved his arm out from underneath his head and rubbed his eyes before sitting up in his bed.

"Yeah it is. I was only about seven in that picture," he replied as he started pushing the rest of the covers off of him.

"Easy there, I didn't come down here to see Jase junior," I told him.

He shook his head and finished pulling the covers off the rest of the way until he was out of the bed completely only wearing a pair of boxer shorts. I must have been staring at his bare chest again. It was by all means more captivating than the picture I was so interested in earlier. It had just enough definition that made me want to whimper, until Jase cleared his throat, bringing me back to the picture.

"Um, so the picture." I tried to recover my embarrassment.

He took another look at me, letting a quiet chuckle escape before standing right next to me.

"We were so young," he said, as though he was picturing the day in his mind. "It was at our friends' farm. They had horses, we went riding that day, and it was our first time. Our moms had us sit down on the hay to take a picture, but before we did I put a piece of hay in my mouth so I could be like my dad," he said, still staring at the picture. "And then the others followed suit."

"You were an adorable child, just look at the wild curly hair peeking out of that hat," I said, picking up the picture to look at it closer. "Looks like a fun day for you three."

"It was," he said, smiling over my shoulder at the picture in my hands.

"So who are the other two kids with you?" I asked him.

"My brother and a friend," he answered quietly.

"You said you didn't have any siblings." I questioned him, confused by what I thought I knew.

"No. I said it was just me in the house." He let out a long, deep breath. "Cassie… we just don't talk about him much, that's all."

"Why is it such a big secret?" I asked, concerned there was something deeper going on.

"It's not a big secret." He shrugged. I couldn't take my eyes off of him though; I would need a better answer than that.

"Listen, families have problems. It seems normal nowadays. There are just some things better left unsaid, okay?" he asked gently.

"Yeah, I guess." I didn't think I would be getting any other answers than the one he just gave me. Not to mention, I completely and whole-heartedly understood about families having problems because I was used to them too.

"Thank you," he said.

I took my focus from the picture to the other side of the dresser. Another picture showed an older version of him standing with his mom, smiling at the camera, and giving a big thumbs-up. His mom wore scrubs, and it looked like they were at the hospital where she worked now. "Did you go to work with your mom a lot?"

He walked behind me, his chest almost touching my back, causing a small shiver to run down my spine. He looked closer at the picture. "Yeah, on summer break especially. It was fun as a kid to roam the halls of a hospital, it lost its entertainment the older I got," he said, walking back to his bed, sitting down on the edge of it.

"I couldn't imagine hospitals being entertaining at any age," I said, taking a seat next to him.

He shook his head as he stretched his arms over his head. "So what brought you down here? Kudos on not getting lost by the way," he said with a yawn.

Ugh. I slapped the side of his arm that was next to me. "Normally you are up at the crack of dawn and ready to go, waking *me* up… so when I woke this morning and the house was quiet, I was just making sure you were okay," I confessed, slouching, as I felt silly for worrying so much over him.

"I was just tired from yesterday and then I stayed up a little later."

"Why were you up so late?" I asked, pulling up a leg underneath me.

He looked at me, his eyes steady. "Can you keep a secret?" he whispered.

"Of course," I whispered back, leaning closer to him, eager for him to be confiding in me.

"So can I."

"You are such a brat, you know that?"

"I was reading, Cassie," he said. "You don't take well to teasing do you?"

"I guess not," I answered him. "And what did you say? That you were *reading*?" I questioned him, never having heard that answer come out of a guy's mouth who wasn't in college, and even that was rare.

"Did I say reading? What I meant was, I was watching television," he said, nodding his head.

"Too late Jase, you already spilled the beans. Come on now, what were you reading?" I asked intrigued.

"Don't get too excited, I was just reading some letters from a friend," he answered.

"You mean emails?" I asked confused.

"No. I mean snail mail. Like the good old fashioned hand written letters that the mailman delivers. None of that electronic stuff, Sweetheart."

He seemed to enjoy the old-fashioned things in life, the letters, and the memories. It was really cute. "I'm going to say that's probably why you still have a flip phone." I dropped my gaze down, peering at him.

"People become too reliant on having the world at their fingertips. Enjoying the moment and not knowing what's going to come next, that's the real deal, Cassie," he said.

"Well that's not nearly as exciting as a book. But I get it, sort of," I admitted to him as I heard a vibrating noise coming from his nightstand.

"Speaking of phones," he said, leaning up and reaching for his phone.

"Hello?" he answered.

"Yes ma'am. Who's this?" he asked.

"Ah, I've been expecting your call."

"As a matter a fact she is," he said, looking over at me. It was either Melanie or, well it had to be Melanie.

"She's in my room. Definitely not being held hostage. I promise she's in good hands Melanie," he said as he nodded into the phone with each answer.

"I know you will," he said cringing. I could only imagine the words that were coming out of her mouth. Not to mention the half frightened look on Jase's face as he answered her questions.

"Yes ma'am, I will. Okay here she is." He pulled the phone from his ear and let out a breath, handing the phone over to me.

"She's a feisty one," he said, making me giggle. She was most certainly a feisty chick and I loved her for it.

"Hey Mel," I said, glad to hear her voice.

"He said he isn't holding you captive, is this true?" she asked in a half teasing manner.

"No, he's not holding me captive." I could see Jase shaking his head.

"Okay then," she said. "He sounds really cute, Cass. Is that why you were okay waiting for your car?"

"Melanie. Oh my gosh. I can't believe you. Call me tomorrow, love you."

"Love you too, Cass," she said, giggling before hanging up the phone.

I handed Jason back his phone. "She's a little protective," I told Jase, who was looking at me with a questioning glance.

"Just a little," he said. "It's good though, she just wants to make sure you're being taken care of."

My heart pumped a little faster as I thought about how he was doing just that, taking care of me.

He yawned as he leaned up from the bed. "So, how about we get ready and then I want to take you somewhere today," he said, turning to look at me.

"Is it to get my car?" I asked.

"No, sorry to burst your bubble. I want to take you somewhere and then tonight we have dinner at my grandmother's house."

I turned my hand pointing to myself, "Me. I'm going with you?"

"Yes you. I'm not leaving you here," he said. "So hurry up and go get ready. I'll do the same. Meet you upstairs in five?"

"Five minutes? Ha... I don't know what planet you live on." I got up from his bed.

"Wishful thinking?"

"Just a bit," I said as I walked toward to his door. "I'll be as quick as possible, but no guarantees."

"I'm just excited to get you in a pair of boots, that's all," he said with his lips curling up at the corners and his eyes fixed on mine.

"Boots?" I asked him with a shocked expression plastered on my face. Why did I need boots?

Chapter thirteen

I COULDN'T STOP STARING DOWN at my feet; they were nothing like I imagined when Jase had told me where he was taking me. I never thought cowgirl boots were my thing but I was in love. They were a gorgeous dark turquoise color with gold studs lining the rim and gold swirls on the sides.

"You like 'em?" he asked as he drove us to his grandma's house.

"Like them? I love them Jason," I gushed, still staring down at my newly decorated feet, I couldn't stop admiring them. "You didn't need to buy them though, I wish you'd let me pay you back," I said, still miffed he used his money on me. It was thoughtful and the sweetest gesture, but I felt bad for it.

"Cassie, it was the only way I was going to get you in those boots. You would never have bought yourself a pair," he said, shifting his eyes between the road and me, with a stern look on his face. "I wanted to do something nice for you to keep your mind off your car and all."

"Maybe not then, but now that I love them, you can bet your ass I'll be buying more," I admitted, making him smile before he returned his gaze to the road ahead. "You have no idea how amazing today was for me. It's been a long time since I've gone out and done something like that."

I looked down again, admiring my new boots and going over our day in my head. It really did keep my mind off of things. I've never once had a guy offer to go shopping with me let alone have it be his idea. So when Jason drove us all the way out to the next town just to buy boots, I was already impressed. Not to mention, he took me into not one, but three different stores just to find the perfect pair of boots. I thought he might have regretted the whole thing after having no luck at the first and second store, but he kept trudging on as if it was no big deal. I'm pretty sure I even saw him smile when the staff was admiring his boots. I had one of those 'Ahhh' moments the minute I put on the turquoise boots. I felt like Cinderella as the guy slipped the boot on for me. A first ever for me and I could tell my color choice freaked Jason out a bit, but I knew the minute I saw myself in the mirror they were a perfect fit. We ended our shopping trip with a lunch of the "usual". A truly perfect way to end it all.

"Well I'm glad you had such an awesome day," he answered back. "I *was* a little apprehensive about your color choice, but they look really good on you." I saw his lips curl up a little bit as his eyes remained focused forward.

"It's a bold choice for me, trust me," I admitted as we came up to a stoplight.

"The only stoplight in town," I said, glancing at it as if it were a national landmark. It was not like what I pictured. It was a four-way intersection with only one light segment hanging from each intersection. And by hanging, I meant dangling; the structure was not at all what I was used to seeing back in Denver. I giggled as I took in the small town stoplight, thinking how silly it was that I was so easily amused by it.

"I hear you over there," he said.

The light turned green but he didn't move forward. He kept his foot on the brake and turned his head in my direction, wearing a grin that was spread at least six inches wide.

"Do I want to know why that smile is plastered on your face and you aren't driving even though we have a green light?"

He turned his head in either direction. "No one is behind us. Is it making you nervous that I'm not driving when the light is green?" he asked playfully.

"Yes, as a matter of fact, it *is* making me anxious... normal people don't sit at a green light Jase," I told him, staring right back at him, eyes locked on his. "Well, are we going to drive or just sit here and stare at each other?"

He didn't reply. He put the truck in park and slowly turned his body toward the door and grabbed the handle. He stepped out of his truck, making his way to my side and stopping. I raised my hands, wanting to know why on earth he got out of his truck in the middle of a light. He opened my door and stood there smiling, holding out his hand for me to take.

"What are you doing?" I hesitated.

"You need to learn how to relax and let go. Cassie, you are way too uptight, Sweetheart."

"How is getting out of the truck going to ease my nerves? It's only making it worse, Jase. What if a car pulls up?" I asked him with a hitch in my voice, scared of becoming road kill.

"Then we'll move. Don't worry so much about what might happen. Just enjoy the moment," he told me softly.

I took a deep breath and closed my eyes. I was trying to do as he said and began to place my hand in his when the moment was cut short.

HONK! HONK! HONK!

"Holy shit," I yelled. Not even once looking to see where it was coming from, I pulled my hand from his and got back in touch with the reality that I was about to get out in the street. I tucked myself into my seat and cowered down.

Jason was now busting up laughing as he held his stomach, while I was trying to catch my breath from the scare the horn gave me. He looked across the street and cupped his hands around his mouth to say something to the driver who had his head out of the window.

"What the hell man?" Jason yelled to someone that I assumed he knew.

"Dude what are you doing?" he asked.

Jason raised his hands up at him. "Having a moment, what does is look like to you?"

"Well your grandma is going to be all sorts of mad cow if you don't hurry your ass up. We're going to be late," he hollered over to us.

Jason waved him on as he walked slowly back to his side of the truck.

"Scared?" he asked chuckling.

I crossed my arms over my chest, and although seeing him laugh only made me want to do the same, I was able to keep myself under control and the scowl on my face. I was embarrassed, not to mention angry because I knew I was right. I knew what was going to happen. It was too risky and dangerous. I couldn't believe I almost let myself get out of the truck.

"I'm done laughing now," he whispered to me while he drove us down the street. I kept my eyes straight ahead of me watching the road in front of us. "It was a little funny, Cassie," he said, teasingly.

I sat biting on my bottom lip, unsure of whether to give into his humor or to keep my embarrassment to myself.

He reached over and put his hand on my knee. "Come on now; give me a smile. It was fun," he said.

I turned my head to face his direction and held up my thumb and index finger about an inch apart. "Okay it was a little funny, but still not even close to being fun," I told him.

"I'll get you to have some fun in the street, you just watch. Can I at least get a smile pretty girl?" he asked softly.

I turned my head back to the front and let a small smile sweep across my face. "I knew it was in there somewhere," he said.

It was in there, and an even bigger one wanted to rise to the surface too, but I was still too embarrassed over my reaction to let it out. Not to mention I was still wondering over and over again why he wanted me in the street.

"Are you nervous about tonight?" he asked, interrupting my over thinking brain.

"Actually, I am," I admitted to him. I was unsure of what to expect at his grandma's house, it had been a long time since I was with grandparents.

"Don't be, you'll have fun. It's not hanging in the street with me, but it's a good time," he smirked.

"Very funny Jase. But really, what if they don't like me and what if I don't like the food, and what if-" I tried to finish but he cut me off, holding his hand up.

"Whoa there, you need to calm down," he said, putting his hand back down.

"First of all, they will like you. Just don't be so nervous and uptight. Relax, okay?" I nodded yes, trying to think of how I could be less uptight, because I didn't even realize I was. "Second of all, the food is delicious and you'll love it. It's not salads and burgers," he said. "But if you don't, we can use a code word," he suggested.

"A code word? What do you mean?" I questioned him.

He turned down a dirt road that was quite bumpy, making it hard for me to try and sit still. "Hang on Sweetheart," he told me as we made our way further down the road. "A code word, it's like something you can use in place of the real word so people don't catch on."

"I know what a code word is Jason," I replied.

"Well then why did you ask?"

"I just was unsure of what you meant by using a code word for food," I told him.

"Well, let's use green light, since you are so fond of them," he said, turning his head, smiling in my direction.

"Hahaha, you're so funny," I sassed him.

"Green light will be love, yellow light will be like, and red light, obviously, you hate it," he said.

"I'm just supposed to shout out green light while I'm eating to let you know I love the food?" I asked.

"Of course, why not? That way if there *is* something you 'red light', then I'll know and I'll eat it for you. We don't want you making a bad impression do we?" I slapped his arm and started laughing along with him.

"Fine, but if people give me strange looks, I'm stopping," I told him, unsure of how his code word plan was really going to pan out.

"Deal," he said with a wink as we pulled up to a very car packed dead end dirt road.

My eyes had to look as wide as saucers as we parked and headed up to the house, the house that was busting at the seams, it was so full of people. "Don't worry. They are going to love you, Cassie," he told me as he put his hand on the small of my back, guiding me through the front door.

Here we go.

Chapter
fourteen

"MOOSE!" JASON YELLED AS WE walked through the door. Scared to death, I pivoted behind Jason and ducked for cover. I've never come close to a moose and as loud as he yelled it, I definitely didn't want to start now.

"Cassie?" he questioned before he bent down, looking me straight in the eyes with a confused look on his face. "What are you doing?" he whispered with a raised brow. I began to hear a few whispers and chuckles from others in the room.

"You yelled moose, and correct me if I'm wrong, but those aren't gentle animals," I whispered back even more confused than I already was.

Jason closed his eyes and let out a breath before shaking his head. "You are correct, but this moose, he's as gentle as they come," he said before grabbing my hand and standing us both up. I kept my body behind him as I clutched onto his arm, preparing myself to meet a moose in person. There was always a first for everything.

"Where is it?" I raised myself on my toes, whispering into his ear.

"You're looking at him," he smirked. "Moose, meet Cassandra. Cassandra, meet Moose," he said as the guy from the intersection walked forward.

I released my grip on Jason's arm giving the guy a questioning glance. "Oh." Letting out a sigh, I was mortified that

I just now caught on. "I'm really humiliated now." I reached my hand out to shake his.

Between the laughter of Jason, his friend 'Moose', and the giggles coming from around the room, I was ready to escape to his truck and hide.

"Name's TJ," he said, letting go of my hand.

"So how'd you get a name like Moose?" *The poor guy.*

"Not by choice. That's for damn sure." TJ shrugged.

"Yeah, we just kind of ran with it," Jase smirked as he continued. "A few years ago we had spent the day in Estes Park. We walked around, went to lunch, and just had a good time. Before we left, we decided to take a picture of the scenery. I'm ready to take the picture and TJ decided to jump in it. I started to count and by the time I got to three his face was just priceless." He paused, letting out another chuckle, trying so hard to control his amusement of his own story.

I started getting the giggles, not even knowing what for, but hearing his laugh was just too much not to join in.

"Could you just get on with the story?" TJ asked, apparently getting frustrated.

"He had the biggest look of shock and horror on his face that I've ever seen in my life. His jaw was literally on the floor. I snapped the photo and right after I did, TJ came running toward the car yelling 'MOOSE, MOOSE', so I looked behind me and sure enough there he was... the biggest moose we'd ever seen," he said, showing me the size of the animal with his hands.

"It's the only moose you guys have ever seen," a girl's voice said from behind me.

"We dashed into the car and thankfully the moose must have been spooked because it stopped and took off in the other direction, but the picture, Cassie, oh my God," he said. "It was priceless. Never will I ever forget his face. We kept the picture and forever named him Moose."

I looked over at TJ who was clearly sick of hearing this story, yet was obviously trying to hold back a smile.

"That's classic. I've got to see this picture," I told the guys.

"Too bad we don't have time to. Looks like it's dinner time," TJ said, walking away with his head down.

"I have a copy of the picture, I'll show you," he said before placing his hand on my shoulder, leading us down the hall amongst others for dinner. "Before we eat, I want you to meet my grandma," Jase said with a smile a mile wide. You could tell he really cherished her.

"Can't wait," I told him only half-nervous, the other half excited to meet a lady who wanted to have everyone over for dinner. It takes a special lady to tolerate this many people in her house.

We walked into the kitchen. It was mad chaos as people loaded their plates with food served buffet style. I spotted what I thought was his grandma right away. She was the only one in the kitchen with white hair in a cute little bun on top of her head; she was standing next to Trish, both helping pile everyone's plates high.

"Grandma," Jason said, giving her a hug and kiss on the cheek. He stood about a foot over her, which looked ridiculously cute.

"Cassandra, this is Grandma Maggie," he said as he moved back next to me. "Dad's side, of course."

"Cassandra, I've heard so much about you," she said as she grabbed my hands in hers.

I cringed. I could only imagine the things she might have heard. On top of being lost, there was crashing into their precious town tree, and staying in a stranger's house amongst all the gossip. "I hope good things?" I asked coyly.

"Oh, don't worry, all wonderful things," she said as she peered over to Trish who was grinning right with her. "It's a small town dear. We all know when there is a new person here." She gave me a wink, surprising me with her slightly feisty personality. I liked it.

"I had a feeling." I teased, making a chuckle escape her lips.

"Go eat now kids before it gets cold," she said, shooing us away.

"Grandma, get your plate first, please," Jason told her sternly, well, as sternly as you could tell an adorable little lady like her.

She gave him the 'I'm your grandma. I make the rules look'. "You know I will. I just want to make sure everyone gets taken care of first."

He shook his head at her and then gave her a 'Yes Grandma' look before leading us into the line.

Plates in hand, we headed to the back room where a table was set up.

"Saved you guys a seat," TJ said, patting the seat next to him as we made our way to the table.

Jason pulled out the seat next to TJ for me to sit in. This could be extremely awkward, but I tried to replay the words Jason told me in the truck and not to be uptight.

Jason sat down right next to me and everyone immediately got silent and focused on eating. Our plates were full, and thankfully, I was hungry, but I failed to recognize any of the food that Jase piled on my plate. I was sheltered when it came to home cooked meals. I took a deep breath and remembered I had a code word in case of an emergency, which made me feel more awkward at the thought of having to use it. I took my fork and stabbed it into a heaping mound of green beans that were probably my safest bet, but also suspicious because they were drowned in some sauce that I could only imagine was butter and tossed with bacon. As soon as I started chewing, I knew they were the best tasting green beans I've ever had in my life. Before I devoured the mountain of them, I decided to give the chicken dish a go. I took a deep breath and put a bite of the chicken casserole in my mouth. It was wonderful. I could sense Jason's eyes on mine, so I turned my pleased mouth toward him as I finished chewing another bite of the casserole. He leaned his head closer to me, raising his brow, expecting an answer.

"Green freaking light, Jason," I yelled a little too loudly, causing him to shift his gaze to his plate, clearly mortified by my unintentional outburst of excitement.

He raised his head and I mouthed the word 'oops' at him as we both glanced around the table that had gone silent and all eyes were on me.

I could feel my cheeks were on fire as they began getting hotter and hotter the more stares I got. I needed to recover quickly. I thought of the only thing in my mind that made any sense.

"The green light that we passed on the way here, crazy it's the only one. It's not like that where I'm from." I tried to cover my embarrassment, feeling Jason pat my leg under the table as I did.

"Where are you from, Cassandra?" the girl from the front room, whose name I believed was Kasey asked.

"Boulder," I answered in her direction across the round table.

"What brings you to Keaton?" she asked, immediately making Jason choke on his dinner.

"I'm just passing through... was passing through... well actually, I'm not even supposed to be passing through," I said, keeping my eyes on Jason as we both curled our lips into a grin.

I turned my focus back to Kasey. "It's a long story," I said, hopeful to change the subject.

She nodded and went back to eating her food.

I tried to do the same but the silence was reminding me too much of being at dinner with my parents and I couldn't take it anymore.

"Moose? Have you lived here your whole life?" I asked him.

"Yes ma'am."

"What is it that you do?" I asked, curious about who I could only guess was Jason's best friend.

"I work at the mechanical shop," he stated proudly.

Oh, help us all, he was the one working on my car? Shit.

Jason must have seen the look of horror displayed on my face as his eyes found mine.

"He's fixing my car?" I whispered to him. I would be lucky if it was finished next year. This wasn't a mechanic. He was a kid.

"If it makes you feel any better, his dad owns the place, and Moose has been doing this since he could practically walk," he tried to sweet talk me.

"Hey, don't you worry, your car is in good hands."

I was almost positive a code word was in order here. "Red light Jason," I said, looking him straight in the eyes.

His lips curled up. "You might red light it now, but you'll green light it in the end," he whispered to me.

I gave a not so reassuring nod as I looked over at TJ who was staring at us as though we were talking gibberish.

"It's going to be fine, Cassie," he said softly.

I took a deep breath. It was either "Moose" or no mechanic so I guess I had to just trust that Jase knew what he was talking about. "Okay, I'll trust you."

"I haven't steered you wrong yet have I?" He asked, knowing damn well he hadn't.

"No you haven't," I admitted to him, only making his "I told you so" grin even wider.

"See? It'll be okay then."

We continued our stay for quite a while longer as we chatted with everyone at the table. They were polite, entertaining, and treated me like I was a friend from down the street that they grew up with all their lives. It was welcoming and I was grateful for that.

"You ready?" Jason quietly asked me.

"Whenever you are."

"I'm kind of getting tired, so let's go say goodbye to the family and head home." He grabbed our plates as we got up from the table. I waved at TJ and the rest of the table, and both of us said goodbye to the group.

"See you later man," TJ yelled to Jase.

"We'll come see you soon to check on the car," he told him.

That would be a hard visit. I almost wanted to miss it.

He set our plates down in the kitchen sink before walking us over to the table in the dining room where all the adults sat, his parents and grandma included.

"Cassandra, did you enjoy dinner?" I heard Bart ask as he put his napkin on his plate.

"Yes!" I exclaimed. "Best home cooked meal by far," I said, nudging Jason's shoulder next to me. "Except, of course, for the breakfast Jason made me the other day."

"Is that so?" he asked, grinning slightly at Trish.

"It was nothing," Jason muttered.

"It's been a long time since you've cooked Jason. He really must have wanted to show off his cooking skills," Trish said.

"Are you blushing honey?" his grandma asked him, getting all too excited.

The whole table was about to start laughing before Jason closed his eyes and let out a sigh in what appeared to be red colored cheeks. I wasn't sure what the blushing was for, but I could only guess he didn't cook often anymore and it meant something to his family that he did.

"Well now that everyone has met Cassandra, I think we're going to head back home now," he said, walking over and giving his grandma a hug.

"I hope to see you around, Cassandra dear," Maggie told me.

"Thanks for having me over, Maggie," I said.

"See you guys at home," Jason said to his parents before guiding us away from the kitchen.

"Your grandma is seriously adorable."

His lips curled up as he started shaking his head, "She's too much sometimes."

Obviously, he was still a little embarrassed. I thought it was cute.

We got into his truck and began our trek home again. I thought it was a good time to *tease* him.

"You know, your cheeks look good in blush." I teased him.

"Oh yeah?" he asked.

"You're clearly on the other end of the teasing now mister. Not so fun, is it?"

"Touché. You know, for being a stranger in this family, you fit in all too well."

"I like your family. They're really nice Jason. You're a lucky guy."

"I am, aren't I?"

"More than you know," I replied as we pulled back up to the only damn light in town.

The light was red and it was as if I could sense something stewing in his mind. I turned my eyes to face the window, hoping not to acknowledge the infamous light we were under. It would always be embedded in my mind no matter what streetlight I looked at from now on.

I could see the green illuminating the intersection and beaming off of the hood of his truck. He slowly put the truck in park and stepped out with a sexy grin on his face. I kept my eyes on him as he sauntered over to my side, opened the door, and put his hand out for me to grab.

"Can I have this dance?" he asked softly.

My heart was racing but for other reasons than a horn honking. I hesitated for only a second before I placed my hand in his. I didn't know if it was him, or just the way he asked, but saying no wasn't an option. He helped me out and walked us into the middle of the intersection.

The green light changed to yellow and then to red, keeping the road lit up just enough for us to see each other. My breathing was getting heavy as we did something out of character for me, but in this moment, I was here, all of me. He twirled me around so I was now in front of him. He put my left hand around his waist and took my right hand in his, holding it tightly to his chest. He began to sway us back and forth to absolutely no music or noise around us but the slight sound of the breeze that was blowing.

"Jase," I whispered as though people could hear me, despite the fact that it was only the two of us in the street. "There's no music?"

"Stay here," he whispered in my ear before running to the truck. Then I heard it; the sound of country music coming out of the doors he left open. He turned the volume up so we now had music. Mush. I was turning into mush, what was going on with me?

"Jase?" I said his name quietly. I wanted to talk to him, but he didn't reply.

He put my hands back into place and pulled my waist closer to his, putting our cheeks side by side, continuing to sway in the dark, under the stars. I started to hear a slight hum echoing out of his throat and noticed he was singing to the song on the radio. The sweet sound of his voice was so velvety and smooth, I closed my eyes and rested my head next to his, taking in his silky effortless voice. I moved my hand from his waist, slowly sliding it up his back so that I could hold onto him tighter, feeling the need to be closer to him. My breathing was getting slower as I relaxed and yet my heart was racing all too rapidly. I was enjoying the feel of his warm cheek with rough stubble on it pressed hard against mine. He slid his cheek away as he moved his head directly facing me and pierced his green eyes right into mine. He took his hand off of my waist and moved it to the side of my head, pushing back a stray piece of hair before he gently cupped my cheek. I let it rest in his hand that he held so softly against my skin. It felt warm and slightly rough, and I loved it. I opened my eyes only to see he was still holding his gaze on me. He slowly put his other hand up to my other cheek so that both of his rough hands were ever so gently holding my face. His eyes were glistening as the green light was catching them just right, making them look even more striking. I was losing my train of thought. I was losing my sense of where I was; all I could see was the green in his eyes and all I could feel was the touch of his hands warming my cheeks. His face was slowly inching closer to mine, making my heartbeat spiral out of control. I wasn't sure if this was really happening, it all seemed too wonderful. His lips parted and I took a breath in, waiting for what was about to happen, the anticipation was too much.

"God, you are so beautiful, Cassandra," he said quietly as he looked reluctant to be taking his hands off my face and his body away from mine.

I was taken aback, certainly not expecting a comment like that to come out of his mouth. He grabbed my hand gently before I had any chance to respond and walked me to my side of the truck helping me in. I grabbed his arm before he could close my door, turning down the music first so he could hear me. He looked down at my hand on his arm and then up to me. "Thank you Jase," I told him, it was soft like a whisper but loud enough that I felt like the world around us heard me. He smiled softly and then walked back to his side of the truck.

My mind was racing. My body tingling all over because of what he said and how it made me feel and but also because I didn't do stuff like that. I wasn't raised to let myself dance in the street, but now it was all I could think about. Thinking about how I was feeling every wonderful moment of being out there and dancing with him. I wasn't sure what was going on with me, but being into someone like Jason wasn't like me. Yet for some reason, in that moment he just created, I had felt something. My stomach was full of butterflies fluttering around as though they had the time of their life. My life was already a mess and falling for a guy I didn't know was entirely out of the question. I knew that I had to talk to him about it to find out what was going on or maybe I didn't. Maybe not talking about anything was easier for everyone. For all I knew, he could have just been showing me a good time, and I was entirely over thinking the situation.

Chapter
fifteen

WE ARRIVED BACK TO THE house quickly. Everything in this town was less than ten minutes away. I liked that, less time to stew over things in the truck. We walked in the house, both of us silent. It was almost eerie and I didn't like not talking to him.

We stopped once we reached the kitchen. I wasn't ready to call it a night and was hoping this wasn't the end of it. I wanted to talk more, I missed hearing him speak about things in his life, and part of me wanted to find a way to talk about what happened earlier. I knew the chicken in me wouldn't though.

"You want to come downstairs for a bit?" he asked cautiously. He didn't have to be cautious though. I knew him well enough now to know he wasn't that kind of guy. I knew we would just be hanging out, nothing more.

My chest eased. I was relieved to know he didn't want our night to end either. "Yeah, I'd really like that," I told him.

His hand reached for mine and held it as we walked downstairs to his room.

"You cold at all? The basement can get pretty chilly."

"I'm okay right now, but thank you," I said, walking over to his sofa.

"So what's the story with your grandma Maggie? Why the dinners and stuff?" I asked him once he sat down.

He sunk himself down into the sofa, getting comfortable. He rested his arm over the side of the small couch. Open invitation to move closer to him or just being comfy; I couldn't read the body language.

"She's the only grandparent we have left. She's been doing dinners ever since my grandpa died. We all went over there after the funeral, everyone bringing something over to eat. Ever since then, no one wanted her to be alone, so we all decided once a week we would continue with the dinners. Whoever in town that wanted to come was welcome. It gives her something to look forward to."

My heart melted as I listened to his story. It was sad in so many ways, but also very loving and uplifting. It's remarkable that the entire town was there to support his grandma. "That's a tight knit community."

"My grandma wasn't joking when she said it's a small town, we're all family, blood or not," he said. I pulled up a leg underneath me as he put his over his knee.

"I like that." I said, twisting my fingers together in my lap. "I wished it was something I had grown up with."

He inched a little closer to me, gently resting his hand that was on the back of the couch, on my shoulder. "You have it here. Blood or not, Cassie. When you leave Keaton, you'll be taking a little part of this town with you, and you'll also be leaving a little piece of you behind."

I looked up and gave him a surprised glance. "What? You'll be chopping off a piece of my body to keep as a souvenir?"

"Shit. That's not what I meant," he said.

"I sure hope so," I said, a few goose bumps prickling down my bare arms.

He stood up and walked over to another door, disappearing inside what had to be his closet.

"You looked cold," he said, draping the dark blue blanket around my body, wrapping me up like a burrito.

"Much better. Thank you," I told him. He sat back down taking the same position he was in earlier, making sure to rest his hand on my now covered shoulder.

"Grandma Helen made it. She's my mother's mother. She died before I was born. Cancer."

"That's horrible," I replied, my lips started to turn downward.

"She made the one on your bed too. My mom was pregnant with her second child and Grandma Helen made sure to start a quilt for the baby. She was certain it was a little girl that time, but my mom miscarried three months into the pregnancy."

"Okay, we're going to have to stop with the sad stories," I told him as my heartstrings started tugging too much. I was feeling a pool of tears swell up in my eyes. I wasn't positive, but it had to have been another side effect of this damn pregnancy. My heart ached for Jason though. These stories of his childhood, losing his grandparents, his mother miscarrying, it was like a depressing novel.

He scooted over to me and wrapped his arm around my shoulder. "Not all of it is sad Sweetheart. My mom had me after she had her miscarriage." He peered down, smiling.

"That does make it better." I said, blinking away the tears. "My grandparents are still alive; my father's parents live in Florida. I've only seen them a handful of times. My mom's parents live in Arizona. I used to see them often as they would always stay in their summer home here, but when winter came, they scurried off to Phoenix. They've been staying in Arizona for the past three years now with no visits to Denver. I think they are just getting too old to travel," I shared with him. I loved those grandparents. They would always let me stay with them during the summers when I was a child. My grandmother taught me to play the piano and my grandfather tried to teach me to golf, but it was harder than he and I both expected.

"I didn't even have to ask you for that information," he smirked. "Grandparents are great. You should make some time to go visit them."

"We'll see," I answered, entertaining the idea of doing just that. Until I remembered how disappointed they would be at me given my current state.

"What's wrong?"

I shook my head. "Nothing, just a little," I let a yawn out, "tired is all."

"Let's get you to bed then," he said, helping me out of the quilt he bundled me in.

We got upstairs to my room, but there was still something eating me up inside. "Jase," I said quietly, part of me hoping he didn't even hear me.

"Yeah," he answered back just as quietly.

"What was tonight about? The dancing, the touching, telling me I was beautiful," I unwillingly asked him. I wanted to know, but I didn't. It was as if the words just slipped out of my mouth like vomit, uncontrollable. The chicken in me lost the fight.

He stood there still as a statue, taking in a deep breath and releasing it slowly. "Why do you need to know? Why can't you just enjoy the fact that you had fun? I know you did."

"Because I need to know, you can't just do something like that and not have a reason for it. Why can't you just commit to saying what it was about, why are you leaving this open-ended?"

Amusement surfaced over his face, as if he was enjoying the torment he was causing me. "Sweetheart, why can't you just learn to let things be? Let the chips fall where they may. Enjoy all the moments without worrying about the who, what, when, where, and why of everything."

"That's not who I am," I told him.

"I'm beginning to see that, Cassandra," he stated as he walked out of the bedroom, closing the door behind him.

Ugh, why was he so difficult and why did I care so much? *I red light all of this.* I couldn't help but huff as those words ran through my mind. Who would have thought code words could have been so amusing and exciting to use, let alone catch on to someone so quickly. It didn't take away the fact I was still upset for the way we ended things tonight. I hit a trigger with him and it made me mad. I didn't understand why he couldn't just answer me, why he had to leave it out in the air. Was it because he knew I would be leaving when my car was done? I didn't want to stop thinking about it, but sadly, exhaustion won, and out cold I went.

Chapter
sixteen

"GOOD MORNING," I SAID as I pulled a mug from the cabinet, filling it with steaming coffee. I grabbed my mug and sat in the chair directly across from Jason. There was a plate of toast sitting in front of me. I was about to get up from the chair, worried I just took someone's seat when Jason told me to sit back down.

"I made the toast for you. I heard you getting sick again. I figured this would help your stomach."

Shit. He heard me. I didn't even know what kind of excuse to use this time. My accident was days behind us and there was no logical explanation to use. "Thank you," I said coyly, trying to avoid the subject. I was also unsure of what his mood was like after he abruptly left my room last night. I definitely pushed some wrong buttons and I felt guilty for pressing the issue. He was the one being so helpful to me. I had to remember that.

He put his paper down and looked straight at me. I waited patiently for his response, prepared for anything at this point.

"Listen. I'm sorry, Cassie. I didn't like how we left things last night. I wasn't being nice to you and that's not me. You had a question and I dodged it. I'm sorry," he apologized.

What? Since when did men say they were sorry and for that matter, without even being told they did anything wrong? This was a very new revelation in all my studies of men over the past few years.

"Thanks Jase, but really I'm the one that's sorry. I'm sorry I badgered you about it. I'll let it go or try to at least," I replied.

"Thank you, but I really am sorry Sweetheart," he said, pressing his lips together. I could tell he felt like shit about it. I can't deny he made me feel terrible for asking, but it was nice to have things smoothed over with him.

And just like that we were back to being normal, whatever our normal was. No questions about my persistent nausea, and no more urging on my part about unexplained feelings. Except I still had questions, but I really was going to put forth the effort of learning to let things be. It was going to be hard, but if it was working for Jase, it had to work for me too.

"So what's on the agenda for today?" I asked, enjoying the toast he made me. He put his mug down. "I have an errand to run this morning but this afternoon, I have some things in mind for us. I'll be back later, why don't you take the morning off and relax," he said.

"Okay. Where are you going, though? Can I come with you? I promise I won't ask questions, aside from the ones I just asked."

He let out a chuckle. "No. It's easier if I just do it by myself. I have to, uh, help my dad with something."

He stood up from his chair and made his way to my side of the table. He slowly placed his hand gently against my cheek. "I'll be back soon," he told me, before walking out of the kitchen.

Don't think too much into that. Let it go... Don't think, Cassandra. Don't think. It wasn't working. Trying not to think about it made me think about it more. Either he was feeling something for me, or he was just a very sweet and sensitive guy. *Stop thinking, Cassandra Elizabeth. Stop thinking.* Ugh, my stomach was starting to bundle itself into knots as I thought about the way that simple gesture made me feel. I've never had a guy do something like that before; it was caring, gentle and turned me to mush. Was it possible to feel something for a guy I just met? It wasn't as if I didn't know him, but I certainly didn't know everything he kept hidden inside him. Which normally should scare a girl, but I couldn't help feeling a strong pull toward him.

Worrying about it was useless, unless I had answers from the source himself, and that wasn't going to happen. Ugh, maybe

Jase was right, I just needed to let it be and enjoy the fact that it made me happy. Because that is exactly what it did, whatever was going on, the bottom line was that I was enjoying myself. I was feeling content inside. He was starting to bring out the Cassandra I knew existed but could never find. I thought maybe she was lost for good, but perhaps getting lost was the real secret to being able to find myself, and Jase was the one helping to make all of it happen. A wide smile spread across my face as I realized for the first time in a very long time, I was smiling because I was happy, not because I was being forced to.

I finished my toast and coffee, again feeling a pang of guilt for consuming caffeine when I felt it was in no way good for me, and this soon-to-be stomach hog growing inside of me. I had to figure out what route I was going to take, but my mind wasn't ready to think about it yet. I had too much Jason on the brain.

I was lying down on my bed, resting after a long hot shower. My brain had finally shut off all things Jase and I was suddenly wishing I had the world at my fingertips as Jason called it. I wanted to check in with Mel. Without being near him and his phone, I was without a way to talk to her. I wondered if she called him, what they talked about, wishing it was me that got to talk to her instead. And then boom it hit me like a ton of bricks. My stomach was hungry and growling. I grumbled as I got off the bed and decided to go do what Trish said, eat some crackers. My eyes ventured over to the bag hiding next to the dresser, the one they gave me at the hospital. Curiosity suddenly struck. I grabbed the bag and put it on the bed. I wanted to read the pamphlets. I didn't know why now, but the curiosity of what information they had was beginning to intrigue me.

I walked into the kitchen and opened the door that Jason assured me was not the door to his room but the pantry and began my search. "Ah-ha," I screamed to myself when I saw the big red box that housed the crackers. I grabbed a pack and then a can of ginger ale in the fridge and made my way back to my room.

I sat with my legs crossed on the bed as I opened my package of crackers and can of soda. That was much better. What a difference it made. Trish was obviously a mom, one I wish was more like mine, and one I wish I could be someday, just not today.

I pulled one of the pamphlets titled 'Your New Changing Body' out of the bag. Gah. I opened it up and began reading. The section discussed my breasts becoming tender. My new mood swings and lastly, the nausea. Well, check, check, and check. I was without a doubt more pregnant than I realized. I looked down at my stomach that had yet to start growing; I was sure that information was in another pamphlet. "Why is it that so many women out there want a baby, yet here I am dreading every minute of this? I'm wishing and praying too hard, that you weren't in my stomach trying to make yourself a nice home," I said. "I don't have a good mom little seed. I'm not a good daughter. I lied, I ruined my life, yours included, and now our future as we know it is gone." I was talking to it, and the things I was saying were cruel and hurtful. I was an awful mother. I started crying, letting the tears soak the pamphlet that was in my lap. This was just another reason that this baby shouldn't be mine; I would be a horrible mother. I put the pamphlet back in the bag on my bed, wiped away the tears, and ate another cracker before putting the package next to my bed. "I guess those will be good to keep for emergencies," I told myself.

"Do you always talk to yourself Sweetheart?"

I jumped up from my spot, almost spilling the soda that was in my hands. I shoved the bag from my bed to the floor in one quick movement before putting my hand to my chest. "Jason, good God, you scared the shit out of me."

"Clearly. I just heard you talking when I came down the hall and had to see who or what you were talking to."

I put my hand down from my chest. Then another wave hit. What all did he hear? "How long have you been listening to me?"

"You've been talking to yourself that long?" he asked with a slightly scared look on his face. "Maybe you are my Crazy Cousin Cassandra."

"Very funny," I said. He clearly didn't hear me earlier. *Thank God.* "It was quiet in the house and I tend to talk to myself when I get lonely." Or when I'm telling my growing seed how bad of a mother I'm going to be.

As I sat waiting for Jase to respond, I couldn't help but notice something seemed different, he didn't seem like himself. Something was off.

"Hey, are you okay?" I asked him.

"Yeah I'm good," he answered me with his eyes gazing at his feet. "You hungry?" He looked over at the nightstand with the crackers on it.

"I only had a few, but yes, I could still eat," I said. If he were telling me he was okay, then I would try my best to believe him.

"Perfect, I grabbed lunch on my way home. Let's go eat."

I got up from the bed and made my way to the door where he was standing. "You'll want shoes."

Shoes?

"Or boots. You pick, but I personally like the boots better," he said before he left my room.

Boots it was. I was glad I had on my yellow, summer sundress today as it matched my turquoise boots perfectly.

Chapter seventeen

HE PULLED INTO A PARKING spot across the street from the infamous tree that I damaged.

"Jase?" I peered over to him before we got out of the truck.

He smiled as I said his name. "Trust me."

I let out a sigh and got out of the truck, making my way toward him. He was carrying the bag of food he'd picked up on his way home and the blue quilt he had wrapped around me the night before.

"This way." He motioned for me to follow him, except we weren't going to the tree; we were staying on this side of the street.

We made our way over to a large, grassy area in front of an old building that appeared abandoned. He spread out the quilt and set the bag on it before slipping his boots off. "Boots off, Sweetheart."

I slipped off my socks and boots. The feel of the grass underneath my feet was refreshing. I stood there wiggling my toes in the grass when I felt Jase come up next to me, barefoot and all, proceeding to do the same.

"What are we doing?" he asked me.

"Have you ever just stopped and felt the cool grass under your feet before?" I asked.

He let out a huff. "You're learning to enjoy your moments."

I watched my feet for a second longer and realized, I sure the shit was. I couldn't help but laugh. "You're wearing off on me I guess," I said.

"What can I say? I'm pretty amazing. Now let's eat, I got your favorite."

I didn't know what I expected to come out of the bag but a chicken Cesar salad was not it. I guess I was waiting for the usual to come out.

"Why do you look so stunned?" he asked, handing over my container and a fork.

"Not stunned, just pleasantly surprised."

"I actually eat salads, I just really felt like splurging this week with you and wanted to get you to eat a burger or two." He grinned.

"I did enjoy the burgers, but I do love my salads," I said.

We were almost through with our lunch when I saw Jason grab his phone from his pocket.

"Hi Melanie," he answered.

"Sorry I wasn't able to answer earlier."

He laughed. "No, she's still well and breathing."

"Actually right next to me."

"Just finishing up lunch outside on a blanket."

"Oh really? Well I can tell you without a doubt she is."

"I'll let her know. Here she is."

"She says you're not an outdoor girl and she's proud of you," Jase told me as he handed me his phone.

I shook my head. I wasn't an outdoor girl, but in my defense, I really hadn't been given much opportunity to be.

"Hey Mel."

"Hot Damn. Did he seriously just give you a picnic lunch?"

"Can you excuse me for a sec?" I asked Jason quietly as I got off the blanket. I made my way over to the truck, so I could talk privately.

"Yes. Pretty incredible, right?"

"Is he as hot as he sounds? Cause he sounds damn hot."

"Very," I sighed into the phone. He was hot, but his sweet disposition made him even more attractive.

"Alright I'm more than okay with you staying now."

"It's not like that. You know my situation. No way in hell am I dragging this nice guy into it." I leaned against the passenger side of the truck, crossing my ankles as I stared at the ground.

"If he is this nice now, something tells me he wouldn't be stupid and let a girl like you go, regardless of your situation."

"I don't even think he likes me like that. I think he's just genuinely a nice guy." I told her honestly. I knew there was a connection between us, but I wasn't sure if it was just me that was feeling it.

"Please tell me you're joking? A guy who's not interested does not, and I repeat, does not go through the trouble of taking a girl on a picnic, let her stay in his house, stay with her at the hospital, and talk to her friend like it's not a problem if he doesn't feel some sort of connection."

"Mel," I said as my lips curled up. "That's not all. He also got me to dance in the street under the stars, took me to his grandma's for dinner, and took me shopping for boots."

"Holy shit! If you don't jump on him, then I will."

"It's not even like that. There is so much more to him. He's not like other guys, like Parker. He's not just into ass and boobs. He's the guy that takes you home to meet the parents because he's proud of you. Not the guy that keeps you a secret. I'm the secret. I'm the girl you hide from your parents because for one, the mom already knows I'm trouble. I'm with child Mel, not real girlfriend, long-term relationship material."

"Are you done talking now?"

"Um, yeah?" I said, making it sound more like a question than an answer, unsure where she was taking this.

"I don't think you give Jason enough credit. You're judging him. You're being a hypocrite. You don't want people to judge you like your parents do which is why you come to me instead. Yet you're judging Jason on how you think he'll react to your situation when you don't even know what he'll say. Stop preplanning every conversation in your head before it happens, because nine times out of ten, the conversation will go differently. Go finish lunch and think about what I've said. I love you girl."

I wasn't sure how else to respond other than to do as she said. "Love you too Mel." I snapped the phone closed and absorbed her words. I somberly walked back to our picnic in the grass and handed Jason back his phone.

"You okay?"

"Yeah."

"What was that all about? You know I could have left if you wanted to gush to your friend about me and my awesome picnic," he said, as if he knew exactly why I walked away.

"Were you eavesdropping?" I asked, teasing him.

"No, but you did come back looking upset. Talk to me." He patted the open spot next to him on the blanket. I sat down next to him, noticing he cleaned up our empty lunch containers.

"Okay. Can I ask you a question?"

He looked over at me with a raised eyebrow.

"No not like the game. It's a question about life." I said.

"Go for it," he said.

"Do you ever go over in your head how someone will react to something you tell them, you know, like a conversation playing out?"

"All the time, but only because I'm scared... I'm scared that I'm going to get hurt, so I reason with myself by saying it's okay not to tell the person because I already know the outcome, but I don't. The future is unknown; you can't pre-plan in your head how life will play out until it does. Conversations included. I learned that a while ago, Cassie. If you never take the chance to let things play out, then how will you ever learn how to trust in other people? You're just assuming you know, and remember what you told me about assuming," he said, flashing me a wink. "Does that answer your question Sweetheart?"

Between him and Mel, I wasn't sure who was more spot on with how I've been acting lately, but it took Jason's reasoning for me to realize how much I've been doing what I was always told not to... assume. "More than you'll ever know."

He grabbed his socks and boots and slipped them on. I looked at him, waiting for him to say what he was doing because I wasn't ready to leave yet.

"Come here. I want to show you something. I know you already left your mark on the tree but I want you to leave another one," he said with a devilish smile.

I shook my head and laughed. I slipped on my socks and boots before grabbing his hand as he took us across the street.

When we got to the tree, the visible damage that I did to it could have been seen a mile away, but up close, it was far worse. "Damn. I didn't think I hit it that hard," I told him as I grabbed onto the tree trunk.

"I tried to tell you," he told me. "Over here, this side."

I followed him around to the other side of the tree and saw initial after initial carved into the tree. Some were inside hearts, and others were alone. "Wow, is this like a town thing or something?" I asked, intrigued with all the letters engraved in the tree. I saw too many letters. I tried to find Jason's but I didn't see a J or a B next to each other. I did see a J next to an A that wasn't in a heart, but I wasn't sure whom the A was for.

"The town legend says that it brings you good luck," he whispered as he came up behind me, "if you believe hard enough."

I could feel the goose bumps trickle down my skin as I felt him breathing on my shoulder. "Is that so?" I asked, turning my head to the side to meet his gaze.

"That's what they say."

"Why are there initials inside the hearts then?"

"Couples that want good luck. Are you not romantic, Cassie?" he asked me as he walked to my side, leaning up against the tree.

"I guess I just haven't found the right person to make me believe romance like that exists," I said truthfully. I believed it had to be out there somewhere, but wherever it was, I had yet to find it, or him.

He took a pocket knife out of his back pocket and flipped it open. "Well I guess we'll just have to give you some luck then, won't we?" he asked as he took the knife to the tree.

"Oh really? And whose initial is going next to mine?" I asked curiously. My heart started racing the moment he started carving. I knew there was something with Jason, but I wasn't ready to admit it yet.

He made a heart and put a letter C inside of it. "You'll have to leave it open until you find the guy. Then you can come back and put his initial next to yours."

"And where will I find this guy? I seem to be looking in all the wrong places," I said. I rested my hand casually over my stomach as I thought about the worst place I ever looked, the place that caused the growing seed inside me. I was most definitely looking in all the wrong places.

"I don't know where, but I have a feeling he's close by," he said as he slid the knife back in his pocket.

I was sure my heart skipped more than a beat; try ten. I was more off base than I realized. He had to feel it too. A person just doesn't make a comment like that. Mel was right.

"You ready to head back?"

"Yeah, I guess so," I replied. Not ready to head back just yet, but not knowing if I was going to be able to keep my feelings to myself the longer we stood here talking about romance and guys.

"You seem unsure of that?"

"No, I'm fine."

"Okay see, there's that word. 'Fine.' It does not mean what it sounds like. It's obviously not fine, so are you trying to figure out in your mind what we are going to do next? Is that what's bothering you?" he asked. God, he was too much. I couldn't believe he was a guy who knew the word fine meant anything but what it sounded like.

"You're good Jason, too good," I told him. "I really had a good afternoon with you and I'm not ready for it to end."

"Who said it has to end?"

I could see the blush coloring his cheeks again. Damn, he looked too gorgeous with the rosy cheeks that I caused. "You're blushing again," I said.

"That seems to happen a lot around you."

"So what's next then Mr. Rosy Cheeks?"

His cheeks became an even deeper shade of pink. "We were doing so well too, with the grass and all. I really thought you were catching on Sweetheart," he said. "I'll figure out something to do, but you won't get to know what it is until I say so."

"You really know how to get my anxiety going don't you?" I teased him.

"Just as much as you know how to get me to blush." He smiled back.

Chapter eighteen

"SO THIS IS YOUR IDEA OF FUN?" I asked as we sat on the sofa in his room.

"I said I had something in mind, give it a chance before you cross it off as not being fun," he told me as he walked over to his closet.

He came walking out, carrying the board game Scrabble. "Alright, I got it, let's go."

I gave him a questioning glance as he left his room and headed back upstairs stopping at the kitchen table. Trish and Bart were already in the kitchen when we got up there.

"Hi Trish, Hi Bart," I said to them as we made our way through the kitchen to the table.

"Cassandra," Bart said. "Good to see you again."

"You too," I replied.

"I see Jason has been keeping you busy this week," Trish said, sounding all too excited.

"Mom," Jason said quietly to Trish as he put the game on the table. "Not now."

"He's been a great tour guide this week," I told her.

"Good," she said.

"Alright, let's get this game started shall we?" Bart asked as he took a seat at the table.

I felt Jason come up behind me. "You're in for a fun night," he said so quietly only I could hear him. My arms and neck erupted in goose bumps. "You cold?" he whispered in my other ear. No, they're from your soft sexy voice Jason... I thought to myself. "No, I'm good."

I could see him smile as he walked by me. I had to get a grip.

"Have you played before?" Trish asked, bringing my thoughts back to the game.

"Yeah, all the time," I lied. I had never played Scrabble before, but honestly how hard could it be? I was really good with words and English; I had to be good at this too.

"You're totally lying," Jase said as he laid out the board on the table.

It didn't matter; I was going to win this game. "Are you prepared to lose?" I asked him with full certainty that he would.

"I think you might have met your match son," Bart said.

"Alright Sweetheart, let's see what you've got," he said as he passed out the letters to each of us.

I laid out my letters, and already had a word, it was small, but it would do. Trish started, then we were to continue clockwise, which meant Bart and Jason had to go before it was my turn. I watched as Trish put down her word and then Bart exchanged a couple of tiles. I wasn't that familiar with the game, but it didn't take long to catch on.

Jason bit down on his lower lip as he put his tiles down for his first word.

"A double word and that makes twenty two points for me." He looked over, giving me a shrug with a slightly cocky grin. He wasn't normally cocky about things, but I actually enjoyed seeing this side of him. He was more competitive than I thought.

Trish broke my thoughts to let me know that it was my turn.

"Hmm, I guess I'll just have to play this word, which just so happens to tie me up with Jason." I looked over at him after I was finished laying out my tiles for the word 'MAKER', giving me exactly twenty-two points. "I tried to tell you, Jason," I said teasingly.

"It's not over yet Sweetheart," he said, batting those perfectly long eyelashes over his green gems.

"Not even close," I whispered to him as Trish took her turn.

So, this is what a family night felt like. It was more than refreshing to see parents like this, parents who showed affection and who had fun with their kid. I would have never guessed a night of Scrabble would have been just the ticket for a fun evening. Normally family nights for me were awkward and uncomfortable, especially the older I got. Now I realized what I'd really been missing. It made me sad, but also happy that I had the chance to experience it, even if it was only for this one time.

The game continued for over an hour. Bart was the first one out, Trish followed him, leaving Jase and me to finish for the winning spot. This was a true cowboy showdown, or so Bart told me. You'd have thought this was a national contest on television as intent as they sat with their eyes on the board, waiting for Jase to make his move.

If I wasn't able to connect my letters to his next word that he laid out, I would lose the game. I sat fidgeting with my hands on my lap as I waited impatiently for him to take his turn.

He finally put down his last letter and glanced over at me. 'LUCKY'.

I could tell by the way he looked at me that there was more meaning behind the word than anyone could ever know. I felt the same way too, but right now, this time, I had to put my letters out for a win that Jason just made possible.

"Fourteen points, Jason," Trish said, keeping score for us.

I started grinning ear to ear, knowing the word I was able to spell. He was either going to laugh or get pissed, and if I knew him as well as I thought I did, he was going to do exactly what my word spelled out.

I laid out all my letters, spelling the word 'BLUSH'. I sat back in my chair after I finished placing all the tiles. I looked over at Jason immediately.

"Seriously?" he asked, shaking his head as his cheeks started to turn that color of red that I loved seeing.

"Oh you better believe it. I couldn't have worked it out more perfectly if I had planned it myself," I said.

Trish and Bart were now laughing hysterically along with us.

Trish lifted her head up after putting the score down even though I already knew my numbers. I was unfortunately too good at adding in my head. "Our new winner is Cassandra," she gushed.

"What? That's impossible," Jason said as he grabbed the score sheet.

"Read it and weep mister. Triple word and my H landed on a double letter score. Correct me if I'm wrong but that puts me twenty-four points over you. I win, I win!" I realized after saying it out loud.

"WOOHOO!" I screamed. I might have also done a little dance as I got up from my chair, cheering myself on. I looked over at Trish and Bart who were still in hysterics at my word and for my pure enthusiasm for winning. It had been awhile, but I finally did something without failing. *Baby steps, Cassandra, baby steps.* I couldn't help but giggle at myself. I had just compared not failing at life to winning at Scrabble. I really must have been getting too much fresh air this past week. I sat back down before I took my excitement any further.

Jason sat forward in his chair with a sexy look on his face, not at all the face of a loser. That was probably because he was not even close to being one. He was winning me over every day.

"I'll let you have this win, but only because," he paused as he leaned over closer to me, "you look so happy right now and I like seeing you like this."

"Or, how about because I actually really did win," I said, leaning in closer to him. "I also am really happy right now."

He shot me another grin before getting up from his chair.

"I don't think I've ever had that much fun playing a board game before," I told Trish and Bart as we started cleaning the table up.

"We play once a week, but never has it been this competitive or exciting," she said.

We finished cleaning up our board game, putting the tiles in the bag they came in and the board back in the box.

"Okay who's ready for some dinner? I was thinking of grilling tonight." Bart announced as he grabbed a pack of chicken out of the refrigerator.

"Sounds good Dad," Jason said. He made his way closer to me. "That okay with you, Cassie?"

As much as I loved home cooked meals now, I was just too exhausted to stay up any longer. I had a hunch because of the pregnancy that I was starting to feel more tired than usual. "I think I'll pass, I'm actually really tired and was going to head to bed."

Trish came up to me as though she was trying to keep it between us. "Are you sure Sweetie? You really should eat something. Do you feel sick? Do you want a pack of crackers?"

She was too kind. "I have a pack in my room. I think I just had too much fun for one day," I told her.

She nodded her head and went back into the kitchen.

Jason had a worrisome look in his eyes as he made his way over to me, making my stomach feel guilty for lying to him. I knew I had to do as Mel said and give him the chance to respond in his own way, but I was just too afraid. I was protecting my feelings from being hurt beyond repair.

"Night Bart, night Trish," I hollered over to them as they started preparing dinner.

"Hey I have somewhere to take you tomorrow." He nudged his head toward me.

"Where to?" I asked.

"Moose wants me to bring you in to see your car."

I wasn't ready for my car to be done yet. I couldn't place the feeling, but I wanted more time with this man standing in front of me. I wanted to see what these tingles and goose bumps really meant. I just needed more time. I never thought I would say that, as much of a hurry as I was to get away from my life or from Keaton, but my heart was telling me to stay. Mel could tell there was something going on, but I needed to know if he did too.

"You don't seem happy about that?" he asked, inching closer toward me. "We don't have to go look at it. I mean it might be hard for you since it's not done yet, the parts just came in."

And exhale. I looked up at him. "No, we can go. That would be good. Well maybe not good to see the way it is, but to see it progressing, I guess is what I meant," I said, stumbling over my words.

He shook his head and chuckled. "You sure you're alright?"

"Yeah I'm just really tired, I will probably be asleep the minute my head hits the pillow."

"Do you want me to keep you company?" he asked, his eyes looking me over as though he was looking for signs of illness.

Yes. I do want you to stay.

"As much as I would like that I don't think I'll be much company."

"Get some sleep then. Night Cassie," he said quietly.

"Night Jase," I said to him, mirroring his tone. He lingered, his lips parting open. He looked like he wanted to say something else but he didn't. He shut his mouth and left.

As I got into bed, the only thing I could think about was Jase and the tingles he gave me. One I hadn't ever experienced before and goose bumps that weren't because of being cold. I suddenly smiled as I thought about how it was good to have these feelings.

Chapter
nineteen

THE NEXT DAY WE WALKED into the garage and it was nothing like I was expecting. It wasn't like the shops back in Denver, but it certainly wasn't awful like I envisioned and I was glad for that.

A sudden gasp left my mouth as I saw my car sitting there. "Oh my God! She looks terrible," I said, pointing to it in disbelief.

"Well you did do a number on it, Cassandra," Moose said as he rolled out from underneath the car sitting next to mine.

"I know, but I wasn't expecting to see this. It's been a week and she still looks so..." I paused, trying to find the right word.

"Rough?" Moose suggested as he came walking over to us in greasy coveralls and a baseball cap.

Rough was exactly the perfect word.

"I think you were so shaken up from your accident you didn't realize the shape your car was in. Now you see why I wanted you to go to the hospital to get checked out," Jase said as he stood next to me, both of us taking in the shape of the metal before us.

"I definitely get it now." I hadn't understood the severity of the situation before, but I did now.

Moose walked over to the front left of the car, pointing to various places explaining to me in gibberish what he had already done and what was still left to do. "We had to pull the door off. The windshield will have to be replaced. We also had to pull your hood off, your front bumper, the left fender, and that don't even cover the frame damage underneath, the radiator, the radiator core support, the alignment it will need, or the tire and wheel that will have to be replaced too," he finished.

"Huh?" I asked, gawking at him.

"Your car is hurt badly, but I'm going to fix it," Moose said, giving me a 'you are such a girl' look.

Jase and I both looked at each other and laughed. I hated that I had no clue what he was telling me, but I wasn't raised around fixing cars.

"Your car is in good hands, don't worry," Jason said.

Moose walked over to a large toolbox and pulled something out.

"Dad found this when he was pulling your car apart, I believe this belongs to you," he said, handing over a white phone. MY white phone.

I looked at him, my eyes not even believing what was in front of them. My stomach was doing a happy dance inside as I let out a sigh of relief. "Oh my God. Seriously. You, Moose, are too awesome. Thank you so much."

"Man, you don't realize how long we have been looking for that thing," Jase said to Moose who had a look on his face like he just saved a kitten from a tree. This was no kitten, but it was my only connection to the world and I was more than glad to have it back.

I looked up at Jase who had the same excited look on his face as I hit the button on the front illuminating the screen. "It works!" I gasped.

"So this means no more calls from the feisty one. I'm bummed," Jase said sarcastically.

I rolled my eyes at him as I slid my finger across the screen.

"Forty five missed calls," I said out loud. I clicked on the phone icon bringing up all my missed calls. "And all from Mel. I should have known." I sunk my shoulders. I didn't know why I thought I would have any from my parents. Even though my week had been flipped upside down, it didn't mean theirs had. I also never let them know, so I only had myself to blame for the absence of calls from them.

"Hey," Jase said, catching my attention.

"It's fine. I didn't tell them. It's my own fault for thinking they would just know that something was wrong with their daughter," I said.

"It's not okay, Cassie, but if you want to call them, we can give you some privacy," he offered, being the sweet Jason I've come to know.

I shook my head. "No, I'm okay. Really," I lied, my eyes blinking away a few tears that wanted to push through. This wasn't anything out of the normal I hadn't dealt with before.

I felt his hands on my shoulders, squeezing them as he whispered in my ear from behind me. "They really do care about you, Cassie. Sometimes parents just have an odd way of showing it."

"I know," I whispered back.

"Big D could relate," Moose said.

"Big D?" I asked.

Jase walked back around standing in front of me. "My brother; he has parent issues, so I see what you're going through. It'll be okay," he tried to assure me.

"But you said you didn't talk about your brother. So how is it going to be okay?" I tried to understand, but I couldn't. His parents didn't discuss his brother but he said everything would be okay. How would he know for sure?

"Because in the end, everything will be okay. It has to be," he said.

"I guess." I shrugged, trying hard to trust him.

"Sorry man," Moose said to Jason with an apologetic look.

"Don't worry about it," he said, nodding his head.

"So are we all going out tonight or what?" Moose asked, twirling his dirty rag around in his hand.

"That's up to Cassie," Jason said, glancing in my direction.

"I guess that depends on where "out" is," I said.

"It's just a bar," Moose piped up.

I wasn't familiar with much when it came to babies, but I did know that was bad, so no drinking was going to happen for me tonight. "It sounds like it could be fun."

"Could be? Cassandra, it's not a question. It's definitely a great time," Moose said, tossing his rag over his shoulder.

"We don't have to go if you don't want to," Jason assured me.

"No, we can. It'll be fun," I answered.

"See, there's the spirit," Moose said. "Not to mention, we go at least once a week. It's kind of a thing in this town."

"I wouldn't want to break tradition," I said.

"Alright Moose, we'll see you tonight buddy." Jason waved as we left the garage with my horrible excuse for a car in it.

I was relieved that it wasn't ready yet, but also in a state of shock for how truly bad it did look. I also couldn't help but cringe at the thought of what my father would think if he saw my car in its present condition. Just the image of him in my mind caused shivers to run down my spine, and not the kind Jason gave me. That was not a conversation I was even remotely ready to have with him. I would get the car fixed and aside from a large bill that I was going to have to pay off, he would never know. That was the plan, and I was going to stick to it.

"You're awfully quiet over there. What are you thinking about?" Jason asked as we pulled back up to the house.

"Nothing. I'm just not looking forward to having to tell my father about my car."

"Tonight will be good for you then. You look like you could use a night out," he said as he opened his door.

Yeah it would be good for me, I hoped.

Chapter
twenty

I STEPPED OUT OF MY ROOM wearing my new boots, of course, and a little strapless black dress with a belt that had gold on it to match the studs on my boots. It was nothing I would normally wear all together, but it was perfect for tonight as these boots were starting to become my new favorite wardrobe item.

"Oh Sweetie." Trish said from behind me. "You look beautiful."

"Thank you," I said as I looked back down at my dress and boots.

"Where are you guys going tonight?"

I cocked my head up trying to think of the name, but I never got one. "A bar, but I don't know the name," I shrugged.

"Oh, you must be going to Dog Gone," she said, nodding her head.

I lifted my brow at her. "I'm sorry, where?"

"The Dog Gone bar. You'll have fun," she said.

She put her hand on my shoulder as we made our way to the family room. "I hope so," I said.

"Wow." I heard him saying as I came around the corner. "You look g-gorgeous." His voice caught as he tried to get the last word out.

His eyes traveled from my boots up to my hair that I left down and wavy with the help of Trish's blow dryer.

"It's not too much?" I asked, hoping not to be over dressed to a place with the word 'dog' in it.

He cleared his throat as he continued to look me over. "Definitely not."

"You look pretty nice too," I said, doing a once over on him. This must have been his cleaned up look and I was glad I got to see it. He wore a pair of dark, tight jeans with a different pair of black cowboy boots; I had yet to see them on him until tonight. He completed his outfit with a dark V-neck tee and a matching cowboy hat.

"I *really* like the hat Jase," I told him.

He flashed me a wink.

"Let's get this show on the road," he said as we walked to the door. "Night mom," he said to Trish as he gave her a kiss on the cheek before closing the door behind us.

"So, you failed to mention the name of the bar to me. Dog Gone?"

"Catchy huh?"

"Yeah, if I'm an animal, which I'm not," I said sarcastically.

We arrived quickly as always, I couldn't help but chuckle a little. Getting around town was too easy, I could seriously get used to it.

"Uh, this looks more like a barn than a bar," I stated as we walked up to the doors.

"The only barn in town Sweetheart." He placed his hand in the middle of my back as we made our way in. A shiver ran down my spine, enjoying the feel of his hand there too much. I took in a deep breath as we walked through the double doors and decided to try and let my guard down a little. I was going to find out if that was even possible.

The place was already busy. The dance floor looked packed and the tables around the bar were completely full. There were people I had recognized from around town along with many others that I had yet to meet. Moose and the girl Kasey from dinner were waving to us at the bar as we headed that direction.

"I know I already told you, but I have to say it again, you look incredible tonight," Jason said quietly behind me as he kept his hand on my lower back leading us over to the bar. My pulse was now completely racing.

Moose and Jason immediately gave each other a slap on the back as we walked up to the few open seats left. "Wow, Cassie, you clean up nice," Moose said teasing.

"You too. The little bit of grease on your left cheek really completes the look," I told him.

We started laughing as we watched him trying to figure out where the grease was until he realized I was joking.

"You are a cruel woman, you know that?" he said as he came up behind me squeezing my shoulders.

"You remember Kasey right?" Jason asked as she came walking up to my other side.

"Of course I do, it's nice to see you again," I said.

"Hey Cassandra," Kasey said as she extended her hand for me to take.

She looked just as cute as she did at dinner. Her short hair had a few curls in it, her long legs covered in a nice pair of jeans, and then something completely caught my eyes.

"Oh I love your cowgirl boots," I told her. They were lipstick red and gorgeous.

"Thanks," she said as she turned her feet in either direction showing them off. I was certain I would need a pair.

"I think I may have started something bad," Jason said.

"You have no idea," I said, still eyeing the boots.

"Come with me, Cassandra. We'll get some drinks. The bartender hasn't left that end in a while," Kasey said as she pulled my arm toward her.

I looked over at Jason as I walked away with Kasey as she all but dragged me away.

"What are you having?" she asked as we took over two empty seats at the end. The bar curved so it was easy to see everyone; Jason and Moose were sitting in the seats we originally had, looking as though they were deep in conversation.

"Water with lemon, please," I told her, getting a shocked expression on her face in return.

"I'm just really parched," I said as she shrugged in acceptance.

"One water and a beer please," she yelled to the bartender over the music blaring through the speakers.

We got our drinks and continued to stay where we were. She was friendly enough and some girl time might do me some good, since I was more than missing Mel.

"So you like him don't you?" she bluntly asked, my water almost spraying out my lips.

I swallowed my water and turned my gaze to the glass of clear contents that I wished was actually liquid courage. "Kasey, I'm not quite sure I'm his type. My life is too complex for him," I told her honestly. I knew I deserved a good guy when the time was right but this guy deserved someone who didn't come with baggage and whose life wasn't in disarray.

"Well, the way he is looking at you right now tells me that he definitely would disagree with everything you just said."

I looked up at her and saw the knowing grin she had on her face. I twisted my neck to see what she was looking at and sure enough, Jason had his eyes fixated on me with a sultry expression. He didn't even bother to turn his head the minute I looked at him. He flashed a wink at me, causing my cheeks to warm up quickly. I turned back to face Kasey.

"See what I mean," she said.

I couldn't help but smile at the thought of him staring at me. "I guess so."

"Oh Cassandra, I've known Jason for a long time. We grew up together: him, Moose, and me. And I've never seen him this smitten before."

My cheeks were now on fire as her words seeped through me.

"He's been through a lot, but I can tell a nice girl when I see one, and you, Cassandra, seem really sweet," she said.

"He's the sweet one. I can't figure how on earth he's still single?" I asked her.

"Like I said, he's been through a lot. Then there was a girl, but she was bad news. I think that really jacked him up, kind of shut him down on the girl front anyway."

Before I could reply, Moose walked up between us. "Sorry, I promised this one a dance, go keep Jason company," he told me.

He took off with Kasey to the dance floor and nudged his head in Jason's direction. I could take a hint.

"Hey, there. This seat taken?" I asked before I sat down.

"For a girl like you? It's never taken," he said, flashing me a grin.

I loved his grins, his sweet ones, his cocky ones, and most of all, his sexy ones. Yet, looking at him right now, I could sense there was something hiding behind his gorgeous green eyes of his that was plaguing him. I wanted to help him, I wanted to tell him whatever was haunting him he could tell me, he could confide in me, but how could I tell him that when I couldn't even come clean about the demons I kept hidden away? I started biting the inside of my cheek, feeling like such a hypocrite.

"What are you thinking about over there, Cassie?" he asked, breaking my thoughts. I swiveled my stool to face him. He had his elbow leaning on the bar, resting his head against his hand.

"Nothing," I said, I didn't have the courage to battle him.

"I can tell you're lying," he said. I took in a deep breath and exhaled it slowly trying to ease the drumming in my chest.

"Fine, you seem sad Jase," I told him. His gaze immediately shifted down to the floor as he fidgeted with his drink, which looked like water too. "You can talk to me," I offered. I put my hand on his knee, trying to get him to look at me, but he didn't.

I moved my hand and grabbed my water, taking a long sip when he finally looked up at me. He didn't have to say anything; his eyes said it all. They were warm and even though they still were sad; I could see through them, he was glad about something. I wasn't sure what, but I was hoping he was about to tell me. He put his glass on the counter and jumped off his bar stool. I could feel his breath behind my ear as he spoke softly.

"You can talk to me too you know," he whispered, making a shiver run from my neck to my toes.

It wasn't what I wanted to hear. I longed to hear him divulge his deepest secrets to me so I could help try and take the pain away, but that wasn't going to happen tonight. He pushed my water back and took my hand in his, then swiveled my stool so I was facing him.

"Let's dance pretty girl," he said.

I was thankful to change the subject. As much as I was not in the mood to talk about myself, clearly he wasn't either. I was also ecstatic to have someone ask me to dance. The only other time I was asked to dance was at my high school prom, and that was with some cheese ball jock that didn't dance with me. Instead, he hit on every other girl at prom while he was there with me. Something inside told me that this would be much different, that Jase actually knew how to dance and treat a lady. The only problem? Honky-tonk wasn't really my strong suit, let alone my suit at all. My breathing suddenly turned heavy as I stayed still on the stool that Jase was trying to pull me off of.

"There's a slight problem," I said quietly. He moved in closer to me putting his hands on my knees as he leaned his ear by my mouth. "I don't know how to dance country," I confessed.

He moved his ear away from my mouth and started laughing, his loud contagious laugh was rumbling through his body. I put my hand over his mouth to try and stop the rest of the bar from hearing and looking over at us.

"Stop it, this is serious," I told him. He stopped and took my hand off of his lips.

"I'll lead, you just follow. You'll be okay. Just go with it, Cassie," he said, pulling me off of the stool, like a parent helping a toddler off of a chair.

I guess this meant we were going.

He walked us out to the dance floor where Moose and Kasey were already getting their country on. The music running through the speakers changed immediately from drums and guitars to a sweet soft melody. Jason grabbed my right hand with his left. My eyes stared at them, admiring how perfectly they fit together. His other hand touched the side of my cheek, gently pushing it to face him. Our eyes intently locked together, and like I was a doll and had no control over my own body, he moved my other hand and put it around his upper back. He placed his hand around my lower back and pushed us closer, body to body.

"Don't be scared, just like we practiced in the street." He looked at me. His eyes glistened as the spotlights above us hit them just perfectly, showing their true emerald color.

I was locked in on them; they had every bit of my attention. I let the music sway us, almost as though I was reliving our moment in the street and not here in the bar. He moved his head closer to my cheek. Feeling the scruff on his face against my skin was like déjà vu and we were literally back under the streetlights for sure this time. I closed my eyes and let him lead us as we danced together, our bodies fitting together like two puzzle pieces connecting for the first time. I fit perfectly against his chest as I hit right where his cheek could rest against mine, feeling every bit of him against my body. It was too much, and I shouldn't be letting myself get carried away by the moment we were sharing, but I was and I let myself go with it.

I could hear him humming softly in my ear the melody of the song that was playing. Every time his voice got low, it would send shivers down my spine. I was listening to the song lyrics along with the sweet sound of Jason's voice. The words were beautiful, and jogged my memory. I had heard this melody before, I just couldn't remember where. I didn't listen to country music, so I know it wasn't something I put on purposefully, but then it hit me. I slid my cheek away from Jason and put my face directly in front of his, leaving a few inches of space between us. Jason's eyes were smiling, he was enjoying this moment too.

"This is the song you were humming in the street isn't it?" I asked him, even though I already knew the answer.

A big smile swept over his face, his eyes softened even more. He didn't respond with a verbal answer, giving me all the confirmation that I needed. He pulled our bodies closer together without hesitation and placed his mouth next to my ear.

"It's called *Wanted* by Hunter Hayes," he gently whispered, making every nerve in my body pulsate.

My chest dropped into my stomach, not because of bad nerves or being upset either, this was the first time it had been because of a guy... because of a guy that made me feel like the luckiest girl in the world just knowing him. He made me feel more than wanted. He was helping me in more ways than I could even count on one hand.

We kept our bodies close as I moved my face from the side of his to the front. I couldn't tell if we were still swaying to the music anymore or if we were floating in the air like I felt we were. I took my hand out of his and placed them both behind his neck latching them together. He must have got the hint because he moved his hands around my back, hooking them together; we were now completely linked together. Our gazes were engrossed on each other. I couldn't take my eyes off of his, and I didn't want to. The heat between our bodies was more than just radiating and I could feel my lips start to venture their way toward his, slowly closing the gap between our mouths. His breath felt warm against my lips and I wanted nothing more than to feel them on mine. I could feel his body hugging me tighter each second that went by. The music was getting softer and quieter, but my heartbeat was getting louder. I was nervous and scared. All the reasons why I shouldn't kiss Jason were screaming through my head yelling at me to stop, but my heart was ready to jump in full force. It felt the connection with Jason, getting stronger as each minute I knew him passed by. Every beat that drummed in my chest was my heart telling me to go for it, to let it happen, that maybe just maybe, our two lost souls could help fix each other.

The music stopped as our lips were barely touching, almost grazing each other. I heard a loud country song come on next followed by hoots and hollers from the crowd and a very excited Moose running toward us. We both shook out of the trance we were in, our eyes still locked on each other. I wasn't ready for our dance to end. I wanted to see where it would take us, but there was something inside telling me that I was playing with fire. Both times, we danced. Both times, we were close to kissing, and both times, we stopped before it happened. I couldn't help but think of the coincidence. The look in Jase's eyes told me he was thinking the same things. The wheels were turning in both our minds, going over all the reasons a good guy like him needed to stay away from a mess like me.

"My turn next," Moose exclaimed as he grabbed my hand. The one that was just around Jase's neck, I could still feel his warm skin underneath it.

Jason shot me a smile as Kasey took a hold of his hands leading him further away from me. Moose took my hand in the air and started to spin me around. He caught me off guard because my thoughts were still on Jason, and I almost tripped over my own feet.

"Whoa there, Cassie. You okay?" he asked while he stopped me up from falling.

"Sorry, Moose, I just wasn't ready for that," I admitted. His eyes were wide as if I just scared him. "I'm ready to go now," I said, trying to ease the tension in his eyes. They started to relax more as he took my hand again more firmly this time.

"Do you want to go sit at the bar?" he asked with a concerned look on his face. He was a lot like Jase; they both were very cautious people.

I curled my lips up and shook my head no. "No, let's dance. I'm okay, you just caught me off guard," I shouted to him over the music.

It was a loud, fast, guitar-filled song, and I just hoped I could keep up. It wasn't a dance with Jase, but Moose seemed like a good guy and I was eager to get to know him better. It also probably wasn't a bad idea to take a little break from the moment Jason and I had just shared.

"Atta girl," he shouted, this time motioning with his head that he was going to spin me.

I was ready for it this time and landed right around, meeting his hand in mine as he started moving his feet quickly to the beat of the music, practically giving us a tour of the dance floor. My eyes must have been wide and my feet clumsy because I could hear Moose starting to giggle.

"Just let me lead," he yelled over the music.

"Easier said than done Moose. Have you ever let someone lead you on the dance floor?" I asked him with a smirk.

He threw his head back and slowed down, continuing to shuffle us across the dance floor. After numerous turns, pivots and glides, I was out of breath. When the dance was over and we were both covered in sweat, he took my hand and guided us outside of the bar to a bench by the front door. The cool air felt nice as I aired out, regaining my breath. Moose did the same.

"What in the world was that dance?" I questioned him.

He let out a breathy chuckle as he took a seat on the bench patting the empty space next to him. I quickly took a seat and leaned back into the bench.

"It's called the country two-step," he answered.

"More like the country twenty step," I suggested.

He let out another breath before going silent as though there was a reason he brought me out here alone. I sat silent, waiting for him to tell me to stay away from his friend. It was possible Jason talked to him about me, and he probably thought I was wrong to be interested in him when he knew I would be leaving in my car soon, probably never to return. But that was just it, I didn't know if I would be able to stay away now, even though I knew deep down I should. Jase didn't need me ruining his life. I could feel the damn tears starting to pool up in my eyes, as they were slowly tumbling down my cheek one by one. I turned my head to the side so Moose didn't see, while I tried to pull myself back together, but I wasn't quick enough.

"Hey, what's the matter?" he asked in a soft voice.

I tried to hold the tears back and get my voice ready to speak. "I'll back off, I'm sorry." I told him.

He moved his head back and arched his brow. "What?" he asked.

I turned to face him, wiping the rest of the tears off my face. "I know you brought me out here to tell me to stay away from Jase... Jason. And I get it, I do. I'll back off. I don't honestly know what even happened in there on the dance floor," I mumbled, trying to remain calm and remember that it's for the best.

"Cassie," he said. "I didn't bring you out here to say any of that."

"You didn't?" I questioned him. He shook his head and wiped the sweat off of his forehead.

"No, not at all. Actually, I came out here to get some fresh air."

I felt incredibly absurd. I put my head in my hands and moved my head back and forth, feeling his hand on my back. "Oh my God, I'm so embarrassed," I muttered out through my hands. I lifted my head up to see him smiling. "I've been really emotional lately," I tried to apologize to him.

"Aren't all women?" He shrugged.

"Touché," I answered him. What he didn't know was that it was most women, especially the pregnant ones like me who couldn't control their emotions.

"So I take it you're pretty fond of him?" he asked curiously. I pressed my lips together. I didn't want to be honest, but with the emotional outburst I just had, he needed to hear the truth.

"Jason is a great guy, Cassie," he said, leaning back into the bench.

"Too great," I replied.

"I haven't seen him smile this much in a long time. He really needs someone like you right now and from what I see in your eyes when you look at him, you need him too. If there is one thing I learned from him, it's to enjoy the moment you're in, because you'll never get it back. If you worry too much about the future, you'll miss out on building a past you'll want to look back at," he said as he gazed into the dark street across from us.

I sat there, pondering what Moose just told me. He was right, neither of us knew what the other was going through, but for whatever reason we both clung to each other trying to help the other out. It was like a force we, especially I, couldn't control. Then there were all of the moments, the ones Moose just explained that Jason kept creating for me, but why was he so caught up in them? It's as if he's afraid of his future for some reason, yet so laid back that he didn't care about it. Either way, from what Kasey and Moose just said, he's happy right now and I couldn't help but smile because I was too.

"You know, he's lucky to have a friend like you."

"No." He shook his head. "I'm lucky to have him."

"Should we go back inside?" I asked, overly anxious to see Jason again.

"Yeah, I could use a drink after the 'twenty step'," he said.

I playfully smacked his arm as we walked back inside to find Jason at the bar.

"There you two are, I was beginning to think I was going to be alone tonight," Jason said as I took a seat on the stool to his right.

"Not a chance," I whispered. "We just needed some fresh air after Moose tried to make me tour the whole God damn dance floor."

"You really need to teach this girl how to two-step man," Moose said.

"In good time," Jason replied.

"You know who's back in town right? I guess just for the weekend. It's her dad's fiftieth birthday." Moose said to Jason who dropped his gaze down.

"Damn it," Jase muffled under his breath.

"Sorry Man. Kasey just told me this afternoon," Moose said.

"Who is it?" I asked, trying to search either of their faces for answers.

"No one," Jase said, trying to smile but it looked painful for him.

"Just some bitch that broke his heart," Moose piped up.

Whoa. I wasn't expecting that. I was shocked by the harshness of his tone and the words that came out of his mouth. I looked over to Jase for an explanation.

"Let's not worry about her okay? Like Moose said, she's just some bitch," he mumbled to me. I cringed as he called her a bitch. She must have really broken his heart if he was using that word. From the time I met Jason, he had never used that kind of language.

"Damn, I guess that's what I get for opening my mouth. I didn't think she would be coming here tonight. You might want to leave now," Moose whispered to us as the bar suddenly grew quiet, watching a girl and the guy hooked around her waist walking through the door. I could only assume it was...the bitch.

"Shit," Jason muttered under his breath. "I'm sorry, Cassie."

"For what? I'm not even quite sure what the whole deal is," I said honestly, as I thought back to the conversation I had with Kasey about some girl that messed him up, but I wasn't sure if this was the same girl.

"That's a story for another day, Sweetheart," he said, giving me a nervous look.

The bar seemed on high alert, as the tension grew stronger. The eyes of almost everyone were shifting between the bitch, who quite frankly just looked like some average girl, not a bitch by any means, and to Jason who was keeping his focus on his hands placed on the bar. Whatever the 'story' was, it seemed everyone knew it but me.

"Seriously, what's going on? Why is everyone staring?" I asked quietly, getting a quick headshake from Moose letting me know to stop prying.

"Hey there. It's Cassandra, right?" a voice asked from behind us. I turned my chair at the same time Jase did only to see Jeff, the guy from the motel, behind me with a beer in his hand.

"Hey man," Jase muttered, his mind obviously still lingering on the dark cloud in the room.

"Yeah, it's Cassandra. How are you?" I said to him.

"Can I take you for a spin on the dance floor?" he asked, doing a weird shimmy with his body. I must have given him a strange look as he did because both Moose and Jase let out a quiet chuckle.

"If you promise not to do that again," I giggled. I looked over to Jason who now looked more in tune to what was going on.

"Not too long, Jeff," Jason told him. Was that Jason getting protective? I had a spark of excitement as I realized that is exactly what it felt like. It was as if I finally got some sort of verbal confirmation from him that he was in fact interested in me. Yet the timing was wrong because I was going back to the dance floor with Jeff, not Jase.

He set his beer down in front of my seat as he helped me off the stool, dragging me to the dance floor. My eyes couldn't help but look back at Jase who had sorrow written all over his face. I wanted nothing more than to know the story so I could help him, and the other part of me, perhaps because of the pregnancy hormones, wanted to knock her ass so hard she fell to the floor. I was most certain it had to be the hormones because I was neither aggressive or a fighter.

Jason turned his stool around, his soft eyes catching mine before Jeff had twirled me around and started up with his weird shimmy dance move. I wanted to look back at Jason again, but I stopped myself. It was clear to me now that I had to talk to him; I had to know what was going on between us, if it was even anything.

I locked my eyes back on Jeff who had some seriously bad dance moves. Not that mine was much better, but these were awful. I took my hands, put them on his arms, and told him to stop. He looked up at me bewildered.

"A little less shimmy and a little more steady," I told him.

"Can you show me?" he asked in a sultry voice I wasn't prepared for. I assumed it was the beer talking. I shrugged it off.

I looked over to Jason before I showed Jeff the correct way to dance with a girl and noticed *her*. She was in front of him and they were talking. She had on a short skirt and a cute top with a pair of cowboy boots. She looked perfect. She was heavily flirting, but the guy who came in with her stood next to her until she shooed him away.

"Cassandra?" Jeff said, getting my attention.

I looked back at him and remembered I was out here to dance with him. "Sorry. So about that dance."

I put my hand to the side of me getting ready to show him a better way to shimmy when another slow song came over the speakers. Damn.

"Oh." I felt Jeff's hands immediately on my waist and his hot-liquored breath warmed my face. My stomach started to feel homesick as I realized this was not even close to what it felt like slow dancing with Jason.

"Like this, right?" he asked in another voice that almost made me want to run for the hills.

"Yeah, just not so tight, okay," I said, trying to be firm but nice.

I glanced over in Jason's direction only to see the girl sitting down on my barstool. My pulse started racing, a fire started building inside. I tilted my head. Was I getting jealous and protective over my seat? I shook my head a little to try and get myself out of this feeling. He must have been looking at me because I saw him grin when my eyes found his. I gave him one back and then watched the girl continue to talk to Jase. Her seat was facing him, but he kept facing forward. My thoughts were overtaken and brought back to dancing when I felt Jeff gripping my waist a little tighter.

"Wow, you are a great dancer," he said in a hushed voice, making me shiver in disgust. I was not feeling comfortable with this anymore. I was trying to be less uptight and enjoy myself but he was making it difficult.

I felt his hand move further down my waist and start to grab my ass cheek. I was getting ready to leave before I smacked him across the face and perhaps another place when he was suddenly jerked away. Looking up, I saw Jason pulling him off of me. I gasped, "Oh My God." It was like watching it in slow motion. I saw Jase throw him to the floor, punch him in the face, and as he went to punch him again Moose pulled Jason off, hauling him to the bathroom. The crowd around us that halted to watch the commotion had now gone back to dancing before a few guys came to get Jeff off the floor.

Kasey came running toward me. "Are you okay?"

"Holy shit. What just happened?" I searched her face for answers.

"You are about to get an answer to a question you might not want to know the answer to," she said. "I told you; he likes you, Cassandra. That was Jason being protective of you."

I wanted to believe her. I wanted to confirm what I felt earlier, but without hearing it out of Jase's mouth, I couldn't.

"You still don't believe me?" she asked, shaking her head. "Come on, let's go wait at the bar for the guys."

I looked back over to the guys who were helping Jeff walk over to the other side of the bar. "He thought what Jase did to him was bad?" I looked over to Kasey who had her eyes on me. "He's lucky Jason got to him first. I was about to smack him in both heads," I told her. She started laughing and then grabbed me by my arm.

"He's harmless but tonight he's clearly had way too much to drink," she replied.

We walked over to the bar and asked the bartender for a fresh glass of water, when really what I wanted yet again was a shot of vodka. I could feel the tension in my shoulders as I rolled them back. Kasey sat down to my right as we quietly sipped on our drinks while waiting for Jason and Moose.

"Hey there… Yeah you. I need a tall vodka and cranberry. Thanks." I heard a high-pitched voice saying next to me. I gave

Kasey a look as the voice continued, only to see her eyes widening.

I turned my head to see what was going on. Sitting right next to me was the so-called bitch. It was like watching a show about an animal and finally getting the close up shot of it.

"Hi. I'm Anna," she said as she sipped her tall drink.

I froze, not knowing what to do in front of said animal. Out of the corner of my eye, I watched Kasey quickly get up from her seat and walk away. My eyes frantically went back and forth from Kasey to Anna, unsure of what to do. It was like taking a test you didn't study for. I took a deep breath and decided to start the exam.

"Hi. Cassandra," I told her.

"Well, Cassandra," she said, making me cringe the way she said my name. She looked normal on the outside, but I fully understood the bitch part after hearing her speak. It was like a baby voice stuck in a grown ass woman's body. Nails on a chalkboard. "Listen, I don't know who you are, and seeing how he won't give me the time of day here, I'm assuming it's because of you, especially since you're the one he keeps staring at. He'll never choose you. You'll never come first. I know you probably know everything, but you'll just end up doing what I did and leave him. Take it from me and leave him now," she said. I watched as her little body sat down on the stool next to me.

"And why would I take advice from you? I don't even know you." I raised my brow at her.

"Because honey," she said slowly. "He's never gotten over me and he won't change, not even for some city girl. Yeah, I know why you're here. The town is small and people talk. I just had to come see for myself the girl who he's been following around like a little lost puppy. You're just the shiny new toy. Now me," she said, pointing to herself, "I'm the real deal. We grew up together and were high school sweethearts. You don't stand a chance."

I didn't have the slightest clue what she was talking about, but I'd had enough of her voice for one night. This girl clearly missed out and couldn't help but try and ruin us, even though there wasn't an 'us', but now understood why there wasn't a 'them' anymore either. "Well that's a shame for you, because I like him just the way he is. Not to mention, I might be the shiny new toy, but you're the old one that gets sold for cheap," I practically growled at her. I swung my chair in the other direction only to be saved by Jason, Moose, and Kasey who were quickly walking toward us.

"Jason, we need to talk," Anna barked as Jason stopped in front of me, his eyes staying only on mine.

"We're done Anna. It's taken me a long time to realize it, but I don't deserve you." He finally shifted his eyes at Anna.

"You do deserve me Jason. Can we talk in private please?" She begged like a toddler, whining out the last word slowly. Jason let out a huff and then looked at me.

"No Anna, I deserve better than you."

I didn't know much about Anna, but anyone with two thumbs and a brain could tell he absolutely deserved better.

"Jason!" She slammed her palm on the counter and stared him down. I looked up at him and said what I knew I had to say.

"Red light, Jase," I smirked.

"Me too, Sweetheart. Let's get out of here," he said, reaching for my hand. "Anna, I don't want to hear from you again, ever."

The look on her face was like a kid being told no in a candy store. Upset and clearly as though she had never been told no before. It was glorious to watch. I looked at Moose and Kasey who were watching this final goodbye unfold in front of their eyes too.

"Bye guys." I quickly waved at them as we exchanged shocked glances.

"See you later Moose and Kasey," he said before hauling us out of the bar, one that I was glad to be leaving.

"What all did Anna tell you?" he asked, his eyes firm as we hustled through the doors.

"Nothing really, but it's okay because I'm pretty sure I shut her up on my end," I told him. "She really is quite the bitch you know."

"You have no idea," he huffed.

Jason was opening my door as we approached the truck, but my heart stopped my body from moving. I grabbed his arm and stopped him.

"What was all that back there? With Jeff, why did you take him out like he was your punching bag? I've never seen you like that before Jason," I told him, pausing long enough to take a breath. "I may not have known you a long time, but I know you well enough to see that this isn't your normal behavior."

He closed his eyes and took a deep breath, his fists clenching by his side.

"I couldn't stand his hands touring your backside, Cassie. I lost it, okay?" His eyes finally peeled open, piercing mine. "He doesn't need to be hitting on you." He inched closer to me, placing a hand on my cheek. "You have enough going on in your life than to worry about being hit on by him."

I swallowed back the lump in my throat. "What do you mean I have enough going on in my life Jase?" I questioned him.

"I mean, you need someone who won't run when they find out you're pregnant." He stood motionless as his eyes pierced mine.

Holy. Shit. "You know?" I gasped, almost losing my balance and falling down to the ground.

"Yes, and you need someone who will help you through it, realizing there's more to you than just a hot piece of ass, like Jeff sees. Drunk or not, what Jeff did wasn't okay. I was raised better than that. I had to protect you."

I pulled his hand away from my cheek. I wanted to cry. I wanted to heave. Anything, but be standing here in front him. "How do you know? Did your mom tell you?" I asked panicked, terrified that my secret was out without me even knowing. I knew I needed to tell him, but having him find out from someone other than me was hard to take.

He cocked his head. "My mom knows? What?" He looked upset and shocked as his eyes stayed trained on mine.

"I had to tell her at the hospital Jason. I had to see if I was still pregnant. You didn't answer my damn question. How do you know Jason?"

"Sweetheart, I may be from a small town, but I'm not stupid," he said deviously.

I let out a deep sigh. I was completely shocked. It wasn't that I thought he was stupid; it was that I thought I was better at lying.

"Come on, Cassie!" He yelled at me as he threw his hands in the air. "If you constantly getting sick weren't a dead giveaway, then maybe the fact you were running away was. It doesn't take an idiot to put two and two together."

"Oh my God." I put my head in my hands and began weeping, letting the turning feeling in my stomach match the outside of my body; tears streaming down my face.

"Get in the truck Sweetheart. We need to talk," he said, holding the door open for me.

I got in, not thinking that I really had much choice in the matter. It was me who lied to him to begin with. The ice was already broken. How bad could the rest of the conversation go?

Chapter
twenty-one

NOT A WORD WAS SAID as we headed in a direction we had yet to go in this town. I kept my eyes in front of me and Jason did the same. It was awkward and it was killing me, but I was hurt. He lied to me. He knew what was going on the whole time and made me believe I was hiding it from him. I wiped the tears that were slipping out in a continuous flow now as I thought of how he had to feel about me now, pregnant, lost, and apparently not as good of a liar as I once believed.

"You probably think I'm a terrible person and I'm sorry I lied to you, but I was afraid. I was terrified of what you would think of me once you found out. I was scared of losing you and your friendship that I've grown to enjoy too much," I said quietly as I closed my eyes, wondering if he even heard me.

"Look, I'm not going anywhere, you have to believe me. I want to help you; you don't have to go through this alone. I know you have your friend, but you have me too."

I looked over at him, his eyes still shying away from mine. "You should have told me you knew Jason. You shouldn't have let me continue to hide everything if you knew."

"It wasn't my place to say, Cassie. *You* needed to tell me, but then tonight, seeing Jeff and his damn hands, I couldn't take it anymore," he said, his hands slamming down on his steering wheel. "I knew you would want answers so I just had to come clean. Listen, I'm not proud of what I did, but I'll be damned if I let someone put their hands on you."

"Where are you taking us?" I asked lost, hurt, and scared. I didn't want to hear about his feelings, how he didn't want someone else to touch me, yet he wouldn't. I just wanted to run, go back to his house, and cry into my pillow.

"You'll see," he said quietly.

Before I knew it, we had arrived at what looked like a farm. I could only guess it was theirs. "Your farm?" I asked as he parked in front of a huge wheat field.

"Yeah," he said, finally looking at me. "It's the only place far enough from the town that you actually feel far away from the world, I like it here." He grabbed a blanket from the truck, the same blue quilt from his room as he stepped out. I did the same and followed him to the back, watching as he quickly spread the blanket across the bed of the truck before hopping down.

"Give me your hand," he said, reaching his out for mine. "Let's take a walk and talk first." I placed my shaking hand into his. We started walking into the field, the wheat stalks tickling the bare skin in between the boots and my dress.

I followed him, our hands intertwined, as we got further into the field. It didn't take long for the nerves to take over my whole body. I stopped and let go of his hand. I couldn't take the silence anymore. "Jason, my heart is racing. I am so nervous right now. I just... I need to tell you what happened, I need you to know the whole story," I told him.

"I want to know what happened, Cassie, but only if you're okay with telling me," he said, his body facing mine.

I wasn't okay with confessing it, but he had to know. I just feared for what was to come after he heard it. I knew he wouldn't be so inclined to help me anymore. He would think horrible things about me; I knew this, because I thought them myself.

I took a deep breath and gripped my hands together. "My roommate insisted that I go to a party at her boyfriend's house. It was a kickoff party for the beginning of the school year. For most like me, it was our last year. I never went out, especially to parties. I wasn't the college party girl. I had too much to work for and riding on me to be that girl. She begged me, saying her boyfriend had a friend that she wanted me to meet and I needed to get out of the apartment and act like a college student for once. I let her words sink in this time for some reason."

My shoulders slouched as I looked at Jase. His face held a blank expression I hadn't seen on him before. I peered down; I couldn't look at him while I told him the rest.

"It could have been the brunch with my parents. They'd let me know how disappointed they were that I wasn't graduating a year early. I wasn't sure, but I think that could have been the straw that broke the camel's back. My roommate went out, did the college thing on the weekends, and studied hard during the week. We had moved in together our junior year, so I knew her pretty well. She wasn't the A student I was, but she wasn't failing by any means either. I said yes to going. She helped me pick a dress out of her closet, and off we went." My hand covered over my face. I wished, I prayed I could go back and change the course of history. I felt his hand gently pull mine away from my face. I looked up and watched as Jase's eyes fixed on mine. They pleaded with me to finish.

"I knew too. I knew that it was a bad choice to go, but the devil on my shoulder won, and so I went. I was actually having a lot of fun when we first got there. It wasn't out of control like I thought it would be. There were a lot of people, but there weren't people vomiting in the halls and girls dancing on the tables like I was expecting. I was naïve. I had never been to a party before, so I wasn't sure what to expect, but I was pleasantly surprised."

I closed my eyes. I couldn't watch his anymore as I talked about the other guy. My heart wouldn't let me.

"My roomy introduced me to her boyfriend's friend, Parker. He was nice. Said all the right things. I could tell he was a ladies' man and I was very interested. After a couple of hours, the drinks were flowing and the touching was getting more intense. Before I knew it, we were kissing on the couch. We knew exactly what we were doing, and the sad part was, I thought it was what I wanted, Jase. I was having fun. This hot guy who was interested in me was good company. There wasn't one thing to complain about, except the fact that we moved our make out session to his room upstairs. If I needed Mel more than ever, it would have been to stop me from going upstairs." I started to feel the stinging pain behind my eyes. The tears were forming.

Jase put his hand on my back and rubbed it gently, not saying a word, but letting me know he was there. That was worth more than anything he could have said.

"When I woke up in his bed the next day, it was like nothing happened. We both got out of bed, said our goodbyes and I had my first walk of shame along with a few other girls. I felt disgusting and I wanted to vomit right there in the house. This was obviously normal for him, as it didn't faze him when I walked out of his room. The rest of the day, I was useless. I was battling a major hangover and I was feeling more than lonely. All I wanted and needed was for Melanie to be with me. That was my first one-night stand, and I needed someone to tell me it was okay, that things were going to be fine. It wasn't until the next night before bed that I realized I missed two birth control pills that month. I didn't think much of it when it happened since I wasn't having sex. Then, I vaguely recalled our conversation right before we had sex. We didn't use protection, we both assured the other that we were clean and I told him I was on birth control. It was a night of too many drinks, being in the moment and not thinking clearly. Panicked wasn't even the right word for what was going through my head after I let the actions of that night settle in even more."

I began to pace, traipsing over the wheat stalks, flattening them as I made a small path in each direction. I stole a few glances of Jase. He stood in the same spot, still as a statue.

"My roommate came in, saw me terrified, and tried to calm me down, telling me that the odds were low. It's almost 99% effective and I'd be okay. She reminded me it was only one time, it had happened to her before and she was fine. I let her words sink in and realized it was only one time, what are the odds, and that I did have a good time, I wouldn't do it again, but I did something because I chose to, not because of my parents. I didn't think things could go wrong at this point so I started to relax and breathe again. I was so wrong, Jase."

I stopped pacing and let the tears pour out of me, the sobs now uncontrollable. He snaked his arms around me, pulling me close to him, telling me it would be okay. I wanted to believe him, I really did, and even though he made me feel comforted, my life was still in shambles. I wiped away a few tears, still with plenty left on my face, and tried my best to control the sobs long enough to finish.

"I let the fun, free flying Cassandra take over and I did the dumbest thing I could have. I dropped out of school. I walked into the administration office and withdrew from all of my classes. I hated what I was going to school for, and that party, as silly as it sounds, changed things for me. I realized how much my life wasn't mine, how much it was what everyone else wanted *but* the most important person living it, me. I didn't tell my parents I dropped out because they would have gone ballistic Jason. I was scared, but I also felt relief from taking charge of my own life. I called Mel and told her what I did. She was stunned to say the least, but then begged me to come down and see her. I told her I would soon. I had to try and figure out what I wanted to do next. I knew I had to tell my parents, but before I dropped the bomb on them, I needed to come up with a new plan for my life that I was taking back. By the time I figured out a few classes I was going to start taking in the fall for creative writing and journalism, I was hit with another obstacle. I missed my period. It was like taking charge of my life was the worst thing I could have ever done. I was scared, terrified, and alone. I went to the only place I could think of, to see Melanie."

"And that's how you ended up here?" he asked.

I nodded my head.

"God, Cassie, I'm so sorry you had to go through that alone," he said as he continued holding me. "Does Parker know?"

"No, I didn't want to tell anyone."

"You need to tell him," he said, pulling back to look at me. "If I got a girl pregnant, I would want to know."

"Yeah, but you're not like most guys Jase. You'd actually stick around to help. Guys like Parker have their whole lives already planned out. They wouldn't even be a part of a kid's life; they would just write a check and wash their hands of the rest."

"Cassie." His eyes were steady on mine, as he looked overly concerned.

"Yes."

"Promise me that you'll tell him."

"Jase," I said, trying to get the strength to tell him why telling Parker wasn't in the plans. "I don't plan on keeping this baby." I looked down at my stomach as I said baby.

"What?" he asked, his brows furrowed.

"I can't. I'm not ready to be a mom."

"What do you plan on doing then?"

"I haven't decided yet. I've thought about abortion, but I've also thought about adoption," And the tears were back, raining down hard. It broke my heart that I felt this way, but I couldn't throw my future away on a one night stand, even though I didn't even know what my future held for me anymore. "I don't know what to do, that's why I was going to see Mel. She was going to help me figure it out."

He looked down at the wheat between our legs, shuffling his boots in it. I knew the wheels were turning in his head. I could only imagine the horrendous things he was thinking of me for what I did, for what I had to do, for who I was becoming.

"Should I pack and go to the motel now?" I asked, saying what I knew he was probably thinking. I was relieved that he finally knew why I was running, but scared shitless I was going to lose his friendship or even worse, him.

He looked up, his gaze piercing me. "No way in hell would I ask you to leave."

"I don't make you want to run the other way?" I asked shocked.

"Not even close."

"Why? Because honestly I want to run in the other direction from myself," I admitted.

"I saw it in your eyes when they wanted to take you to the hospital and then when I saw you again lying in your bed in the ER. I knew you had more going on and you were scared. I knew the look all too well because I had it once myself. I wanted to help you; I felt this instant connection to you. I can't explain it, and it sounds cliché but." He paused and let out a deep sigh before continuing, "But maybe you got lost for a reason."

I felt an ounce of weight being lifted off my shoulders as his words escaped him, hearing from him what I thought about myself. "I think about that too. That maybe, getting lost was all part of this master plan for my life and that I got lost for a reason."

I took a deep breath and searched his face. I was waiting for him to respond but he didn't. He wasn't going to bring it up, so I would have to just ask him.

"Why did you have the look in your eyes? Why were you scared?"

He closed his eyes for a split second, his Adam's apple moving as he gulped. "Some stuff happened years ago and I just remember being scared, not knowing what was going to happen in the future. But as I got older, I just learned to let things go and go with the flow."

"What are you hiding? What's going on?" I asked him, my heart pumping harder, needing to know what happened.

"You'll just have to trust me, when I'm ready to talk about it I will, but right now all I can think about is you. I don't know what it is, but you drive me wild inside. You make me want to protect you from everything; even though I know you're strong enough to take care of yourself. I just want to be with you, letting you know every day how amazing you are, giving you the courage you need to kick back when life tries to throw another hurdle your way."

He placed his hand against my cheek. I couldn't help but lean into it, feeling the warmth of his hand against my skin. My heart was racing so fast I thought it was going to beat out of my chest. "I want to kiss you so bad right now."

Those were the words that I had only dreamed of hearing. "Jase, I would love for you to wrap your arms around me and kiss me. That's all I've ever wanted in a guy. Now you're here right in front of me telling me you want these things too, but it feels like the timing is just all wrong," I said with a crack in my voice. I reluctantly pulled my cheek from his hand and stepped back until I was several feet away from him. I put my hand to my chest as I could feel the pain inside aching for him. I couldn't get close though; I couldn't let my feelings take over for someone who I knew deserved better.

"If you wait for the right time for anything, it will always be too late," he said quietly as he motioned with his head for me to walk back to him. "Come here."

I slowly took in a breath and brought my eyes up to his. They locked me in; they were gleaming as though this was exactly what he wanted. I couldn't deny it was what I wanted too. My heart was screaming for me to walk faster to him. I took another deep breath as I raced to him, jumping in his arms the second I was in front of him, his arms wrapping around me as I did. I looked into his eyes for only a moment before I felt his soft lips pressed against mine. My whole body went limp as he cradled me against him, feeling for the first time the true notion of being wanted. Not just physically, but that a weight lifted off my shoulders knowing I had Jase with me, holding me tightly.

I felt his grip tighten as his tongue found mine, massaging it tenderly as he held onto me like his life depended on it. He walked us back to his truck and sat me down gently on the bed of it. I kept my legs wrapped tightly around him as he stood in front of me, taking his cowboy hat off and putting it down next to me. I slid my hands back in his hair and wrapped my fingers in the gorgeous wavy hair I had wanted to touch since I saw it. His lips sadly left mine, but only for good reason as he planted his soft kisses down the delicate curve of my neck until he reached my bare shoulder, blanketing my arms and back in goose bumps. I never was more grateful for wearing a strapless dress than I was right now. I turned my neck to see his face as he stopped with his lips still pressed to my skin. My heart was all but pounding out of my chest as his eyes connected with mine. "Cold?" he asked quietly as he lifted his lips up enough to talk.

I shook my head no. "It's you," I whispered as my pulse raced. My breathing was becoming even more rapid each second that I watched his lips hovering over my shoulder.

"Hmmm," he said. He slowly lifted his head and placed a finger on each arm, softly running them up creating more goose bumps as his fingers reached my neck.

He arched his brow as he looked at me. I knew what he wanted to hear. "Still you," I said quietly, watching his lips curl up knowing he did that to me.

He brought his lips back to mine as he took both hands and tangled them in my hair, causing a moan to escape my throat. I took my hands and pulled him even closer, wanting to pull him up onto the bed of the truck with me. He got the hint and let me go, hopping up and going to the back to lay down, patting his chest before putting his arms behind his head. "Right here," he said, taking an arm out as he patted his chest.

I crawled over, snuggled myself next to him, and laid my head on his chest, loving the feel of his hand caressing my hair. I could hear his heart beat in his chest; it was as fast as mine was. My lips immediately grinned, as I knew our emotions matched. It couldn't have felt more right than to be here with him. I was suddenly angry with myself for trying so hard to get out of this town, when all I wanted now was to stay as long as I could.

We laid there for a while without talking, just listening to the wind blow through the wheat behind us, but it wasn't long enough. I could have stayed in his arms all night.

"We should get back Sweetheart. It's getting late," he said softly as he continued to push my hair back.

I didn't want to leave, I wanted to fall asleep right here tonight, but as I moved from his chest, I realized how hard the truck bed was and how uncomfortable it was for him to lie on.

"If we have to," I said as I sat up, looking at him. His hand found my cheek after he sat up.

"I don't want to, but my back is killing me," he said.

"We didn't really think this one through, did we?"

He shook his head before pulling my face toward his for what I assumed was our last kiss tonight, not knowing what was in store for us after this moment. His lips roughly pressed against mine as though he was hungrier than before. The urge for more was growing faster than before and suddenly kissing wasn't enough. I rose to my knees and grabbed the back of his head, pushing our lips together even harder, deepening the kiss as I knotted my hands in his hair. He let his lips tour down as he made his way to my collarbone, tickling my neck with his stubble brushing against my chest. He pulled me onto his lap as he kissed his way across my chest to my other bare shoulder. I let my head fall back, enjoying the feel of his moist lips marking my skin with his kisses.

I brought my head back up, ready to steal more of him, when I felt his pants vibrating and it suddenly took me back to reality.

He closed his eyes, putting his forehead against mine. "Damn it," he said almost out of breath. He looked down and reached in his pants to grab his phone, answering as he pulled it out.

"Hello?" he answered, still keeping his head against mine.

"Yeah we're good."

"No, just took a little detour before heading home."

"You too, talk to you later man." He flipped his phone closed as he moved his head back.

"I guess that's our sign to stop," I said to him before planting a kiss on his cheek. I grabbed his hat from beside me and placed it on his even messier hair than before.

"Moose was just checking up on us, making sure we were okay." He grabbed my cheeks pressing his lips to my forehead.

"He sounds like Mel," I said.

"A little less feisty but just as protective. It's getting late, let's get out of here," he said as he helped scoot me across the bed of the truck before lifting me down off the tailgate.

I wasn't in any way ready to come off of the incredible high I was on from Jason's lips, but my body was slowly running on fumes, as I was positive it was far past midnight.

He came around opening my door for me. "You know," I said. "I do know how to open a door."

"You know," he said, mirroring my tone. "I wasn't raised that way, I will open your door for you as long as I still have arms to do it with." With that, he helped me in the truck, made his way to the driver's side, and drove us home. I would have been sad that we were leaving the spot that would now hold a special place in my heart, but when I felt his hand reach over to grab mine, the sadness was replaced with comfort and happiness.

Chapter

twenty-two

IT WAS HARD TO SLEEP; I was tossing and turning more than ever before. The butterflies in my stomach were in full force as I recollected about each kiss Jason gave me; on my lips and on my bare skin. My thoughts were interrupted as I heard the beeping on my phone. I saw the light illuminating my room as I reached over to grab it; it was a text from Jason. I was suddenly extremely grateful I let him plug his number into my phone after we left the garage earlier today.

Are you asleep yet?

How could I be sleeping? His lips just rocked my world; my heart was racing too much to be sleeping.

Not a chance.

Me either.

I put my phone down and got out of bed. I didn't know what else to do so I let my body decide. It would have argued with my brain either way. I let my infectious craving for his lips guide me downstairs to his room as I quietly crept to his door.

I took a deep breath and tapped on his door. He swung it open immediately as if he knew I was on the other side. The room was dimly lit, but I could see just enough. He was standing there in nothing but boxers; I couldn't help but look him up and down from head to toe. His mouth was open and his breathing was heavy as his chest rose and fell quickly, matching mine. It didn't take long for the hunger inside to take over. He stepped forward and grabbed a hold of me, pulling me close to him as he took us over to his bed. I didn't know where we were going to take this tonight, and quite frankly, I just didn't care; all I knew was I needed to be with him. It could have been Jase, it could have been my hormones, but every part of me was craving his touch. I got a taste and I needed more.

"Cassie," he whispered.

"Shhh," I whispered back. I put my finger over his mouth. I didn't want to hear what he was going to say, we had done enough talking for the night.

I stepped up closer to him, raising myself on my tippy toes so I was closer to his lips as I pressed mine hard against his. I heard a small moan escape him as he tangled his hands in my loose hair, pulling us onto the bed.

We fell onto the bed and I positioned myself with my back against it as Jason hovered over me, his arms on either side. I took my hands, placed them on his scruffy face, and pulled him closer to me. Somewhere between being pulled onto the bed and Jason hovering over me, our lips had lost each other; this was not going to work for me. I didn't even have to pull hard as his lips curled up and lowered down to my face. "I've never seen you like this Sweetheart," he whispered into my ear as he nibbled on it.

I was sure a soft moan escaped my lips as he took my ear into his mouth. "I've been holding it in," I told him.

"I can tell," he said quietly before running his lips down my neck then into the curve of my shoulder. It was making me shiver from my neck all the way down to the aching spot between my legs. He was trailing his way down my neck when I suddenly realized I needed to take off what was keeping him from continuing further down.

"Wait," I breathed out. Jason lifted his lips from my skin as I wiggled my arms enough to slip off the cami I was wearing, throwing it to the side of the bed. He closed his eyes and let out a deep breath.

"Damn Cassie, you are going to be the death of me." He opened his eyes back up, piercing them into mine. I needed more.

"Please keep going," I begged him.

"You don't have to beg, but it's so damn sexy when you do," he said softly as he brought his lips back to my skin, taking his time as he moved further down to my bare chest. He slowly grazed his lips across each breast before making his way down, trailing kisses until he got to the top of my yoga pants. He was driving me wild; I was having a hard time not ripping all my clothes off. This was not normal for me, but I loved every moment of it. He was bringing out a side of me that hadn't existed before, and I hoped it didn't go away.

I grabbed his upper arms and rolled us over so I was on top of him. I could feel that this was just as good for him as it was for me, as his excitement was sitting between my legs.

"Enjoying yourself?" I asked in the sexiest voice I could find.

"You have no idea. Now get down here," he said as he pulled me down to his lips, biting down on my lower one before smiling and finally pressing our lips together again. Kissing him was what I always imagined it should feel like. Not wanting our lips to ever be apart because they felt too good pressed together. I knew deep down kissing had to be that amazing or people wouldn't be so passionate about it. I completely understood it now and I could finally say the feeling happened to me. Jason, he made it happen, he was the spark that lit my lips on fire. I couldn't help but go insane inside as his lips continued to kiss me like his life depended on it. I slowly released my lips from his and began placing kisses on his chin, running them all the way down from his chest to the very top of his boxers. I slowly raised myself up and loved seeing the satisfied grin plastered on his face. I put my hands on his shoulders and caressed them all the way down, feeling his chest form goose bumps as I did. I took my index finger and traced a line along the top of his boxers, making a soft moan rumble through him. I lowered myself back down on top of him; his hands grabbing my back as our bare chests collided together. I leaned my mouth close to his ear, whispering into it. "I know you green light this."

That must have sparked something in him because I heard a growl escape his throat as he rolled us back so he was now hovering over me once again.

"Just so you know, I'm not this guy. I'm not normally the guy who has a hard time controlling himself. You seriously have me going crazy right now," he said with a heavy breath.

"Just so you know. I like it."

His lips were back on mine as he slipped his tongue back in devouring mine; his hands touring my body, not missing one square inch as he massaged my peaks gently then rough, making my body not know what hit it.

I rubbed my hands up his arms that were still holding him up over my quivering body and felt something rough on his left arm. I broke from our kiss and looked at it. I realized that I never noticed it before, but it was as though something was under his skin. It was probably because every time I looked at him I was too fixated on his damn gorgeous eyes to look at anything else.

"I had something happen when I was younger. Don't mind it, it's just a scar." He shrugged.

He was sweet, protective, and had a scar to show for himself. I was in heaven. "It's sexy," I said. It looked painful and if he didn't want to talk more about it, I wasn't about to push him. This moment was too intense for that.

"I like to think so," he said back before moving his lips that I craved over mine as he sucked my lower lip into his mouth, making my whole body quiver. I grabbed the back of his hair and gripped the curls tightly, forcing his lips even harder on mine. I heard another growl escape his throat as I did. His enjoyment was making me want more. I slid my hand down his chest, taking my time as I felt his skin tingle under my touch. I let my fingers tease the top of his boxers again but this time slipped them under his waistband. I felt another moan from Jason as we continued kissing. Before I could make it any further, he pulled his lips off of mine.

"We need to stop Sweetheart," he said, breathing heavier than before. "I don't think I'll be able to stop and we need to."

"I don't want to stop," I confessed as I slowly removed my hand from his boxers.

"I want you, badly, but I also don't want to complicate things more for you. If lying here with you is all we do, I will be the happiest man alive. Getting to hold you tightly in my arms, feeling your cheek on my shoulder, your lips against my skin, that's all I need. I could do this until I died and never once would I want anything more. Well," he said. "I would, but what I meant was I don't need anything more with you to be happy. You are amazing as you are and anything more with you is just the icing on the cake."

I swallowed hard, trying to absorb his words, trying to place where he was taking this. I knew what he was trying to say but it also had a way of making me feel like he didn't want me.

"Okay. There's that look. Sweetheart, every guy wants it, but knowing when it's right is what makes the moment of making love so special. It has to be something that you give, not something that I take."

"Wow. How is it you're still single?" I asked him, because that right there just made me turn into a puddle of mush.

He was right. I wanted it right now, but how would I feel in the morning? I didn't need another walk of shame. Something inside told me this wouldn't be like that, but I also didn't want to regret anything. I had never in my life been with a guy the way I was with Jason. The one-night stand with Parker was a sloppy drunken mess. My ex would have never been like this, and this was the first time my heart didn't stop racing, anticipating his next move, craving his hands on my skin and never wanting his lips to leave mine. It was as though he knew every single thing I wanted, because he wanted it too. It didn't go far, but it didn't need to; my body received the craving fix it needed, for now.

He moved beside me, extending his arm out for me to fit perfectly next to him as I laid my head on his chest. I snuggled myself closer to him as he pulled his comforter over us. It didn't take long for me to fall asleep with the beat of his heart in my ear rocking me to sleep.

Chapter
twenty-three

"GOOD MORNING." I HEARD his voice beside me. I opened my eyes all the way and suddenly remembered I was still in his bed. I rolled over to see him, feeling guilty that I didn't even ask to stay in his room and I just fell asleep, but that feeling went away the moment I saw his smile. It was warm and made me feel anything but guilty.

"Good morning," I said in a quiet voice, still trying to wake up. I wiggled my way closer to him under the covers, noticing I was still without my cami that I came down in. His arm grabbed my waist as I did and pulled me closer than I expected, his bare chest feeling warm against mine.

"Sleep good?" he asked in a husky morning voice. I liked it.

"Too good," I said. "I'd like to say it was the bed, but I'm pretty sure it was you."

He placed his lips to my forehead. "You are so damn cute in the morning."

"I find that really hard to believe, but if you say so."

"I definitely say so," he whispered in my ear, his lips grazing the skin just enough to send a small shiver down my spine.

"I have to go to work, or you better believe I would replay last night with you at least ten more times."

"I'm thinking you should call in sick then," I suggested.

"I wish," he said quietly as he got out of the bed, his excitement more than visible. I couldn't help but look and unfortunately got caught doing so.

"Like I said, I would stay if I could." He laughed as he walked over to his dresser. He pulled out a shirt and tossed it on the bed. "You can put this on when you go upstairs. Don't rush though. Stay and sleep."

He pulled out a pair of jeans, another shirt, boxers, and socks, cradling them in his hands as he walked over to me, now lying in his spot on the bed. "I need to go take a shower. The bathroom is around the corner from my room, on the opposite side of the basement in case you need it." He raised his brow.

"Okay." I knew exactly what he meant and it was more than a possibility that I would.

"I'll be back later," he said as he walked out of the room, closing the door behind him.

I grabbed the shirt he threw over to me and couldn't help but put it up to my nose, inhaling his scent. It was spicy and earthy and made a shiver trail down my spine as his scent warmed over me. I sat up and slipped it on with no intentions of going upstairs yet, but wanting only to be in his shirt. If I couldn't have his arms wrapped around me, I could at least have this. I laid back down and pulled the comforter around me, surrounding myself with everything Jason as I immediately closed my eyes and drifted back to sleep.

I woke up a couple of hours later not remembering saying goodbye to him; I must have been out cold.

I headed back upstairs after making his bed look like a girl just made it, and noticed no one in the kitchen when I quietly opened the door. That would be one less awkward thing to explain to Trish or Bart if they were home.

As I took off Jason's shirt in the bathroom, I couldn't help but sniff it one more time before setting it on the counter as I stepped into the steamy shower.

For once, I felt a moment of relaxation as I realized I didn't think about anything in the shower. I didn't spend an obscene amount of time contemplating life. I actually just showered, nothing more. I was proud of myself.

After putting on clean clothes and towel drying my hair, I made my way down the hall.

"Good morning Sweetie," I heard Trish's voice as I came into the kitchen. She was making herself a cup of coffee.

"Good morning," I replied. "You don't work today?"

"No, I have the weekends off. Do you have plans today?" she asked.

I walked over to the coffee pot grabbing a cup to fill up. "No plans today," I answered.

"Cassandra, Sweetie, what are you doing?" The look on her face was cause for alarm.

"What do you mean?"

"You shouldn't be drinking coffee; the caffeine isn't good for the baby, Sweetie."

I looked down at my stomach and shook my head. "Thanks, just one more thing I can't have or do," I grumbled to the damn seed.

I heard a giggle out of Trish. "Isn't it wonderful talking to your baby?"

I looked up at her and huffed. "Trish, I'm not talking to my baby. I'm yelling at this seed growing inside of me."

"You are about seven weeks now Sweetie. It's bigger now, about the size of a blueberry. It's growing hands and feet now," she continued to gush.

I didn't respond. I didn't know how. I took my cup of coffee that I shouldn't be drinking and sat at the table putting my head in my hands.

"Cassandra, something is bothering you. I can tell." Trish said quietly as she walked over to the table taking a seat next to me. "I know this was unplanned, but I really thought you wanted this baby. I thought that's why you were so concerned at the hospital."

"I don't know what I want, but being a mother right now isn't it. I'm not ready. Can't you see, I didn't even care or think about the damages coffee would cause the 'blueberry'? I'm horrible."

I felt her hand on my back, rubbing it gently. "You're not horrible honey. You're young. There's a big difference. Every new mom has to start somewhere."

"Trish, what if I don't want to start anywhere?"

She looked at me with sad eyes. "Have you talked to anyone about your options?"

I shook my head no. "That is where I was headed when I got lost and crashed. I was going to see my friend, she was going to help me through it, decide what to do."

She put both of my hands in hers. "Is there anything I can tell you? Do you feel like you can talk to me?"

I let out a sigh. "Trish, I feel like you are the only one I can talk to aside from my friend."

"Come here. Let's go talk on the couch."

We both took a seat on the sofa next to one another. I looked down at my hands, my stomach feeling like it was in shreds as this was the first time I had discussed options with anyone. "I'm scared Trish," I said quietly with my eyes closed.

I felt her hand on my back. "I can only imagine, Sweetie," she said softly.

"I've thought of my only two options, abortion, and adoption. I've read online about things, but not much. I get a pit in my stomach the more I read, the more I realize how sad both options are."

I opened my eyes and looked over at her. "There is no easy option here, unfortunately you need to do what you think is best for you. As a mom who miscarried at one point in her life, I can't even tell you how much my heart was set on a baby and how hard it was to lose it." She stopped and took a breather. I had already known about this from Jason, but I wanted to listen to what she had to say. "It was horrible, because we had tried to conceive for about a year. When I finally got pregnant, I had told a lot of people, my mom included. She couldn't contain the excitement long enough to start making things for the baby. Then not too long after that I had an obscene amount of blood on the bed when I was suddenly woken up by terrible cramps in the middle of the night." I leaned my hand over for her to take. She has been here for me, and I wanted to do the same for her. She grabbed a hold of it tightly.

"Bart and I went to the hospital, but I already knew. I could feel it inside that I lost the baby. It was hard not to think horrible thoughts like that when you had that much bright red blood coming out of you when you knew you weren't supposed to. It was confirmed and I sat quiet and depressed for some time. I thought that perhaps my childbearing days were over. It took us so long to get pregnant again that the worst thoughts come to mind. I started to focus on the next step. I wanted another child. I knew in my heart that I wanted another child to call me mom, to raise and love, just like my first." She paused long enough to wipe the sadness from her eyes.

"I looked into adoption. There are so many parents, like Bart and me, that knew in our hearts we wanted nothing more than to be a big family with kids. I was looking for a back-up plan in case we couldn't get pregnant again. Cassandra, Sweetheart, there are so many kids that need loving families just as badly as parents need kids to call their own. If I can give you honest advice, it's to give this 'blueberry' inside of you the best home you can until you deliver. It won't be easy. It will probably be the hardest moment of your life handing that baby that just spent nine months of its life growing inside of you to another set of parents. Those parents though Sweetie, they want nothing more than to raise a wonderful baby of their own. If you don't want this baby, if you are not ready to be a mom yet, then that's fine, but don't let this baby not be a gift to someone else. There is a family out there that will love it unconditionally and this baby deserves that. Just like you deserve to be loved unconditionally by your parents."

I wiped away the tears that fell, smearing them across my cheek, not able to keep up with the outpour. "Jesus, you must think I'm awful."

"No, not at all. I think you're in a tough spot and that you have a hard decision to make."

I let out a sigh not even knowing what to say. Trish just made my decision twenty times harder.

"I'm not trying to sway you either way. I'm just giving you some insight from a parent who wanted so badly to have a baby, and would have wanted to adopt a sweet baby like yours if it came to it. I also know there are plenty of other parents out there like that too. I can go with you to see a doctor if you want someone there with you."

"Trish, you just made this so much more confusing, I really thought abortion was my best option, but now it seems like the exact opposite of what I need to do."

I felt her hand on my back again rubbing it gently. "I'm sorry Sweetie. I didn't mean to make it harder for you."

"It's not a bad thing; it's a parent thing, and you have no clue how wonderful it is to have that. To have a parent give you advice and not just tell you what you *have* to do." I was still more confused than ever, but my thoughts were becoming a little clearer after talking with Trish.

"Nothing in life is ever easy, Cassandra. It only gets harder the older you get," she said. I believed every word too.

"So what happened after your miscarriage if you don't mind me asking?"

"Of course I don't mind. Well, after about seven months of trying, but not really trying. I was focusing myself on other things. Not really obsessing over getting pregnant as my doctor told me to do, we just got pregnant. It was the most exciting moments to look down at the results on the test. I was relieved and told myself to learn to relax a little and things will work out, and they did. That was how we had Jason, he's my little baby," she gushed. I couldn't help but smile with her. I also needed to take note of her advice about relaxing more.

As much as I wanted to ask about her other son, I remembered Jason had told me that they don't talk much about him, and so I decided to keep my questions to myself.

"I really have to stop calling him my baby though, the boy is more of an adult than most kids I see these days."

I couldn't help but think of the irony. My parents would never be caught dead calling me their little baby, yet they treated me like I was still a child.

"He's a good guy," I told her.

"He really is." She took in a deep breath. "Well, Cassandra, I was going to run out to the farm to take Bart and the guys some lunch. Would you like to join me?"

"I'm actually feeling a little nauseous this morning. As much as I would love to join you, I think I better just stay in today and rest a little," I told her, saddened that I had to forgo joining her, as I really did like spending time with Trish.

"I understand Sweetie," she said. "Don't forget, crackers and ginger ale, they will soon become your best friend."

"I'm slowly learning that," I told her, and with that, Trish and I went our separate ways, I to my room to rest and Trish to the farm.

I grabbed my phone from the dresser and saw two missed calls from Mel. Shit. I quickly hit the button to dial her back, her panicked voice answered.

"Cassandra, seriously, you better be okay. Neither you or Jason are answering your phones," she said before lowering her voice an octave. "Unless of course, you were *busy*."

I couldn't help but laugh.

"Oh my gosh, spill girl."

"It wasn't like that, or maybe it was, I don't know Mel, I'm scared, but I'm happy."

"I need details, who kissed who first?"

I took a deep breath. "We went to a bar last night, it was actually really fun. We had a moment on the dance floor Mel, we were so close to kissing, but then we got interrupted by his friend."

"Damn friend," Mel interrupted me.

I continued with my story only to relive the night of his ex, Anna, and Jeff.

"Oh hell no, did you smack him like I showed you, a hand to the face and a knee to his manhood?"

I told her how Jason showed his protective side, and took care of Jeff before I even had the chance to use her move.

"Holy shit. I miss all the good stuff," she said. "Are you okay?"

"I'm okay, I was just shaken up. After that, we got the hell out of that place. Although, Jason, he…" I said, my voice trailing off as I thought about what happened next. "Mel he knows. He knows that I'm pregnant. He told me in the parking lot."

I heard a gasp on her end of the phone as I told her how I found out he knew and then about our talk back at their farm.

"And he didn't run away, did he? I know I'm right, but go ahead and tell me anyway."

She was too good. "No, he didn't. He told me how he would be there for me and that he wanted so badly to kiss me."

"And then you kissed?"

"No," I replied, telling her how it happened as I closed my eyes, remembering the feel of his soft lips pressed onto mine.

"Was it a movie moment?"

"You have no idea Mel. It was like my first real kiss from a guy who actually wanted me. The sparks, the fire, the butterflies, it was all there. I can't even describe how amazing it felt."

"I told you he wouldn't run when he found out. He's too good of a guy, Cass. I understand why you think it's bad timing, but he's right you know. You can't wait until your life is ready for someone, you don't get to choose when the right person gets to walk into your life."

"I woke up in his arms this morning and never felt more relaxed or happy in my life."

"Did you, uh... ya know?"

"No." I shook my head as if she could see it through the phone. I reflected on that moment for a second before telling her why we didn't take it further. I also couldn't help but try and blame the frisky behavior on my hormones even though deep down I knew it was more than that.

"You can blame the hormones all you want, but my guess is it's just that you really like this guy."

"Well you're filled in now. I don't know what's going to happen next though. I'll keep you posted," I said.

"As if you have a choice. You okay otherwise?" she asked.

"Yeah for the most part," I replied, feeling an overwhelming sadness, I missed her so much. I was closer to her than before, but still so far away.

"Alright, I better get back to class, call me soon. Love you."

"Love you too," I replied and ended the call.

I spent the afternoon thinking, only making myself more confused. I thought about what I wanted to do, what Trish told me, and then about my conversation with Mel. My brain was exhausted. I decided it was time for a break. I took out a book that I had stashed in my purse and began to read it. It was a contemporary romance novel by one of my favorite authors. I had read it at least twenty times and it still never got old. It always brought me comfort when I read it. I was lost in a story where I wasn't the main character, where I didn't have near as much to lose as this couple in love did. I only made it about half way until I fell asleep only to wake up with the book still open, lying flat on my chest. It reminded me of when I was a little girl and I would fall asleep reading on my bed at night, of course only to get yelled at by my parents for staying up too late reading what they liked to call garbage. If it wasn't a textbook, it wasn't worth my time in their minds. I shook my head and stretched before getting up and straightening out my hair.

"How was the farm?" I asked Trish as I made my way to the kitchen.

"It was good, hot though. Those boys worked up a sweat today. How was your afternoon? Did you rest any?"

"I did. It was definitely needed."

"Jason should be home in about an hour, I'm just getting ready to start making dinner."

"Can I help with anything?"

"Oh no, why don't you go relax outside, get some fresh air," she said.

"Okay, if you insist."

The warm air felt nice on my skin as a slight breeze kept it from being overly hot. I took a seat on the swing that was on the porch and rocked myself back and forth, enjoying the moment. Jason was wearing off on me more and more each day. It had been a long time since I was able to sit anywhere, let alone on a porch swing doing absolutely nothing. It felt wonderful.

Chapter
twenty-four

I DIDN'T KNOW WHAT it was but when I saw his truck pull onto the gravel drive, my stomach suddenly did more flips than a gymnastics routine. I was overly excited to see him tonight and the butterflies were in full force. He didn't get out of the truck right away; he sat in it for a few moments before finally stepping out. His normal little kid in a candy store smile was replaced by one I hadn't seen on him before, it was indifferent, expressionless. I tilted my head to look at him, trying to study what was different about him tonight. He slowly walked up to the swing and took the open seat next to me, only it felt like a mile away as he sat as close to the other end as possible.

"Hey Jase," I said to him.

"Hey," he muttered, shifting in his seat. Something was off, something wasn't right. I could feel the flips in my stomach being replaced with knots. I knew it was only a matter of time before he sat long enough in his own thoughts that he would finally realize I was a girl who had more problems than he wanted.

"How was work?" I asked, trying to get something out of him.

He ran his hand through his tousled hair. "It was fine," he said quietly, keeping his eyes in front of him.

The minute his mouth let out the word "fine" my heart sank. He and I both knew how much that word meant the opposite of what it was. He was definitely not fine. I could feel my pulse start to race the longer we sat in silence. I scared him; he had time to think today and I knew it was me that he was having a hard time with. I guess I was the one percent that had the pre-planned conversation in her head actually end the way I thought it would.

"How was your day?" he asked, finally looking over in my direction but giving me the worst excuse for a smile that he could.

"It was fine," I replied. It seemed as if we weren't even friends, let alone two people who had kissed. We felt like strangers.

He let out a long breath as he grabbed the back of his neck and began rubbing it. "Cassandra," he began to say until Trish interrupted.

"Guys, time to eat," she said in her normal cheery voice.

I felt relief that she came out when she did. I wasn't sure if I could have handled what Jason was about to say. I got up from the swing with Jason behind me and walked inside to the kitchen. I was beginning to love the smell of home cooked meals all too much.

"Smells wonderful you guys." I tried to put on a happy face in front of Trish and Bart. They were doing me such a big favor by letting me stay here. They didn't need to get involved in the problem that was clearly between Jason and me, one that after last night I honestly didn't see coming.

"Thank you, it's one of our favorites," Trish said.

From the looks of what was cooked and from the scent traveling under my nose, tonight we were having lasagna. We all grabbed platters of food and sat them down on the table that was set with forks and plates. Jason sat next to me but not once did he even call me Sweetheart, let alone act as though we just spent the night together. Dinner felt awkward between us. I only hoped it didn't feel that way for Bart or Trish. My heart was hurting, badly. I was feeling embarrassed and my mind was laced with confusion. He interacted with his parents the same as usual but he was completely different toward me tonight. I tried my best to eat the meal that was cooked, it was delicious but the nausea hit and this time it wasn't because I was pregnant.

The conversation throughout dinner was plentiful and seemed normal for them. I tried to participate, but my thoughts were elsewhere. I was going to have to talk to Jason. I didn't want to but it needed to be done. I would just have to wait until after dinner, until we were alone.

When everyone was finished eating and the dishes were cleaned, courtesy of Bart and Jason, I knew my opportunity to talk to him was approaching. The knots in my stomach grew.

Bart and Trish excused themselves to go swing on the porch, something they said they loved to do. Jason and I were finally alone. I could feel the tension building as he stood in the kitchen, his arms holding him up on the counter top as he kept his head lowered.

I stood on the other side of the countertop waiting for him to say something… anything. It never happened though. I had to be the one to break this frigid ice that was going on between us for whatever reason.

"Jason?" I asked quietly, placing my hand on top of his. He didn't move. "You seem, off tonight. What's going on?" It was the hardest thing to have to ask him, partially because I didn't know if I was prepared for his response.

He slowly raised his head, his eyes found mine. Nothing. There was nothing in them. "Cassie," he sighed. "I'm… Well, I mean we… Damn it." He took his hand and rubbed it over his face. "Just forget it. I don't know what I'm trying to say." He looked at me with another fake smile.

I could take a hint. I slid my hand off of his and across the counter top until it was next to me again. I took in a deep breath and felt the pain in my stomach. I didn't have to pre-plan any of this conversation in my head to know what was really going on; it was called woman's intuition.

"Listen," he muttered, breaking the silence between us. "I'm just really tired. I need to get some sleep okay?"

I pressed my lips together. Sleep was a good idea, except I knew I wouldn't get any, thinking about what just happened.

"Good idea," I replied and gave him the fake, horrendous smile he showed me, before letting out a sigh and walking to my room.

I sat on the bed watching the doorknob, waiting for it to turn for at least an hour before finally realizing that wasn't going to happen. I'd be lying if I said I didn't wish he had come walking through that door. Wanting to tell me what was wrong, or even better, that he was sorry for being distant, but that didn't happen. I finally got up from the bed and got ready to go to sleep. I didn't know why, but I put on Jason's shirt he had me wear this morning. I was either a glutton for punishment or just sad and wishing it was his body that was wrapping itself around me and not his shirt. I got under the covers and hugged myself tightly until I fell asleep.

Chapter
twenty-five

"You don't deserve this baby. I'm keeping it. Get out of here and don't come back."

I SHOT STRAIGHT UP AND LOOKED around confused, until I finally realized it was just a dream. I put my hand to my chest and tried to calm my erratic breathing.

"It was just a dream, Cassandra, just a dream." I tried to tell myself, but I couldn't help but feel the realness of it.

It was vivid. It started off with me waking up, just like I did this morning, except Jason was in my room taking my clothes out of the closet and literally shoving them into my suitcase. He didn't say a word as he finished, but then he saw me wearing his shirt. He told me to take it off and give it back. So that's what I did as I cried, soaking the shirt before handing it over to him. He didn't even let me put anything else on as he took me outside where everyone I had met in this town was standing out front waiting. It didn't take long to see what he was waiting for as it headed toward us. Moose was driving my wrecked car that was still in shambles, down the street. He parked it up front, as Jason told me to get in it, yelling at me to leave, and get out of his life. I got in the car that was missing the windshield and looked the same way it did in the garage the other day and started driving off. I looked out the window one last time only to see him holding a baby, my baby, and he took it and kept it. I stopped and asked him what he was doing with my baby, telling him it wasn't his, that I needed to give it to a family that would adopt it. He told me I didn't deserve it, so he was keeping it. Then I woke up. Talk about heartache. I still wasn't sure what to think of it as I replayed the dream in my head. It was troubling and left me distraught. I needed to get out of this house; I needed some fresh air, badly. I reluctantly looked over at the nightstand where my phone was. Nothing. Not a damn message or anything.

After getting ready, I knew I needed out of the house. I made a sandwich, took a ginger ale, grabbed my phone and I locked up the house. It was gorgeous out. The wind was steady providing a slight breeze through the hot rays that were beaming down, warming my skin. I remembered the spot Jason took me to eat lunch the one day in the grass, my wonderful picnic lunch, ugh. I didn't know why, but I decided to go there. It was shaded and just far enough away from the house that I could sit and think.

Once I got there, I sat down on the cool grass and slipped my boots off. I looked at them as I set them beside me. I loved them, but what I loved more was who got them for me, Jason. I let out a sigh as I ate my sandwich with my legs stretched out, my toes touching the grass underneath them.

I felt my phone next to me vibrating. Looking down, my heart did a little flip until I saw it was Mel, not Jason.

"Hey," I answered quietly.

"Whoa, you don't sound like someone who just kissed a hot guy. What's up?" she asked, sounding concerned.

"That obvious?" I asked as I put the empty sandwich wrapper to the side of me.

"Uh. Yeah. Spill. What's going on?"

I took a sip of my ginger ale and put the can next to me. "I honestly don't know what happened. I just know something is definitely wrong. He was fine yesterday morning. I talked to you and then when he got home, he was a completely different Jason. Shut off, didn't want to talk to me, barely wanting to make small talk. His sorry pathetic attempts at smiles were what hurt the most."

"Maybe he just had a bad day. Where was he all day?"

"Work and it wasn't a bad day, it was clearly a horrible day for him. He obviously sat at work and stewed about us, about me.

He probably realized what a shitty mess he got himself into. I've been thinking, and I might just try and find a way to come see you. Maybe staying here was a bad idea." I didn't like the words that were coming out of my mouth, and neither did my eyes that were stinging with tears.

"Don't say that. You're thinking too much into it. People can have off days. They're allowed that. You have them. I have them. My gut tells me it's nothing. Just stay and see what happens tonight. Is he at work again today?"

"Yeah. I'm hoping to just spend the day alone, but I can't help think it would be better if I just left and came to see you. Get my car later. I don't even have to see him when I leave. He has dinner at his grandma's tonight I think."

"Whoa, Cass. I want to see you badly, but don't leave like that. Don't run. Where are you right now?"

I looked around; I was in a perfect spot. "Outside, in the grass. I just finished eating."

"Cass, promise me you won't run from him?"

"It's not just that. I had a weird dream last night too, so I'm all funky right now," I said.

"A weird dream?"

"It was so weird." I said, going over the horrid details with her.

"Okay, that's just creepy."

"You're telling me. I'm the one that had to wake up from it, thinking it was real."

"Listen, stop over thinking, and just relax. Don't leave. Take some deep breaths and relax. Enjoy the fresh air."

"Okay, I'll trust you. I'll stay for now."

"Good. Call me later. Love you."

"Love you too, Mel." I ended the call and put the phone down next to me. I realized how nice it was to just sit and do nothing again. I was getting too used to it. I laid myself back and decided to close my eyes and think.

I thought about everything as I replayed my whole journey down here in my head. I beamed at the good times and cringed at the scary moments, but nothing prepared me for how I felt about this guy. This guy who had me so wrapped up in him I didn't know which direction I was heading. Running away wasn't the right option and I'm glad Mel talked me out of it. It still didn't help the knots in my stomach as I thought about the way Jase was acting toward me. I continued to let my mind wander where it wanted to as the breeze blew over me and the grass tickled my arms and legs for what felt like a few hours of pure alone time.

Chapter twenty-six

"HEY PRETTY GIRL," I heard his familiar voice say from behind me. I didn't move as I continued to lay with my eyes closed. Hearing the words pretty girl only confused me more. Yesterday I was nothing, this morning I wasn't even worth a goodbye, and then tonight I was back to being called a nickname. My head was overwhelmed.

"Is this spot taken?"

"No," I answered quietly.

I heard him take a seat next to me, and the ruffle of a bag he placed down on the grass. "You've been out here a long time."

"How do you know that?" I asked, curious if he had some sort of spy cam on me or not.

"The shop is just down the street. I saw you."

"Well, it's a nice spot to think," I told him.

"It's my favorite spot to think," he said quietly as his body shuffled in the grass. "Will you look at me?"

I slowly opened my eyes to see him leaning close to me. His eyes were happy, his lips curled into a smile. He was a completely different guy from yesterday.

"Hey there," he whispered, his hand brushing away a loose piece of hair from my face.

"Hey."

"I brought dinner," he said as he lifted the bag next to him.

"Thanks, but I thought you had dinner at your grandma's tonight?" I asked.

He shrugged his shoulders. "We can miss one night."

He pulled the bag over as I sat up, crossing my legs underneath me.

"Chopped salad," I said surprised.

"A different 'usual'," he said. "So why did you need to come out here to think?"

I looked down at my salad as I used my fork to push the lettuce around, trying to dodge his question.

"Do we need to play a game so I can get some answers out of you?"

"No, no trivia. I was just thinking about things, nothing in particular." I was such a liar. It was all I did these days. I hated it.

"Hmmm." That was all he responded with. His eyes looked back down to his food, mine did the same.

The clouds were getting darker the longer we sat. It was looking as though a storm was about to roll in.

I took a bite as the wind picked up, making my fork move to the side before I was able to put the salad in my mouth. I saw Jason start to chuckle as he reached his hand out to my face. My body froze as I felt the warmth of his fingers on my cheek. I couldn't help but close my eyes for just a moment, remembering how much I loved feeling his touch. I pried them open and watched as he used the pad of his thumb to wipe something off the side of my lips.

He slowly took his hand off of my cheek, leaving it feeling cold again. "You had some dressing on the side of your mouth," he said quietly.

The wind picked up again and then a few sprinkles dropped from the sky. I continued to sit there as I watched the small drops hit my flesh. He didn't seem to want to move either as we both sat there finishing our dinner.

I couldn't eat anymore though; my stomach was shredding itself as I continued to think about Jason. I was confused, frustrated, and needed to know what we were, if we were even anything at all. I couldn't take not knowing anymore. One day he was kissing the shit out of me, making the world come undone around me, and then the next day he ignored me like the plague. Now tonight, he's all smiles and taking my breath away as his hand touched my cheek. More drops were now falling out of the dark ominous clouds that hovered over our heads, no longer feeling like sprinkles.

"You ready to get out of here, Sweetheart?" he asked, wiping away the rain that was hitting his face.

That was all the confirmation I needed, the second he called me Sweetheart my heart had to know, I just had to know. I put my salad container in the bag and stood up, Jason doing the same thing. I didn't move though, my body wouldn't let me. Instead, I felt hard raindrops hitting my skin as a crash of thunder barreled through the town making me close my eyes as it rumbled through my body. It seemed like the storm was right above us.

"What are you doing? Let's go!" he yelled.

My hair was now completely drenched to match Jason's; our clothes looked as though we just jumped in a pool with everything on. My heart was pounding with every second that passed. Thud. Thud. Thud. I opened my quivering lips; this was it.

"Tell me you feel it Jase. You feel your heart on fire every time we get close. That you try not to even think because all you want to think about is what it would feel like to have our lips touch again, knowing that it will be just as earth shattering as the first time. That everything inside tells you it's too fast to fall this hard for someone you just met. That it can't be real even though your heart screams to you that it is. Damn it Jase!" I screamed as the rain soaked my face. "Tell me you feel it too."

"I do. I feel all of it, every goddamn bit of it, Cassie. From day one, you had me, you owned me, my thoughts, my everything. I couldn't stop thinking about you. I didn't want to."

"So what happened yesterday and this morning Jason? What the hell was that about?"

"I was scared. I was afraid of what would happen the moment you left. I knew that I wouldn't be able to handle it. So I thought by giving us some distance, it would be easier for the both of us, but it's not. I was wrong. I was so fucking wrong. If you're in this, then so am I, but you're stuck with me forever because my heart won't be able to handle losing you now Sweetheart," he said as the rain continued to run down him, soaking every inch of his body.

"I'm in Jase, I was already in," I admitted.

A large grin swept over his face as he took three large steps and was standing in front of me. His hands cupped my cheeks as his wet lips found mine.

"I'm sorry, I'm so sorry," he said through the kisses that felt like our lips were starving for them.

"Don't be sorry, just don't do it again, please," I said against his mouth.

"Never again, I promise," he said, pushing our lips even harder together, deepening the kiss that we both craved.

It didn't take long for our affection to stop as another crash of thunder radiated through the town followed by a bright streak of lightning, a little too close for comfort. I screamed like a girl as he grabbed our trash and my hand as we ran. I thought we were headed for the truck but he took us into the abandoned building behind us. We went around to the back entrance, which was unlocked and made our way into the building. It was dark but I could still see enough, especially when the lightning would strike, lighting up the room. There was a desk and a few tables around along with carpet still on the ground.

I couldn't help but notice our drenched bodies from the downpour of rain outside. "We are soaked," I said, looking at him.

"Just a little. Let's wait out the storm in here. Wait there a sec." I saw him walk into a closet only to return with a lit candle and a smile on his face, the one I loved seeing.

"Where are we?" I asked, trying to figure out what this building once was.

He put the candle on the table next to him as he walked closer to me. "It's the old library. They moved it to a new location. No one has bought this place yet though, so for the time being, I've used it as my thinking spot. When the weather gets bad, I come inside, though I love the spot outside."

"That makes much more sense now, but why is there still furniture left in here then?"

"Well," he said as he sauntered even closer to me. "The person who moved it bought all new stuff, so they just left everything else behind."

"Are there any books left?" I asked.

"Let's go look." He took my hand as he pulled us away from the back door, and grabbed the lit candle from the table.

We walked out of the back room and down a dark hallway, and then finally back to an open space filled with rows and rows of bookshelves so tall that they almost reached the ceiling. When we stopped in front of one of the aisles, Jason looked back at me.

"What?"

He let out a quiet chuckle. "Are you doing okay?"

"Yeah, this is actually really fun," I replied.

"I think so too," he said.

He pulled my hand and we walked down the row of bookshelves. Even though they appeared empty, we kept looking. He sat the candlestick down on an empty shelf and walked down to look at the end.

"Anything?" I asked.

"No, grab the candle; let's go look on the other side."

I did as he asked and grabbed the candlestick, followed him to the end of the aisle, and slowly trailed him down the next one. I put the candle down and looked at the bookshelves; there were no books left anywhere. I should have guessed they would all be gone, but it was still a good, fun way to pass the time while waiting for the storm to pass. I looked around and suddenly realized that Jason wasn't next to me or even behind me anymore. I called his name, but he didn't answer.

"Come on, Jase. This isn't funny," I said, getting slightly panicked.

"I'm over here," I heard a faint whisper from the aisle next to me.

I quickly walked over and saw his shadow walking back toward me. "What are you doing?" I asked.

He looked up at me. "I was looking for a book for you," he said quietly.

"You left. It scared me," I told him, embarrassed by my fear of being alone in this dark, vacant library.

"I'm right here." He reached out his hand. At the same time I grabbed his hand, a loud rumble of thunder roared through the old building making everything in my body tense. I screamed like a little girl and all but jumped into Jason's arms.

"You're okay. I've got you," he whispered into my ear as I clung onto him. His hands slid down my back to my waist, soothing me from the thunder's jolt.

The candle in the aisle next to us did little to break the darkness that surrounded us, but I could clearly see his eyes. I would always be able to see those eyes. They pierced mine as my hands leisurely moved up his chest and around his neck. He slowly took a step closer, moving us so that my back was now against the bookshelf. His hands left my waist to rest on the shelf behind me. My chest was rising and falling as quickly as his was, and it was as though our bodies were in sync. I could tell we both were feeling everything. Every butterfly that fluttered in our stomachs, every breath exhaled and inhaled, and every bit of self-control lost the longer our bodies held this position.

I couldn't help but lick my lips. I wanted his on mine badly, they needed the taste of Jason on them again. It was as if the storm now raged inside of us, ready to be unleashed. Another loud roar of thunder around us, and then, there it was. A growl escaped Jason as I bowed my back to take a tighter hold of him. His eyes watched as my teeth captured my bottom lip, and his lips immediately found mine. For a split second, a crash of lightning appeared, lighting up the row around us. Our tongues immediately intertwined, kissing frantically as though it was our first kiss.

I slid my hands from around his neck, and up his arms, until I reached his hands, placing mine inside his. He gripped them tightly as he pulled his lips from mine and began softly placing kisses down my neck into the curve of my shoulder. I let out a soft moan, loving the feel of his wet lips against my skin. His grip tightened as his body pressed harder against mine, and his teeth bit down softly on my ear. I wanted to melt into a puddle right here on the floor. Turning my head toward him, my lips were ready to taste more of him. I kissed him and then like something fierce had stricken inside me, I bit his bottom lip. His answering growl made every pulse in my body race. I trailed my lips down his neck but enjoyed the feel of his scruff against my soft cheek first. When I got to his neck, he moved back slightly. With my hands still gripped tightly in his, I was stuck, unable to continue kissing his neck.

"This isn't funny," I said, my voice husky.

He leaned closer, his hold still firm on my hands. "Cassandra, I don't know if I'll have the ability to stop, so I have to keep your hands locked in mine where they're safe."

I slowly shook my head. "I don't want to beg for this. I have never wanted anything more in my life. I'm giving this to you, and I want you to take it and never give it back. I want you, Jason."

His eyes closed, and with a heavy sigh, he let my hands go without saying a word. That said more than any verbal response he could have given me. I smiled and could make out his as the lightning flashed through the windows. I placed my hands on his chest and slowly pushed away, sauntering down the aisle past him. I glanced over my shoulder and saw his confusion before I made my way around the corner. That was exactly what I wanted. I pulled my boots off and placed them in the middle of the aisle. I quickly slipped my wet shirt over my head, and left it peeking out of the bookshelf. I made my way down the next aisle, leaving my shorts on another bookshelf making the trail of clothes easy to follow. I slowly slipped each bra strap off my shoulders, and then hung it on the end of the last bookshelf. When I reached the middle of the aisle, I casually stood with my arms crossed over my chest.

My heart raced as I waited for him. I saw the toe of his boot peeking around the corner as he finally made his way to the front of the aisle. He was carrying my boots, shirt, shorts, and bra as he walked closer to me.

"You are doing a number on me right now," he said breathlessly.

I could only bite my lip and grin. I didn't know what had gotten into me, but I was more than positive it was Jason. He made me want him as I had never wanted anything before in my life. He made my insides rage with desire for him. I felt myself getting even hotter the longer I thought about it. I uncrossed my arms and let them fall to my sides. My chest was now fully exposed. He dropped my clothes to the floor as he made his way to me. He pushed his body close against mine. The wetness from his shirt against the bare skin on my chest gave me goose bumps. He gazed deeply into my eyes almost as if he was unsure of something.

"I don't have a condom, Cassie."

I peered into his conflicted green eyes and gave him an honest response. "I had a feeling, but it doesn't matter Jason. I know I'm clean. If you say you're clean, I trust you. It might not make sense to you, but being with you, this way, feels right. I trust you and I want this intimate moment between us."

His eyes searched mine before he replied in a soft whisper. "I swear I'm clean. It does feel right, doesn't it?"

My heart raced because I knew what was coming. It seemed like I was going into this as a virgin again, except this time was with a guy that meant more to me than he would ever know. This time, it was special. I nodded my head gently. "Yes. More than you know."

As he pressed closer against me, my eyes drifted closed as I savored the feel of his body on mine. He put his hand to my face, slowly moved it back, and tangled his fingers in my wet hair before pressing his lips hard to mine. I opened my mouth, welcoming his tongue; I was being too impatient for him. He pushed his body harder against mine, making it impossible to think about anything other than the feel of his body on mine. A soft moan rumbled through my throat as I felt his hardness against my thigh. As I broke the kiss, I impatiently pulled his shirt up over his head, and tossed it on the growing pile of wet clothing. A sexy smile appeared on his face before his lips found their way back to my skin, tracing a line from my chin to my ear.

"You are so sexy," he whispered before untangling his hands from my hair.

The goose bumps that he just gave me were too apparent as his lips curled up to the side. "All you," I whispered.

He chuckled as he put his arms around my waist and pulled my body away from the shelf. My hands fumbled with his belt buckle. Finally taking the hint, he moved my hands, unbuckled his belt, and unzipped his pants. He heel-toed his boots off and slowly lowered his pants to the floor and kicked them to the side.

"Now we match," I said quietly.

"That's about to change," he said.

When he picked me up as if I were a rag doll, a shiver traveled all the way down my spine. I threw my arms around his neck and wrapped my legs around his waist, as he slowly carried me to the middle of the aisle.

"I'm going to lower you down. Don't let go," he told me.

I held on tight, needing him to understand that I would never let go. He should know better. With one hand under my ass and the other on my back, he slowly but surely lowered me to the floor. His lips immediately settled on my tingling skin that ached for his touch, his love. Kisses trailed from my neck to my stomach to the top of my lacy panties. His finger traced an outline on the top of them, sending my body into a heated frenzy. He was teasing and he knew it. I closed my eyes, enjoying the feel of his light touch on my skin. A soft moan escaped me as his fingers gently pulled the lace, tickling my legs as they moved down and then off. I opened my eyes to see him kneeling over me.

"We don't match anymore," I said in a sexy voice that probably cracked because he had me so anxious for more.

"That's a problem," he said quietly as his lips curled up. God, I was going to come undone right here without any help from him. Between his delicious lips curling up into sexy grins, his gorgeous eyes shooting me winks every time he was up to something, or his soft caressing touch, I wasn't sure that I would be able to hold on much longer.

"It's a major problem," I said, putting my hands on his chest as I quickly raised myself up.

As he leaned back, I kept one hand on his chest and crawled over him until he was flat on the floor and I was completely hovered over him. He ran his hands up my legs until they perfectly gripped my waist, pulling me down until our lips were together once again. My wet hair cascaded around us until his hands swept it back, and holding it in place, forced our lips together even harder. I couldn't help but feel pleased when a moan escaped him as I continued to move back and forth against his rock hard excitement between my legs. Now who was teasing whom? My lips left his to taste his skin, doing what he did to me until I got to the top of his boxers. Those needed to come off immediately. As I sat up to remedy that problem, his hands gripped the tops of my thighs. I traced my fingers along the top band of his boxers, and took pleasure in giving him goose bumps all over his body. I slowly inched his boxers lower and lower until he was bare. I couldn't help but stare at his body after I tossed his boxers on top of my panties. He sat up and gripped my waist, pulling me closer to him.

"Are you sure you want this?" he whispered as both hands cupped my face.

I put a hand on top of his. "I am more sure of this than I am about anything else in my life."

"Me too." He let go of my face, took my hand, and pulled it to his mouth, placing a soft kiss on it.

He crawled over me and placed a hand behind my back, lowering me to the floor.

"You are so beautiful, Cassie," he said as his eyes toured my excited, bare body.

I wrapped my legs around his waist and my hands behind his head. I couldn't wait any longer; I needed him now. He got the hint and his cold hand cupped my warm, aching spot. I softly moaned as his fingers slid in with ease. It wasn't going to take long as every flutter inside my body brought me closer and closer to my eager release. His other hand gently massaged my taut peak. His scruff scraped against my neck and his teeth gently bit my ear, forcing more moans from my throat. My hands ran through his hair, gripping it tightly as I was so close and could feel it.

"Jase…" I moaned out, ready for him to go faster and harder, but he didn't. He stopped, pulling his fingers out quickly.

"Shhh," he said, giving me that damn sexy grin that just kept turning me on even more.

He pulled back and positioned himself perfectly between my legs. He put an arm on either side of me and my legs hugged his body. His lips found mine as he slowly eased into me. It was as though his key found the perfect lock to fit into, filling every bit of me as though we were made for each other.

"Oh my God," I cried out as he began rocking in and out of me.

He stayed quiet as his lips claimed mine. With every gentle thrust he made, the ecstasy building inside of me rushed through my veins, hitting every sensitive nerve in my body. I wanted to moan, yell, and scream Jason's name but I couldn't. His lips covered mine, not once releasing, not even to take a breath. I grabbed his neck as we continued to rock our bodies back and forth, devouring each other until the intensity that built was too much. It was coming, the end, and the orgasm that my body was so ready to have. I wasn't prepared to leave this moment with him, but the feelings that were building needed release, needed to explode inside my body. Our breathing was heavier and the kissing was hungrier as we clung to one another, both getting closer, knowing what was waiting for us at the end. And like a flash of lightning that had lit the sky earlier, it struck my body, bolting through every vein in me. It was every moment, from seeing him at the scene of my accident to dancing under the stars, to our first kiss, and all the buildup in between, raging through my body as the orgasm took over. I felt Jase's body tremble over mine as we both let the release take over until our bodies slowly collapsed against one another. My legs and arms fell to my side as the euphoric sensations rapidly raced through me. His breathing slowly returning to normal, but his heart still beat fast as he lay on top of my chest. He slowly raised his body, hovering over mine, and I didn't want to let go of the tingles still shooting through my body like aftershocks of an earthquake.

He took a long deep breath and closed his eyes. "Wow, Cassie. That was…" He paused.

I took my hand and put it under his chin, pulling his face down toward mine. "I know, Jase. I know," I panted before placing soft kisses with my swollen lips onto his.

He eased his body down next to mine, pulled my waist toward him and my back against his chest, and we laid there while he cradled me in his arms. We were both calm and relaxed, just like the weather now that the storm had passed.

"How often does it storm here?" I asked him as I ran my fingers across his arm around my waist.

"Why?" he asked quietly.

"Because we need to repeat this every time it storms, and all the other moments in between." I teased, but not really, because I would be more than okay repeating that with him.

That wasn't like sex with Parker or even my ex-boyfriend. Their kind was raunchy and quick, whereas this was powerful. It was meaningful. This was the type of sex you took slowly. You didn't want it to end because you'd miss being inside, feeling everything the other person felt. This was making love. I finally understood what it meant.

"It just so happens to storm here a lot," he whispered into my ear as he softly tickled my side causing me to giggle.

"Even better," I replied.

We held onto each other for what seemed like mere minutes before we realized the sun was setting. We grabbed our damp clothes and put them on before leaving the abandoned building. I took one last look at the library that now forever held a special place in my heart, before Jason helped me get in the truck. He placed his lips on mine and gave me a quick wink before closing my door. This man had me, all of me. I didn't think I would ever be able to drive away now, fixed car or not. I was his like he'd said, and I couldn't bear to lose him either. I finally had something in my life that made sense. When everything else around me seemed to spin out of control, he was my center, my balance. I grabbed his hand as we drove home. It wasn't my hom

I wasn't able to fall sleep, yet again. My mind and body were back at the library with the thunder, the lightning, the kissing, the moaning, the growls, everything. I couldn't stop replaying the night in my head. It was like reliving every moment. I was definitely not going to fall asleep. I saw my phone light up, heard it vibrate on the nightstand next to me, and couldn't help but get excited. My heart already knew who it was.

I can't sleep.

Me either.

Will you come down here and lay with me?

He didn't even have to ask. I wanted nothing more than to be wrapped in his arms again tonight. I pulled the covers off and slipped out of my bed, put a pair of yoga pants on, and quietly left my room. I crept downstairs and opened his door, tiptoeing over to his bed. It was dark but it didn't matter, I didn't have to see anything. His arms pulled me into his bed, and I couldn't help but giggle as he did. He pulled me against him, snuggling my body with his warm one.

"Much better," he said.

"Almost," I said as I pulled off my constricting yoga pants, threw them next to the bed and intertwined my legs with his. "Now that's much better," I said.

"Goodnight," he whispered into my ear.

"Night, Jase," I replied, before nestling my head on his chest and falling asleep in his arms for the second time.

Chapter
twenty-seven

I WOKE UP IMMEDIATELY feeling a cramp run through my stomach. I shot up in the bed as another pain followed. I grabbed my stomach and could feel that something wasn't right. I took off, trying to be quiet so I didn't wake Jason. I closed the bedroom door behind me and all but ran to his bathroom. I stopped at the sink, put a hand on the counter, and a hand on my stomach as another cramp hit me. They weren't excruciating, but they were painful enough to let me know something was not right.

I felt something damp between my legs and quickly lowered my panties to see what it was. An overwhelming dizzying sensation hit me like a truckload of bricks as I saw bright red spotted on my panties. I grabbed hold of the counter so I didn't fall over. As I steadied myself, I pulled the panties down the rest of the way and suddenly needed to see if there was more. I grabbed a handful of toilet paper, and closing my eyes, wiped myself.

Something had changed from the previous days of not wanting this baby. My feelings immediately went into protective mother mode. I knew that whatever was going on had to do with the baby, with *my* baby. My chest hurt as my breathing became painful. "Please Lord, please, let there be no blood," I whispered before looking at the tissue. My heart sank. There was blood, more blood than I knew was okay. Oh my God. I stopped moving; my body became numb as I let the situation sink in. Miscarriage came to mind and thoughts of Trish losing her baby, and then the reality hit, losing my baby. I couldn't lose it. It was mine. I didn't want the baby before, but something inside pulled on my heart as it told me I might not need the baby, but my baby needed me.

I didn't even remember walking back to Jason's room. The light was on and Jason was sitting on the edge of his bed. I didn't know what to say so I stopped in front of him, feeling lifeless as I looked past him. All I could think about was what was happening inside my body. My fear had frozen me.

"Cassie? What's wrong? You look like you just saw a ghost."

"I'm-I'm scared, I don't know what to do."

"What's going on?" he asked, sounding panicked.

"There's blood. I'm bleeding, and I know it's not okay," I cried. I buried my face in my hands, and within seconds, his arms wrapped around me, holding me to him, as if he knew this *was* bad.

"Shit," he muttered as he continued to hold me. "We need to get to the hospital."

"I didn't want the baby. I wanted more than anything for it to just disappear, to disintegrate inside me. I prayed the accident took care of it. Then it didn't, and I cursed the damn thing growing inside of me. I hated it," I screamed out, my forehead leaning against his chest. "It was ruining my life, and now, I just ruined its life. What am I going to do? I will never forgive myself if I knew I did this, if my praying and wishing were actually what caused this. I'll never forgive myself."

"Don't think about that right now. Just focus on breathing in and out, slowly."

I couldn't stop thinking though. Losing my blueberry because I didn't take care of myself was all I could think about. His hands grabbed my face as he pulled his body away from mine, peering down into my panic-laced eyes. He was trying to be strong for me, and I was grateful. I didn't have the strength in me right now to do anything but cry.

"I'm calling my mom. Let's get you upstairs to put some clothes on and then I'm taking you to the hospital. Just breathe, Sweetheart. It's going to be okay," he said as he pressed his lips to my forehead. "It just has to be," he mumbled against my forehead. It had to, but that didn't mean it would.

He grabbed my hand and never let go as we walked upstairs to my room. I didn't even care about the silence between us as he dressed me like a child. He slipped on a new pair of panties as I hung on to his shoulders, putting one leg through each hole at a time. He did the same as he dressed me in a pair of yoga capris, my bra, and lastly, a tank top. The whole time he moved my body, putting on each article of clothing, I stood numbly in the room. I thought about each time I yelled at my baby and told it I didn't want it. Each Goddamn time I thought about the ways it was ruining my life.

It was going to ruin my future.
I didn't have a clue what was good and what was considered negligent.
"Why is it that so many women out there want a baby like you, yet here I am dreading every minute of this?"
"I've thought about abortion and adoption."
"I don't plan on keeping the baby."

I didn't even know what a gift I had until I was about to lose it, if I hadn't already.

He pulled my hands from my face, holding them gently in his. I looked down through the wetness covering my eyes and noticed I had on my sandals. How could I ever repay him for this?

"Let's go. Remember, just breathe. Focus on your breathing," he said cautiously.

Unfortunately, I couldn't focus on anything at the moment, let alone think about my breathing. He let go of my hands and pulled his phone out of his pocket.

"Mom, no, it's Cassandra."

"She's... bleeding," he whispered into the phone.

"Okay. Yeah. We're on our way now."

He slammed his phone shut and off we went to the truck, driving quickly out of the neighborhood. My eyes immediately went to the floor as nausea from the nerves pitted in my stomach. How could I have been so cruel?

"Hey, look at me, Sweetheart," he said, grabbing my hand from my lap, lacing our fingers together. "Look at me," he said with authority this time.

My neck turned as I did what he asked, my eyes connecting with his.

"You're going to be fine and so is your baby."

My heart squeezed tight at his words. I loved that he seemed so sure of things, that he had this positive outlook. I wish I had it, but I didn't.

"Let's play a game. Take your mind off of things until we get there."

I shook my head. I wasn't in the mood to play a game. "We aren't at the diner."

"It's truck trivia and we have until we get to the hospital. I'll go first," he said as he kept one hand on the steering wheel, the other gripping mine even tighter.

I closed my eyes. I would try to play his stupid game, but I didn't know how far trying would get us.

"What's your happiest memory when you were a kid?"

I sighed. I couldn't think about happy right now.

"It's okay. Just answer the question," he said in a soft voice.

I looked over at him, his eyes switching between the road and me, and his thumb gently rubbing my hand. I had to try. I let out a breath and thought of my answer. It wasn't a hard one.

"I remember when I was young, about twelve years old, and my mom finally broke down and bought me a hard backed journal. I had begged for one for what seemed like forever, but my dad kept telling me what nonsense it was to want to write, especially when I could read and learn something instead. She snuck it into my room when I was at school, so when I came home that afternoon, it was on my desk with a little pink ribbon tied around it," I told him, picturing that afternoon in my mind. "A note tied to the ribbon said, *'To Cassandra, write away my darling'* in my mother's handwriting. I knew without a doubt that my father had no clue about it. That night, I wrote until my hand cramped. It was our little secret and I'll never forget it. I kept it hidden in my closet behind my clothes and every night I would write. It was my outlet. I could write about anything I wanted and no one could tell me otherwise."

I heard Jason sigh. "God, you should see your smile right now," he said, his neck turning as his eyes found mine. "We're here by the way."

I looked in front of us. Sure enough, we were. I let out a long breath and looked over at him. "Thank you."

He nodded before dashing out of his door. "Mom's waiting for us with the doctor," he said as he helped me out of the truck.

And there she was, waiting with a wheelchair. I sat down and she wheeled me inside of yet another ER room. This was becoming a weekly thing, and I just prayed it was good news like the last time, that everything was fine.

My body shook as Trish had me change into a gown, put me on an IV, and helped me in the bed. She didn't say a word, but every now and then, her soft eyes would find mine. They looked as worried as I felt, but she tried to play it off as though she wasn't. She would flash me a quick smile before continuing the check of my vitals. I could only guess that my blood pressure was high.

"You need to try and calm down. Dr. Rich will be in here soon. Just try and think positive, okay Sweetie?"

I nodded, unsure if I could do as she asked. She of all people knew I wouldn't. It helped though that she was here. Jason was told to sit in the waiting room, but I knew by the way Trish kept looking at the closed curtain that he was on the other side. Trish caught me looking at her as she stared at the curtain.

"He can come in when we are all done, okay," she said quietly.

"I'm right here, Cassie. I'm not going anywhere," I heard Jason's voice say from the other side of the curtain. I was sure a tear or two fell from my eyes as his sweet voice echoed through my room.

I wanted him to hold my trembling hand, but I also needed the doctor to come in so I knew what was going on. My mind raced with every thought imaginable, good and bad, but mostly the terrible.

Trish was finally finished writing in my chart when Dr. Rich came in. He adjusted his glasses and focused on the chart for what felt like an hour, but was only mere minutes. He walked over to the bed and as he did, I inhaled a deep breath. This was it.

"Cassandra, Trish says you are bleeding. When did it start?" he asked, looking down at me.

I clasped my hands together and held them tightly as I got ready to answer his question. "I woke up this morning with a strange cramp. I had two before I decided to go to the bathroom to see what was wrong. I looked down after I felt something wet between my legs and noticed the-the blood."

"Okay," he muttered as he wrote in his file. "How much blood and what do the cramps feel like?"

I closed my eyes, remembering the blood that I saw this morning. "There was enough to see it on the toilet paper and on my panties. The cramps are not at all what they feel like during my periods. They are light. They don't really hurt; they just feel strange. What's happening to me?"

He handed Trish the folder and sat on the stool. "A lot could be happening right now. We're going to do an exam first and see what's going on."

"Is my baby going to make it?" I asked, my voice trembling. I didn't care about the gibberish he was speaking, I needed to know the answer. I needed to know it was going to be okay, that this sort of stuff happened all the time and ended with good results.

He closed his folder and looked at me with a smile. It wasn't a fake, or an out-of-pity smile, but a genuine one. He pulled his glasses off and held them in his hand while he looked at me.

"Cassandra, we don't know much right now, but I promise you we will find out. Why don't you take a couple of deep breaths for me while we get you set up for the exam, okay?"

"Okay." I took in a few deep breaths while he prepared.

Trish came over and stood by me, grabbing my hand in hers. "We got through the first exam just fine, Sweetie. We're going to get through this one too."

I squeezed her hand. I hoped so. I seriously fucking hoped so.

My legs were propped into the stirrups once again and the screen of the ultrasound was in place, the back facing me.

"Are you ready?" Dr. Rich asked.

"Yeah," I mumbled as I gripped Trish's hand tighter, feeling like I was crushing it.

"Go ahead and relax for me. I am inserting the probe now. You might feel some slight pressure," he said as he slowly inserted the probe.

There was pressure, but nothing was worse than the agonizing pain of waiting; it was tearing me up from the inside out. Dr. Rich continued moving the probe around as he looked at the screen while mumbling to himself. Sometimes I would see Trish trying to look at him or the screen, but he was being too quiet. Not one word slipped out of his mouth. I put my hand to my eyes and closed them. The suspense was eating me alive. Every ounce of hope I had coming in here was slowly fading the longer Dr. Rich was silent.

"Okay," he said, his voice flat. I slowly tore my hand off my eyes and lifted my eyelids to see Trish staring at Dr. Rich, waiting for an answer too. I looked over at him and just as his voice was impassive, so was his face.

"Cassandra," he said softly as his hand quickly moved the screen to face Trish and me. "Your baby is doing just fine."

"Oh my God," I said, letting out the breath I had been holding in all too long. I felt Trish's hand squeezing mine as she heard the news.

Dr. Rich pointed to the screen. "We are measuring at about seven weeks now and there is the heartbeat. It is measuring at 123, which is perfect. And, the spot right there," he said, pointing to it, "is your baby."

I looked at Trish who had a tear rolling down her cheek. Her face matched mine, happy and relieved. "Thank you," I mouthed to her, letting my tears stream freely. Dr. Rich pulled the probe out and turned the ultrasound machine off.

"Can I see Jason now?" I asked Trish. She looked over to Dr. Rich.

"I'll be back in to talk to you about what's going on," Dr. Rich told me as he and Trish left my room.

Jason didn't take long to come in. I knew he already heard the news, but I couldn't help telling him myself. "Jase, my baby is okay."

He immediately walked to my bed, sat on the side, and pulled me into his arms. "Thank God," he said quietly as he held me tightly.

"You told me everything was going to be okay, and it was. How do you stay so positive all the time?" I asked as he pulled back from me.

"It's a choice I make. If something is going to happen, why not think positive about it? Then, at least it won't scare you so much," he said quietly as he put his hand to my cheek.

"You amaze me every day," I said as I held his hand on my cheek.

He placed his lips on my forehead before getting off of the bed. "They said I only had a few minutes, but as soon as the doctor is out of here, I'll be back in, okay?"

"I'm counting on it," I said as I grabbed his hand, reluctant to let it go.

He kissed the top of my hand before slowly pulling away and leaving, closing the curtain behind him.

Dr. Rich walked back in looking overly perplexed. My eyes followed as he walked to the counter with my file, and then finally stood in front of my bed. I lifted a brow up to him; this happy moment of finding out my baby was still okay started to dissipate as Dr. Rich silently stood there.

"Cassandra," he said, looking down at my file. "We need to discuss a few things about the bleeding and cramping."

"Okay," I replied, my shaky voice returning.

He finally looked up and took off his glasses before taking a breath and sitting on the edge of my bed. "Women in their first trimester can bleed; they can bleed for no reason or for extremely problematic ones. From the exam we just did, I am going to rule out any problematic reasons as your baby is still fine and growing healthy inside of you," he said. I swallowed the golf ball sized lump that was stuck in my throat. "Many women who have first trimester bleeding go on to have very healthy babies. There is, however, nothing you can do to prevent a miscarriage. They happen for no reason, at any time. I don't want to scare you, but I need you to know this."

My heart fell to the floor. I closed my eyes and shook my head.

"I'm not saying it's going to happen, but I want you to know there is nothing you can do to prevent it from happening. You need to just do the best you can to relax, not stress, take care of yourself, and think positively, okay?"

I heard his words, pictured him in my mind as I kept my eyes closed. I could feel the salty tears reach my mouth before I finally opened my eyes. "What caused the bleeding then? Was it something I did?"

"Cassandra, your cervix is closed and we saw the heartbeat on the monitor. Bleeding happens. In fact, it always amazes me that we can make phones smarter than most humans, but we have yet to figure out what causes bleeding in pregnant women."

"So there's nothing I can do to prevent it?" I didn't believe him; I didn't understand how something so horrible could happen to me without explanation.

He shook his head. "No, there is nothing, but what I would like you to do is start taking it easy. Go rest for the remainder of the day, no walking around, and no exercising. I want you to stay calm and lie down. Doctor's orders."

I felt like I was already doing that, aside from stressing about life. I would do this though; I would make damn sure I was resting today.

"If the bleeding or cramping gets worse, you rush right back in here. Okay?"

"Yes Dr. Rich. Thank you."

"Of course," he replied, grabbed the file, and left the room.

A few moments later, Trish came walking in. "Doing okay Sweetie?"

"I was when I found out the baby was okay, and now, my stomach is back to shreds. Dr. Rich said there is nothing I can do to prevent a miscarriage. I can't even protect my own child." I put a hand protectively over my stomach.

She walked over to me and rested her hand on my shoulder. "I know, Sweetie. I know this all too well, but you need to allow yourself to stay positive right now. Don't stress over the 'what if's'. Take all of the energy in the part of you that wants to play every bad scenario there could be, and wash it out with happy thoughts, positive emotions. Anything, but what you're thinking right now. You can't change the outcome of this, so worrying is making it worse." She kept her motherly brown eyes on mine. She always seemed to know the right words to say.

I let out a deep breath. "Thanks Trish. I don't even know how to repay you for how kind you've been to me."

"Keep that smile on your face. That's how you can repay me," she said before starting to take my IV out.

"I can do that," I said.

"Good. So all of your blood work came back great. Dr. Rich says it's okay to release you now, but if you have any more problems, let Jason know and get right back okay?"

"Okay. Where is he?" I asked her as she put a cotton ball and then a Band-Aid over the spot where she removed my IV.

"Right outside the curtain still," she said quietly. "Go ahead and get dressed. I'll be back in a few minutes with a wheelchair."

I pulled the cover off and sat for a moment on the edge of the bed. I was scared to look down at the bed once I got up. I didn't want to see if there was any blood, or how much. I knew it wouldn't help to think about it once I saw it, but like a bad accident, I couldn't help but look. I took a deep breath and held it in as I put both feet on the cold hospital floor. Standing up, I closed my eyes and turned my head behind me, slowly letting out my breath and opening each eyelid one at a time, only to see... blood. It tainted the positive pep talk that Trish just gave, smearing its hopelessness all over me. I swallowed hard as I tried hard to hold the tears that were stinging behind my eyes. I dragged my feet across the room to the chair where my clothes were. A maxi pad sat on top. Trish must have put it there. She must have known that I would still be bleeding. I felt the slight tinge of the anxiety that I carried on my shoulders leave as I realized this must be normal; this had to be. It was going to be okay I thought to myself. As I put on my clothes, I tried to focus on dressing, breathing, anything but the color red.

I perched myself on the edge of the bed when I finished and waited for my two-wheeled ride out of here. I wasn't consumed in my own thoughts long as Jason's voice came from the other side of the curtain.

"You all done in there, Sweetheart?" he asked.

"Yes, but why do I feel like this is the worst case of déjà vu I've ever had?" I asked him, feeling all too familiar with this scenario.

He came through the curtain wearing the adorable smile that I loved seeing. "No, it's really not, because this time, I've known you for a lot longer than 8 hours. So now, I get to call you much more than just a friend." He parked the wheelchair and sat down next to me on the bed.

"Oh really? Am I your best friend then?"

He shook his head. "No, you're more than a best friend. You're mine, Sweetheart." He placed his lips on my bare shoulder and kissed me. If Trish's pep talk didn't help, then I knew with all that I was, that this moment right now led me to believe I had everything to be positive about. I was his.

"I'm yours?" I asked as he slowly took his lips off of my shoulder, gazing up at me. I couldn't help but feel the flutters inside as his words sank deep into my heart.

He stood and placed a kiss on my forehead. "Yes, mine," he whispered back. My heart was pounding; he had me. He had me so much that he wouldn't even be able to comprehend. I had my baby and we had each other. Things were going to be okay. I was beginning to believe what everyone else was trying to get through my stubborn, thick-headed skull. I smiled to let him know he made me happy, how everything around me was going crazy, yet he balanced it. He was my sanity in this crazy, insane situation I had myself in.

"Let's get you home to rest." He reached out a hand for me to grab as I got off the bed and sat down in the wheelchair.

"Doctor's orders," I told him.

"My orders too," he said.

Chapter
twenty-eight

WE GOT BACK TO HIS HOUSE, his hand laced through mine as he took me downstairs to his room. I stopped in the doorway waiting for him to say something. He turned when he noticed that I wasn't moving and kept trying to pull me further into his bedroom.

"What?" he asked, his eyes scanning me over.

"I can rest in the room upstairs, you know?"

"I know that, but you seem to sleep so much better down here with me. You make these really cute little moans as you fall asleep, and you just look so peaceful in my bed."

I hid my face behind my hands, embarrassed by his words. I loved that he wanted me down here, but I made noises while I slept? Good Lord. His hands pulled mine from my face, his eyes peering down at me.

"Don't be bashful now. It's pretty adorable."

I rolled my eyes playfully at him. "I seriously doubt it."

"Doubt it all you want. It's cute. Now go sit on the bed, Sweetheart," he commanded as he walked over to his dresser.

"Yes sir." I teased as I walked over and sat down on his bed.

He sauntered over to me, carrying a shirt in his arms. "Why don't you put this on, and I'll be right back." He flashed me a wink before walking out of his room and closing the door behind him.

Yes, I did it again; I held his soft, white t-shirt up to my nose, inhaling the scent of Jason. As his smell engulfed me, I allowed every spicy scent tingle my senses. I reluctantly pulled it from my face, quickly pulled off my tank top and bra, and let his shirt slowly slide itself down my body. He was so much larger than me, and his shirt was more like a dress, which made it perfect for resting and sleeping. I pulled down my yoga pants and finally felt even more free and relaxed. I was now extremely grateful for the maxi pad. I wanted the bleeding to stop more than anything, but if it continued, at least I was covered. I folded my clothes and walked over to put them neatly on his dresser before walking back to his bed.

"Taking over my room already, I see." I heard his sweet voice behind me. I quickly turned on my heels and saw him smiling, holding a few things in his arms.

"Yes, I just might. I like it down here," I said, teasing him. "What are you carrying?"

He walked over to the bed as I sat down and crossed my legs. "Well," he said, putting down a water bottle and a couple cans of ginger ale. "I thought you might be hungry, so I made us a picnic."

"Really?" I asked, stunned and surprised, but entirely grateful.

"Yes, *really*." He chuckled. "Now get comfy so I can spread our picnic out."

I did as he said, crawling over to the side where I normally slept, getting under the covers, and leaning against his wooden headboard. He laid out a few paper towels along with two sandwiches, saltine crackers, and a bundle of grapes.

"Quite the spread here," I told him as he sat down on the bed.

"You impressed?"

"I'll let you know after I taste the sandwich," I said. He looked over at me, shook his head, and handed me a peanut butter and jelly sandwich wrapped in a paper towel.

"Hmmm." I looked down, admiring his choice in simplicity.

I took a bite of it and looked over at Jason, who had his brows pushed together waiting for a response.

"You have impressed me. No one puts peanut butter and jelly together quite like you do," I told him, his eye lowering like he knew I was being sarcastic. "It's perfect. I really appreciate it, all of it."

"I know," he said as he started eating his peanut butter and jelly sandwich.

I was thankful for the lunch. I had felt nauseated all day, but luckily, nothing came up. I blamed it on my preoccupied mind. I would have rather just vomited this morning than had to have dealt with the blood.

"Crackers?" he asked as he handed me the pack. He must have known they were a staple item for me these days.

"Thanks," I replied, opening the package and taking a few out.

We continued to eat, making some small chitchat, but for the most part, it was quiet. Not awkward, just pleasantly silent while we finished our picnic on the bed.

"So," Jason said, sounding unsure of what he was about to say. I put my napkin down, looked over to him, and saw his teeth biting down on his lower lip. God, it was sexy, but I had to stay focused. I felt he was about to lay something on me, and it left an uneasy feeling in my stomach.

"Yes?" I asked, leery of the answer.

"I talked to Melanie at the hospital. She called my phone. She said you didn't answer yours. I explained to her what was going on. I don't want you to be upset, but I know how much she means to you, so I didn't want to leave her hanging."

I put my hand over my gaping mouth. I was taken aback. Not at the fact that Melanie called, but that he cared enough about the relationship I had with her and knew that I'd want her to know what was going on.

"You're mad, aren't you? Damn it, I'm sorry, Cassie."

I peeled my hand off of my mouth and placed it on his knee. "I'm not mad. Not at all. I'm more shocked that you did that for us. Thank you so much. You really are a sweet guy."

"I know how much she means to you, and I also know how she would castrate me if I didn't answer the phone. She wants you to call her. So, I'm going to take our trash upstairs and give you some time to talk to her."

"You don't have to leave," I told him.

"I know," he said, grabbing his phone and handing it to me. "But, girls like to talk in private."

"Ah yes. The girl code of needing privacy to talk. You know this means that now I have the perfect opportunity to talk about you," I told him while he picked up the picnic items on the bed.

"Exactly," he responded before leaving his room.

I clicked Mel's name on Jason's phone.

"Jason? Is everything okay?" Melanie asked hastily as she answered on the second ring.

I let my jaw drop a little when she thought I was him and not me. "No, it's not Jason. How about your best *friend*?"

"Oh, well, where is your phone?" she asked.

"Upstairs in my room."

"Ohhh. So you are in his room, then?"

"Yes and I'm resting in his bed *and* shirt." If anyone would understand the excitement of this, it was Mel.

"Well, I'm jealous," she said.

"He told me he talked to you about what happened this morning."

"Yes, I've been so worried. What's going on?"

I gave her the full rundown of what happened when I woke up this morning to what the doctor told me. Down to the part where he told me that I wouldn't be able to prevent a miscarriage, which only made my heart break.

"Oh my God. How do you feel about this?"

"Honestly Mel, something clicked. Something changed inside me when I saw the blood. I was terrified I just let this baby down. I became extremely protective and guilty. I want this baby," I told her as I felt a tear trickle down my cheek and land on the comforter. She was silent on the other end. I didn't even hear a gasp from her. "Say something," I pleaded.

"Sorry, I'm just not sure what to say other than the fact that I'm happy you finally figured out what you want. You are going to be a great mom."

I let the tears of happiness roll down my cheeks. Hearing it from Melanie, my best friend, my rock, the sister I never had, made me realize it was real. This was all real.

"Thanks, Mel," I cried.

"Oh, don't cry. I need to hear more about your man candy before you start the water works."

I wiped the few tears that had fallen down my cheeks. "Man candy?"

"Yes. You heard me. Spill."

"I feel as though you should have plenty of man candy where you're at. You know, college and all?"

"Uh? No. That is college candy. While it's good to enjoy a few times a year, it loses its sweet flavor once it decides to be an obnoxious, video playing, college guy again," she replied.

"Oh geez. Well, *this* man candy is perfect. It's like he's permanently flavored sweet. I haven't found a sour moment yet," I said, teasing her.

"I can taste it now," she said. "Okay, I know you've tasted his lips, but what about…"

"MELANIE!" I exclaimed.

"Hey," she said. "I am just trying to get a good visual of the guy."

"I have a better idea then. Why don't you come out here?"

"Hmmm. That's actually not a bad idea. I don't have class the day after tomorrow. So I can come out then. Does that work?"

"Uh. YES!"

"Ha-ha, are you sure about this?"

"Um, more than sure. I want to see you badly. I'll talk to Trish, but I can honestly say as amazing as this family is, they would have no problem with you staying here for the night too. And if not, you can just stay at the motel, but with that one, I bid you good luck, and you'll be on your own."

"Perfect. It's planned, Cass. Let's just hope it's not the latter though. I'll need an address too."

"I'll have Jason text it to you, seeing how I'm not the best with directions these days," I said, rolling my eyes at myself.

"I can't tell you how excited I am to see you and this man candy you have. So you'll have to spill the beans about what else you've tasted when I get there, ya know?"

"Fine," I said, shaking my head. She wouldn't let it go, but I honestly could say I was more than eager to share with her all the moments I had spent with Jason.

"Can I at least get an inkling of what you two have been up to?"

"Well, there was this one moment we had. It was storming, our bodies were drenched from the rain, and there was an abandoned library and nothing to do. I think you can figure the rest out for yourself." I loved teasing her.

"Oh, hot damn, does he have a brother?" she asked, practically panting into the phone.

"As a matter of fact, he does, but I don't know much about him."

"Find some out before I see you, would ya?"

"You make it sound so easy. Whatever you say." I giggled.

"See you soon. Love you, and I'm glad you're okay. You had me really worried."

"I love you too," I replied before ending the call.

I could barely contain the excitement running through me, knowing I would get to see her soon. So much that I didn't even notice Jason leaning against the doorframe. Shit.

"You don't even need to tell me what you talked about because I heard it all, Sweetheart," he said in a husky voice as he sauntered over to me.

I could feel my cheeks getting hot as I slapped a hand over my face. Damn, damn, damn.

"I actually only heard the tail end. I just assumed you were talking about me because you looked so damn happy when you hung up."

He sat down on the bed and scooted up so his back was against the headboard. I looked over to him and was relieved to know he didn't hear me talking about our steamy library moment.

"I was, in fact, gossiping about you," I told him. "But I asked Mel if she would come down here. I miss her like all sorts of crazy right now and I think she is eager to meet you." I looked at him, hoping, and praying that it was okay she was coming down.

"As long as she doesn't have any knives in her hand and stays away from my manhood, I'm eager to meet her too."

"Do you think it would be okay if she stayed the night here? I hate to ask, or even impose, so if not I completely understand." I asked, scrunching my face as though I was asking my mother for something.

"Of course. Why wouldn't it be?"

"Really? She can share my bed with me, and you won't even know she is here."

"I have a better idea. How about you share a bed with me, and she can have your bed upstairs?" He popped a brow up as he asked me.

"Tempting," I said. "I think I like that. In fact, I like it a lot."

"Good, me too. When is she coming down?"

"The day after tomorrow," I replied.

"That works out perfectly. I was going to take you out tonight. I wanted to talk to you about a few things, but I would rather you just relax the rest of the day. So how about I take you out tomorrow night before she gets here?"

"Talk about what, Jase?" I eyed him with concern. He could have been saying anything, but it wouldn't have mattered. All I heard of what he just said was that he had to tell me something.

"There are just some things I want to talk about. A few things about me I want to share with you. I'm not a serial killer or anything, so get that out of your head." He let out a chuckle.

"That wasn't what I was thinking, but thanks for reassuring me. Okay then, tomorrow night, it's a date."

"Good, it's a date," he said as he lifted up his right arm. "Now get on over here so I can snuggle the shit out of you."

He didn't have to ask me twice. I scooted over to him and rested perfectly in the nook of his body. His arm wrapped around me and his hand rested on my waist as he pulled me closer to him. I could feel myself relaxing immensely as I closed my eyes and listened to his calm breathing and the rhythmic beat of his heart.

Chapter
twenty-nine

Mom said Mel was good to stay here tomorrow. I had to run out real quick, be back soon. Be ready for our date later.

Jase

I READ THE NOTE FROM Jason and couldn't help but feel like a kid that just got two cupcakes instead of one. The day was turning out too good. First, date night with Jason, and then my best friend was coming tomorrow. Before anything else though, I knew I had to check on something that was sitting in the front of my mind. It would not let me forget about what happened yesterday.

Once in the bathroom, I took a deep breath in because I wasn't ready to look, but I also knew in every beat of my heart that was racing that I needed an answer. I had no choice but to look down. Blood or no blood, I had to stay positive. I let the breath out and looked down and there it was, or rather wasn't. I felt like I had just won a small battle. The toilet paper was clean, spot free; there wasn't any blood. Holy shit. My body relaxed and a smile took over my once-worried expression.

I knew with certainty that after the scare I had yesterday, my heart now belonged to this baby. It was mine and I wasn't about to let it go without a fight. I was petrified though. I needed to speak to my mom, but she didn't even know I was pregnant so I couldn't talk to her yet. The only other person to talk to was Trish. I needed her. Jason was out running an errand, but I had to talk to her now. I had to know if my feelings of being mortified for what I was doing were normal or if it meant I was too weak to be a mom. I put on my running shoes and grabbed the front door key that Jason had left me in case of emergencies and started my journey to see Trish at the hospital.

Staying on my feet that long was probably not even remotely okay since I was told to take it easy, but I needed answers and the 'preplanning Cassandra' had to know what to do. I wasn't patient and it was showing. It only took me thirty minutes at a slow pace to walk to the hospital. It was hot which left me exhausted. I stepped through the front doors, immediately feeling the cool air-conditioning on my sweaty skin and stood for a moment enjoying it. I walked over to the front desk and the eyes of the nurse who was here yesterday caught mine.

"Cassandra, is everything okay?" she asked panicked.

Everyone in this small town seemed to already know me. "I'm fine. I just came here to see Trish. Is she around?"

The helpful nurse took me to the other side of the hospital toward the ER. That was one place that I've become all too familiar with.

"Trish? Cassandra is here to see you," she said as we walked by the ER check in desk.

Trish looked surprised. "What are you doing here, Sweetie? Did you walk?"

"Yes," I said ashamed. "I needed to talk to someone, to you. I need help... Please," I begged.

"Is it the baby? Are you still bleeding and having more cramps?"

"No." I shook my head. "My bleeding seemed to stop and so have the cramps. It's about the baby though. I need to talk through my feelings with to a real mom, someone like you. Someone who can tell me if what I'm feeling is normal," I told her, feeling the exhaustion finally catching up with me as I felt the need to sit down.

"Okay, come with me. You need to sit down; you shouldn't have walked here, Sweetie. I'll get you some water and then we can talk. Whatever you need, know that I'm here for you," she replied, taking us back into the staff lounge. She had me sit on the couch as she grabbed a bottle of water and then sat down next to me.

"I'm scared Trish. I'm more horrified than before, because now I want this baby. I want it more than anything, but I don't know how to overcome this fear that I'm not good enough to be its mom." I paused to drink more water. "I can't talk with my own mother because she doesn't know what's going on, let alone will she even accept the fact that I'm going to keep my baby and soon be a mother myself. She will never accept it. My heart hurts for this baby. How will I give it the life it deserves?"

She looked at me as if she knew something I didn't. "Congratulations, Cassandra. You're a mom. Worrying about your baby before anything else is what makes you a mother." She reached a hand over my shoulder and gave me a squeeze. Tears were running down my face as her words sunk in deep. I was a mother. "You'll never stop worrying, not even when they're adults. I was younger than you are when I was pregnant with my first. It's okay to be scared. Lord knows I was petrified and questioned everything. But when you hold your baby for the first time, all those fears, those questions, fly right out the window, because at that moment, nothing else in the world seems to matter. All you know is that you would do anything to protect and take care of this child of yours. Sweetie, you're going to be fine."

"I hope so. I want to be fine, and I want to know that everything is going to work out. Now that I know in my heart I want to keep it, I hope this baby is fine and I don't end up miscarrying."

"You have to trust that everything will work out, and it will," she said, grabbing my hand in hers, and squeezing it tightly. "I knew the minute I saw Jason come to the hospital to see you, he thought you were something special. That boy has the biggest heart I've ever seen, but the way he waited to see you and stuck around to make sure you were okay, he was drawn to you. And that's because you are something great and special. You may not see it or feel it, but you have a way of making the whole room light up."

"That's exactly how I feel about Jason. He's special and wonderful and I don't know what is going to become of all of this, but I don't want to lose him. He means so much to me." I felt something wet hit my hand and as I looked up at Trish. I saw them, the tears, dropping down one by one.

"Oh Trish, why are you crying?"

"Just talking about Jason, I just love him so much. You'll understand when you have your baby. There is no stronger love than the one you have for your child, Cassandra."

"I'm just such a mess right now. I'm not good for Jase. I dropped out of school. I'm pregnant. My parents don't have a clue about out any of this, and I'm in a town I've never even heard of. I'm so lost right now."

"You're not though, Sweetie. I think you're right where you need to be. No matter the girl, perfect or flawed, she's still the light of somebody's life. Jason knows this and whatever you think you are, he sees none of it. He sees your big heart, your brave face, and he also sees the side of you that needs someone to be there. He sees all of you and he hasn't run away yet. He's not like that."

"He's too good," I said, relieved to hear her confirming in her own words that Jason and I were good together.

"He's battling things too, but you both bring out so much good in each other. You don't even realize how much he's a different person when he's with you. Also, Sweetie, you can stay with us as long as you like. Just because your car will be done soon doesn't mean you have to leave. We all like having you here," she said, giving me another hug.

"I really appreciate it Trish, more than you'll ever know," I said, hugging her back. "I also wanted to thank you for allowing my friend to come here tomorrow night."

"Anything for you, Sweetie. Any friend of yours is a friend of ours. Jason told me she means a lot to you."

"She does. You have no idea how thankful I am that you are letting her stay and me too. I owe you guys so much."

"Like I said, anything for you, Sweetie and anytime you need to talk, I'm here for you," she said as we stood up and walked back to the front of the hospital.

"Thanks again." She was the rock of this family and she was suddenly becoming my rock too. I wished more than anything I had the courage to talk to my own mother the way I do with

Trish, but it wouldn't happen. I had to get that through my head. I had to be strong now, for my baby's sake.

"Okay honey, take my keys, and drive yourself home. No more of this walking business, you hear me," she said as she handed me her car keys.

I was ashamed that I walked the long way even after what happened yesterday, but it was important. The relief I felt now was far greater than I could have expected. The nerves were still there. The fear that I was going to be like my own mother was consuming me, but the happiness of knowing every mother had fears calmed me. "Thanks Trish, I won't be walking that far again. Trust me," I told her, rubbing my belly that was still flat with nothing to show, but I knew my blueberry was in there. It had to make it; it just had to.

"Trish?" A nurse from behind us grabbed her attention. "Jason is almost done. He asked to see you when he was finished."

Trish quickly shook her head to the other nurse. It felt weird, like it was something she didn't want to talk about in front of me.

"Jason's here? What is he almost done with?" I asked the nurse then looked over at Trish, who had trouble keeping her eyes on mine.

My stomach dropped, I knew immediately something was wrong. Something wasn't right about this.

"Almost done with what, Trish?" I demanded her to answer.

I could feel my breath getting more rapid as my heartbeat escalated so much that I could feel it through every pulse in my body. Something was horribly wrong. I looked at the other nurse who had her face down as if she had just been shamed, and looked back at Trish whose eyes were getting red. The look on her face was pleading with me to let this go. "I can't talk about it. Jason will be home soon," she said in a muffled voice.

That was all the confirmation I needed. I had to find him. I left the keys on the counter and walked away from the desk.

"Please don't do this." I heard Trish yell as I headed down the hall.

My heart sunk even further as I raced down the hall looking for any sign of Jason, his voice, his laugh, anything. There was nothing. Jason wasn't anywhere, but he had to be. The nurse said herself that he was almost done. I stopped and put my hands on my knees and took a breath. The only words that were racing through my mind were *'what's going on'*. I stood back up and could see Trish coming up behind me. I had to be close. Then I heard his voice and my heart stopped. He was down the hall to the right. I looked back and saw that Trish had stopped. She knew I wouldn't let this go. She knew it was only a matter of time until I found him. I walked up, could see the partially open door, and heard a woman's voice.

"She sounds wonderful, Jason."

"Colleen, you have no idea," I heard him reply.

I took a few more steps until I was in front of the door. I took another deep breath and read the sign on the door. Dialysis. I panicked and pushed the door all the way open so that I was able to see him.

"Oh my God," I gasped. Jason sat in a chair, hooked up to a machine and tubes were coming out of his arm.

"Cassie?" he asked in disbelief that I was standing in front of him. He clearly wasn't expecting to see me.

"Jason?" I breathed out quietly; I put my hands over my mouth as I started to back up.

"Damn it!" he yelled as he closed his eyes.

I shook my head in disbelief as I did the only thing I knew how to these days. I ran. I ran straight into Trish, who had tears running rapid down her face.

"What is going on Trish?"

"He has kidney failure, Sweetie," she said through her soft sobs.

My knees buckled beneath me and I fell to the floor. "No, no, no, this can't be happening!" I screamed in anger. My heart was racing, my breathing was hard, and my mind was spinning. I could feel my insides knotting and pulling as *kidney failure* kept repeating in my brain. I pulled my numb body from the floor and could feel it again. The need to run. I put my hand over my mouth and panicked as I searched for a trashcan, but it was too late. Everything, every feeling, every tear, every moment of my time here with Jason came up, releasing all over the floor in front of me. The heaving was violent and rough as it took me back down to the floor with it.

"Oh my God," I cried, releasing the tears that were stinging behind my eyes.

Trish walked up next to me and reached her hand out for me to take. "Cassandra, let's talk, but you need to calm down first. Think about your baby."

"You will not tell me to calm down right now. This is what he's been hiding from me, isn't it? That's why he keeps leaving for 'errands' too, ISN'T IT?" My emotions were high, my chest was heavy, and my temper was meant for Jason, not for Trish. I felt horrible for taking it out on her but I was hurting. I lifted my head to see her nod yes to all the questions I was asking her. I broke down in sobs again. I wanted to know more. I had to know what was wrong, but my body was weak and in pain. I didn't know if I was able to hear the truth about him, about the guy I accidentally found, the guy I grew too fond of in only a matter of a week. I didn't know if I could bear to hear what she was about to tell me. I slammed my fists on the floor and screamed out in pain with all that I had in me.

"Cassie!" I heard Jason yell from behind me. I got up as quickly as I could and made a dash for a bathroom. I continued to hear his footsteps behind me as I ran inside. It was a single bathroom, so I locked the door and slid down it, pulling my knees up to my chest, letting my tears soak my legs as I wept.

"Please, Sweetheart, we need to talk," he yelled through the door. I grabbed tightly onto my legs. Hearing his voice only made matters worse. It made my heart break for every time I asked him if he was okay. For every time I knew in my heart that something was wrong and how he kept it inside, only for me to find out this way.

"Jason, just give her some time. I'll give her my keys. She'll come home when she's ready." I heard Trish tell him.

"I'm not leaving. I'm staying until she comes out," he replied.

"She needs time, Jason. Go home. Wait for her there." Trish spoke with authority this time. She meant what she said; she knew what I needed. Unfortunately, I didn't know if I would ever come out of this bathroom. I heard a fist slam against the wall next to the door and then their footsteps faded away. I lifted my head up, taking a quick breath.

"Ouch," I felt a mild cramp in my abdomen. I grabbed my stomach and tried to calm myself down. It was hard. It was almost impossible but I was trying. I stretched out my legs in front of me and kept my hand on my stomach.

"Baby, this is your mom. Please don't give up on me. I'm not going to give up on you. You have to calm down with me. I need you right now. I need you to stay inside me. I need you to make it, or I don't think I will. Please baby, for mommy," I said as I looked down at my stomach.

I rubbed my hand gently across my little blueberry and rested my head on the door behind me. I closed my eyes and tried with all my might to see nothing, but it was hopeless. Staring back at me were those emerald eyes that I'd grown so accustomed to seeing every day. His long lashes moving up and down as he blinked over his green gems. I finally knew the sadness hiding behind them. I didn't know what I originally thought he kept hidden from me, but kidney failure was not it. I kept my eyes closed as I stared back at the green ones in my mind. They weren't going anywhere and neither was I. My body needed to relax; I had to take this time to prepare for what I would be dealing with when I saw Jase back at the house. I wasn't ready to face him or his secrets that weren't secrets anymore.

I heard a soft voice behind me on the other side of the door. It was Trish. "Cassandra?"

I listened to the dripping faucet as each drop of water hit the sink in perfect rhythm. I heard each splat of water hit a hundred times or more before I realized how much time had probably passed when Trish interrupted the focus I had on the faucet.

"Sweetie, are you okay?"

"No, Trish. I'm not," I told her honestly.

"Can you come out? You need to get to a bed so you can rest honey. Please? For me," she begged quietly through the door.

My choice was either staying in here on this hard bathroom floor or going back to a nice comfortable bed and possibly seeing Jason before I was able to get some rest. I had to take my chances. I wasn't ready to talk to him yet, but my back was hurting and my body was craving a bed. "Okay Trish, I'll come out," I replied. I slowly stood up and opened the door.

She was standing there with her keys in her hand, her face red and eyes swollen. I felt guilty for knowing my actions made her cry.

"Here you go, Sweetie," she said quietly as she handed me the keys. "Please drive carefully."

I took the keys from her hands. I gave her the only smile in me that I could find. It felt small, pathetic, and forced. I drove myself to their house, pulling into the gravel drive next to Jason's truck. He was home and hopefully in his room.

I unlocked the door and walked inside. The house was quiet, almost too quiet, but at least he wasn't sitting in the front room waiting for me. I let out a breath of relief, shut the door behind me, and made my way to my room. My door was still closed as I left it this morning. I opened the door, ready to just lie in my bed and cry the night away when my heart jumped into my throat. He sat on my bed with his head in his hands. He heard me come into the room and lifted his head. His eyes puffy and swollen, his face had agony written all over it.

"We need to talk," he said quietly.

I shook my head. I didn't want to do this now; I didn't think I could handle anything else filtering my brain. The words *'kidney failure'* were taking up too much space in there. Unfortunately, words came spewing out without even giving me a chance to fight them back.

"Why didn't you tell me? Why would you fucking keep this a secret from me?"

"I was going to tell you tonight. That's why I wanted to take you out. I knew I needed to tell you."

"You could have told me sooner. You had every opportunity under the sun to say, *"Hey Cassandra, by the way, I have kidney failure."* You don't just keep something like that from me."

"You really want to know why I kept it from you for so long?"

"Yes. I think I've made that very clear."

Jason stood up from my bed and made his way over to me, coming close, but keeping a good amount of distance between us. I crossed my arms over my chest, gripping my hands on my arms as tightly as possible as I waited for his answer.

"I didn't want you treating me like I was sick like everyone else in this fucking town. I loved the way you looked at me as if I was *your* hero. For once, I had someone treat me like Jason. Not the guy who was sick and had to be treated three days a week, and not like I was going to shatter into pieces every time I took a step on the sidewalk. You made me feel more alive than I've ever felt before. I should have told you, but I didn't want to because I love the way you made me feel."

I shook my head. Nothing in me comprehended the words coming out of him. All I could concentrate on was what happened when I saw him at the hospital. Finding out the way I did completely surprised me, and in the worst possible way.

"I'm sorry, but I don't even know what to say right now. I need to be alone. Please get out Jason," I told him as I turned my head so I was looking at anything but him.

"It's *Jase*," he smirked before slamming my door shut on his way out.

He could have slammed it a thousand times, harder each time and it still wouldn't match the anger and pain I felt inside. My heart ached, burned, and felt speared by the sharpest of daggers. I felt each and every slash it made as my heart was being ripped slowly from my chest. I threw my phone on the bed and then followed it. As my head sank into the pillow face first, I bawled my eyes out for the pain my heart was enduring and for the way I just spoke to Jason. Neither of which I wanted to feel or do ever again.

After the salty tears had soaked my pillowcase and the sobs had stopped, I took a moment to breathe. I grabbed the drenched pillow, tossed it to the side, and rolled myself over on my back. I took in each breath through my nose and exhaled it through my mouth. I closed my eyes and placed my arms on either side of me. My body felt paralyzed as I laid there, unable to think of what to do or where to go next. Unfortunately, I knew what I needed to do and I could feel the pull my brain was having on my heart, telling me, yelling at me to go speak to him, to find out more of what was really going on. Little by little, I pulled myself up from the bed and perched on the edge, letting my feet touch the floor. They were coming; the tears and sobs were back and approaching quickly as I thought about what I was going to do. What I was about to let myself hear if he would tell me. I honestly wasn't going to give him a choice. He owed me the truth; he owed my breaking heart the truth. I stood up and tried fiercely to keep the sobs back as I walked out my door and through the empty house, making my way to his room. The further I went, the harder it was to contain myself, and when I finally reached his door, the control I had over my sobs had vanished. I let myself have a few moments before I grabbed the handle to his door and turned it, pushing it open.

Chapter
thirty

I LOOKED AT HIM. His eyes were swollen and red, and his face was splotchy like mine. We were a pair right here. A pair of sobbing, frightened people who were no longer strangers. We were brought together by my accident and now I understood why. We had a connection far greater than mutual attraction; we were both brought together for deeper reasons. I was running from my past because it threatened my future and he was hiding from his future because of his past and the threat it had on his unknowing future. We could have been strangers or best friends, but nothing would bring us closer than this moment we were about to share. I took in a deep breath as I approached his bed.

"I need to know everything," I told him through the hard cries that were convulsing through my body.

"Come here, Sweetheart." There it was, his soft voice. The one that let me know he was going to tell me, that I didn't even have to fight him for the truth.

"I want you right here." He lifted his blankets for me to get in. "In my bed with me. If I'm going to tell you what's going on, I need you right next to me so I can hold on to you."

If that didn't make my already soaked eyes release more tears, I didn't know what could. I was a blubbering mess and beyond consolable. I climbed in bed, putting my body so close to his that there was barely any room between us for a blade of grass. I laid my head down on the pillow and looked up at him.

His arm bent and his head was resting in his hand, he was lying on his side, his body open to where I laid next to him. He looked deep in my eyes, and pulled me even closer.

"I didn't mean to yell at you," I told him quietly as he kept his hand on my waist.

"It's okay. You're scared. Believe me; I get it."

"Is that what you meant when you told me you knew scared eyes when you saw them?"

He closed his eyes as a few tears trickled down his cheeks. "When we first found out my kidneys were failing, all I ever saw in everyone's eyes, including my own looking back at me in the mirror, was fear. It was horrifying, and then when I saw the same damn look in your eyes, I knew it wasn't just the accident that had you scared. I knew it was something else and I didn't want you to have to be alone, because it always helped me and my family that we had each other. You needed someone with you and I wanted it to be me."

"I don't even know what to say, but you have no idea how grateful I was to have you there."

"I know." His hand moved from my waist and cupped my cheek, his thumb caressing my skin. "Are you ready for the story?"

"As ready as I'll ever be," I told him. I was scared. No, I was *fucking* scared of what I was about to hear. I didn't want to hear it. I wanted to just close my eyes and fall asleep in his arms again, smell his familiar scent the whole night as I dreamt of what it would be like to stay with him forever. That was not the reality though; this was. I had to hear *his* story.

He inhaled deeply and let it out slowly. "You remember when I told you about my brother?"

"Yeah," I said confused as to where he was going with this.

"He's fine, well, not fine. He and my parents are not on speaking terms right now. That's why he remains unseen. That's a story for another day. But the point I'm trying to make is that..." He inhaled again, struggling to get the words out. "Sorry, it's just been a long time since I've talked about this."

I snuggled closer to him, grabbed the hand that was cupping my cheek, and held onto it tightly. "I'm here and I'm not going anywhere."

He let a smile spread across his tear-stricken face as he squeezed my hand. "My brother was big into sports. He was really good at them too. We always went to his high school games to cheer him on. My parents were busy with work, the farm, and my brother. They were trying to get him a scholarship for college. The money wasn't there to send him without one. I was only fourteen when he started his senior year of high school. Mom and dad were busy, and I didn't mind because I kept busy helping at the farm and our hardware store. I kept getting more and more exhausted, but I didn't stop working because I knew our parents needed my help if we were going to get my brother into college. I wanted him to go, probably more than he did." He started to chuckle a little. "I was a very proud, younger brother and I couldn't wait to go visit him at college. In the meantime, we were busy taking care of Grandma Maggie because a year prior we'd lost my Grandpa Art." He peered down at me. I nodded, letting him know I remembered whom he was talking about. I could never forget Maggie. "He died of a stroke. He rarely took his medication, and they believe that his high blood pressure led to the stroke." He paused to take in a breath. "I'm sure you get the point that we were a busy family, so when I started to feel pain in my back and on my sides, I didn't say anything. I kept trudging on. I didn't want the family to have to worry about me on top of everything else."

I put my hand over my eyes. I didn't want to hear this. I didn't want to hear how he felt he was a burden to others so he kept his pain inside. "I can't hear this, Jase," I said weeping.

His hand pulled mine away from my eyes and he gripped it tight in his, placing it between us. "It's okay, I'm not going anywhere. I'm right here," he whispered. "It wasn't until halfway through the school year that it got worse. I had blood in my urine, and the pain was now excruciating, so I had trouble hiding it. I finally went to my mom who took me to the emergency room. She thought it was a urinary tract infection or possibly a kidney stone. After testing for those and coming up with nothing, they did an imaging scan and saw two cysts on my kidneys. With a lot of doctor visits, probing and prodding, and too many tests to count, we learned the cysts are from a hereditary kidney disease that came from my father's side. Even though Grandpa Art died from a stroke, the problems were created from this disease he didn't know he had because he was too stubborn to go to the doctors. My father then passed it along to me. He has the gene but hasn't developed the symptoms, which is why we never knew about it. My case is rare since I developed symptoms so early. I spent the remainder of high school in and out of the hospital." He stopped to wipe the tears pouring out of my eyes once again.

I clung to him as he spoke, unable to fully digest it all, and yet completely understanding why he was the way he was. My heart was hurting, breaking at the seams as each word slipped out of his mouth.

"So what will happen to your dad?" I asked, scared to hear the answer.

"I don't know. He may live the rest of his life without ever having the symptoms and then again, he could. He goes for regular checkups with his doctors and monitors his blood pressure, which could increase with his symptoms. So right now, he's good."

"This is a lot to take in. I couldn't imagine hearing all of this when you were so young."

"You have no idea. I'll never forget being in the hospital as they were trying to figure out what was wrong with me, thinking that I should have spoken up sooner. But I had the family with me and that helped. I grew to hate that damn place though."

"It makes sense now. I wish you had told me. I could hit you. I'm so mad that you kept this from me, but I understand. I really do," I told him.

"I know. I should have told you sooner."

"What happened next?" I asked him.

"My brother did get a scholarship but he declined. Toward the end of his senior year, I needed a kidney transplant because mine were functioning at less than ten percent. He stayed with me every step of the way, and then he did the bravest thing he could have ever done. He offered up his kidney. At first, we weren't sure if it would work because he could be a carrier of the gene too, but as luck would have it, he wasn't. I was thankful too. I didn't want to have to watch my hero, my brother, go through this same disease. After match testing, we found out his blood type and mine were the same, so the kidney transplant was a go. My brother gave me his kidney. He acted as if it was the easiest thing in the world for him to do, but to me, it was the most courageous thing he could have ever done for me. I thanked him every day for giving me a piece of him that improved my life. He always told me it was nothing, that it was the least he could do, and that he would give me any organ I ever needed to save my life. It broke his heart and mine when just last year the kidney stopped functioning. It was quick for a living donor kidney to go that fast, but I guess it was just in the cards I was dealt. I'm on the waiting list and now under full dialysis until I get another kidney."

"The errands you've been running? They're because of dialysis?" I closed my eyes, seeing him back in the hospital hooked up to the machine.

"Yeah, I have to go three times a week for about four hours each time. I am lucky that, even though it's a small hospital, I was able to get a dialysis machine there. They bring in a special technician three days a week to be there with me for the treatments. It costs a lot of money. That's why we had to sell the farm. I couldn't work there anymore because of the pain I would be in some days because the cysts were growing and making my kidneys larger than normal. We had to pay for everything, and the only way to do it was to start selling off things, the hardware shop included."

"Seriously Jason, I don't know how much more I can take. This is too much to listen to." I cried into the pillow as his hand brushed strands of my hair behind my ear.

"There are some good things. Like when I received my kidney from my brother, it was like a whole new world. I still had to watch myself carefully, eat more salads." He winked. I tried to give him a small smile, but my heart was in too much pain. "I take more pills than an eighty-year-old man, not to mention I have to watch out for cyst bleeds. But things were going okay. So I decided with the encouragement of my family, and especially my brother, to enroll and take a few classes at the community college in Lamar, the only college around. It's about forty five minutes away."

"Those are the college courses you were talking about," I said, starting to piece together the answers he gave me when we first met.

"It was, but it was getting to be too much for me. I struggled with making sure I was okay, dealing with abdominal pain, the pills, and the dietary restrictions. I started to panic and those scared eyes I saw too many times in myself were back. I couldn't do it. So after my first year, I left and came back home. I tried to help out, but Mom and Dad wouldn't let me. I argued until they let me work at the hardware shop on the weekends. In fact–" he paused to look down at me, "–Moose and his family purchased it so that we could keep our family name on it. They let my father and me work there too. They're a good family."

"That's the sweetest thing I've ever heard," I replied, thinking of how special Moose was to him and this family. He had a special place in my heart too.

"There are people with this hereditary disease that are far worse off than I am, and then those that don't even show symptoms. It all just varies case by case. I'm doing the best I can with it. Some days, I wish that it would just take me already, and other days, when I take a moment to appreciate everything around me, I'm glad it hasn't. I don't know what my future holds, and honestly, I don't want to know. What I want is to enjoy each moment that I do have because that's what I've been given."

"What will happen next? I need to know." I asked, not knowing if I was ready for his answer.

"I don't have a timestamp, Sweetheart. People can be on dialysis for a long time. Some get other complications. With my disease, I can have a lot go wrong; we just always have to prepare for the worst but hope for the best. I was supposed to get a kidney last week. When you saw my mother crying, it was because the kidney went to another person. So, I had to break the news to my mom. It's coming. I know it is, but in the meantime I have had the best time of my life being here with you."

I wiggled out of the hold he had on me and sat up. I knew what I had to do.

"I will give you my kidney. I will get tested to see if I'm a match," I said, hoping I was a match.

He rolled on his back, and put his hands under his head. "Sweetheart, you're pregnant. I wouldn't take one from you anyway. You have a baby to take care of now."

"But there has to be something I can do to help Jason. Please, what can I do?" I pleaded with him. I had to know how I could help save him.

He chuckled and pulled me down so I was cradled right next to him. I rested my head on his chest as he put his arm around me, holding me tight. "You're already doing it. Here I was thinking that I was helping you, saving you from your problems. But I haven't felt more alive since the day I received my first kidney. Your being here has shown me how little I've been living all these years."

I glanced up at him; his green eyes were no longer glossy with tears. "Funny, being here with you has shown me how little I've been living too. Only living for everyone else and regretting things in my past, but you've changed my mind about everything I thought I once knew," I said.

"Then I guess it's a good thing we found each other."

"You have no idea how grateful I am for crashing my car. It led me to you." I propped myself up on my elbow, raising my head up so my lips were directly across from his.

His eyes gleamed and his lips moved just a tad closer to mine. "You get to tease about crashing, but I can't tease you?"

"Exactly," I said, keeping my lips close, but still not touching his.

"Typical woman." He took his hand and placed it behind my head, tangling his fingers in my hair. "How about if I say that I want to crash my lips onto yours? Is that use of the word *crash* allowed?"

"I think that would definitely be allowed," I said softly.

"Good, because I wasn't going to take no for an answer," he said, mimicking the softness of my voice.

He brought up his other hand, tangling it in my hair as he *crashed* our lips together. This was more than a good form of crashing. He untangled one hand and pulled me so I was now laying comfortably on top his body. He continued kissing me, but it grew softer and less hungry. His lips gently pressed against mine, and each time, he would open his mouth just enough to let our tongues delicately touch for seconds at a time. It felt like teasing, but it was, in fact, all too pleasing. I loved when he kissed me with hunger and passion, but there was something to be said for gentle, tender kisses. He slowly drew his lips from mine before kissing me one last time, pulled the extra pillow over, and moved it to prop up his head. He wrapped an arm tight around my waist and he held me there. I looked up at his gorgeous eyes.

"You make crashing very enthralling."

"You make it easy," he said, placing a sweet kiss on my forehead.

"Thank you for telling me. For opening up to me about what's going on."

"Thank you for giving me the chance to explain."

I couldn't believe I was mad at him for keeping this from me. It seemed so trivial now that I realized I could have let my emotions get in the way of what Jason was battling. He would never grasp how thankful I was for him filling me in on everything from the beginning to where he was at today. None of it eased my feelings on how scared I still was for him. What he was going through frightened me to my very core. He said he didn't have a time stamp, which was sometimes worse than having one. I could only pray to anyone wanting to listen to me how much I needed this man to stay alive for his family and for me.

I lowered my head and laid my cheek against his chest as he held me in place. For a day that started out well, happy even, it turned unbearable quickly, only to end where it should. I thought about the ending, for the ending was all that mattered. I remembered Jason telling me, *"Because in the end, everything will be okay. It has to be."* And for tonight, it was. I closed my eyes as I listened to his ever-soothing heartbeat.

Chapter
thirty-one

I PLACED EVERYTHING THAT I once put away per Jason's request back into my suitcase. It didn't take long for me to pack up my belongings as I zipped my suitcase closed. It was time. I couldn't be away from him a second longer. I quietly hauled all of my things downstairs to his room. I set my suitcase down by his dresser. It was early in the morning, so his room was just starting to get light from the sun. And from what I could see, he was still in bed.

I barely slept last night while thoughts of yesterday flittered through my head. It would be impossible to sleep upstairs knowing that he was down here. Knowing that he needed me just as much as I needed him tore at me. I wanted to spend every moment that I could with this sweet man.

I inched my way over to his bed and slid under the covers, filling the spot that I was in before. I felt his hand slip around my waist as he pulled me closer to him.

"You were gone for a while. You feeling okay?" he asked in his husky morning voice.

"I'm feeling okay, a little nauseous, but not too bad this morning. I just had to take care of something," I answered, slightly unsure of how he would take me moving down to his room.

"Would it have anything to do with the suitcase you just brought down? You're not leaving me are you?"

"How did you know about my suitcase?"

"I heard you set something heavy down over there, so I just took a wild guess. Unless you're the one I should be worrying about and you just brought down a dead body."

"Definitely not the crazy one. Although you might think I'm crazy for this, but I can't be without you anymore. I don't want to spend one more minute upstairs when I could be down here instead. So to answer your questions, yes, it was my suitcase, and no, I'm most definitely not leaving you. In fact, it's quite the opposite."

"Not the answer I was expecting," he replied as he brushed a hand against my cheek. "But I'd be lying if I didn't say that I've wanted to have you bring your stuff down here for a while now."

"Well, in that case, consider your room officially taken over," I said.

"Well, in that case, consider it okay," he replied back before placing his lips on my forehead. "My room welcomes you with open arms. You can use everything except the bottom right dresser drawer." He looked at me like a parent, telling me the one thing in a room of fun that I couldn't play with.

I searched his face for a moment, waiting for the 'I'm just teasing' to come out, but it never did. "You realize that you just told the person that you called nosey when we first met to stay out of a certain drawer. Why on earth would you trust me? Not to mention, I don't like it when you keep secrets. They aren't the easiest to take." I frowned at him.

He put his hand on my waist and slid it under my cami, gently tracing circles with his finger on my bare skin. "There is nothing hidden in there. It's just personal items that I'm not ready to share yet. And I do trust you because you've had every opportunity to go through my whole house to look for things, and I know you haven't. What's in the drawer is nothing secretive. It's only personal. I have nothing to hide from you. You never have to worry about that again, okay?" His hand had stopped making circles on my skin and was holding me tightly.

"Okay, I believe you," I told him. Even though I believed him, I also had a hard time not knowing what was in the drawer. I needed to show him he could trust me, and honestly, he could. He was right; I had many opportunities and didn't take one of them. I was changing, and for the better.

"So," he said quietly. "Doesn't someone come down today?" His eyebrow arched.

My eyes widened and I put a hand over my agape mouth. Oh. My. God.

"You forgot? Melanie is not going to like that," he said.

"I honestly can't believe I forgot," I said, shaking my head. "My thoughts have been elsewhere." My smile slowly faded as my heart knew the reason why my brain had been so consumed. It hurt even worse when I realized I was going to have to fill her in.

"Hey, Sweetheart," he said, pulling his hand from my waist. He put a finger under my chin, raising my head to look at him. "It'll be okay." His eyes were serious and his lips were pressed together. He truly thought everything was going to be all right all of the time. I wish I had just an ounce of the positivity he had.

"Or if you rather, just don't tell her," he said teasingly. "It worked for a little bit with you."

I frowned and pulled his finger from my chin. "You better be joking right now," I said, giving him a stern look.

"I was only teasing," he said, bringing his hand back to my face and pulling me in for a soft kiss on the lips. "She'll probably be here soon though, so we might want to—" I placed my finger over his lips and cut him off.

"She will most definitely be here soon but I just want five minutes. Five minutes of this," I said, pointing between us. "Okay?"

His eyes found mine, and in a matter of seconds, his lips did too. I knew right then that my five minutes were approved. He knew what I was after and he was delivering. His hand slipped under my cami again, slowly inching higher and higher until he reached one of my taut peaks. My skin erupted with goose bumps as he gently massaged it, puckering my nipples even more. He had the most tender touch. It was the perfect amount of pressure from his hands and lips. They had a way of running tingles from my head to my toes and every place in between. He had my whole body on edge, as every inch of me was sensitive to his affections and thought-out touch or kiss.

His lips left mine as he slowly sat up. The satisfied look on his face was apparent as he took the bottom of my cami and lifted it over my head. I ached to be touched again, which I found unusual because my breasts were very sensitive from the pregnancy. He clearly had a magical way of making them throb for his touch. He straddled my body, his hard-on settling right where I needed it. A soft moan escaped as I felt him pressed against me. His lips grinned before he sealed them against mine. One hand held his weight up, and the other went back to my breast. I took my hands and ran them across his back, using my fingers to lightly trace circles or other random shapes. My mind was in a fog as his tongue continued to stroke against mine. I stopped tracing and gripped his back harder as his lips devoured my neck, making their way to my chest. They were almost there when my phone started making noises next to his on the nightstand.

He lifted his lips off my skin and took in a deep breath. "Time's up, Sweetheart," he said, batting his eyelids over his sultry green eyes.

"Damn it," I said breathlessly.

Jason reached over to the nightstand and handed me my phone. I looked at the screen. There were two text messages, both from Melanie.

4:45am On my way, can't wait to see you

8:21am In town. Be there in a few

Holy shit! I knew she was as eager to see me as was I to see her, but I didn't expect her to leave that early in the morning. Either way, my best friend would be here in mere minutes. I set my phone down to the side.

"Maybe you should tell her to just come tomorrow instead," he said as he placed several kisses on my swollen lips.

"I would. I *so* would, but she'll be here any minute. She's right down the street," I said as he looked down at me like I was joking. "She's really excited to be here," I said, trying hard to contain myself, but the look on his face was hysterical.

"Apparently. She doesn't waste any time." He slowly got off the bed. "Well then, I'd say it's definitely time to get ready. You might want this back." He tossed me the cami he pulled off earlier.

"Probably a good idea," I said. "Hey, is your mom home today?"

He glanced up like he was trying to remember. "No, she should be home around seven tonight. Why?"

"I just wanted her to meet Melanie. I guess we'll have to do meet and greet at seven then."

"Sounds perfect. I'm going to take a quick, cold shower. I'll come upstairs when I'm done." He curled his lips up to the side before walking out and closing the door behind him.

I couldn't help but laugh at the thought of him taking a cold shower. I needed one too, but I didn't have much time. I quickly grabbed a hair tie, threw my hair in a bun, and put on a bra, a tee shirt, and a pair of cotton shorts before heading upstairs. My heart was racing like I was about to start some sort of championship game. It was like the nerves had settled in, realizing that she would be here any second. I peeked through the front curtain; she still wasn't here. These were officially the longest few minutes of my life. I stopped myself as soon as I noticed I was pacing in front of the window. Not even five minutes later, she was pulling up to the house. The minute I saw her car park, all my nerves disappeared and pure excitement set in. I screamed like the excited girl I was and flew through the front door. I ran to Melanie who was running to me, meeting halfway as we threw our arms around each other. One would have thought this was a reunion of two people that hadn't seen one another in years; truth was, it had only been a couple of months, but it didn't matter. It could have been only a week and the enthusiasm would still be the same.

After what felt like the longest, tight-gripped hug we could have had, we pulled away and the relief I had when I saw her face produced instant tears. Or, it could have been the hormones. Either way, the tears trickled down. "I missed you so much," I said as I wiped the tears off my cheeks.

She wiped the tears that trickled from under her aviator sunglasses and smiled back at me. "I missed you more."

We hugged one last time before retrieving her small overnight bag and heading inside.

"It's okay that I stay here, right? Or should I take my bag to the motel you made sound all too appealing?" she asked with a smirk.

I was getting ready to answer her when I saw Jason walking down the hall toward us. I looked over at Mel whose face went from excited to stunned and awe. It seemed she couldn't fully grasp how attractive Jason really was. He wore a striped, short-sleeved, button-up shirt tucked into his delicious, ass-shaping jeans that sat perfectly on his hips. His biceps looked mouthwatering in that shirt, not to mention the cowboy boots and cowboy hat that completed the look. I couldn't help but stare at him too. I saw him a lot, dressed just as good as this, but something about just stopping to admire how gorgeous he really was made me appreciate him even more. I honestly could keep my eyes on him all day, every day, and never get bored.

"Melanie, I presume. It's nice to finally meet you. I'm Jason. And yes, it's more than okay that you stay here," he said, interrupting our apparent gawking as he put his hand out in front of Mel.

Both Mel and I snapped out of our trances. She gave a look that said more than words could ever say. She had just been caught and was clearly mortified. I tried to contain myself as she tried to recover for herself.

She cleared her throat and shook his hand. "I really appreciate you inviting me to stay, Jason. It's good to meet you and to finally put a face to the voice," she said.

"You too," he replied.

"Uh, I need to use the restroom, Cass. It was a long trip," she said, looking over at me.

"At least you didn't get lost," I told her which only made Jason smirk. "Down the hall, first door on your right."

"Thanks. I'll be right back." She scurried off quickly down the hall.

I sauntered over to Jason, wrapping my arms around his waist as I looked up at his still amused face. "What?" I asked coyly.

"Not what I was expecting."

"What do you mean?" I asked.

"She has some harsh words for a girl that looks like that."

I knew exactly what he meant now. She wasn't what you'd expect from only hearing her voice. Her appearance was very polished. Her face was like porcelain. She had big brown eyes. Her hair was a perfect shade of chocolate brown. Her petite stature would never give away her bossy, say what she wants, no fear personality. At first glance, you saw a princess; after she opened her mouth, you witnessed her transform to a sailor. I never understood it. I really didn't care; she won me over the day we met in elementary school. She didn't tolerate bullies, so I always assumed that was why she was the way she was. Or it could have been her parents, the reason she wanted to go to college so damn far away. They weren't like mine. Instead, they didn't care enough about their daughter.

"Harsh words?" I asked, unhooking my hands from his waist and moving to the side of him.

"Uh, yeah. Let's just leave it at that." He chuckled.

"I heard the whole damn conversation, kids. Your walls are paper thin, Jason. Yes, Cass, I used harsh words. I threatened his head, and I'm not talking about the one with a brain. I'm going to protect my friend no matter how cute she says the guy is." Melanie raised a brow with a smirk on her face.

"What? She only called me cute?" Jason looked over at me, slightly blushing, but not nearly as much as I was.

"So, this is fun," I said, trying to break up the embarrassment.

"Don't worry Jason. She used plenty more words to describe you, but no need to embarrass her any more than I already have." She looked over at me and winked. "Not to mention the fact that she never talks about the guys she likes, so consider yourself special." The look on Melanie's face was that of pure enjoyment. She would get hers; one of these days, I was going to be sure to put her through the same thing. For now, all I could do was be glad that my friend was here. No matter the embarrassment, I loved her more than words could say.

We walked into the kitchen and sat down at the table.

"What's the plan?" she asked, her eyes switching from Jason's to mine.

I looked at Jason. "The look on your face says you have a plan, but I know you well enough now to know you don't make plans," I said with an arched brow.

"Well, Sweetheart, I did make plans for today. I'm going to help Moose out with a few things at the shop so you ladies can catch up. I'll be back this afternoon, and then I was thinking we'd go to dinner later." He gave us both a questioning glance as he awaited our responses.

I looked over at Mel as she shrugged. "Doesn't matter to me. I'm just along for the ride," she said.

"This is certainly new for you," I said, teasing him. "But it sounds perfect."

He put his hands on the table, stood up, and looked over at Mel. "Nice to meet you again."

"You too, Jason," she said, eyeing him once again.

"And you," he said, as he walked over to me, placing a kiss on my forehead. "I'll see you later. Have fun ladies."

I noticed we both watched his backside as he walked down the hall and out the door.

Melanie turned back to me. "Moose?" she questioned.

"The friend who kept interrupting our moments." I reminded her.

"Ah, yes, Moose. The cockblocker. Damn friend," she said, making us both chuckle.

"God, I've missed you."

"Me too," she replied. "I mean that I missed you, not myself."

I laughed at her. "You need some coffee?"

"Like you wouldn't believe."

"Alright, I'll start the pot for you and then I'm going to take a quick shower, glam myself up a bit. You can settle in and have your coffee. The room you are sleeping in is the last one on the right."

She nodded as we got up from the table. "Why aren't we just sharing a room? Or are we?"

I bit down on my lower lip. "Um, no, we're not." I quickly scurried away from her as I got the coffee started.

"How many rooms are there?"

"Three," I mumble, watching her calculate in her head, and seeing her figure out that I was most definitely sharing a room, just not with her.

"You little vixen you," she gasped. "Well, I can't say that I blame you. I'm gonna need a damn fan every time he's around. Normally, cowboys don't do it for me, but he's hot."

I turned around and couldn't help but smile as I thought of him. It wasn't just that he was sexy and looked great in clothes and without for that matter. It was how he treated me; he was pure sweetness. It was like every candy shop in the world bottled up all their sweets and poured it into him. I didn't think he had a bad bone in his body. I'd also never felt a connection like this with anyone before, one where my body turned into a puddle of mush every time he was around. I couldn't wait to see where this relationship would take us in the future. My heart fluttered as I thought of the possibilities. And then my heart sank as I thought of his struggles and the secret he'd kept from me. I needed to fill Mel in on it. I'd tell her later today. I put a coffee mug on the counter and quietly shuffled out of the kitchen.

"I'll be right back," I mumbled to her.

She pushed her brows together a bit before she said okay and poured herself a cup of coffee.

I wrapped the towel around my body and walked out of the bathroom.

"What's wrong?" Melanie asked as she sat on the floor opposite the bathroom door, sipping her coffee.

I looked down at her, trying to decide if right here, right now was the time to tell her what I knew. Standing naked under a towel didn't seem to be the appropriate time.

"I know something's wrong. I know because you look like someone just ran over your cat."

"I don't have a cat," I reminded her, trying to keep my voice from cracking.

She tilted her head to the side. "Fine, your *dog* then."

"I don't have a dog, either, Mel."

She stood, her angry eyes meeting mine. "Oh my God. You look like someone just ran over your fucking fake pet, and you're going to burst into tears at any moment. What is going on?" Her voice was softer as she walked closer to me.

"It's not an animal or something fake that's hurt, Mel. It's…" I swallowed, trying to get the lump in my throat to go away, but it was no use. It balled up tighter. "It's Jason."

"What?" Her eyes stunned.

"I need to tell you what's going on with him. I don't want to, but I do. I need my friend to tell me everything is going to be okay." Crying, I fell against her, and she wrapped her arms tightly around me.

"Sweets, what is going on?"

"Jason has kidney failure," I managed between sobs as my tears soaked her shirt.

The quiet whisper of the words 'Oh my God' and the feel of her arms tightening was all the response I got from her.

After taking a moment to re-group, I took Melanie downstairs to his room. I dressed in a pair of white jean capris and a black tank top before sitting down on his bed. I knew it would be a struggle as I told Mel the slightly abridged version of how I found out and the story Jason told me last night.

"Holy shit. This just can't be real," she said, shaking her head in disbelief. "I didn't see this coming." She wiped a few tears that had trickled down her cheeks.

"You?" I gawked at her. "I've been living with him. I could tell something was up, but I honestly thought it was family issues, not this."

"Yeah, I would have never guessed, and then to find out that way. God, I'm so sorry, Cass."

"That's why I moved my stuff down here. It's not because I'm some code red clinger. It's because my heart needs him. It needs to be close to him. If something happens to Jason, I need to know for my own sanity that I did everything I could to support him and spent as much time as possible with him. It sounds crazy, I know."

"No. I don't think it sounds crazy at all. I think it sounds hopelessly romantic. I wish I had a Jase in my life. Speaking of that, we need to discuss that brother of his."

"Yeah, uh, the brother is off limits. He's not really talking to the family. We'll have to work on the brother thing another time."

"Fine," she said. "I guess that's just a chapter for another day, huh?"

"Exactly."

"But, really? Code red clinger? Is that a new phrase or something?"

"It just kinda came out."

"How about crazy-cock clinger? Maybe then we can call it a triple c threat," she suggested.

"I'm not a triple c threat though. I'm just..." I hesitated, thinking of how to say it. I knew what it was, but the words were having trouble leaving my lips.

"I know," she said. She and I both knew that this wasn't just some triple c threat with Jason. This was so much more than that.

"It just breaks my heart. Someone so kind and gentle who has the heart of a saint is going through something like this."

"Yeah," she said. "It would take a saint to be able to handle all of it, though."

"You always know what to say."

"What are friends for?" she asked. "So now that we're both extremely depressed, what do you say we go do some shopping?"

"I'll get my purse," I told her as we both got up from the bed.

After grabbing my purse and slipping on a pair of flip-flops, we headed to the next town to get our shop on. Melanie always had a way of knowing when to change the mood, not to mention finding ways to cheer us both up. As we drove down the street, I couldn't help but think of how much I missed this, missed being with Melanie like we were in high school again. Things were changing though with a baby on the way, a life in Keaton that I had no clue what it held for me, and a guy who fought every day to keep himself healthy. One thing was certain, and that was Melanie. She would always be here and we would always have each other. For this, the smile on my face was permanent. I thought of all the reasons this amazing girl was more of a sister to me than any blood related one could ever be. I would let myself enjoy this afternoon with her and not think of the things going on in life that seemed to be so uncertain or sad.

Chapter
thirty-two

YESTERDAY WENT BY TOO FAST. It was already morning and Mel was leaving. I knew I would see her again soon but it still didn't make seeing her leave any easier. Even though she said her goodbyes and thank yous last night to Trish, Bart, and Jason, I still had to say goodbye.

I snuck upstairs so I didn't wake Jason and met Mel upstairs before she left.

"This was a damn good time, Cass. I'm glad I came up." The happy look on her face was forced. I knew she had a good time, but she was reluctant to go. I couldn't blame her. I didn't want her to go just yet either.

"Best time ever," I said tearfully.

She grabbed her bag, and we quietly walked out of the house to her car. It was still dark, the sun soon to rise as we hugged goodbye on the curb. We pulled away with a single tear rolling down each of our cheeks.

"Goodbyes suck ass," she said with a crack in her voice.

"Tell me about it," I said. "Will you please call me the minute you get back to campus?"

"You know it." She opened the driver side door and threw her bag on the passenger seat.

"Love you, Mel," I said, my heart aching that she was leaving.

"Love you too, Mama." She winked, sitting down in the seat as she closed the door.

I blew her a kiss, then walked into the house, and headed back downstairs.

Today was going to be a hell of a day. Not only did I have to say goodbye to my best friend, but I also knew Jason had dialysis today. I was bound and determined to go with him. I wanted to be there to support every aspect of what he was going through as much as I could. He was always supportive of me, and I wanted to do the same. I quickly brushed my damp hair and finished putting on my clothes before I left Jason's bathroom. I decided to get ready before he could dispute me going with him. When I made my way to his room, his light was on and his door was cracked open.

"There she is," he said to me as he pulled out some clothes from his dresser. "And she is already dressed." He looked me over from head to toe, confusion plastering his face. "I was headed to the bathroom to go check on you. I thought you were getting sick again. Why are you already dressed?"

"You act like you've never seen me ready for the day," I said as I walked by and put his shirt that I slept in by my suitcase.

"This early? No, I haven't," he said.

"I got ready early so I would be ready to leave when you are. I didn't want to give you the chance to use that as an excuse."

"What are you talking about?"

"I don't want you to get mad or even argue with me about this, but I'm going with you today."

He pushed his brows together as he looked at me, shutting the drawer he just pulled a pair of jeans from. "Going where with me today?"

"Dialysis," I answered, walking over to his bed to sit down.

He was shaking his head and turned so he was fully facing me. "Absolutely not."

While his voice was definitely not happy with what I told him, I couldn't help but gawk at him standing in front of me. His bare chest and tight dark blue boxers had me so distracted. I couldn't help but quietly giggle as my eyes caught focus of his morning wood.

"What's so funny about that?"

I got up from the bed and walked over to him. "Nothing, just go shower." I shot him a wink and headed for the stairs.

"You're not going," he shouted.

"Whatever you say, Jase," I shouted back as I made my way upstairs.

I fully intended to go whether he approved or not. I opened the door at the top of the stairs and made my way to the front door. I grabbed his extra set of keys he kept hung by the entryway and went outside to wait for him in his truck.

"What are you doing?" he asked as he pulled his truck door open, his head shaking back and forth in apparent disapproval.

"I'm going. I'm supporting you, and I'm not getting out of this truck."

"You're stubborn," he sassed as he sat down in the driver's seat and closed his door.

"I learned from the best," I said.

"Are you sure about this?" he asked as he started up his truck, the look on his face concerned. It was as if he had never had anyone want to be there for him before, which I knew was impossible. He had support all around him.

"Yes. Stop asking and just drive. I'm not leaving. Like I told you, you have me," I said and reached for his cheek, rubbing my hand against his scruffy face. "I'm in this with you."

He closed his eyes. I leaned over the emptiness between us and placed a kiss on his lips, surprising him as he opened his eyes suddenly. He pressed his lips harder against mine, kissed me back before pulling us out of the driveway, and heading to the hospital.

Trish wasn't around as we walked through the front doors and headed down the hallway that led to the dialysis room. That hallway didn't bring back good memories. In fact, I grabbed Jason's hand and held it tightly until we got to the room.

"There he is," an older lady said as we opened the door and entered the room.

I let go of Jason's hand as he greeted the lady with a hug. "Colleen," he said as he let go of her. "This is Cassandra." I smiled as he pulled me up to his side.

"Cassandra," she said, extending her hand out for me to shake. "I've heard so much about you."

I met her hand with mine and shook it. "It's nice to meet you, Colleen. Sorry for the—"

She put her hand up, cutting me off. "No need, Cassandra. I completely understand. This is hard for anyone to take."

I gave her a grateful look. "Thanks."

"She insisted on coming with me today," Jason told her.

"Yes, I did. I'm here for support," I told Colleen.

"You're a lucky guy," she said to Jason as she walked past him.

He looked over at me and mouthed 'thank you' before walking over to Colleen.

I watched him get his weight, blood pressure, and temperature checked. He was amazing. That was all there was to it. Three days a week was a lot for someone to have to do this. I felt a prickling pain in my chest as I thought of all the times that he told me he had to run an errand. Picturing him sitting here alone almost made me break into tears.

"Cassie?" I heard his voice yell to me. I looked over at him. "You okay over there?"

"Yeah, sorry." I had to stop checking out mentally.

"I have a chair for you right next to Jason," Colleen told me as she finished getting Jason set up in his chair that was next to a large machine.

"Thank you," I said as I sat down in the chair next to Jason.

I watched as Colleen hooked two tubes in his arm. I closed my eyes, remembering when he told me about the scar. Clearly, it wasn't accidental. It was purposeful and most definitely for his dialysis.

"All set, Jason," she told him before walking away.

It was a lot to take in. The machine was huge. There were the tubes coming out of him and a large screen monitoring him as the blood flowed through the tubes. I tried to swallow the lump in my throat as I watched the screen on the machine.

"Don't be afraid of it," he said, interrupting my thoughts.

"It's hard not to be," I replied. "Is this why Anna broke up with you? Because she couldn't handle seeing you like this?"

He shook his head as his eyes found mine. "No. Not even close, Sweetheart. She broke up with me because she couldn't handle me holding her back because I was like this. She was selfish, and as much as she tore my heart to shreds, I'm grateful now because she made me feel like I was sick and breakable. Who wants to feel like that? You look at me like I'm stronger than any other person you've ever met, like I'm your hero."

"Because you are, Jason. You are the strongest person I know. I couldn't even fathom going through what you are, and still keeping a smile on my face. You're a hero Jason."

"Okay, if you two keep this up, I'm going to start bawling my eyes out," Colleen told us as she came walking up to Jason. "But I see what you were saying, Jason. She's a keeper," Colleen said before walking to the other side of the room to look through a few charts.

It was time to change the subject; we didn't need to make anyone cry today. I adjusted myself in the chair and looked over at Jason. "Thanks again for letting Mel come and for taking us out to dinner."

"It was good to meet your other half," he said. "She is a good friend for you. Not what I expected, but in a weird way, it works."

"Her parents, while I love them because they are the opposite of mine, are part of the problem. They don't really give two shits about their daughter. That's why she went to college on the complete opposite side of the state."

"That's horrible," he said.

"Yeah, but she is a tough cookie and she has me. To make sure she knows she is amazing. I'll never let her down."

"You are such a good friend," he said. "What did you guys do yesterday before dinner? I forgot to ask you guys last night."

"I had to tell her about you and that is something I don't ever want to have to do again. I can *slightly* understand why you took so long." I gave him an apologetic look. "Then we talked about the baby and went to the store you took us to when you bought my boots. She wanted a pair of black ones."

"Ah, already starting a new trend with your friends. Look at what I've done," he gloated.

I playfully rolled my eyes at him. "After the boots, we just literally talked the whole time. Even though we've talked over the phone, it's always different in person. You can actually see the emotion and excitement on the other's face. It was a much needed visit. Then we drove back and visited with your mom a bit, and then you came to take us to dinner. Sorry about the dinner conversation by the way." I cringed as I thought about her mouth and the things she said. She always gives out too much information.

He let out a throaty laugh. "It was extremely entertaining. I especially enjoyed the commentary on her past boyfriends and their nicknames."

"She has a way with words and happens to be missing a filter, but she means well. I know there is a good guy out there for her; she just hasn't found him yet." I couldn't help but feel the butterflies releasing in my stomach as I thought of the guy I just found. I'm so lucky to have him in my life and to think, I wasn't even looking.

"What are you thinking about?" he asked softly.

I turned my gaze back toward him and lightly shook my head. "Nothing, just stuff."

"Should I be worried? Is this too much for you?" he asked, sounding concerned that I would bail on him.

"I'm not going to lie to you Jason. It's a bit much, but you definitely shouldn't be worried. So, what do you do in here for four hours?"

He let out a heavy sigh and tilted his head, his beautiful green emerald eyes looking so content while he gazed at me. "I think, sometimes I write letters, sometimes I play card games with Colleen. The four hours go by quick."

"Again with the letters. Who are you writing to?" I asked, curious about his secret pen pal.

"Are you jealous?" he asked as his lips curled up. "You want me to write you a letter?"

"Yes! I'd absolutely love it."

"And where do I mail this letter to?" he asked as he arched his brow up at me.

"Not sure about the mailing address. How about you just leave it on my suitcase? We can just pretend the mailman dropped it off." We both laughed at my teasing.

"I can do that," he said, nodding his head.

"When will I be getting this letter?" I asked him.

"This will be pure torture for you. Not knowing when it will arrive is going to just sit and eat at you isn't it?"

"You're a brat," I sassed.

"You'll get it soon. I have special plans for your letter." He winked.

I felt like a little kid waiting for Christmas. It was going to take all the patience I could muster up to not sit and wait for the 'mailman' to deliver a letter to my suitcase. It was pure hell what he was doing, but I couldn't help loving the torture he was putting me through.

A few hours had passed. Like Jason said, time went quickly. As I stretched my arms in the air, an obnoxious beeping startled me. I looked around to find where it was coming from, and I realized it was the dialysis machine.

"Oh my God, your machine is beeping. Jason, what's going on? Are you okay?" I panicked; I literally panicked. I didn't know if I could handle something going wrong.

"Relax," he said calmly. "The machine is just telling me I'm done. There is nothing wrong." His lips curled to the side in amusement as a chuckle escaped them.

"I do not find this funny in the slightest."

"You're right. It's not funny. It's cute." His eyes went from mine over to Colleen who was walking over to Jason.

"How was your first time here, Cassandra?" Colleen turned her head toward me as she waited for my response.

"It was," I said before pausing, trying to think of the right way to describe what this felt like, "hard at first, but Jason made things okay. He turned something that was scary into a pleasant four hour date." I looked over at Jason and flashed him a sexy wink. His cheeks blushed in return. I would never get sick of seeing him blush an adorable shade of pink.

"She is everything you said she was," Colleen said as she finished up with Jason.

"Yeah, I think I'll keep her," he said. "You ready?" He looked over at me as he stood up from his chair.

"Sure am," I answered as I rose and walked over to him. "I got plans for you, Mister."

He looked over at me with a curious look in eyes. "Oh, you do?"

"Not like that, but yes, I do have plans," I said, grabbing his hand as we walked out of the hospital. "We are going to take it easy because you get so tired after dialysis."

"How did you find that out?"

"Your mom told me yesterday. I can remember the moments that I thought something was different with you, and now I know why. You were just tired, and you hid it well, just so you know."

"It was hard, believe me. I just didn't want to waste time being tired. I wanted to spend and enjoy every moment that I could with you."

"I like that answer, Jase. Well, this afternoon, we are going to relax and have a Scrabble rematch. Just the two of us," I told him. "If I win again though, you realize that means I officially become a Scrabble master."

His head fell back as he let out a throaty laugh. "We'll have to see about that."

We got in his truck and left the hospital. I suddenly realized how my two times going to the emergency room would never compare to the three times a week he had to go for dialysis. I couldn't believe I even complained about having to go in the first place.

I felt his hand grab mine as we drove toward the house. "Thanks for going today. I mean it too. You'll never know how much that meant to me, Cassie." His head turned in my direction, and he had a look on his face that I hadn't seen before. It was warm and thankful, deep down to his very core. I could feel it as his hand held onto mine so tightly that it seemed he wasn't ever letting go. I didn't want him to. My heartstrings pulled tight as the smile stayed on his face once he turned back to the road.

"I'll be at the next one too. Like I said, I'm in," I told him, squeezing his hand tighter.

He squeezed my hand with a firm grip. He didn't have to say anything. I already knew how grateful he was. What he didn't know was how grateful I was for him.

Chapter
thirty-three

BEING WITH JASON WAS EASY. It was as though the sun was always shining down on us, warming our skin, rain or shine. Everything with him was pure bliss and maybe it was what people referred to as the honeymoon stage, but I honestly didn't care. Honeymoon stage or not, the affection and feelings we had for one another couldn't even be classified as a stage. It felt like it was in a category all of its own.

Three days passed so quickly that it seemed as though we were on fast forward. I wanted it to slow down but it wouldn't. The whirlwind never stopped. Between kicking his ass at Scrabble a few more times (which only made him believe that I was for sure cheating), another dialysis trip full of meaningless but powerful conversation, and sleeping in his arms every night, my world started piecing itself back together. I especially loved the moment when I got Jase to agree to attend college with me in the spring. It took some major convincing on my end, but he finally caved. He planned to take only a couple of classes until he felt comfortable enough with a full schedule. It made me proud that he was taking the leap again. I told him that I'd find him a dialysis center and would be there for him in any way I could be. He could count on me, just like I could count on him. He made sure that I knew without a doubt in my mind that he would be there for the baby and me. Knowing I had his support warmed me over. He felt certain it was a boy and I was positive I would be in all sorts of trouble if he were correct.

My car was finally fixed and, just as Jason said it would once Moose finished, looked completely perfect. She was as good as new, and parked out front of the Bradley's house. It wasn't going anywhere, and neither was I. After talking with Trish, Bart, and Jason, we agreed that I would be staying until Jason and I left for college. It was an extremely emotional conversation, but one of the easiest decisions I've ever made. As I said before, these three days were a whirlwind of emotion, love, and happy moments that I would never forget.

It was on day four though when the most magical thing happened. A call came that would change the life of the man who was changing me.

"It's time." Jason said as he flipped his phone closed.

"You're not kidding, are you?" I asked in pure shock and disbelief that it was really happening.

"No," he said, shaking his head. "This is it, Sweetheart. It's real. I have a kidney waiting for me."

"Oh my God," I cried, putting my hands to my face as I tried to keep up with wiping them away, but it wasn't possible. They streamed like a raging river flowing out of control.

I could see his happy face through the pools flooding in my eyes. He walked over and wrapped his arms around me, pulling me in for a hug. "You're going to make me cry," he whispered in my ear, sending shivers down my spine.

"I'm sorry." I bawled into his chest. "I just didn't think you'd get one so soon."

"You're my good luck charm, I guess." He released his arms from around me and cupped his hands on both sides of my face. "We gotta go, Sweetheart."

His lips curled into a smile that I would never get tired of seeing. This one, though, was like watching a kid who just received the ultimate birthday gift. It was like the cherry that topped a towering sundae, and he was finally able to dig in.

"Okay," I replied.

He used his thumbs to wipe the tears from the corners of my eyes, and then gently pressed his lips to my forehead. I inhaled deeply before we both gathered a few things from his room. He had an overnight bag that he was putting together while I grabbed a few items of my own. I looked over at Jason; he looked completely happy. I couldn't help but stop what I was doing to watch him. He was calm and relaxed as he carefully placed items in his bag, his lips curled up as far as they could go. He looked up and caught me staring at him.

"I'm sorry. I'm just astounded that you aren't anxious and freaking out right now. I'm so excited that I feel like I'm going to piss my pants or need to pinch myself to make sure I'm not dreaming."

He zipped his bag shut, set it on the bed, and walking over to me, placed a hand on my cheek. "I'm freaking out inside, Sweetheart," he said as his eyes stayed focused on mine. "But because I have you here with me, I know that everything is going to be okay. It makes all of this that much easier. You, my pretty girl, are the only thing keeping me from having a full out 'can't breathe, can't move', heart-stopping panic attack because I'm so nervous. It's all you, Sweetheart."

I had no clue how I was helping with any of this. His kidney was the gift, not me. Either way, I couldn't help but feel his words washing over me, enveloping me, and warming my soul.

"Do you have everything you need?" he asked, his eyes fixed on mine.

"I do."

"I just need to grab a few more things. I'll meet you upstairs?"

"Okay," I answered, still feeling cozy from his words as I grabbed my few items and walked upstairs to wait.

I pulled out my phone and texted Melanie that he had a kidney and we were on our way to the hospital. She responded exactly as I thought she would, wanting to know which hospital to meet us at. I typed Prairie Medical Hospital. Within seconds, she responded that she was leaving and would be there as soon as she could. I put my phone in my purse and waited for Jase. My body was heavy with anxiety as the surrealism of it all set in. He finally got a kidney, but that didn't take away from what was going to happen today. Receiving an organ was major, life-changing surgery. I started to get more nervous the longer I sat and thought about it. I wasn't left with a wondering mind long as he came walking upstairs, his bag in tow, and a cowboy hat to complete the ecstatic aura that surrounded him.

"Mom is picking dad up, and they are meeting us down there," he said as we made our way out the door.

"Perfect. I guess we better go get you a kidney then, huh?"

He didn't speak, but the way his eyes lit up said it all. We got in the truck and made the hour and a half trip to the hospital.

The hospital was busy, and as chaotic as it was, seemed lonely as I waited for Jason to finish being prepped for surgery. The waiting room had the usual chairs, tables, magazines, and television, but nothing could stop my racing mind as I waited alone.

The time I spent was soon interrupted when I saw Trish and Bart walking out of the elevator with Moose behind them. Relief washed over me as I watched them approach.

"Where is he?" Trish asked as she gave me the type of hug I always wanted, but never got, from my mother. I squeezed her back and told her that Jason was getting prepped and that we would be able to see him shortly.

"Okay, I'm going to see what paperwork I need to fill out. I'll be right back," she said in a hurry to get to the medical counter. Everyone was on edge as the nerves started setting in. This moment, even though exciting, was still extremely scary. Surgery was performed all of the time, but it always held its risks, and while I tried to keep on a brave face, inside I was terrified.

"How's he doing?" Moose asked me as he stood next to me.

"Actually, really good," I answered him. "I wish I could say the same for myself."

He put his arm around me and assured me that everything was going to be fine. He didn't have a reason to lie, so I decided to hold onto his words and keep them with me today. I was going to need them.

Once Jason was prepped, we were allowed to go see him one at a time. Trish was first, followed by Bart, and as much as I insisted Moose go ahead, he made me go before him. I thanked him with a hug, and all but ran into see Jase. I couldn't help but pause a moment before walking through the door. Seeing him in the bed, with a gown, IV, and monitors all around him was a little much to take in.

"Come here, pretty girl. I've been waiting to see you." He reached his arms out to me.

I walked up and hugged him, pulling away for only a second to look him over once more.

"You know? This IV and hospital gown is a good look on you." I winked at him and giggled.

"Now, where have I heard that before?" He knew exactly what I was saying, and it warmed my heart. He literally remembered everything.

"Someone, who I had no clue at the time would become such a big part of my life, told me that," I replied.

We continued our light conversation for another ten minutes before we heard a light knocking and saw Moose standing in the entryway. "Sorry to interrupt you love birds, but Mel just got here, Cassie."

"Melanie's here?" he asked surprised, but he couldn't hide the smile that swept over his face.

"Yes, she made me promise to tell her. She wanted to be here to support you. I'll go see her, and you and Moose can talk." I pressed a soft kiss to his cheek and walked out to go see Mel.

After more visits by everyone, we were back in the waiting room for only a few minutes before my I felt my phone vibrating. I glanced down at the screen and saw it was my mother. With all the things that had happened in the past few weeks, this is the time she chooses to call? I let out a huff and hit the ignore button. That didn't stop her. She called again, so I hit ignore one more time. She was persistent. I now realized where I got it from. I let out a chuckle as I looked over to Mel who was staring at her phone. She peered at me with shocked eyes.

"Your mommy dearest is calling my phone. Does she know what's going on? Any of it? Or that I'm here with you?"

I shook my head and told her that Mom never called me, and I never called her. Mel clicked ignore, and then the damn vibrations were back to my phone. I let out a frustrated sigh and decided to answer the call this time, not even sure what could be so important at a time like this. I slid my finger angrily across the phone and put it to my ear. I heard hysterics on the other end.

"Mother?" I asked, trying to decipher what the background noise was.

"Cassandra, where in the hell are you? I've called you a dozen times." Liar. It was only three, but who was counting.

I gave her a brief answer. "I'm out, Mother. What's so urgent that you needed to call me three times?" I looked over to Mel who just shook her head as I continued talking. Mel never had a warm heart for my mom; they always butted heads.

"It's your father. He's just had a heart attack, and they're taking him to Swedish Medical. You need to meet me there right away."

I put my hand over my mouth and looked down. My heart sank. My father just had a heart attack. Of all the fucking days in the year, it happened today.

"Cassandra? Are you there? Did you hear me?" My mother asked, panicking.

"Oh my God. Yes, I'm here. Is he okay?"

"I don't know, Cassandra. I just don't know. You need to get here right away."

Goddamn it. This was bad. This felt like a dramatic show on television, and now my episode was just unfolding. I could tell that I didn't even want to see how it ended.

"Okay," I said quietly before I hung up and swiped at the tears on my cheeks.

I looked up to see Moose coming down the hall, Bart and Trish who were leaving to go see Jason again, and Mel who was beside me. The look on my face stopped them, and they all stood around me. I gripped the sides of the chair as I tried to digest the news I just received. I needed to figure out who I would end up hurting and which hospital I should be at today.

"What's going on, Sweetie?" Trish was the first to break the silence.

I couldn't look at her. It felt as though the walls and people were closing in on me, making it hard to breathe as I tried to figure out what to say. Trish came and sat on the other side of me while Moose kneeled down in front. Mel grabbed my hand in hers as I sat in a pure state of shock.

"Cass, talk to us. What's going on?"

I looked over at Mel who already knew who had called me. I could see in her bewildered eyes that she knew it was bad. I tried to swallow the lump in my throat that made it difficult to speak.

"My father just had a heart attack." It wasn't two seconds later that I had everyone's arms around me as I cried. "My mother said I need to get to the hospital."

Trish, who was on my right side holding me tightly, spoke softly to me. "Sweetie, you need to go see him."

I shook my head no, but after she said it, the rest of the group all agreed, and without even realizing it, it was decided that I had to go.

With Trish and Mel behind me, I walked in to see Jason. His eyes went wide when I approached his bed. "Cassie? Sweetheart, what is it?" he asked, grabbing my hands in his. The warm, tingling feeling of them holding onto mine made this so much harder.

"My father had a heart attack, and I have to go see him," I said. His facial expression changed to shocked. "I don't want to go, though."

"If it's me you're worried about, don't. I'll be fine. You need to go see him."

I shook my head in protest.

"Take my hat. Hang onto it while you're gone. That way you'll have a piece of me with you today."

"Really?"

"Yes, really." He watched me pick up the hat in my shaking hands. "Now get over here. I really need a kiss."

I walked over to him and hesitated. "Goodbye?" I asked. I didn't want to give him a kiss goodbye, because this couldn't be goodbye.

"No, because I just want a kiss." His lips curled up as I pressed mine to them. I walked out of the room with his hat held tightly to my chest. I told everyone goodbye before heading toward the elevator. Something just didn't feel right about the way I was leaving. I wanted more.

"Stop. Wait. I have to go back. I need more time!" I yelled as I handed her his hat.

"Fine," she said. "But not long," She let go of my arm and walked back to the waiting room.

I rushed to his room and flew through the door, anxiety taking over as I tried hard to catch my breath.

"Cassie?" Jason asked, clearly surprised to see me.

"I just wanted more time," I said, trying to conceal my cracking voice.

"You need to go see your dad. I'm going to be fine, Sweetheart." He pulled me closer to his bed before kissing the top of my hand.

He slid over, making room for me on his bed. I climbed up and made sure to sit as close to him as humanly possible.

"What are you thinking about?" he asked me softly, still holding my hand in his.

"That I want to play a game with you?" I smiled like a cheese ball. Jase did the same when he caught on to what I was doing.

"Oh yeah?" he asked. "But we aren't in the diner."

"I want to play 20 questions."

"Oh, that game, huh?" He chuckled.

"But we only have until Melanie comes to get me," I said, wishing I didn't have to cut my time short with him.

"Okay, you go first." He pulled me closer to him. I didn't think it was possible for our bodies to get any closer, but he made sure there was a way.

I leaned into him as I rested my head on his shoulder. "What's the best memory you have?"

"You picked a tough one," he said, taking in a deep breath. "But I'd have to say I finally have one that I'm sure can never be replaced. Meeting you and seeing your pretty face in that car when I came to your rescue."

I held back a sob. It stung, but I had to stay focused on our game and crying wasn't part of it.

"I like that answer." My whisper in his ear sent goose bumps racing down his arms that tightly held me.

"It's my only answer," he said.

I closed my eyes, feeling as though I couldn't finish the game. They burned as I continued to hold the tears back. I felt his hand run up and down my arm. I opened my eyes and looked over to see him smiling. I had to pull myself together. I tried my best and curled my lips into a small smile.

"What's your next question, Sweetheart?"

I took in a deep breath and let it out slowly. "Are you scared?" My stomach was in knots, and it felt as if someone was pulling the knots tighter and tighter the longer it took him to answer.

He brought his face a few inches from my mine and slid down so that our eyes were at the same level. His eyes glossed over with tears as he took his free hand and placed it on my cheek, and the tears I had tried so hard to hold back slowly released one by one.

"I'm only scared of losing you," he answered back, bringing our foreheads together. I could feel his body releasing soft sobs against mine. My tears, now uncontrollable, were escaping; trying to hold them back was no use. We lay there, letting the tears pour out and holding onto the one thing that finally made sense in our lives. Each other.

"But I won't lose you. I'll be okay. And when I'm feeling scared, Sweetheart, I'll just picture your pretty face, and it will get me through it. I promise to call you as soon as I'm done," he said with a cracked voice and tears streaming as he pulled his forehead off mine and pressed our lips together. I wanted to stay like this forever, never letting go, but we were cut short as Mel tapped her knuckles on the door.

"It's time, Cass. We really have to go," she said.

Jase pulled himself together the best he could and gave me his ever-beautiful smile that I had grown too fond of over the past few weeks.

"Green light, Jase," I whispered before closing my eyes as more tears trickled down my cheek. I felt the pad of his thumb gently wiping them away.

"I love you too, Cassie," he whispered back.

"We'll be back soon," Mel told Jason.

I reluctantly removed myself from the comfort of his arms and stood next to his bed, our hands intertwined. "I'll see you soon," I told him, squeezing his hand like my life depended on it.

"Yes, you will."

I released a deep breath, and let go of his warm hand and curled into Melanie as she took us out of his room.

"He's going to be okay, Cass," she tried to reassure me.

I felt a hand on my shoulder. Lifting my head from Mel to see Trish, I saw eyes as red as mine. "I'll call you the minute he is out, Sweetie," she said. "I know he wants you to check on your dad. You're doing the right thing, Cassandra."

"I don't feel like it," I said quietly, trying to prevent another outburst.

"You are, Sweetie," she said, giving me a hug.

I wanted to just get in the car so that I could bawl my eyes without everyone staring at me.

"We've done this once before, and he came out better than new. He'll be alright, Cassandra," Bart told me before we headed to the elevators.

"Why does it feel like leaving right now is the worst decision I've ever made?" I asked Mel as we rode the elevators down to the lobby.

"We'll be back before you know it." She tried hard to reassure me.

Chapter
thirty-four

IT TOOK ABOUT AN HOUR AND HALF, but we finally pulled up to the hospital and found a parking spot. We looked at each other, pausing before getting out of the car.

"They would have called if something had happened to your father. He'll be okay."

I closed my eyes. I felt like a guilt-ridden monster inside. We were here for my father, and my thoughts were anywhere but on him.

"That's not who you're worried about though, is it?"

I shook my head no. "I'm horrible, aren't I?"

"No, you're not."

"It's not that I don't care about him. I do. He's my father, for crying out loud, but he's an asshole, and he'll fight as hard as he can before he'll let death take him away. Jase, he's just so sweet." I stopped myself and clenched my teeth together. I would not cry. I had to keep it together.

"I understand what you're saying, but Jason, he's a fighter. For you, he'll fight. Alright, let's go check on father dearest. Don't worry; I'm here to change the subject when necessary."

"Thanks, Mel."

As soon as we got in the hospital, we headed straight for the check-in desk. The lady at the counter looked up at me as we approached.

"I'm looking for Henry Pierce."

"Are you family?"

"Yes. I'm his daughter."

"The second floor, room 215. He'll be in the left wing."

"Thank you." Mel and I headed straight for the elevators.

We arrived on the second floor and headed left. We didn't have to find his room because my mother was pacing back and forth, talking on the phone in the waiting room.

She noticed us walking up, quickly ended her conversation, and placed her phone in her purse.

"Hello, Mother." I greeted her with a half hug.

"Cassandra," she said before pressing her lips together as she looked over at Mel.

"Hello, Diane," Mel quietly said.

My mother gave a small nod in Mel's direction. "I didn't know Melanie was with you."

"There's a lot you don't know," Mel mumbled under her breath.

"What was that, Melanie? I couldn't hear you." She gave Melanie a look that said she was giving her one more chance to rephrase her comment.

"I said, I just love your coat."

"This isn't a coat. It's a blazer," my mother said, adjusting the collar on her blazer.

"And a fine blazer it is," she replied in a slightly sarcastic tone.

Melanie looked over and mouthed the word 'sorry' to me. It didn't matter, though. I knew she had just as hard a time being around my mother as I did. I shrugged, letting her know it was fine.

"Mother," I said, getting her attention. "How is he?"

"Considering he just had a heart attack, he's doing okay. They are waiting on some tests to come back, but his assistant called for an ambulance just in time."

"That's a relief to hear," I told her, feeling a slight weight lift off my shoulders.

"He's been waiting to see you. What took you so long?" Her lips pursed together as she peered at me.

"Um." I stalled, looking over at Mel, trying to figure how to explain our two-hour drive.

"Don't say 'um', Cassandra. It's what people say when they don't know what to say. It's a waste of breath."

"Um, Diane." Melanie smiled devilishly at my mother. "Shouldn't we be checking on Mr. Pierce?"

"She's right. Let's go check on him." I urged. My mother agreed as she popped her nose in the air and walked to the room of doom and gloom.

"Thanks," I whispered to Mel as we followed my mother into his room.

It was dim and eerily silent. The blinds were closed and the hum of the monitors was the only thing making any noise. Mel and my mother stood on opposite sides of the room, far away from one another. I cautiously walked up to his bed. His eyes stayed closed until he sensed me next to him. They strained opened, searching until they found mine, his face remaining emotionless as he lay there.

"Cassandra?" he asked, his eyes searching my face.

"Yes. How are you feeling?"

"I'm fine. Don't worry about me. I want to know how school is going."

Ugh, of course he would.

"You just had a heart attack. I don't think it's an appropriate time to discuss my classes." Not to mention, I'm not going to school. There would be nothing to discuss. My stomach pained with guilt as I thought of the things I was withholding from my parents.

"Answer the question," he demanded. His eyes made it hard to focus as they pierced into mine like a dagger. My heart raced harder, the longer he kept staring.

"I'm not talking about this right now."

"Don't you talk to your father that way." My mother raised her voice at me.

I let out a frustrated sigh and looked over at Mel who had a pissed off look on her face. A light knock on the door before the nurse entered the room caused us all to look in the same direction.

"How are you feeling, Henry?" she asked as she checked his IV bag.

"The same as the last time you checked, Sarah. You really need to stop asking so often. I'm not dying," he mouthed off to her.

"Henry, I'm just doing my job. You're not going to die on my watch," she sassed back.

I needed out of this room, and now was my chance to leave. I eyed Mel and as though she read my mind, she nodded her head at me. We both quietly headed for the door.

"Where are you going?" My mother stopped us before we could make our escape.

I looked over my shoulder at her. "We are going to get some coffee."

"Get me a steak while you're out," my father barked at me.

The nurse, Sarah, closed her eyes and shook her head. "Henry. You're not eating a steak." She reminded him, her voice miffed. "How about a piece of grilled chicken or salmon?" she asked, trying her best to remain calm.

"We'll be back." I finally said, grabbing Mel's arm, and dragging her out of the room with me.

Once we were a safe distance from his room, I stopped, took a deep breath, and let it out. "I can't believe I'm here. I can't believe I chose them over him."

"They're your parents. They suck, but in their own weird way, they love you, and you love them."

"Love is such a strong word," I replied.

Deep down, I knew my parents were like this, and at one point, I was okay with it. How? I didn't even know, because now it burned me to my core with frustration.

"He's just being such an asshole right now. Not to mention, what is up with my mother? Could she be any bitchier?"

"It's definitely tense in there. I think the stress of the situation is what's stemming the assholish behavior. Don't let it get to you." She tried to convince me.

I didn't need convincing. My eyes that had once looked up to my parents were now looking down on them, and seeing their true colors.

I looked over at Mel. "Assholish?"

It fit. Let's go get some coffee."

I walked with her to the cafeteria.

We headed back upstairs after two cups of decaf and an hour's worth of sitting. We didn't talk much. My mind sifted through thoughts of Jason and my father. Melanie knew this as she sat silently next to me.

When we got back my father's room, it was instant tension once again. We sat and listened to my father and mother discuss who knows what for who knows how long since I had clearly zoned out. It had to have been awhile though, because my ass was starting to go numb from sitting so long. All I could think about was how gullible I was. How I was stupid to believe that what my parents told me was the way things had to be. It amazed me to think of how much I always worked for their approval, their acceptance, and I was happy doing it because I thought I had no other choice. Being lost in Boulder had led to finding myself in Keaton. I felt like a person who had just won the lottery. I didn't win money, but I won my freedom, and it was worth more than millions to me.

I started to get up when I felt my phone vibrating in my pants pocket. I immediately stood and glanced at Mel as I pulled my phone out. She stood and walked over to me. The number on the screen was Jase's. My chest started hurting as my heart beat like a drum with anticipation. This was it. It felt like time stood still for a moment as I looked over at my mother. She had a questioning look on her face, her mouth agape, as she was about to speak, and my father had his nose in a folder full of work. I looked at Mel, and she looked as anxious as I felt. Without hesitation, I slid my finger across the screen. I dashed from the hospital room. Mel was right behind me as I answered the phone.

"Jase? Please, tell me it's you?" I held my breath and tears as I waited for his voice on the other end. *Please, for the love of all that is holy, let it be him, and let him be okay*, I begged.

"Sweetie, it's me, Trish." Her soft voice answered on the other end. My heart jumped into my throat. I wished more than anything that it was Jase's voice on the other end. I could feel the tears stinging behind my eyes as I tried to answer her.

"Trish, is he… Is he okay?" I managed to ask her.

"He… Um. He…" She stalled, and I could tell she was holding back bad news at this point.

"Trish, please tell me he's okay," I begged her. The tears slid down my cheeks as I tried to hold them back.

"He's okay, Sweetie. He's out and doing well. He wants to talk to you, but he only can have a minute, okay?"

"Okay. I just need to talk to him," I said, practically out of breath as I yearned to hear him. It felt like several minutes passed as I waited impatiently for his voice on the other end of the phone.

"Sweetheart, it's me," he finally said, sounding extremely groggy.

I felt the pain in my chest be replaced by pure happiness. His voice sounded like music to my ears.

"Oh my God." I let the happy tears saturate my cheeks. I looked over at Mel who looked relieved with a smile a mile wide sweeping across her face. "It's so good to hear your voice."

"How is your dad?" he asked slowly.

"He's fine. I only care how you're doing though. How do you feel?"

"Better than new," he answered, still sounding out of it, but little by little, more like himself. "I miss you."

"I bet I miss you more," I told him, knowing how much I couldn't wait to leave this hospital so I could be with him.

"Hurry up so I can see you pretty girl." His voice sounded so happy as he spoke to me. My heart, that felt ice cold with my parents, was melting back to normal just by listening to him.

"I will. I'll be there before you know it. I can't wait to see you, Jase."

"I'm smiling just thinking about it. Green light, Sweetheart."

"Green light."

I sank to the floor as we ended the call, my heart heavy with love and elation. I felt an immense amount of relief. The kind you felt when you ace your final exam or just met a deadline for work by the skin of your teeth. The relief you felt when it counted the most. I felt it and more as Mel knelt down next to me, throwing her arms around me.

"Thank God," she whispered in my ear.

I couldn't thank him enough, I thought to myself. We got up and slowly walked back into my father's room.

"What was that about? Why did you leave?" asked my mother, looking back and forth between Mel and me.

"It was a personal call," Mel chimed in.

"It was my boyfriend." I answered, setting them straight, my pulse picking up quickly as I did. Something burned inside of me and I knew that whatever it was, it was about to show itself sooner rather than later.

"Boyfriend? What boyfriend, Cassandra?" my father hissed from his bed.

"We've never met him?" asked my mother, as though it was some new revelation.

"Maybe because he's new, and she didn't want to scare him off," Mel muttered to them.

"What?" my mother snarled.

It was coming now. I could feel the burning hot, molten lava rising inside me, ready to explode and set this room on fire.

"Yes," I spit out to my patents, looking at them both. "I have a boyfriend, and I don't know if or when you'll get to meet him, because I don't care what you think of him. I love him, and that's all that matters. I also don't know why I vied for your approval so much, because right now, your opinions are the last ones I care about."

I looked over at Melanie, her face in a state of shock as her eyes continued to get wider.

I did it. The lava was pouring out, and, unfortunately for my parents, it wasn't done. The lava was about to sting their hearts with a pain they couldn't even imagine.

"You know what else?" I asked, directing my eyes straight into theirs. My parents' faces were getting angrier by the second. I hated being like this, but I was done. I was pulling off the shackles they kept me in, prepared to suffer the consequences. "I'm pregnant AND I dropped out of school AND I'm keeping the baby."

My mother gasped as she put her delicate hand over her face. The lava wouldn't stop pouring. I had one more bomb to drop and this one would hopefully burn her heart as it burned mine, searing every inch of it until it was burnt to a crisp.

"And you know what? Here's another thing for you. I miss my mom. I miss the mom that loved me. That would let me be myself. Who secretly gave me a journal and took me to ballet class. I miss my mom. I don't know who this woman standing before me is anymore, but she disgusts me and I hope I am nothing like her."

I pressed my lips together as I watched my emotionless mother walk steadily toward me. It felt like slow motion again as I heard muffled words coming from my father and watched my mother raise her hand in the air and slap it across my cheek. The stinging pain lingered behind as I put my hand to my cheek to stop the pain. I swung my head back to face her as the tears streamed down.

"How dare you? What is going on with you?" she asked.

"Woman, you touch my friend one more time, and I'm going to shove your shoe so far up your prissy ass that you'll taste the dirt on the sole of it. The dirt you walk on just like the rest of us. You are no better than anyone here. In fact, I feel sorry for you assholish people. We're out."

With that, Mel led me out of that hospital room faster than I could blink.

She took me to a waiting area and let me cry on her shoulder. It was normal for people to cry in a place like this. What the passersby didn't know was that I wasn't even crying for someone who was here. The lava that I'd unleashed was slowly sliding itself back inside, searing my skin as it did. I unleashed the fury, but wasn't prepared for the burn it would cause me.

"Thanks for standing up for me," I sobbed into her.

"Do you have any idea how proud of you I am?"

"Proud? Look at what I've done."

"Yes. I'm proud. You stood up for yourself. You don't have to be afraid of the monsters anymore, Cass."

After pouring my heart out to her for a good fifteen minutes, we began our drive back down to where my heart knew I should have stayed. They were my parents, yes, but they weren't the people I should have been with today. No. Today was important for Jason, and I needed to be next to him, not my parents. I knew Jason was okay and out of surgery, but that still didn't stop me from being overly anxious to see him. I had a lot to make up to him for being gone when he needed me the most. Thirty minutes into our drive back, I felt my phone vibrate against my leg, breaking me from my restless thoughts.

I looked over at Mel who was peering at me out of the corner of her eyes. "Who is it?" she asked curiously.

I glanced at the unknown number on the screen. I looked up at her and shrugged. "It says 'unknown'. Should I answer it?"

"Yeah, it might be the hospital," she reminded me.

"Good point." I replied as I slid my finger across the phone to answer it. "Hello?"

"Cassie?" I heard a faint voice on the other end of the phone. It sounded like Moose, but I wasn't positive from the muffled voice.

"Moose? Is that you? I can barely hear you."

"Yeah, it's me, Cassie." His voice sounded strained and subdued as he spoke into the phone.

"What's up? Trish already called me a while ago. We're on our way back now."

"Cassie, you need to hurry. It's bad."

"Moose? What are you talking about? What's bad?"

My heart stopped. It literally stopped beating as I froze, trying to understand what he was saying. "You have to tell me what that means. I don't know what you're saying. Please tell me what it means Moose?" I screamed into the phone, my body shaking with nerves, my heart racing a mile a minute as I waited for his response.

"The doctors are doing everything they can. Just get down here fast." He sobbed into the phone, finally stopping the fight against them.

"Moose, No!" I yelled harder into the phone. I put a hand to my chest, the pain too much to bear. My heart was being torn apart, not into, not in pieces, but in shreds.

"Just hurry."

"No!" I screamed into the phone as he hung up.

"What the fuck is going on?" Mel looked over at me, her eyes wide with horror.

I frantically shook my head as I tried to catch my breath between sobs. My whole body convulsed under the immense power. Mel pulled off the side of the highway. I could tell we had stopped, but that was the last thing we should be doing. I just couldn't get a break in between cries to tell Mel we had to go; we had to save Jason. She turned her body to face me, and putting her hands firmly on either side of my face, she peered into my tear soaked eyes.

"Breathe, Cassandra. I need you to breathe," she said with a calm tone.

"I, I, I can't." I managed to stammer. "No. Please, hurry."

"Sweetie, you have to tell me what is going on."

I shook my head. I couldn't talk. Of all the times I needed to, my voice wouldn't allow it. All I could do was panic, and let the sobs take over my body.

"Now!" she screamed at me in a tone she'd never used with me before.

I ripped her hands off my face and screamed as my instinct to get us to Jason kicked in full gear. "Moose said it's bad. We have to HURRY!"

"Oh my God," she muttered under her breath as she looked over at me with the most scared set of eyes I had ever seen.

Her hands gripped the steering wheel so tightly that her knuckles were white. She spun her tires as the car left the side of the road and reentered the highway, leaving a trail of dust behind us. Her hand tightly gripped mine as she drove like a racecar driver down the highway, not once losing speed or caring that we might get pulled over. I was sure she would keep going even if the police were behind us.

We arrived at Prairie Medical Hospital in less than an hour. Mel parked in front, not giving two cares in the world that it wasn't an actual parking spot. We raced out of the car and through the front doors. I was out of breath, and my chest felt weighted with bricks. My body was in immeasurable pain as the sobs and shaking took over. I didn't care though; I didn't care about any of it. I just needed Jason. He was all I could focus on as we made our way up to his floor. The elevator ride felt as though it would never end as each floor passed slower than the last. The doors finally opened, and like a scene out of a horror movie, no one that I knew was in the waiting room. I couldn't see Trish, Bart, or even Moose. I scanned the room two times, but they weren't around. I began to panic until I thought they might be with Jase. The doctors must have fixed whatever was wrong. I had to believe with every fiber of my being that this was why. I looked over at Mel who also scanned the room, and she met my eyes with hers. It seemed we both had the same thoughts running through our minds that Jase was okay, and we let out a breath of relief at the same time. I started walking to find him, with Mel following behind. I couldn't wait to wrap my arms around him after the scare he just gave me.

"Everyone must be in his room. I could hit Moose. I'm so mad for the scare he gave me." I told Mel as we walked.

"Yeah, no kidding," she replied.

We walked down the recovery hall and immediately stopped when we saw everyone standing in the hall around the doorway of a room. I didn't care who I was bumping into as I pushed past them to see whose room it was. After passing a few people, my heart stopped as I saw Trish. Her face would haunt me for the rest of my life. It was ghost white as she cried in Bart's arms. He, too, looked pained, tears streaming down his anguished face. I put my hand to my mouth as I watched and listened. Everyone was in hysterics, screeching, and wailing. It sounded like a pack of wolves howling in pain. Mel put her hand on my shoulder. I couldn't feel it, but I could see it. I was starting to go numb as we continued watching.

Moose came through the crowd and headed toward me as if he was walking to the edge of a cliff. He seemed to have a hard time placing one foot in front of the other as he neared the edge. *Me.* His eyes, almost too swollen to see through, were open as he approached me. He stared at me a moment, a moment that was too long, before he closed his eyes and took in a deep breath. I felt sick, like my insides were about to explode any second if he didn't start talking. He stepped even closer, our toes almost touching, tears trickling from the corners of his eyes.

"What's going on Moose?" I asked him. I needed answers.

"Something went wrong and there were complications." His voice was quiet and cracked as the last of his words came out of his quivering lips.

"He's okay though, right?" I asked, using all the hope I had left in me. Everyone was just crying because they were scared. That had to be the reason.

"No. He went septic and he's gone." His voice was a soft whisper, but it felt like a cannon exploding in my ears.

I watched as Mel's head dropped and her body went limp. One hand went to her face and the other to her stomach as she held herself. It wasn't possible though. It couldn't be real.

"No! I don't believe you. I need to see him." I tried to get past him, but he threw his arms around my flailing ones as I tried to escape the strong hold he had on me.

"Listen to me. They tried everything they could to save him, but it just wasn't enough. He didn't make it. His body shut down," he cried, trying hard to breathe through his own hard sobs. "I'm sorry, Cassie."

"NO! JASE!" I screamed in agony. Moose didn't say anything else as he wept with me. His arms went weak and his hold turned into a hug as he tightly gripped my body. He needed someone to hold him as much as I needed someone to hold me. Except I wanted it to be Jason, needed it to be Jason's arms around me. I held Moose back though, unleashing my heartache on his shoulder. Visions of Jason ran through my brain as I saw his perfectly scruffy face, his bold green eyes, and his sexy infectious grin.

Moose let go of his hold and looked at me through his wet eyes. "The hospital won't take him away until we're ready, so we all have time to say goodbye. Do you want to see him?"

Away

"I do. I have to see him Moose," I sobbed back to him. He shook his head and held my hand, guiding us through a sea of people.

We didn't make it far before I had a feeling to look over to my right. The instant I did, our eyes met. A moment passed between Trish and me that I would never forget. I saw in her eyes that her heart had just been ripped out, and that she had just lost her son, her baby. I all but ran to her and threw my arms around her neck. Bracing ourselves against one another, we poured out our grief together. I hugged her tightly, trying to get any sign of comfort from her, but there was nothing. Nothing would ever be okay or comforting about this. The world had just lost a ray of sunshine. It would never be as bright as it once was. Her arms held me for several minutes, but nothing could be said in this moment. The only thing that could be done was the releasing of the pain inside us. I felt a hand on my arm and looked over to see Moose. It was time. I didn't know how ready I was for this, and as I let go of Trish, her hand touched the side of my face before I walked away. We stepped the few feet and stopped at the door to Jase's room. Moose dropped his gaze, tears streaming down his face as he let go of my hand.

"Take all the time you need," he whispered.

I slowly entered the silent, somber room. I couldn't look at the bed that he was on as I walked up to it. I didn't know how to prepare myself for what I was about to see, but when I finally lifted my gaze and saw him, I realized then that nothing could have prepared me. I held my stomach as hard cries escaped me.

"Jase!" I cried out as I looked at him, shaking my head in utter disbelief. He was lying so still with his eyes closed. He didn't look like he was gone. It only looked like he was sleeping.

"Jase, wake up! Please, wake up. PLEASE!" I screamed as I carefully reached my hand out to touch his face. I prayed my touch would work some kind of Disney magic. I carefully placed my hand on his cheek, the scruff that I loved so much tickling my hand. He didn't wake up though. He didn't look at me and pull me down for a kiss like the reunion we were supposed to have. This wasn't right. It wasn't supposed to be this way.

"You must have been so scared. I should have been here. I'm horrible Jase. I never should have left you." I stepped closer to the bed, leaving no room between us. As I bent down to wrap my arms around him, I laid my head on his still chest and listened for his heartbeat that had soothed me to sleep countless nights. But there was nothing. The beating had stopped. "I need your heart to beat, Jase. It's supposed to be beating." I clenched my eyes closed as I held onto him, letting the tears escape my closed eyes.

"You weren't supposed to leave this way. Not like this. What am I going to do without you?" I asked him, soaking the gown that covered his body with my heartache.

"I'll never forgive myself for leaving. *Never*. All I want is for you to put your arms around me and tell me it's all a dream. Wake me up, Jase. Please." I begged him. I moved my arms from his waist and grabbed his to wrap around me, to hug me back, but it was limp and wouldn't stay around me. I choked out a hard cry and slowly lifted my shattered body from his chest, and placed his lifeless arms by his side.

I looked down through my wet eyes at his unresponsive face. "I can't say goodbye. I can't do it."

I lowered myself down, placed my hands on either side of his face, and put my mouth to his. I pressed hard against his lips, wanting, needing him to kiss me back, but he couldn't. Every ounce of Jase that was once in this body had vanished. It was nothing but a body that looked like Jase. My sweet guy was gone. He was really gone.

I pressed my lips onto his once more, and then gently held his face in my hands. "I love you so much. I'm your Sweetheart forever."

I removed my hands from his cheeks and looked one last time before I cried out, falling to my knees next to his bed. Moose rushed to my side, wrapping his arms around me. My heart squeezed as I bawled into Moose's shoulder, and then it exploded. Torment and pain spread inside of me, piercing through my veins, and every vivid memory of Jason seeped through me. The world around me had just come undone in such a way that no builder would ever be able to piece it back together again. It would never, ever, be the same. I could feel my lungs gasping for air as my chest tightened, making it too hard to breathe. I put my hand to my chest as the pressure built. I needed to get out of here. I had to do what brought me here in the first place. I had to run away.

I got up as best I could, leaving Moose, and the room behind me. I ran down the hall to the elevator, not once looking back, but knowing Mel was right behind me. I dashed inside the elevator as it opened, pushing past a younger man who was rushing to get out. I slammed my hands against the buttons not knowing which ones I was hitting until Mel gripped my hands in hers and pushed the button for the lobby. We started moving down to the bottom level. Ironically, it felt like I had already hit the bottom. I didn't think I could get any further down, but I was about to find out that I was wrong.

We got into the car, but this time, I didn't sit in the passenger seat. I threw myself across the back seat and bawled hard into the fabric underneath my face. I grabbed his cowboy hat that was beside me and held it tightly against me as I sobbed out in pain. Mel was in hysterics as she drove us out of the hospital parking lot and eventually onto the highway. I didn't know where she was taking me; I could only hope it was to a cliff or bridge so I could jump off of it. I needed to see Jase, and that was my only hope. Everything in my life that was finally starting to make sense had vanished within seconds as the tornado of disaster swirled around me, only to drop me and leave me with the aftermath of nothing. My world had just been destroyed, and life had just robbed me of happiness and love. Damn life and its destruction. Damn it to hell, I thought as I hugged the hat tighter, screaming his name, wishing too hard that this hat were him instead.

Chapter
thirty-five

WEARING THE ONLY BLACK DRESS I owned, I walked into the living room of Mel's apartment. A sloppy ponytail on the nape of my neck, the cowboy boots from Jason, and a red swollen face that was splotchy from days of crying completed my look.

"How do I look?" I asked, not even caring of the answer she would give me. I just didn't know what else to say.

"Like a woman who just lost someone they love," she replied quietly.

"I don't want to go Mel. I don't have it in me to say goodbye. I can't say goodbye to him because I know when I do, it means it's real. And it can't be real. It just can't be. I sit and pinch myself, praying that I'm just stuck in some nightmare." I stretched my arm out to show her the pinch marks. Each one stung like a bitch and only reminded me of how real all of this was.

She came rushing over to me. "Jesus, Cass." She gently reached for my arm and inspected the pinch marks. "Why?" she asked as she dropped my arm and let it fall down as she threw her arms around me.

"I just wanted to wake up. Tell me to wake up," I told her, crying on her shoulder, and quickly covering it in tears.

"I can't because you're not sleeping, Sweetie. This whole fucked up nightmare is real. It's so real and you better believe I would give anything to make it go away, to wake you up, but it's not a dream and I can't do anything but be here for you."

She held me for what seemed an eternity but in reality was only ten minutes. Life could have fooled me. We somberly got in the car, and with his black cowboy hat in my lap, we began our drive to Keaton. We weren't an hour into our drive when I had a panic attack and needed Mel to pull over. Everything inside of me purged itself three times on the side of the highway before the dry heaving came. I finally went numb. I sat on the side of the road with my knees tucked under my chin and my legs tightly gripped. Mel sat next to me rubbing my back. Cars flew by, whirling up dust and debris around us until Mel said we had to go or we'd miss his burial. My mind, body, and soul didn't know if it could handle such a thing anymore. I always thought a broken heart was just that, broken. I didn't believe it could break even more after it had already been broken, but I knew my theory would prove wrong once we got back to Keaton and to the cemetery.

We got back into the car and my phone showed that I had a text message. I opened it up and saw it was from Moose. He had been texting and calling since that horrible day at the hospital, keeping me updated on the burial. Like the good friend Jason said he was, Moose checked up on me. He even drove my car down to Alamosa where I was staying with Mel. He looked as horrible as I felt inside and out, our eyes puffy and swollen, our faces red and burned from the salty tears. He tried to convince me that I saved Jason, that I gave him hope and life, and a reason to live again. How could I have saved him when he was gone? I fought him on it but he wouldn't let me believe otherwise. He really was an amazing friend, and I was glad for the support and concern, but nothing was going to help me. Not today. Not text messages. Not *anything*. I read the message from Moose.

Are you okay? Are you guys coming?

I texted him back two simple words, no and yes. His response was quick, telling me he'd see us soon. I put my phone in the cup holder next to me as Mel continued driving.

We arrived, but the parking lot was already starting to fill up. People wearing black and cowboy hats and boots quietly left their cars and trucks. The vision sliced through my chest as a picture of Jason in his hat and boots stole my sight for a moment. We stepped out the car and braced ourselves.

My eyes immediately went to Trish and Bart who were standing close by. I knew how they would look today, but seeing their faces was enough to make me want to run the other way. A nauseous feeling grew inside me as I walked up to them. I threw my arms around Trish, and she held me tight as her somber tears ran down my shoulder. She pulled me back and again, there was nothing to be said. Nothing that could help right now. I was then being hugged by Bart. He always seemed like an easy-going man even though he had the weight of the world on his shoulders. Today though, he was breaking. We all needed each other. I hugged him back tightly before letting go.

I walked across the grass with the cowboy hat in hand, and dragged my feet past several chairs until I got to him. I pulled my boots off one at a time and placed them next to his casket that waited to be lowered into the ground. I set them side by side as they leaned on each other for support. I couldn't wear them anymore. The only reason I had them was because of Jason. Now he was the only reason I couldn't wear them; he was gone. I couldn't look down at them and see the gorgeous cowgirl boots that he bought me. All I could see was heartache. They needed to be buried; they belonged with him. I lifted the cowboy hat to my lips and placing a kiss goodbye on the front of it, I set it down next to my boots.

I stepped closer and put my hand on the top of the casket, feeling the smoothness underneath my skin. I closed my eyes, picturing him lying so still, pretending he was sleeping, and wishing I could see him and hold him. I prayed his eyelids would open and those green eyes that I loved so much would be staring back at me. I opened my eyes, gazing at the casket underneath my hand. I had to talk to him. I didn't care who was walking up behind me, or staring at me.

"I want to play a game with you Jase. I'll go first." I took a deep breath, letting the tears roll down my cheeks.

"Why did you leave me? We had plans. You and I were going to finish college together. You said you'd be okay, so why are you gone? Why did you leave me?" There was nothing, only a slight breeze whistling through the trees in front of me. "Please answer the question. I need you."

I heard a few sobs and gasps from the audience building up behind me, but I didn't care. He needed to answer or he would forfeit, and he *never* forfeited. I lost it. I screamed phrases that I had never screamed before in my life. I threw my hands in the air when it hit me that he wasn't going to answer. Never again would he answer one of my questions. Never again would I get to play a game with Jase.

I felt a strong pair of arms around me as I was getting ready to slam my hands on the casket. His casket. Jase's new home.

"Let me GO!" I screamed to the stranger holding me, my back pinned tightly against his chest.

"Shhh," he said gently in my ear.

"No! He has to answer or he'll lose his turn," I cried out.

"It's alright. I've got you," he said quietly, keeping his arms around me. I didn't know what it was, but his soft soothing voice and reassuring words were calming me over, and for a minute, I was able to take a breath. I closed my eyes, inhaling and exhaling deeply as the stranger kept his arms around me.

"That's it. Just breathe. You're okay," he said, whispering in my ear, his lips so close that they were almost touching me. His voice caused a shiver to run down my spine as his hold kept a strange calm over me.

I opened my eyes and turned to see who was holding me. His eyes held mine as I did. They were hazel and had a striking, green color laced through them. I was about to speak to him when I saw Mel walk up, and suddenly, his consoling arms left my body and released me to her. The calmness that had run over me instantly vanished. I felt my breath become rapid again as I ran into her arms, hiding my face in her neck, her hair covering the world around me. She held me as we walked to her car, not once looking back. I couldn't. There was no point. He wasn't going to wake up and step out of his casket. Nope, he would be lowered six feet down, the dirt covering him until it filled the hole that perfectly surrounded his body. There was no use in looking back. What's done was done. What he once was, he was no more, and what we once had, had forever gone away.

"Sweetie, we need to stop by their house. We have to pick up your stuff."

I knew this. I knew that my belongings were still in that damn house, sitting, waiting for me to go back to it. I left it the day of his transplant. I left it, knowing that I would be back. Moose felt bad for delivering my car and not my belongings, but I honestly didn't know if I could take them back. They held too many painful memories. "No! Absolutely not. Please, just get me out of Keaton, right now."

"How about I just run in and grab it then?"

"Why?" I looked over at her, my hands in the air.

"Cass, you need your stuff. It will only take a second," she said in a tone that told me I wasn't going to win this battle.

I dropped my hands to my lap. I didn't have any fight left in me. "God, I just don't even care anymore. Do whatever you want."

It felt like we'd been on the shortest stretch of road when we pulled up to the house that I once considered a happy place. Now all I saw was heartache and death. I could see Melanie unbuckling her seatbelt while she kept her eyes on me. The stinging behind my eyes felt like blades trying to dig out of my sockets. It was brutal and there was nothing I could do to stop it.

"Where are your things?"

I closed my eyes, and saw my suitcase that I put in his room. It felt like I put it there ages ago. "In, it's in." I let out a hard sob. "His room," I said as I struggled to breathe in-between the hard cries.

I felt her hand on my shoulder. "I'll be right back. Can I have your keys?"

I knew that I was picking up my purse with my hands as I reached behind me to get it, but I couldn't feel anything. I felt like a puppet, and someone else had moved my limbs. She pulled out my keys and quietly got out of the car. I wished I could be brave. I wished I could walk into the house that once felt so warm and welcoming, but I couldn't. Everything I became was because of him and that house, and I couldn't even bring myself to look at it again. I dropped my head to my lap and let the tears soak my bare legs, drenching them, as the pain inside poured out of me like a waterfall.

It didn't take long for Melanie to come back. She opened the door, and I could hear her sniffling. I slowly pulled my body up from my lap and looked over at her through my tear-soaked eyes. Her face was red, her eyes swollen with tears, and her demeanor matched mine. She wasn't the friend trying to walk on eggshells around me just moments before. She was in pain. She placed my luggage in the back and sat down on the front seat, holding something in her hand.

"Mel?" I sobbed. "What is it?"

"Cass, I'm sorry. I'm so sorry." She put the item in her lap as she laid her forehead against the steering wheel in front of her. "I went in. I was doing okay. I tried so hard to hold myself together for you. I'm your friend and I was trying to be brave. Then I went down to his room. I could feel the tears coming as I grabbed your suitcase, and then this... This fucking thing. I saw it and I lost it." She lifted her head, her eyes drenched with tears. I was hurting for him, for me, and now for Melanie. *Damn it*. I shook my head. I didn't understand what she meant though; I didn't know what 'this' was. She took in a deep breath between a hard sob and handed me the item on her lap.

I took the item in my hands. It was hard and looked like a book. I looked over at Melanie. "Turn it over, Sweetie," she whimpered.

I didn't think I could. I didn't think it would be possible for my hands to turn it over, but as I watched the look on Melanie's face, I knew I had to find just an ounce of strength in me to do what she asked.

I closed my eyes as I turned it over. It was soft and smooth, and I could feel the pages in-between the front and back casing. My heart slowly crumbled in my chest as I opened my eyes. I gasped as I saw it. I didn't think my heart could possibly break any more than it already had, but it just did.

I looked at Melanie who was in hysterics and shaking her head. "I'm so sorry, Cass."

I put my hand over the black, hard-backed journal that had the prettiest, delicate, pink bow attached to the front of it. The tears streaming down rapidly were drenching the beautiful journal. "No!" I sobbed out, shaking my head back and forth while reading the note attached to it.

"To Cassie. Write away, Sweetheart."

I opened the journal to the first page, and like a kid at Christmas, knew that underneath that gorgeous wrapping paper was a gift. Jason left me something special; he left me my letter. I handed it to Mel to read to me. I couldn't do it. She took it in her hands and closing her eyes, took a moment to gather herself so she could read me the letter that he'd promised me I'd get.

Cassie,
I told you I had special plans for your letter! You are peacefully sleeping next to me as I write this. You have absolutely no clue about it and that makes me smile.
One of the best memories I will always have was watching your face light up as you told me about the journal your mother gave you. I knew instantly that I had to get you one, and I can only hope that this will light your face up just as much. Not to mention, my impressive skills by incorporating the letter you so badly wanted, and I so badly wanted to write you in with your gift.
Follow your dreams, Sweetheart. Don't ever let anyone or anything get in your way. Remember to stop and enjoy the little things in life. Enjoy the grass under your feet, have a picnic on the bed, and enjoy a good old-fashioned board game. Those are the moments that pass by too quickly but stay in your mind for years to come. I know with everything that I am that every little amazing thing about you will always stay in my mind forever and all the years to come.
Life has a funny way of showing us our true paths in life and I'm glad yours led you here to Keaton. I know deep down, though, that life has big things in store for you, just as much as I know that you will leave your mark on this world in an even bigger way. Getting lost and meeting me was just the beginning Sweetheart.
Now, my pretty girl, it's time to write away.
Green light,
Jase

As the last of the letter poured out of Mel's crying mouth, I couldn't help but scream. I felt my heart as it ripped from the very cavity where it once was happy. I wanted Jason back. I wanted his smile, his kisses, and his warm embrace to come rushing back to me. I needed him badly so that he could put my heart back where it belonged. It was never going to happen though, and all I had now were the memories and his final gift goodbye: my journal, his letter, and his words forever embedded in my soul.

The term away comes in many forms and phrases. Get away, stay away, far away, go away, run away, move away, but the term that best fits this situation... Went away. He went away. He left me. He left everyone. You went away, Jason.

Epilogue

1 Year Later

"ARE YOU READY?" Moose asked me.

"My mind is as ready as it'll ever be, but my heart isn't so certain." I replied back.

As I drove us down the street toward him, my mind suddenly took sides with my heart. I had been so sure that I was ready to see him, but now that I was actually doing it, I was ready to turn back. But it was too late; I was already there. Damn small towns for having every place so close. Nerves that were unable to control themselves caused my palms to slip from the steering wheel as I tried to park my car.

"I'll wait in here," he told me.

I nodded as I got out of the car.

You can do this, Cassandra. You can do this. Talking myself into seeing him was easier said than done. I took a deep breath and tightly gripped my hands to keep them from shaking as I walked up to it.

I knelt down and unclenched my hands. Running my fingers across the cold hard stone, I traced the outline of his name as I read it aloud. "Jason Dean Bradley." I could feel the lump in my throat growing, making it harder for me to hold back the tears that wanted to escape.

It was real. Everything was done; it was literally set in stone. "Oh, Jase, I thought this would be okay, but it's far from that."

A tear ran down my cheek. I watched as it landed on my lap and tried to think of where to start.

"I miss you so damn much. I'm sorry it took me this long to come and see you. I was hurting and miserable. I was being selfish. I thought I was the only one who lost someone special, but the truth is, everyone in this town lost you too. God, I wish this was a dream. I thought I could handle coming here and seeing you, but it makes it worse. It brings up every amazing memory I have of you. It makes me realize how much I wish you were sitting here next to me, looking back at me with those green eyes of yours, smiling at me, holding me tight."

I let my chin fall to my chest and held my hand against his headstone. It was all that I could do to not lose it again. I let the stream flow out of my eyes and down my cheeks, now soaking my pants.

"Jason, I miss you. I want you to come back to me so badly." I lifted my head up and wiped the tears that covered my eyes so I could see. "I came here to say hi and I had every intention of being strong and brave, but seeing this just makes it so official. I knew in my head that you weren't coming back, but being here really puts it into perspective that you really are gone." I took in a breath and released it slowly trying to calm myself. "Life has been so lonely without you. I think about you every day. I miss you calling me Sweetheart, and I miss playing trivia and Scrabble with you. You said forever, and I believed you. I believed we really would get our forever, but then fate told us no and took you away. It was as if my world was buried with you, and I didn't even want it back. It's been a struggle to dig myself out, but inch-by-inch and day-by-day, I tried my best and finally did."

I took another breath, ready to prepare myself for what I was about to tell him next.

"Thank you for the journal and my letter. I never got the chance to tell you. Jesus, Jase, it was so perfect, so wonderfully perfect. You gave me something to always have that was from you, but I hated that I couldn't even tell you thank you in person. You'll never understand how much that gift meant to me. You told me you had a plan for my letter, and sweet guy, you delivered. You gave me something from you that I could hold onto forever, and I did. I held onto it day after day and I did what you told me to do. I wrote away. I wrote every day until I couldn't any longer. I wrote about running away, hitting the tree, meeting you, the diner, the bar, our first kiss, the library, my baby, finding out about you, everything. I wrote my story and I wrote your story."

I stopped for a moment as my mind went back to the day I began writing it all down. Word after word and page after page my notebook had filled up quickly.

"It was about us, two strangers finding friendship and love in a crazy situation, and in the end, what I ended up with was our story. I took what I wrote and let Melanie read it. She finally understood exactly what we had, and how much you truly meant to me. She loved it. She told me I needed to turn it into a book, get it published, and put it out there. She told me that people needed to read our story. I didn't think I could, so I held onto to it. I held it close to my heart and I slept by it every night until it was as if I had an epiphany. I had to get our story out there, for you; it was going to be my gift to *you,* Jase. I found some amazing people to help me, and with their hard work and help, *Away* was published. You gave me that journal and I gave you our story. I hope I did you proud," I told him, my voice cracking too much to carry on.

I placed my hands over my face and bawled. I let it all out, as I poured my heart into my hands, as I felt relieved for having told Jason what I did, and finally getting to tell him thanks in 'person'. I removed my hands from my wet face, took a few deep breaths, and finished telling him the rest.

"Another moment I wish you could have been there for is when I held my sweet baby in my arms for the first time. God, he is so beautiful too. You would love him so much. I didn't know what to expect, but he was full term when I delivered, and he is perfect. He is three months old now, and he amazes me every day. I wanted so much for him to have met you, so the best I could do was honor you by giving him a name you'd approve of.

I named him Jase Timothy Pierce. His middle name is after Moose. He's been such a rock to Jase and me."

I turned my neck for a brief moment as I looked back at my car that Moose was waiting in. He was every bit of the friend Jason always said he was. With a heavy heart I looked back at the stone in front of me.

"I remember sitting at Melanie's, waiting for the moment I would deliver this baby, and wondering on how earth I was going to do it. I didn't think I had it in me to be his mom without you by my side, but when I saw his beautiful little face looking back at me, I knew with every ounce I had in me that there was no way I could give him up. He is with your mom right now. I forgot how much I missed your parents. I don't think Jase will ever have to worry about not being loved." My heart warmed at the thought of him never being without it.

With a deep sigh I went on, telling Jason the last of what I needed to.

"You told me that life had a funny way of showing us our paths. I am still trying to figure out what mine is. I'm still trying to figure out why you were taken so early, why life chose that path for you. They said I saved you, but really, you saved me. My life was a tornado spiraling out of control until it crashed into your life. You saved me Jase. Somewhere, somehow, I know you are watching down on us. Making sure that life keeps leading us in the right path. Maybe that's what it is; maybe you are supposed to be showing me my new path. I need to know what to do next. I need a sign. Please, just send me a sign." My breath caught as the rest of the tears rained down.

I put my hand over his name as I closed my eyes once again. I pictured his beautiful eyes looking into mine and his lips curled up, smiling back at me.

"I love you, Jase. Green light forever."

Dan's pov

ONLY A WEEK AFTER MY little brother died, I received a letter from him that would change my future. As I read it, the pain in my chest tightened from knowing that he was gone, and that this would be the last letter that I would ever receive from him; this was his final goodbye. I read it a dozen times, and each time I felt more heartache as the reality of it all set in. I knew what I had to do. I had to honor my brother's last wish.

> Dan,
> We've been through this once already. I've been in this bed waiting for a transplant before, so I know it's going to be fine. I really feel that everything is going to be okay, but something is different this time. It's Cassie. If something does go wrong, and if I don't make it, I don't know what will happen to her. I know Mom and Dad will have you, but Cassie won't have anyone. She needs someone to be there for her. To push her, to let her know she has her whole future ahead of her. Dan, you have to do that for me, Brother. You have to be there for her. I know it's a big favor to ask, but I also know that when you meet her, she'll win you over. She wins everyone over.
> As much as I want it to be me with her, I couldn't think of a better man to watch over her than you. I know her. She'll be

282

pissed at you, and she'll hate you for going behind her back and doing this. She'll come around, though, and when she does, you'll know it. Her hazel eyes will be light and soft, and her smile will never leave her face. She might not forgive you right away, but I know you brother. You won't give up.

I don't know where she'll be. We were supposed to go back to college together, but clearly, that isn't happening if you're reading this letter and I'm gone. Find her, watch over her, take care of her, and be there for her when I couldn't be.

I love you, Big Brother, more than you know. Please patch things up with Mom and Dad. Make them realize that it was me who pushed you to be the best you could be. That I knew you were more than just a small town man. You had big things to do in this world, and I wanted to make sure you didn't waste time on making them happen. Take care man, and know I'll be watching over you too.

Jase

I looked up and imagined he was looking down on me, and quietly told him the words he'd want to hear. "Anything for you, little brother. I'll make sure she's okay." I folded the letter back up and put it with a note to Cassandra from Jason that he'd left for me to give her when the time was right. My stomach pained as I sat and held the letters in my hand. My brother was gone. He was truly gone, and this would be the last time I would be able to do anything for him. I wouldn't let him down.

Acknowledgements

I KEPT MY WRITING, THIS BOOK, and all things Indie related a secret from my family and friends for some time. Why? Simple. I was afraid of chasing a dream that was huge and, in my mind, out of reach. I always kept my dreams and aspirations within a reach that I knew were achievable. I didn't dare reach higher, because I was afraid of failure. While I wrote *AWAY* in secrecy, it wasn't until I had about 23K words when I needed to know in my mind and my heart if I even had anything decent. Several emails and encouraging words later I was on the prowl for a beta reader. Fast forward a couple of weeks and I had feedback; some good, some bad, and some really amazing suggestions.

It's crazy to think how long ago that was, especially when it really feels as if it was just yesterday. I broke down and finally told my husband. He was shocked and surprised and above all, supportive. I had a sense of relief that finally someone knew.

Fast forward a month and I had a team of betas, an editor lined up, and family who still were in the dark on all that I had accomplished. While I was happy in the world of Jase and Cassie, I still had a weight on my shoulders for all those that had no clue of the 'nights' I claimed I was just 'watching my shows' or 'reading'. When in reality I was glued to my computer, laughing, crying and enjoying being with Jase and Cassie. My fear of failure was not just for letting myself down, it was for knowing that if I told family and friends, and if things didn't pan out, and my book never made it out to the world, I would have to explain with my tail between my legs. My heart sank every time I thought about it. I hated lying, but I hated the unknown even more.

So I purged on and fast forward three more months, I had a finished book. Unedited, and in need of 'tightening,' but alas, I had a whole book; 110K words worth of a book if you will. After some heavy discussion with my betas, this book was a go. They wouldn't let me turn my back now. They encouraged me and pushed me off the ledge. I needed to tell my family and friends, I needed a Facebook page, I needed a whole slew of things in order to get *AWAY* in the hands of readers. Fast forward to today and the story I just told you would have made me laugh. Never in all my life did I think this is where I would be, and I wouldn't change a thing.

Everything plays out and happens for a reason in my opinion, and the way this all presented itself was just how it was supposed to. I still feel this process and what I am doing is more than surreal. I owe many thanks to every single person who spent long hours with me and *AWAY*. I know I can be a pain in the butt at times, I'm nitpicky, and I analyze every single thing, but you all stuck with me. Through thick and thin no one left my side. Instead, you all encouraged me more. I can't thank you all enough, and even though I know I've told you all thank you, I will never stop.

My list of acknowledgements could go on for pages, but it would feel less than right if I didn't take the time to honor all of the amazing people who helped bring *AWAY* to life. With that said, please grab some popcorn, a chair, and enjoy reading about the people who will forever have a special place in my heart.

Danny, aka Mr. Wolfe — I'll never forget the day I told you I was writing a book. My hands trembled so much I had to sit on them to hide my nervousness. The reaction I received from you was that of a true husband and best friend. You always have been since high school and you always will be. Your support, your helpfulness and your interest in this book has, and never will, go unnoticed. Your queries into this 'all time consuming book world' make me smile each time as I realize, even though you have no clue what an HEA and MS mean, it shows just how much you really do care! Thanks for eating horrible meals, eating take-out more than a person should, warding off the dust bunnies with a forced smile, and stepping over the piles of laundry that sit there because I'm writing. To that, you deserve the biggest thank you in the world. To the man behind the teaser pics that were never an easy task, thank you, they are gorgeous and I'll have them forever! I love you and thank you for standing by me while I reached for my dream.

Mom — I can't forget the day I told you. The look in your eyes will forever make me smile. You were right! Thanks for being a mom a girl can count on and always have in her corner. You'll never realize how much your words mean to me. Love you!

Danielle — A huge thank you for sitting with me and supporting me while I told you what I was doing. I'll never forget the tears in your eyes and the goose bumps down your arm as I told you the story of Jase. Thanks for the encouragement!

Aunt Lori — Thank you for listening to my worries and always supporting me no matter what. For always being my positive words when I needed to hear them.

Sarah — My always helpful nurse! Thank you for taking the time to read about Jase & Cassie. For helping with all things medical related, guiding me with a plethora of knowledge, and going through my research with me.

Laura — Thank you for capturing *Away* in a way I never thought possible. You had a vision and I had a wish for the emotion and love in *Away* to be shown on the cover and my gosh did you deliver! Thank you for being a joy to work with and making this process one that was truly magical!

Sarah — You are just simply a perfect "Cassie". You brought her to life and helped make this cover as beautiful as it could be! Thank you for playing the part so well!

Brad — Your talents will never go unnoticed. From taking pictures for high-end magazines to doing book photo shoots, you have such an eye for beauty. Thank you for taking my ideas and making them a reality!

Kassi — It has been a pleasure to work with you. You are the final step before this book is out to the real world, and I can't say enough good things about working with you! You've made this process easy, enjoyable, and fun. Thank you!

Katie, aka my BPF! — Thank you for the endless laughs on what 'should' be in a romance novel. Your cover ideas are duly noted and, unfortunately, will never see the light of day on my books. Haha! Thanks for listening to me rant on my off days, and gush to you on my happy ones. For your tips and tricks on the ever confusing English language, and for being there for me, no matter what! Love your face!

To the rest of my family and friends — You know who you are and I love you all. I sound like a broken record, but the support you've given me is what helps me along each day. Some days you want to give up, some days you don't think you have it in you anymore. Then you remember the team of family and friends behind you, pushing you day after day because they believe in you and the insecurities vanish. Thanks to each and every one of you. xoxo

Kathryn, aka Katie Mac — I will NEVER forget the day I received an email telling me to contact you. That email brought me a new found sense of hope. Moments before I was told to contact you I had decided to stop pursuing my dream. I had lost hope trying to get settled into the 'indie' world. You helped to make my dream a reality. Thank you for everything — for my beta group, for talking to a panicked girl several times on the phone, and for answering all my million questions. Thank you most for working with me and my book. We were a scary pair to take on but you did it with a smile on your face. Here is to hugs, chocolate, and copious amounts of wine!

Becky — For sending the email that saved my books life! You are one in a million and I can't thank you enough for all your help and kind words! Thank you for your friendship and the chats! I truly appreciate it all!

Kim — KIMMY! I don't know what I would do without you. I mean it. From the first words you read, to the completed book today, you've stuck with me through and through. It's also safe to say this book has changed immensely from the first time we met. It wouldn't even be close to what it is today without your suggestions, help, and advice. And, I too, wouldn't be what I am today without your pep talks, encouragement, and support. You are in fact the best book manager out there! P.s. I'm still waiting for my salt!

1) I will never forget our countless hours of conversation with this book and even life.
2) You brought tears to my eyes and made my stomach hurt from laughing so hard.
3) Kimmy, there is no other way to put it, you are simply the best. (And three makes a list!)

Jodie — You were meant to read *AWAY* from the start! You left for a bit, but then I got you back in the end! Thank you for reading *AWAY* and for being a part of the process! I'll never, in a million years forget the chat we all had while you were reading it. You girls had me crying, laughing, and smiling from ear to ear! You are an amazing beta and the book wouldn't be what it is without you!

JJ — I can't thank you enough for taking the time to beta read *AWAY*. Reading your notes, comments, and reactions to this book was more helpful than you'll ever realize! You were honest, supportive, and exactly what this book needed. Thank you for sticking it out with me and for your encouragement. You'll never know how much it meant to me!

Megan — I hope you're reading this and not out on a secret mission! Your honesty and words as you read *AWAY* will stay with me forever. You have no idea how much I appreciated you beta reading and sharing your true feelings with me. You made me laugh, and cry, and want to hug you through the computer. Thank you for everything!

To my Secret Squirrels — You all took an oath, don't forget. We are stuck with each other forever! We must prepare for our next secret squirrel mission... the sequel! Love you girls!

Debi — Wonderful. There is no other way to describe you. Every time I messaged or called you with one of my many panic attacks, you calmed me right back down. You always gave it to me straight and told me what I needed to hear. For that, I owe you many thanks! You also helped me jump off many 'ledges', so thank you for keeping me on track and cheering me on when I was close to the finish line. For every conversation we had about *AWAY*, the sequel, and all our funny comments about life, I'll cherish every single one! You are one in a million and I'm so honored to have you as a beta!

Elle — I can't say it enough, I'm so glad you were on my beta team. Thank you for always messaging me back when I had a question, for reassuring me more times than I can count, for helping me when I needed to fix a problem area, and for always making me laugh when I needed it! There is no one out there like you, and I'm glad I am one of the lucky ones that got to know you and have you as a beta!

Julie — My grammar queen! Julie, I don't know what any writer would do without you. Not just for your grammar expertise, but for your well-rounded beta reading. You have an eagle eye for finding the things that others never do! Thank you for taking the time to help make sure *AWAY* was the best it could be. I'll send you Kleenex! Hugs!

Lisa — my non-stop encourager! I absolutely loved and still love, talking with you! You kept me going when I thought everything I had written was junk. Here is to our obsession with candy and junk food!! I'm honored to have had you beta read *AWAY*! Thank you for all the fun times. Here is to many more!

Kathy — I still have your email you sent after you finished *AWAY*. It was one that I'll never be able to delete because I love to go back and re-read it. Your notes, your words, your reactions… they all brought me to tears. You helped me in so many ways, I can't even begin to count them all. Thank you for taking the time to read *AWAY*, talking through scenes with me and making sure Away was ready for the world!

To all my betas… I love you all and THANK YOU AGAIN!

Rose, Faith, Gail, and Lauren — the wonderful Indie authors who will always hold a special place in my heart. For emailing back this scared girl when she didn't have a clue in the world what she was doing. For putting me under your wings and helping in any way you could. I'm so appreciative for your help, and I can't thank you enough. I am so glad I took the leap to email you all. Had I not, I wouldn't have met you and had the opportunity to call you friends! You are all so wonderful and I am more than honored to know you and even more grateful for all of our chats!

Brenda, Faith, Livia, Niecey, Lisa, Celeste, Elisabeth — There is not enough I can say about you all. You bring me laughs, warm fuzzies, and encouragement when I need it the most. You all are always there, not just for me, but for each other as well. This group of girls is completely full of love and support and I couldn't be happier to be a part of it. You are the most wonderful friends a girl could ask for. Love you all!

To my wonderful Indie groups — Indie Girls Connection & Indie Chicks Rock — Every single one of you has helped me in one way or other. Without those groups and your words of either encouragement or help, I would still be a lost puppy! For letting me join and ask question after question only to receive responses, guiding me in the right direction. Thank you all! I'd mention all your names, but that would be a book in itself. You are all so special to me and I thank you all from the bottom of my heart for helping me and welcoming me with open arms!

Lustful Literature — You girls are... I don't even have a word. There is no word out there than can pull together how much I appreciate, love, and cherish you girls! You took me under your wing, you guided me, and you promoted me to the ends of the earth. You stood by me through every single crazy moment and every single happy one. Wonderful, amazing, brilliant, great, remarkable, and extraordinary are just a few words that come to mind. I wouldn't be what I am, my book wouldn't be what it is without each of your and Lustful Literature's support behind it. Thank you, from the bottom of my heart, for everything.

Blogs — To all of the blogs and bloggers out there. You have no idea how grateful I am for all of your support. For helping this new girl along any way you could, thank you! I owe a multitude of thanks to each and every one of you who post, share, like, and promote not just me, but other authors out there. We wouldn't be where we are if it weren't for your help and kindness. A HUGE THANK YOU goes out to all of you!

About
the author

B.A. WOLFE IS A GIRL WITH a passion for reading and writing, and lives in the good ol' state of Colorado with her husband (her biggest cheerleader), and her two crazy min pin fur babies. These days, her life is anything but calm, and there isn't one thing she'd want to change. She spends all her free time either furiously typing stories on her laptop or happily reading through her endless TBR on her Kindle. Her list of favorites would be long enough to fill a book, but most would likely fall under the romance category. She is a sucker for a good love story that makes her cry, and an amazing book boyfriend who will melt her heart. *Away* is B.A. Wolfe's debut novel.

Made in the USA
San Bernardino, CA
27 February 2016